Gemini

Kerry Williams

Skye High Publishing

Copyright © 2023 by Kerry Williams

All rights reserved.

No part of this book may be reproduced in any form or by any electronic or mechanical means, including information storage and retrieval systems, without written permission from the author, except for the use of brief quotations in a book review.

Cover Design: Moonshot Covers

Interior Design: SSB Covers and Design

Editor: Swish Design and Editing

Publisher: Skye High Publishing

For Ivy, my darling daughter.
My own Gemini.
May you always march to the beat of your own drum, the way you do now.
And teaching me about a love unconditional.

Chapter One

Connie

Never, ever will I get tired of seeing his body.
    Peter's tall form stands at the large open window, his back lean and strong, observing. He's always watching the placid waters of the Ganges. I can see the vast rivers from where I lie in our bed, a thin sheet covering me. Right now, the waters look black and unforgiving, and there is a rare night Peter doesn't dream of them. Even more so now that we are here. So much has changed, and yet, nothing has changed at all. Peter gives no thought to who might be able to see him below. I sometimes feel grateful that being around him has made me so much more comfortable in my own skin.
    Peter's nightly vigil of the waters has stretched on for months with no signs of a single witch, let alone a coven. Although stories are plentiful, who knows what is real and what is not? This city is one of the most ancient in the world, and Peter is convinced we are in the right place. But the water has become something of an obsession for him, never far from his thoughts, always longing to be in it. Sometimes I think I should push myself to be more concerned, to think more about the water holding Peter's fixation. How Anna watches him like a hawk when he enters it. I try not to think too much about

the great burning ghat not so far away from where Peter wades in and the hundreds of bodies that are burned there every day. He tells me the water is alive, that it's sacred, and that he can feel the souls wash through him.

Best not to think about that, Connie.

So, as the twelve months we planned for our trip turns into fifteen, we have all spent our birthdays and one Christmas on the riverbanks of the Ganges in the holy city of Varanasi. Our beautiful home now, where there are no signs of us leaving. Truth be told, none of us have any interest in leaving. We have set up a firm residence in the Sunshine Hostel.

The thin net of a curtain billows, sending in a fresh, cooling breeze from the night. At last Peter fixes his eyes back on me. Same confident Peter, watching me as I pull the sheets up to expose my legs, silently inviting him back to bed. His lips curl a bit as he walks to me, stalking me like a predator. Coming to rest his knee on the bottom of the bed, he grabs my ankle and pulls me toward him. I give a small shriek at the surprise of the movement.

Peter's dark eyes dance in the candlelight of our room.

"Say it," he commands as he towers over me, his voice low, like velvet.

"You are a god," I whisper.

He closes his eyes against my words, letting out a caressing sigh as he runs his hand up my leg, sending a wave of electricity that ripples across my body. My back arches as he crawls onto the bed.

"I worship you," I murmur.

Biting his lip, he pushes the sheet up, exposing me until his face is at my tummy, where he places a whisper of a kiss.

"You are my religion, Connie," he says against my skin, the goose bumps firing down my legs. "You are my god. I worship you," he repeats back to me before his kisses travel downward.

This boy is my undoing, again and again.

Different Peter. Worship is his thing of late. Worshiping him, worshiping me. It's easy to get carried away in this city of worship, and while I'm all in to kneel at the altar of Peter, it is something new. Anna told me Peter once said to her that he didn't know how to be just part of who he is, so when he learned he was a god, how does he cope with that being *all* of him?

It has occurred to me Peter handled everything that happened with his father quite well, but Peter "after the crash" was different. For the most part, because he felt like he had failed, even with me. The tips of his fingers often trace the small scar that now travels across my collarbone. He'd passed out before he could put me back together in full. The scar serves as a constant reminder that even he has limitations, a reminder of all of our loss. In reality, he saved my life, and Anna's, that day, but he can't forgive himself for being unable to save Brady.

Peter is the only one who walked away without a scratch. My memory is still incredibly hazy, only bits and pieces coming back to me. I remember the sun shining so bright and the world was the wrong way up, with strangers all around the car. Anna had already been removed from the car when I came to, blood everywhere. Everyone's blood. I sort of remember someone saying I would be all right and they were going to get me out.

That's when I saw Peter through the windscreen with blood dried all down the front of his face, I couldn't comprehend what I was seeing or why he was shouting. I watched as the police struggled to restrain him, two, then three, until a total of four of them were needed to take him down before he gave up. Before his shouts died down, he was pushed onto the front hood of a car. His eyes found mine, noticing I was awake. Then his eyes moved to glance at the driver's seat for just a second before turning away from me. In that moment, Peter's distraught expression told me all I needed to know, but I still looked. The driver's seat. Brady. He had been trying to get to Brady, who was still in the car, unmoving.

It was too late.

He was already gone.

I can't even remember the weeks that followed Brady's death and the numbness that followed us all. Peter seemed to take it the worst. He never spelled it out to me, but I know for a long time, he wished he had died instead of Brady.

With time, his grief changed, transformed. His dreams led us to Varanasi, and its waters helped to heal him. Now, he waits—we all wait—for a sign.

Peter's fingers entwine with mine, and I gasp, opening my eyes in time to see the ripple of electricity pass over my knuckles and crackle over my skin. The power takes me higher before his lips find mine.

Sometimes I think I am the only way he stays grounded, keeps his powers in check.

Peter doesn't need the sky or a storm to create the lightning anymore. He can be its source. And it's an easy way to expel the energy he needs to use to keep him balanced. I can't say I mind. With Peter as the source, the energy is all him. On nights like these, I don't know where I end or he begins.

Chapter Two

Anna

"Jesus. Do those two ever stop?" Lorna looks up from the book she is reading, raising her eyebrow as the dull thud of the headboard from next door begins banging.

I chuckle before returning to my own book. "I dread to think what he is doing to her in there."

"Anna, he's your brother." Lorna laughs, throwing a small cushion at me.

After over a year here, our room looks more like a bedroom than a hostel.

"Yes." I throw it back. "And he has always been a terrible show-off."

"Gross."

"It's best to pretend it's not happening," I advise, rolling over onto my belly.

Lorna nods in fervent agreement.

I don't know what I would do without Lorna. She's become a rock this past year. There was never any question about me joining Peter here. A large part of me wanted to come, to travel so far, and to see the country I was born in, but it would have been so lonely without Lorna.

The hairs on my arms stand on end, sending a shiver down my body. I cast an instinctive glance at the thin wall that separates our room from my brother's. To be honest, I don't want to think about what he is doing, but more than anything, I wish whatever it is didn't do this to me.

"Hey," Lorna says, catching my expression. "Do you want to get out of here?"

I give her a grateful nod and follow Lorna's example, throwing on my thin sweater and flip-flops. Escaping the noise without another word, we make our ascent to the roof. We take our seats at its edge, peering out across the river with the beautiful starry sky reflected in its water. It appears so peaceful now.

Lorna puts her cigarette to her plump lips, taking a long, satisfying drag. "Maybe it's time you talk to him about it, Anna."

"Mmm... that sounds like a good idea, Lor." I mock. "Just give Peter another reason to get into his own head." Lorna is the only person I've told about the veil between my brother and me becoming thinner. I've always been in tune with my brother's emotions, but when he drained some of my life force to heal himself, the wall weakened. "Besides, I only feel it when he uses his powers."

"Which is every night at the moment. It's not nice for you, Anna. Maybe if you told him, he would slow down."

I take a moment to consider the idea as Lorna passes me the cigarette. "It will settle down again soon." I let my lungs fill with smoke. "Besides, it would be worse if he wasn't doing, whatever he calls it, balancing out."

I blow the smoke cloud out into the cool night, and the hairs on my arms start to settle.

"He might decide to 'balance' himself in a different way if he knew how you were feeling," she points out as I pass the cigarette back to her.

"It's better he doesn't know," I mutter, my thoughts becoming busy.

Lorna's hair is so long now it almost reaches the tops of her legs and seems to have a life of its own as it dances in the breeze. I cut all of mine off when Brady died. Somehow, I needed to change myself once he was gone. Peter had felt exceedingly guilty about Brady, and I can tell he is not altogether over it. I still feel the raw sadness wash over him sometimes, and I know Connie can feel it too. If he knew how much what he'd taken has affected me, I'm not sure how he would handle it.

"What?" Lorna fidgets a little.

I hadn't realized I am still looking at her, lost in thought. I take the cigarette from her, pulling in a long drag and draining the last of it. A thought occurs to me for the first time. "He took some from you too, once. How did you feel after?"

Lorna shakes her head a fraction, casting her gaze back out into the night. "I don't even remember it happening. It all felt like a dream afterward, far away."

"Could you feel him?"

Lorna shakes her head. We both stare back out into the night, hearing only the docile sounds of the water.

"But," she says after a while, unhurriedly, as if measuring the word.

"But what?" I ask when she doesn't continue.

Lorna eyes me for a second before moving to stand. "I don't know how to describe it. Connie is my best friend. I've known her forever. And with you, I feel like this last year, you've been there for me in a way no one ever has. Brady died, and I don't know what I would have done without you, Anna."

I get up to face her, taking both of her hands. "I feel the same way about you. But what does that have to do with Peter?"

"It's so hard to put into words." Lorna's face searches mine. "I think it's like this. Without him, you and Connie wouldn't be here. Maybe it's more like I feel grateful and... I don't know, loyal to him maybe."

I nod in understanding, deciding it's time to call it a night. I'm tired and don't know why Lorna's words worry me. It's perfectly natural for her to feel grateful two of her friends are alive, especially because he is the reason. I should be happy she is loyal to my brother. I know Lorna has been a loyal friend to Connie, to me, but something in my gut makes me feel like it means something else with him.

A good night's sleep helps to melt away my worries and, when I wake in the morning, I feel refreshed and rested. It's another beautiful day in this gorgeous city. There are worse ways to wake than overlooking the sacred waters of the Ganges.

Lorna isn't in her bed, so I assume she's already gone down for breakfast. I do a few stretches before changing into a long-sleeve top and leggings and heading down to join her a flight below our room.

I see her sitting cross-legged on a bean bag out on the balcony overlooking the busy street below. Lorna loves to people-watch.

"Morning," I chirp once I join her.

"You look better." She beams up at me as she pours me a small cup of chai from the pot on her table.

Observing the busy scene below before taking a seat on the cushion next to her, I don't think it will ever cease to amaze me. There's no way to truly prepare for how many people live here.

Vik, who owns the hostel, is probably the kindest gentleman on the planet. His skin creases into deep laugh lines around his eyes as he brings Lorna a plate of papaya and yogurt.

I give him my warmest smile before he retreats away from our table. Noticing Connie now approaching us, greeting Vik as he passes, she has a broad smile when we catch her eye.

"Is there coffee?" she asks as she arrives at the table.

Lorna gives a small shake of her head as she points to the pot. "That's chai."

Connie yawns into the back of her hand. "I need coffee," she says before reaching up into a high stretch, giving her back an audible crack and lifting her black shirt up to expose her belly.

Connie has always been small, but her already tiny frame seems to be shrinking, her hip bones jutting out where her trousers hang loose on them.

I'm not the only one to notice Connie's nonexistent stomach.

"Jesus, Con. You're looking really skinny," Lorna says, her eyes traveling up Connie's tiny body.

Connie takes a moment to look down, rubbing her belly like it's a buddha. "I know. I'm starving." Connie leans across and pops three pieces of Lorna's papaya into her mouth.

"Hey, I'm eating that." Lorna slaps her hand away before she can eat any more.

"Where's Peter?" I ask her as she tries to chew the three pieces of papaya now in her mouth, it being clear that she has overindulged.

She points upward. "He's on the roof, meditating with sadhu," she gets out between chews, then she motions to Lorna's papaya. "That's good."

"I know. That's why I ordered it." Lorna moves her plate protectively out of Connie's reach. "Get your own, Con."

Connie pouts. "Fine. I'm going to the market. I need carbs. Plus, we need to stock up on water. Can you ask Vik for coffee for when I get back? Do you two want anything?"

Lorna and I shake our heads, then Lorna goes back to her sketch while I sip my chai. Connie is almost at the stairs before Lorna yells, "Cigarettes, Connie."

Connie gives a wave without looking back to acknowledge she's heard Lorna's request.

Lorna glances up at me for a second to say, "I swear that girl has worms."

I glance down at my chai. Our life has become one of relative ease, with many days spent lazing around our hostel. Lorna has taken up drawing. Connie lazily plays her guitar, as well as teaches me how to play, amidst exploring as much of the city as we can.

More than generous, Vik moved us into his best rooms after a few weeks of us being here. We don't have to share a bathroom, and they have views of the river, as Peter requested. It wasn't long after sadhu arrived at the hostel that Vik let him board for free.

Our host explained that sadhu is a hindu holy man who wanders. He doesn't visit often, and it is an honor to have him stay. The first time he stayed at the hostel, he spent a week teaching Peter how to meditate.

Sadhu doesn't speak a word of English, yet Peter understands every word he says. It's only because of this we even learned Peter was able to understand everyone, and had since we arrived. He explained it away as unimportant because he couldn't speak Hindi or Urdu, or any of the other languages spoken here. He can't speak any language other than English, but he can understand all languages. Nothing seems to shock us about him these days. It more annoys us that he doesn't deem it necessary to tell us these things. Peter has never been one to talk a lot, but he is quieter now than I've ever known him to be. Meditation is the other way Peter "balances" himself, and he says it works better when sadhu is around. Sadhu has visited five times in the last year, and Vik is overjoyed by this.

Speak of the devil.

Peter swings down the staircase, cricking his neck as he joins us, planting a small kiss on my head before plonking himself down next to me. We haven't slept side by side in over a year. When I was in the hospital after the crash, Peter slept next to me on my bed the whole time. I miss having him close.

"How's sadhu?" I ask.

"He's good," he replies.

"And you?"

"Good," he states, leaning forward to take a piece of Lorna's papaya.

"Jesus. Can everyone leave my breakfast alone?"

Peter gives her a wicked smirk resting his arm around the back of my cushion and pulling at the edge of my hair.

"How much do you think sadhu knows about you?" I ask.

Peter shrugs. "Not sure." He leans a little closer. "You know, he calls me demigod."

"Really?" I feel Lorna beside me angle herself so she's closer as well. "What do you say?"

"Nothing. I'm not sure if he knows I understand what he is saying."

"What are you going to do about it?"

"Nothing. Sadhu is a holy man. He's pure."

"What does that mean?" I ask, but he doesn't answer. He only shrugs his shoulders again.

I take the last cigarette from the packet on the table, knowing Peter hates it and that it will bother him as much as his cryptic answers exasperate me.

"Do you have to do that?" he quips as I blow out.

"What? You can just heal me, right?"

Peter rolls his eyes. "I believe that would be called an abuse of power."

"Please, like we can't hear what you're doing to Connie night after night." The words are out of my mouth before I knew I was going to say them.

Lorna lets out a low whistle, averting her gaze and fixating back on her drawing. When she said I should talk to Peter, I know she didn't mean like this.

Out of character for him, I see the heat rising in his face. It's not easy to embarrass my brother. He stares at me, not knowing what to say. Typical Peter, with no idea of himself or the fact that we are in the next room. I press my lips together, overcome with the urge to laugh as he maintains the silence between us. He's quick—too quick. His arm disappears from around me and he jabs his finger into my side, giving me a sharp shock.

"Ouch. Peter." I'm on my feet. "Did you seriously just shock me?"

He goes to move again, and I jump over the table as he gets to his feet ever so slowly, with purpose, to try and intimidate me, but I can see the humor in his eyes.

"Oh, you want this?" he asks me, pointing his jabbing finger at me.

"No." I shake my head.

"Come here." He points to the space in front of him.

"No, Peter. I take it back." I laugh. "Please don't do that again."

He laughs, relenting and returning to his sitting position, letting me relax again. I choose to maintain my distance, though, and sit on the beanbag opposite Lorna instead. Peter picks up the pot to pour himself some chai and looks from me to Lorna, noticing the absence.

"Where's Connie?"

"She went to the market," Lorna answers.

"On her own?"

I can almost feel the anxiety flare in him.

"She'll be fine. The market is close, and she's been there a hundred times before." I try to reassure him, but Peter is already on his feet.

"None of you should be going anywhere on your own." Peter rubs his eyes.

"Peter, you would know if she was in danger, wouldn't you? You would feel it. You have to let this go at some point," I say as I rise and take his arm, trying to make my voice soothing.

This has been Peter since the accident. Our protector. He wants all of us close all the time. It's no way to live. He needs to let us get on with our lives at some point.

He runs his hands through his hair, then closes his eyes, taking my arms to steady himself. Looking lost, deep in concentration, I can feel it, what he's doing. He's looking for Connie in his mind, finding her in the crowds.

His eyes snap open, looking into mine. We have the exact same eyes.

"Anna, something is there. We have to go."

Chapter Three

Peter

Anna and Lorna move fast, but it doesn't feel quick enough. Each stride I take toward the market feels like it's taking too long. I breathe deeply, filtering out the crowd around me. I imagine them melting away, clearing a path. When I flex my fingers, the electricity crackles there before folding them into a fist. The last thing I need is to explode in a crowded marketplace.

I close my eyes momentarily and reach out. Connie is close. Whatever I detected earlier is still here. The energy it's giving off is massive, but I can't quite place where it's coming from. This feels different to Arjun. Not feeding me energy, like my father had, but rather vibrating against my own. It seems it should be obvious where the source is. The power it is projecting crushes like it's carving a path through the earth, destroying everything in its way.

The market is winding, narrow pathways full of bustling people carrying on their daily lives close to the temple. Row upon rows of stalls covered with bright, fragrant flowers for the shrines, spices stacked tall in huge Hessian sacks, the clattering of bangles. So much life, it makes it difficult to concentrate. I only know Connie is here with the mass of energy, and I need to find her. Get her out.

I turn to my sister and Lorna, who are a few steps behind me. "We need to split up. She's still here with whatever that thing is. We need to find her and get away."

Lorna looks a bit bewildered at my panic. "Peter, are you sure this isn't what we've been looking for? Could it be a witch?"

"I don't think so." The only witch I ever met besides my mother was my father, so I don't have much to compare to. "Maybe? Regardless, I don't want Connie coming into contact with whatever it is on her own."

"We'll find her." Anna gives my arm a reassuring rub.

They take a different path as I continue my search for Connie. I'm able to see over most of the heads in front of me, but it's still like searching for a needle in a haystack. Out of the corner of my eye, I catch a flash of someone looking at me, but when I look back, no one is there.

I pick up my pace, the energy of whatever is out here pressing on me. Uncomfortable. I flex my back muscles, pushing back against the sensation.

There it is.

An eye on me, I am sure of it. A face in the crowd, but I couldn't grasp onto it.

A silver eye?

I force my feet forward, keeping my breathing steady and shaking out my arms beside me. My powers are pretty balanced these days, but I can feel them buzz under my skin with my growing anxiety. I scan the market, past the overpowering floral scent, the stacks of fruit and vegetables, the people's faces that turn to mine. That's when I see her animatedly talking to a stall holder handing her a fresh slice of mango, which she readily accepts. Her small canvas bag is so full it must be too big for her tiny body to carry.

How can one person emit so much light?

I could live a thousand years and feel the same every time I see her. She is the home I never had.

The breath leaves my body, and a sense of relief at the sight of her washes over me like a wave, restoring the calm inside. Connie hasn't seen me yet. As she gives the stall holder a few notes, I make my way behind her and lift the heavy bag off her shoulder.

On instinct, she grabs onto it, whipping around, ready to push the thief away.

"Hi," I say as she takes in that it's me, bringing her palm to her chest. "I thought this looked heavy."

"What are you doing sneaking up on me like that?" she berates, but her eyes are full of warmth.

"I missed you." I don't want to worry her. "Let's get out of here."

I pull her close, putting my arm around her shoulder to lead her back the way from which I've come. Now to find my sister. I make it two paces before I'm stopped in my tracks.

Connie glances up at me to find out why I've stopped.

The full force of what I sensed before is back.

Not just back, but standing in front of me.

Ten feet in front of me.

Silver eyes.

It's her.

All that power is radiating out of her like an atom bomb.

Her eyes, deadly.

Every hair on my body stands on end as she takes one step forward.

A fleeting thought passes through my mind. *Is this what I feel like to be around?*

I already know what she is.

Her face gives nothing away. She looks unlike anyone I've ever seen before. Full dark lips and even darker skin, contrasted by the long, pure white hair that frames her face and stands out against the red of her kaftan.

My arm falls from Connie's shoulder as I take a step toward the woman. It's hard to tell how old she is. *Ageless,* my brain tells me, *just like you.*

I don't sense any danger from her, and she seems to have made the same assessment of me. Our steps remain tentative, but we more readily close the distance, the earlier push of her energy now becoming more of a pull until we are no more than a foot from each other.

Her face is unreadable, and it almost catches me off guard when her hand reaches out to touch my hair.

"Touched by the universe," she whispers, and the reserve on her face gives way to one of wonder. "I can't believe it. You are real. I have been so alone for so long." Her lips pull into an easy smile.

"I'm Peter," I manage to say, my words returning to me.

"I'm Sorcha."

Unable to look away, I smile back at her. She holds my gaze for what feels like years.

I can't breathe.

Not until Sorcha looks away, her eyes widening in disbelief at what she is seeing. I've been too distracted to notice Lorna and Anna have caught up to us and are standing a little way behind me. I follow Sorcha's astonished gaze to Anna before she looks back at me.

"How is this possible?"

I give my head a little shake, bringing me back to myself. When I see Lorna and Anna eyeing Sorcha with suspicion, there is something I can't place on Connie's face. *Hurt?*

I take a deep breath.

What the hell was that?

Sorcha brings her attention back to me once more. "Are these your only followers?"

"Followers?"

Something resembling humor flashes across her face. "Oh. You really are a baby."

She walks away from me, leaving me dumbfounded as she approaches the others. My initial feelings of wonder give way to irritation.

"I'm Sorcha," she introduces herself to Anna. "It is so, so wonderful to meet you. What's your name?" Sorcha extends her hands for Anna to take, allowing me to notice the tattoos adorning her dark skin for the first time.

Anna gives me a confused expression, and I shrug, not knowing what to make of it either.

"Anna," she answers like she's not sure of it herself. Giving Sorcha her hands, the woman immediately pulls her closer.

"How wonderful you are, Anna. I did not even know it was possible for a twin to survive. I have so many questions for you."

"Peter, who is this person?" Anna looks at me.

I shake my head. "I literally just met her a second before you did."

"You certainly seem to know her." Connie's voice has a definite edge to it.

"She's like me, Connie."

All of them take a reflexive step away from the strange woman.

Sorcha gives a small musical laugh. "Don't worry, I won't smite you all." She addresses Connie. "And who are you?"

"His girlfriend."

Sorcha's head whips round back to me in... what? Disbelief? Amusement? She looks me up and down in a way that puts my hackles up.

"How did you find me?" I ask her.

"Find you?" She laughs again, approaching me, and once again, my body flexes against her.

I'm sure she can feel it too.

"Baby god. It is impossible *not* to find you. You're stomping around like a toddler with no regard for anyone in your path."

"Funny. I was going to say the same thing about you."

She circles me where I stand, and there is something extremely vexing about it.

"If you are not here for me, then what are you here for?"

"The same reason as you, no?" Her eyes glitter at me, and I can feel the mockery there. "The waters?"

"I am here for answers." My patience wearing thin, I catch her wrist—putting a stop to her circling—and pull her in closer.

She looks surprised for a second, her eyes drifting to my hand clamped around her.

Something ugly deep inside of me rears its head. Something primitive, a need for dominance. I stare into her silver eyes, all humor gone now. "Do you have the answers?" The question sounds more like a growl.

Her chest heaves. "I am not your enemy," she states, and although she averts her eyes, I feel her energy pushing against mine.

I release my grasp, peeling back one digit at a time to flex my fingers.

She takes a deep breath, looking relieved for being released, although she must have many years on me, and I would imagine more than enough power to take me down.

I walk away from her, making my way back to Connie. This is my luck. Over a year of waiting wasted—no witches, no coven, no answers, just another god.

"Peter," she says after me. "I am not the one to answer your questions. But I can take you to the ones who can."

Her words draw my attention back to her. Sorcha's perceived hostility is melting away, and she seems more relaxed as she throws her arms in the air.

"Look, I had to come and make sure you were not a danger to them. You didn't honestly think they would welcome you into their home without any protection, did you?"

"Who?"

She places her hand on her hip like it should be obvious. "Well, the coven, of course."

My pulse quickens. *The coven.* Over a year of waiting, holding fast to the feeling that somehow I am in the right place has paid off. I cast an expectant gaze over the others, trying to gauge their thoughts, but they all look as wide-eyed as me and a little shell-shocked that we have finally found what we came here for. Or rather, it found us.

Gemini

"We can all come?" I clarify with Sorcha.

"Sure," she says flippantly, spinning around to leave. "Your followers will be welcome."

I follow her. Her hair is the purest white, and it's hard to take my eyes off of, but irritation with her flares in me again. "Why are you calling them that?"

"Is that not what they are?" She stops to raise her eyebrow at me.

"They're my friends," I reply, feeling childish for some reason.

Sorcha doesn't answer but instead looks a few paces behind me to where the others haven't moved. "Are you coming or not?" she calls to them.

Glancing back, it hits me. I hadn't noticed they weren't following. They are unsure about the decision to join us, but I know this is it. The way to answers.

Anna, who is standing just behind Connie, gives her a delicate shove forward to get her moving. Connie's eyes remain on Sorcha's back as she leads the way.

I hang back and fall into step with her, pushing my fingers through hers. Finding a slight resistance there, she doesn't look at me but stares ahead. I am desperate to catch up to Sorcha and ask her what she meant about the waters. I also want to ask her about the souls. Can she feel them also? What does it mean? But I'm pretty sure Connie is mad at me for some reason, and Connie never gets mad at me. Well, almost never. Unless I've done something stupid.

"Connie, are you annoyed with me?" I whisper.

"I don't know. Should I be, Peter?" she quips, still not looking at me.

Yes, she's vexed. Maybe I should've asked her if she thought it was a good idea to follow Sorcha. I chance a look back at Lorna and Anna, who are a few paces behind us, their expressions give nothing away. My eyes linger back on Connie, who is being careful not to look at me now. I don't understand. I am positive that this is the way to answers.

I don't say anything else to Connie. Instead, I notice the way we are heading is straight toward the temple. Sorcha's gossamer-like hair shimmers and sways in time to the way her body moves as she walks, and for some reason, I find it fascinating. She is almost as tall as me and I imagine she is what Amazons would have looked like.

"We are almost there," she calls over her shoulder.

The announcement was unnecessary.

As she leads us up a small passageway running down the side of the temple, we seem to step over an invisible barrier, and the full force of the coven's power hits me like a brick wall. For the first time since we entrusted Sorcha, Connie stops to look up at me as the force sends me backward, pushing me against the pull of her hand. The unexpected hit sends my powers into overdrive. I rake my hand down my face, trying to pull myself together. The wall next to me shudders with the deep roots of the trees on the hillside of the temple, trying to find their way to me.

Focus.

Find my center.

The way sadhu has shown me.

Bring myself back inside my own body. Focus on my heartbeat, not the effects of the outside world.

With a shaky breath, I bring them to a stop, receding the power back into the depths of my body.

"Is there a problem?" The note of humor is back in Sorcha's face as she watches me pull myself together, probably enjoying my reaction to the power she feels in them too.

"Nope," I say, now fully back in control. Pulling Connie, who is looking a little concerned, forward, I don't do anything except wiggle my eyebrows at her. I'm excited with the anticipation of what is about to happen.

There must be about twenty witches in there—the collective power of the coven is massive.

"Are you okay, Peter?" Anna asks from behind me.

"You should feel it in here, Anna..." I whisper as we advance. I feel a tad drunk. This is nothing like the black presence of Arjun or whatever he was doing to feed me. Twenty powerful witches gathered in one room, all little shining centers of the universe, every one of them. "It's like nothing I have ever felt."

The long passage leads us to a wide, open room that looks quite similar to the open front space of the temple itself. It's basic, with an earth floor and stone tables. We cut through the middle of the room, following Sorcha's lead straight toward the front. Witches watch us as we pass. Men, women, and even some children who must be no older than twelve, all eyeing us with innate curiosity.

Our escort approaches a witch who sits on a large stone chair up a small flight of dirt steps. She looks like the oldest person here, but there is also something warm and youthful about her. Sorcha mounts the stairs and whispers a few words to the woman, who eases herself out of her chair and stands to take us in. This woman commands authority—it's clear she is the high priestess.

"Peter." She extends her hands to me. "You are very welcome."

"Thank you," I say, accepting them. "We are so pleased to finally be here."

Her dark eyes sparkle with warmth and familiarity. "And you...," she moves toward my sister, "... Anna. It is an honor to have you here as well." She brings Anna into a warm embrace before also greeting Connie and Lorna, then takes her seat once more.

I sit on the step and give her my attention.

"I am Kali, the high priestess of this coven."

"Kali?" Lorna questions.

Kali gives a slight chuckle. "Yes. But, my dear, I am no god. Though it is a true honor to have two in our presence today." She smiles at Sorcha before returning her warm gaze to me. "I am sure you can understand our need to call Sorcha to us before we revealed ourselves to you, Peter. When I felt Arjun's passing, I knew he must have found you."

"You knew Arjun?" My face drops. "Was he the high priest of this coven?"

Kali's kind face turns bitter. "High priest? Is that what he told you? My son was no high priest of this, or any, coven."

"Arjun was your son?" Anna asks from her place on the steps, staring up at Kali in shock.

"That he was. You might think me cold, but believe me when I say I did not mourn his passing." Kali's eyes stay soft on Anna for a while, causing my sister to shift in discomfort. After a few moments, Kali comes out of her reverie and extends her hands to mine, wearing a broad smile. "My dear boy, please do show us. What did the eternal gift to you?"

Everyone's eyes shift to me, Sorcha's hard and challenging. I reach into my pockets for any seeds I have there, a ghost of a smile passing my lips when I find the one I want. The full power of the coven saturates the air around me as I move to my knees in front of Kali. Bringing my palms together as if in prayer, I focus my energy. The coven's vitality is so strong I can draw on it. A hazy glow begins to shine within my hands, and I take my time to ease myself higher, the glow of the light warming my face as I inch my palms open to reveal the lotus flower now nestled there.

Kali's face lights up in the soft glow receding from my palms. The coven takes a collective gasp. I can't help but grin at Kali's joy. Knowing what I can do impresses her as she rises from her seat, and I place the lotus flower in her hands.

"What a rare gift." She marvels at the flower, gently placing the tips of her fingers to my cheek. Then, looking to Anna, she says, "What a rare gift to have you both here." Her voice almost shaking, she adds, "I am sure we will learn a great deal from each other."

I glance across to Anna. Now that I am here, it is almost too much to bear. I feel like our journey is only beginning, but Anna looks confused, even more unsure of herself.

Kali notices.

"My dear child, what is troubling you?" She lifts Anna's chin to raise her face to her own.

Anna looks almost apologetic, her big brown eyes, so similar to my own, full of uncertainty. "I'm sorry, but Arjun said all I am is Peter's human half. I'm nothing special."

"Arjun. Pah!" Kali throws her arms into the air, spitting at the name. "Arjun was a zealot and cast out of this coven."

I glance back to Anna, who also looks elated with this news.

"He was thrown out. What for?"

Kali takes her stone seat once more. "For his obsession with his quest to revive the dead practice of bringing gods onto this planet once more. The ritual is barbaric and forbidden in this modern age."

"Barbaric how?" Anna asks.

"The amount of power needed to harness that energy is unimaginable, my dear. To find a host able to contain it, near impossible. It is far more likely to rip them apart than be able to summon and contain that energy in human form." Kali shakes her head, looking at Anna. "Can you imagine gestating the sun, my child?"

Anna's eyes flash back to mine. "Our mother?"

"Your mother was lucky to walk away from your birth with her life. How she survived for another seventeen years is quite beyond me. A witch so powerful, human beings are not built that way anymore."

My brain struggles to keep up. "What do you mean? Anymore?"

"You must understand the gods have not walked this Earth in over two thousand years. Mankind at that time was primitive and savage. The great tribes of that time called forth the gods to fight their wars and build their empires strong. I am sorry, Peter, it is nothing personal, but gods have no place in this modern world. Mankind has evolved, and the old ways are not needed, nor are they wanted."

My chest heaves as I try to make sense of this information. "So why do it? Arjun said it was for the good of the coven."

"Arjun thought we would all come crawling back when we saw what he had achieved. He believed he had found a way to tether you to him, Peter, the way the first witches did to gods of old. It was a dangerous, dangerous mission. A deadly one if he had succeeded, for all of us."

I shudder at the thought. "So, what? I really am a monster? Doomed for this Earth like he told me I was?"

Kali's face lights up once more. Taking Anna and me by our shoulders and giving us a good shake, she says, "No. No, don't you see? Of course you do not. How could you? Anna is the unknown quantity. None of us, not even Sorcha here, could believe your twin was alive. We did not think this possible. It should *not* be possible."

Appearing every bit as uncertain as me, Anna shakes as she replies, "But I am just human."

Kali takes Anna's face in her hands once more. "You are the human half of a god, my sweet girl. Do you think that makes you *just* human?" She laughs. "No one in this world has heard of an adult one of you, let alone met one like you before."

Anna beams up at Kali, but the grim reality of what this meant for all of those who came before me—perhaps every other god this world has ever known—is stark. "Sooo..." I stretch out the word, "...you mean all of the twins, the human twins—"

"Were the first sacrifices made to the new god? Yes." Sorcha's voice is sarcastic, her eyes hard on me, like it is somehow my fault her twin died where mine lived. Her twin had been sacrificed. To her.

I stare back at Sorcha, unable to imagine anything more horrific, but I suppose she has never known any different. Until now.

"Why else do you think human sacrifice became so popular?" Kali says with such nonchalance, her countenance so calm and at such odds with the weight of her words. "Thousands and thousands of human lives have been lost to increase the power of the gods."

Chapter Four

Connie

Peter and Anna babble away in front of me, talking to each other in the way only they can understand. They seem elated. The news that Arjun was not a man to be trusted, while not surprising, confirms there is hope for them both. I kind of hate myself for not being happier for them, for how my mind can't get past Sorcha.

The way Peter can't take his eyes off her.

How she cannot keep her eyes off him.

All the old insecurities seep back into me.

She is the same as him and beyond beautiful. How can I begin to keep up?

"My head hurts," Lorna says, holding onto my elbow as we near the edge of the winding market.

Kali had decided to call it a night and welcomed us all to come back whenever we wished. Another pang of jealousy flares knowing Peter will always want to spend his time here now.

I am officially a clingy, annoying girlfriend.

"Earth to Connie." Lorna waves her hand in front of my face.

I grasp her hand in mine. "Sorry. I'm a million miles away. Today has been something else, right?"

"Do you think there is a chance they'll be able to save Anna?"

"Save Anna?" I take in the earnest expression Lorna is wearing. What a strange choice of words. "Anna isn't in any danger here. You heard them. They are all fascinated by her."

"What I mean to say is, will they be able to find a way to separate her from Peter? So she can live her own life."

I give it some thought. "It's beginning to sound like most of the things out of Arjun's mouth were lies. It might not have been true in the first place. Anna may already be able to do exactly that." The expression on Lorna's face tells me she is not convinced. "Lor, do you know something I don't?"

"No. Of course not," she reassures me. "I guess they will get to it. We can't learn everything in one night, and there are still so many questions. Peter didn't even ask them anything about how to suppress his powers yet."

No, he did not.

Peter is a bundle of energy. I don't know if I've ever seen him so happy, or at least so excited that his very being seems to vibrate. Unable to sit still.

At dinner, he sits next to Anna, animated while he talks to us all. Anna and Lorna appear happy to be swept along in his good mood. It's doing the opposite to me. More and more, I feel frustrated with him for being so perfectly oblivious.

By the time we get to our room later that night, I am seething. I throw my bag down on the chair and observe myself in the mirror.

Are you really doing this, Connie? You're going to kick off with Peter about some girl you've all just met?

Peter moves behind me, snaking his arms around my waist, then planting kisses on my neck that make all my hairs stand on end. My own body betraying me irks me even more.

Yes, I am going to do this.

"Peter. Stop," I command.

Gemini

"Connie, don't be mad at me."

I nudge him away from me. "I am so not in the mood right now."

Something in Peter shifts, and he takes a step back. "Are you scared of me?" He gears up for a ramble. "Because of all that stuff about human sacrifice? About increasing the power of the gods. I promise I knew nothing about that. You said you understood why I killed Arjun. I did *not* do it for his power, Connie. I did absorb the power out of him as I killed him, but I didn't even realize at the time what I was doing. It seemed more like poetic justice after what he tried to make me do to Anna." He stands there looking at me, his breath ragged.

I couldn't feel more stupid. Of course, that would make so much more sense. His brain hasn't even registered that Sorcha is who I'm mad about.

He turns away from me, running his hands through his hair again, hard enough to pull it. It dawns on me that this is what *he* is upset about, despite him charming his sister and Lorna all evening. Being a god and what it means keeps throwing curveballs at him.

"Talk to me, Connie. I hate that I can't read your mind. You have to tell me what you're thinking."

"That's not what I was talking about." I can hear it in my voice. I've lost all the courage of my convictions with Peter here, right in front of me.

"So tell me," he coaxes.

I roll my eyes. "Sorcha."

Peter's eyes narrow in slight confusion for a few moments before his lips spread into a broad grin, and then he laughs, taking a few steps back and holding his stomach. "You're jealous?"

"Don't laugh at me. She is really pretty." *Wow. That is a weak argument.*

"So?"

"So, do you think she's pretty?" I can't stop myself from asking, even though I hate how it sounds.

Peter's expression is one of utter disbelief. "I think Lorna is pretty too. It doesn't mean anything, Connie."

"No, it's more than that. You should see yourself around her, Peter. At how she looks at you. I felt so small next to the both of you. Insignificant."

Peter lets out a long sigh and sits on the edge of the bed. "Connie, everything I am, *what* I am, is yours and no one else's." He reaches out to take my hand, pulling me closer. "I don't want anyone else. I love *you*."

Crawling onto his knees, all my anger and insecurities banished. I rest my lips on him as his hands find my hips, lifting me and placing me behind him on the bed in one smooth motion, which takes me by surprise.

"Let me make it up to you," he says, his irresistible smile back. "Just you. No magic."

I bite my lip, his deft fingers finding their way under my clothes. "Don't you need to? What with the energy balance and all?"

"I can live without for one night," he says into my skin, his kisses already coming fast and clouding my ability to think straight.

The brilliant morning sun pours through our large window. The heat of Peter next to me keeps me drowsy. Usually, he is up long before me, his dreams making him restless. This morning, he looks so peaceful his face and features are soft. His limbs are entwined with mine, his arm drapes across my chest, and one of his legs rests over one of mine, keeping me pinned.

My movement begins to wake him, and he drags his fingers across my belly, the slightest crackles of static on his fingertips. I should've let him use his powers on me last night. The last thing we need is for him to feel out of balance, given his initial reaction when he walked into the coven yesterday.

The coven seems friendly enough, but I'm not sure how they will react to knowing what a knife edge Peter has to live on. And while Kali seems to pose no immediate danger for now, thinking about it in the new light of day, Peter only revealed a minuscule part of what he can do. Although the trick with the lotus is something I've never seen him do before.

Peter's hand clamps on my waist, and while it shouldn't be possible, he pulls me even closer.

"Hey," I whisper, wiggling onto my side to look at him. Pushing the hair from his eyes, I ask, "How did you do that with the flower yesterday?"

Peter runs his fingers up my back and into my hair. "I'm not awake yet, Connie." But he's smiling, keeping his eyes closed on purpose.

I use all of my strength to push his shoulder so he is on his side. "Tell me." I move over him, kissing his jaw. "Don't make me beg."

He bites his lip but keeps his eyes closed. "You, beg? I am *definitely* not going to tell you now. I need to hear this."

I push him until he rolls onto his back and then move on top of him. "Please, Peter." I pout, letting my hand tease down his torso until his breath catches in his throat. "Please, please, please, Peter," I sing. "Tell me."

It's good to put him in this position sometimes, one where I feel powerful even if I am begging him for information. His hands comb through his hair as his eyes open to find me, and his fingers dig into my legs.

"What was the question again?" he asks, his breaths coming heavy.

"The flower. How did you make it?" I smile slyly.

"Connie." He bites down on his lip. "I can't... I can't concentrate when you are doing... that."

I've not realized until this exact moment how much I need the feeling too. That I crave the feeling of his power flowing through me, I want it as much as he needs to use it.

"So? Do something about it," I order.

Anna and Lorna are already at breakfast when we go down later.

"You two are up early," I say and plonk myself down at the low table across from Lorna.

"Hmm..." She doesn't look up at me but continues to read her book, taking a drag of her cigarette. "Couldn't sleep."

As I'm about to ask her more, sensing a bit of grumpiness, Vik approaches me with a cup of black coffee, which I readily accept, offering him a wide smile. Anna yawns, stretching her arms back across the wall of the balcony she and Lorna are sitting against. They both look tired. Peter pours himself some chai from their pot, taking a small sip before spitting it back into his cup.

"Ugh. This is stone cold. How long have you two been up?"

Lorna's face flashes with exasperation as she opens her mouth to say something to him, but Anna cuts her off with, "I was wondering. About what you did yesterday." Anna rests her chin on her hands as Peter motions to Vik for more chai.

"What did I do?"

"With the flower? How did you do that?"

Peter smirks at me, and I feel the color rising on my face. So aggravating. *I thought my body was passed this.* Thankfully, he doesn't dwell on me for too long and instead leans a little closer to Anna from across the table.

"It's the coven. It's hard to explain. Arjun fed me energy on purpose to send my powers into overdrive. Comparing how he was to how the coven is, they're so open and welcoming. In a way, I think he was protecting himself. They feel so different. I think this is why we can trust them."

"Different how?" Anna asks.

We are all enraptured because it's not like Peter to try to explain himself.

Peter looks to the ceiling, bouncing his knees like a small child. "How can I describe it?" He shakes his head, giving her his most brilliant smile. "It feels like creation, Anna. Like pure creation. I made that flower without the earth because of the power of the coven. I could use *their* power, not because of anything they were doing, but because I could feel it all around them."

"Wow," Lorna says, her previous bad mood forgotten. "So they will definitely be able to help, right? With suppressing your powers?"

Peter's face drops a fraction, almost imperceivable, as her words bring him back to himself. "Yes," he says after a beat while pouring the hot chai. "Absolutely. They should be able to help."

Peter slides his fingers into mine. "I'm going back there after we've eaten. Will you come?" His eyes search mine in earnest.

I agree, thankful for his reassurance.

But first, breakfast. I am starving. I always feel hungry these days.

When we do make our way back to the coven's large hall to discover Sorcha is nowhere in sight, I'm happy. Peter either doesn't care or is sensible enough not to ask where she is, making me even happier.

Instead, Kali takes great pleasure in introducing us to the rest of the coven. She is warm and compassionate, and it is soon clear that she is the one in charge. They all treat her with the utmost respect. What's funniest is seeing Peter and Anna's reactions to being here.

Peter is at total ease and comfortable being revered—he is all smiles and charm, happy to meet them as they gaze up at him in wonder.

Anna, however, is hilarious. She is the complete opposite, uncomfortable being the center of attention, and she tries to hide behind her brother or Lorna.

We soon learn the coven is a family with most of the people here related. Their practices have been passed down through the generations. Hundreds, maybe thousands of years' worth of knowledge amassed about the cosmic, not just children of nature as Kali had said, but students of the universe and its unlimited potential. Peter and Anna are spellbound at their connection to such a family, and I can't say I blame them.

After a while, we're left to our own devices to mingle as we wish and make ourselves comfortable in the coven's home. It resembles the temple, maybe more of a commune, with their living quarters off corridors, which all lead to the main hall.

Anna and Lorna drift away from us, moving over to witches who are sitting and reading. Peter keeps me close, rarely letting go of my hand. He leads me back in the direction of a young witch who appears to be about thirteen.

She'd been too shy to say anything when Kali did introductions earlier. I think her name is Mahi. She stands at a small table on her own, planting seeds.

"Hi," Peter says to her, his tone warm. "Mahi, right?"

She nods her head and appears terrified.

"I'm Peter." He holds out his hand to her, which she tentatively takes. "It's nice to meet you, Mahi."

She gives him the tiniest of smiles.

"I was just interested in what you are doing." He continues, unfazed by her silence. "You see, I love plants too. They're my favorite things. Well, except for my friend Connie here." He grins, putting his arm around my shoulders.

Mahi lets her smile stretch a fraction. "I am planting pansies, sir. For our food."

Peter shakes his head at her. "Please don't call me sir, Mahi. Peter will do."

She nods, smiling fully now.

"You know pansies are used for anti-inflammatory—"

"Yes, and they're good for your lungs and your skin. My mother, she is teaching me," she interrupts, her smile flickering a little brighter.

Peter leans down to the little table where she stands. "My mother taught me the same things."

Mahi beams, watching as he places his forefinger into the pot of pansy seeds she has been planting and forces the flowers to life before her eyes. Mahi clasps her hands together, giving a little jump up and down on the spot as Peter beams back at her.

I've never seen Peter with kids before, never given any thought to him being good with them or not. I wonder if everything he's been through makes him feel like he missed out on having a real childhood. Whether he ever thinks about it or if he thinks about having a family of his own. In many ways, Peter is still so naive. I never did discuss with him how there'd been any possibility I could be pregnant last year. I didn't allow myself to entertain it being a reality. I wasn't sure what we would have done. When I wasn't, I didn't feel the need to mention it.

I don't know if I want children myself. I've never spent any time around babies, and besides, nineteen is still too young, in my personal opinion. I try to push a small niggle to the back of my mind, something that has been coming back to me recently with more frequency. And now seeing Peter with Mahi has brought it back front and center.

It's Lorna who brings me back to those thoughts when I am lying next to her on her bed later, demolishing a huge bag of crisps while on my back with my feet against her wall.

"Con, are you going to eat that whole bag? Or will you give me some?"

I eye the measly crumbs left before offering them to her.

She looks from the bag back to me. "Where are you putting it all?"

"What do you mean?"

"You eat like a horse. And yet, if anything, you keep getting thinner."

"Lor, can I tell you something?" My heart starts to pick up.

She looks up from her magazine from where she lies on her stomach. "Of course."

"I haven't had a period in about two months," I say as fast as I can.

Lorna is up on her knees in a flash, and I already regret the decision to mention it.

"Connie, are you..."

"No." I shake my head. "I can't be. I mean, look at me, Lorna." I gesture down to my flat stomach.

"Are you still taking the pill?"

"Yes. But I ran out of the ones from home, so I've been getting the ones from the pharmacy here. Do you think they might be making me ill or something?"

"I think it's more likely that you are pregnant, Connie."

I take a big gulp. "Surely not. You heard Kali. She said it would be like gestating the sun."

"Maybe not at first. Shit, Connie."

"Don't freak out. Please. I wish I hadn't said anything."

"Connie," Lorna says, completely serious. "Peter is a freaking god. Who is to say he can't burn straight through the bloody contraceptive pill?"

I gawk at my best friend, and we stay in silence for a minute, staring at each other. I try not to let my lips twitch but I can feel the corners of my mouth starting to turn. I manage to hold it in for longer than Lorna. She crumbles into a heap next to me, descending into hysterics.

She covers her eyes, rolling side to side. "I can't believe I said that," she gets out between laughs. "That is so gross."

I am crying now, ugly crying. "Stop it." I hit her arm. "I'm going to pee myself."

But we can't stop.

"Hey, what's so funny?" Anna asks, a bewildered half-smile on her face as she comes back into the room. Peter is carrying two bottles of water behind her. "We can hear the two of you down the hall."

"Nothing. The moment passed," I say, waving my hand dismissively and picking up my phone to skip to the next song. I push my hair out of my eyes and readjust to my previous position, flat on my back with my legs extended up the wall.

Upside down, I watch Peter sit on Anna's bed opposite me. As he does, he tilts his head, I presume to see down my top. So I wiggle my shoulders for him. He shakes his head and looks away, the slightest color rising on his face.

I push the thought out of my mind. It's not possible.

"Shall we play cards?" Anna asks.

"I feel like I need a drink." Lorna laughs, and I roll off my back and nod in agreement. "Too bad you can't turn water into wine, Peter."

"Now that would be a trick," he agrees.

We all stop at the small knock at the door. Lorna looks at me, bewildered, but Peter is already on his feet, opening it to reveal Sorcha standing in the doorway.

"What do you want?" To my relief, he doesn't sound friendly.

Sorcha drapes her body against the doorframe, looking up at him. "I come in peace, I promise." She holds up her hands, and although she's not touching him, she seems too close.

The old expression crosses my mind, *"When an unstoppable force meets an immovable object."*

She skirts around Peter and moves into the room. "The coven is abuzz about you all. And honestly, I came here to see if we can be friends." She turns back to look at Peter, making it clear his opinion is the only one that matters.

Peter glares at her, and Sorcha stares back.

I shift, moving to a sitting position to see them better. They seem to take all the air out of the room.

"Of course, Sorcha." Anna breaks the silence. "Come and sit down."

"Thanks." Sorcha moves to sit next to Anna, where Peter had been sitting only a moment ago.

"Are you closing the door, Peter?" Anna asks.

Peter hasn't moved, but the question is enough to make him stop staring at her. I notice him flex his neck before closing the door and sitting next to Lorna.

"So, what's your story?" Lorna asks Sorcha. "What can you do?"

"My story is a long one..." Sorcha smiles, "... but what I can do, I will show you." With a small wave of her hands, the room fills with rain.

In an instant, we are all on our feet, trying to shelter ourselves from the downpour. Everything is getting soaked, except Peter, who is watching Lorna jump up on the bed in confusion.

Sorcha gets to her feet, and in one movement of her arms, the rain is gone and the room is dry.

"What was that?" Peter asks.

"You couldn't see it?" Sorcha looks taken aback for a second as Peter shakes his head with some satisfaction.

"It was rain," Anna answers him, looking at her now dry clothes then to Sorcha in amazement.

"Well, it was the illusion of rain," Sorcha corrects. "Basically, I can make you see what I want."

"But not me," Peter says from his place on the bed.

"No, not you apparently, baby god."

A flicker of annoyance passes over his face at her words. *Maybe I got it all wrong before and they don't like each other at all.*

"It's not very useful, is it?" he bites back.

"Peter." Anna gives him a shove. "Why are you being so rude?"

Sorcha crosses her arms, moving to stand above him. "I can give illusion to all of the senses. How would you like it if your tiny girl-friend smelled rotting fish every time she is close to you?"

Peter is on his feet so fast even Sorcha takes a step away from him. But that is about all he does, stand and stare down at her, as if daring her to make the first move. For a moment, I think they'll start throwing punches. To my surprise, Sorcha backs down, moving away from him, not following through on her threat.

"Look..." she smooths out her ice-white hair, "... I really am here to be friends. I came at the coven's request to offer them protection. They're not worried, so now, neither am I. Let me do something, a gesture." Sorcha looks to all of us. "My powers can be really fun. Imagine the best ecstasy you've ever taken but with none of the comedown."

Anna snorts. "Peter doesn't even like us smoking."

A smile spreads across Sorcha's face. "Are you the boss of these women, Peter?"

Peter lets out a deep breath before shaking his head.

Lorna and Anna glance at each other in excitement. "Really, Peter?" Anna asks.

"I am not the boss of any of you."

I can tell it pains him to say the words—that he would rather us not feel whatever Sorcha is about to feed us even if it is an illusion—but he says no more. Lorna and Anna look to me, and I have to admit, I am curious. I give them a small smile, much to their delight.

Sorcha gives Peter a sly smirk. "That settles it. Your girls have decided to have a little fun."

Peter retakes his seat as Sorcha moves her body in time with the music, slow and sensual, looking at us now, the feeling radiating from her.

Working its way into my body, traveling up my spine, an incredible sensation of letting go overwhelms me. Being free. That's when need makes me want to move my body as well. Soon, my hands find Lorna's, entwining myself with her and Anna, who are both smiling and giggling.

Sorcha joins us as we all move together, connected.

Feeling so unbelievably good.

A bliss only outmatched by one thing I have felt before—when I am with Peter. When the ripples of his electricity pass over my body, nothing compares to that.

It takes me a minute to realize his dark eyes are on me, watching. I dance my way over and urge him to his feet. He may not be able to experience this—not the same way the girls and I are—but he can still feel me. I reach out and thread my fingers in his, lifting his arm over my head and pushing my body into him. It's enough for a reaction. He bites his lip, holding me closer, and starts to dance with me. Sorcha's illusion makes it even easier to focus on him, my world shrinking until it is just the two of us. His dark eyes look amused at the effects as he pushes his fingers through my hair to get a better look at my face.

"I wish I could feel what you are feeling," he whispers to me.

Sorcha is at our side—I hadn't noticed her join us—and she whispers to him, "The reason you cannot feel it is because you are fighting it."

She wraps her fingers around his, coming into rhythm with the two of us. I can see the moment it takes him when he closes his eyes against the fight, letting out a low breath. His head moves from side to side, slowly at first, as he opens his eyes to look at her, his soft brown eyes like obsidian with the rush of Sorcha's drug. Then he starts moving again in time to the music, Sorcha doing the same, pressing her body to his the way I had only moments before.

I feel too good to be bothered. Peter's other hand is clamped around my waist. Something in the back of my mind marks the way he looks at her, something I haven't seen there before.

Coolness.

Arrogance.

I have never seen him look so powerful.

Chapter Five

Anna

Life with the coven has become all too normal after so long in India, where we spent day upon day waiting for a sign of one. The truth is, it's been a long time since I felt like we were still looking for a witch or any answers. In my mind, Peter seemed content on living with his powers. Even now that we have found the coven—our coven—life has changed little. Peter is in no rush to ask the question we came here for, and I suppose I shouldn't mind. The coven has far more interesting insights.

When Peter made the promise we would return to Wixford after a year, he'd done so with the intention of returning me to Brady. What do we have to go back for now? Connie and Lorna's parents are not particularly happy with their decision not to go to university. Peter has assured me he had nothing to do with their decisions.

I sit, as I so often do, on the roof of our hostel, looking out across the waters. It looks so peaceful now. From behind me, I hear Connie laugh and turn to see her at the other end of the roof, leaning against the wall, her guitar on her belly with Peter at her feet, giving her a foot massage. I have no idea what's going on with them lately. Their relationship seems to have gone up a notch, not that I could've thought it possible.

The last few weeks, Peter has kept Connie glued to his side, hardly able to let her out of his sight and even less able to keep his hands off her.

I'm worried about her. I know Lorna is too, although Lorna is evasive as to why. Every night, I know he plows more and more of his power into her, a sensation I never wanted to encounter. But I do, and now I'm too far gone to tell him I know exactly what he is doing. Everyone is keeping secrets, and somehow, I know this all has something to do with Sorcha.

Since the night of the party, Sorcha hasn't given us any reason not to trust her. Although she comes and goes, her carefree spirit seems to grate on Peter for some reason. Often, we'll see her at the temple, or she'll turn up at the hostel at random times. She is fun to be around, and she often has Lorna and me in stitches with her stories. She isn't the friendliest toward Connie, but then again, Con is all but attached to Peter, and he isn't all that amicable toward her. Boy, it's easy to tell when they're in the same room together because they are either bickering or staring daggers at each other.

It's hard to get Peter alone to ask him questions now that he is using Connie as a human shield. I don't want to think badly of my brother, but I can't help wondering if he is doing it to stop himself from doing something he will regret. I have a weird sense of foreboding that something is coming.

Footsteps on metal.

Someone is climbing the old rusted ladder to the roof. I assume it must be Lorna, who has been napping, but when I look up, Sorcha is walking over to join me.

"Hi. Where have you been the past few days?" I greet her as she takes a seat next to me.

"The mountains. It's a great place to clear your mind." She smiles. "You should join me sometime."

I snort at the notion of Peter ever entertaining the idea of letting me go anywhere with her.

"Do you want to party tonight?" She flashes me a wicked grin.

Every now and then, Sorcha comes with this invite, which we all accept with eagerness. Well, Lorna and I do. It's fun. It is the only time Peter even talks to Sorcha and gives Connie a single moment away from him. It's good for her, even though I know she has mixed feelings about Sorcha's hands being on him.

"Maybe," I tell her. "Lorna isn't feeling too good."

Sorcha nods.

"Sorcha..." I start, deciding on an honest approach. "What's going on with you and my brother?"

Sorcha gives a musical laugh. "To be honest, I have no idea, Anna. I think Kali put it best on the first day we met. Can you imagine sitting in the same room as the sun? Now, put two suns in that room. It's uncomfortable, for both of us." She glances back at Peter. "But, just like the suns in the sky when they get too close, there is gravity between them." She observes him with Connie once more—they are decidedly ignoring her. "I see his girlfriend takes the brunt of his frustrations."

I pick up the tone of condescension in her voice and I say in his defense, "He needs to do it."

Sorcha looks back at me, her face soft. "I only mean to say... as long as he knows what he is doing, that's all."

I laugh at that. I don't know how many times I've spoken those exact words to him. "Peter not knowing what he is doing is the understatement of the century, Sorcha."

She cackles at those words. "I believe you." She shakes her head, putting her arm around me. "Tell me... what was it like for you growing up with him?"

It takes me a minute to think.

"No one has ever asked you that, have they?"

"Honestly? No." I snicker. "You know what's funny? I never knew life any different until two years ago. Our mother, she was paranoid. She hid us away from the world for seventeen years. My whole life *he* is the only thing I've ever known. It's been just me and him for so long." I try to put my thoughts into words. "Sometimes it's hard to separate the two."

Sorcha looks at me and slowly releases a deep breath. "Seventeen years. How did you do it?"

"He's not that bad." I laugh. "He's actually pretty gentle."

Sorcha considers me. "That's not what I meant. You and your brother, you defy the laws of this universe."

"What do you mean?" Something about her words makes all the hairs on my arms stand on end.

"Everything has balance, Anna. Light and dark, day and night, life and death. The universe demands balance." Sorcha lowers her head to mine. "Your souls, they want to be joined."

"Do you think it would be better for him if I died?" I look down at my hands, a sensation close to terror filling my entire being.

"Of course not." Sorcha takes my arms, trying to ease my shaking. "I think you two are some kind of miracle. Anna, I don't understand how the two of you can exist side by side. The imbalance should make it impossible."

I know Sorcha doesn't mean to scare me. Maybe what she's been led to believe her whole life is not true. Then, a thought occurs to me. "Thinking about it, he's only been like this since our mother died. We think she bound his powers. Kept them buried somehow."

Sorcha's pale eyes widen. "How interesting. Don't tell your brother I said this... his head is already big enough. He is very young, but he is extraordinarily strong. Even though he is incomplete." She blows out a puff of air that flutters her hair. "Your mother must have been awfully powerful to be able to do that."

"Did your powers get stronger over time?"

Sorcha inclines her head a fraction in confirmation.

"Why is he so strong?" My voice is but a whisper dreading what the answer might be.

Sorcha shrugs. "You? Your mother? Your father? I don't know." Sorcha matches my whisper. "But what he is doing to your human friend, you should try to get him to stop. It's dangerous for her. There is a reason I wouldn't use my powers on you all the time."

"What are you saying?" My heart hammers.

I knew it.

I knew something was going on.

Sorcha's eyes flick back to Peter, who is now approaching with Connie in tow. "Just don't tell him I told you. He will believe it more if it comes from you."

"We're heading over to the temple," he says to me, his arm slung around Connie's shoulder. "You coming?"

"Sure," I reply, replaying Sorcha's words in my mind. I have no idea how I'll talk to him about this. "I'll catch up with you, though. I want to go check in on Lorna first. Do you want to come, Sorcha?"

"No, I'll stay here for a bit. I think I'll dip my feet in the river."

Peter's eyes lock onto hers at the mention of the river, staring into her only for a moment before he turns back to me as he goes to leave, saying, "See you there, then."

I make my way back to my room, where Lorna is under her bed covers. She stirs a bit as I crouch next to her, then gives me a warm groggy smile when I push the hair out of her face. Her skin feels a little too warm.

"How are you feeling?" I ask.

"My tummy is not my friend."

"Do you want me to get Peter? He might be able to do something to help."

"No. It's fine. I just want to stay in bed."

"Okay. I'm heading over to the temple to join him and Connie." I get up and put a fresh bottle of water by her bedside. "Do you need me to get you anything?"

"No. I am just going to sleep it off. Thanks for looking after me."

"Anytime," I tell her, stroking her hair. Lorna is one of those girls who looks pretty no matter how she feels.

When I get to the temple, I spot Peter and Connie at the front, sitting on the steps with Mahi. Connie is nestled between Peter's legs as they watch Mahi levitate small stones about an inch off the ground with a lot of effort. Every time she manages to, they cheer so loud they attract the attention of everyone in the room and cause Mahi's face to flood scarlet. Mahi has become a bit of a favorite, and I get the feeling from the coven that they feel this means something. I'm overcome by a sudden feeling of guilt watching him with the girl, giving her high fives and encouraging her to try again. I shouldn't question his intentions. He would never knowingly do anything bad—to Connie or anyone else.

For once, Kali is on her own, not on her usual stone chair but toward the back of the room on a soft cushion, sewing. It reminds me of our mother, who used to sew our clothes. Being raised in complete isolation, our clothes were practically rags our whole lives. Reproductions and reimaginings of things either our mother or we had worn.

"Do you mind if I join you?" I ask her.

"I would love it if you did." She puts aside her sewing, anticipating my questions.

"Kali, what do you know about my mother? How did she meet our father? Our aunt told us she was mentally ill. Is that true, or was it just her witch powers?"

Kali gives a gentle chuckle. "That is a lot of questions there, my child. I will try to tell you what I know. Your mother had already run away from her home when your father found her in Ireland."

"She went to Ireland? Why?"

"It's hard to explain, but most witches are not born, Anna. They are taught. Every now and then, a person is born with a natural talent, an affinity that is not taught, like your mother. Her powers and her illness were one and the same, impossible to distinguish between."

"That's so sad," I whisper.

Kali nods. "It is. When Arjun met your mother, she had no training, just a natural ability, raw and easily manipulated. Now, you asked why Ireland. You see, your mother being a natural witch, she was drawn to places of significant energy. There are many places like this across the world. We're in one right now. It drew Peter here as it did us. There is also a place similar in Ireland, which is what brought your mother there. I am sorry to say it wasn't hard for Arjun to convince her of his plans, as her delusions matched his agenda."

I nod. "The second coming."

"That is what I believe." Her eyes cut toward Peter. "It would not be a stretch to convince her of what would need to be done. I can't imagine he told her what a danger the whole process would be to herself, or maybe she simply did not care."

My stomach turns to ice. "So, she knew? That I would be sacrificed."

Kali nods as I gulp down my words.

"If it weren't for that fire, they would have gone ahead with their plan."

Kali gently rests her hand on my face. "My dear, your mother started that fire."

My eyes snap back to her. "Why?"

"Something she never expected after all she had been through." Kali's smile is compassionate. "Love. She loved her children. She knew her time was running out, that one day the powers one of you was gifted with would show themselves, and the ritual would be completed by your father. Your poor brother would have been raised to be a beast at his hands. So, she found us, and we helped her escape. The original plan was she would come here once the deed was done, where we would protect her and you two. We did warn her that her human child would not survive. She obviously didn't accept this, so she fled, hiding you all and binding Peter for as long as she could hold on."

Tears prick my eyes, threatening to spill. "You mean she died because of the spell?"

"My child, you had what... seventeen long years with her? Your mother did everything she did out of love."

"How can you say that?" My tears now flow. "She was cruel. Everything she taught us about nature, life, and death. She always kept us at arm's length, used just enough of Peter's power to make him useful, taught us about connection and the stupid cycle, knowing it was not going to happen for him." The pain in my chest builds. "She was a drunk, and Peter took care of us all. Since we were kids, he's carried everything, Kali. No wonder he's messed up."

"Anna..." Kali joins me on my cushion, wrapping her arms around me, "... don't be so hard on her. I know you love your brother, and this may be a hard truth to hear, but gods are ancient creatures. His very nature is against him. He is what he is today because of your mother."

"What do you mean?" I ask as Kali wipes away the last of my tears.

"She taught him to be human. That life is precious. Look at him, Anna..." We look over to where Peter and Connie are still playing with Mahi. "He wants human connection, a home, love. He thinks of himself as more human than god. The binding spell may no longer be in place, but she saved us all from what he could have been."

Something in her words makes my heart break for him. "It's all temporary for him, though, Kali."

Kali gives a thoughtful nod. "It is true. The path you walk side by side is not an easy one. But you have a home here." Kali pulls me into an embrace. "For as long as you want it. Somewhere where he can feel at home, for generations."

I know I should feel comforted by Kali's words. It was how she had meant them. But I can't help thinking there is something dangerous about Peter considering himself as more human. It brings me back to Sorcha's words. Except, what's the alternative? The creature Arjun had envisioned—an ancient, savage creature—that is not my brother.

Instead, he is doomed, as he says. Despite all of his love and his humanity, one day, we will all die as is right, and Peter will live. I peek over at him as he smiles down at Connie.

How does he bear it? I shudder at the thought and leave the temple.

I take my time walking back to the hostel, trying to clear my head and organize my thoughts.

When I get back, Sorcha is nowhere in sight, and Lorna is fast asleep. My regular post on the roof calls to me, where I watch as the skies turn pinky-orange. Peter and Connie are down below, walking toward the river.

I know what he is going to do and I'm on my feet in an instant, following them down.

"Hey. *Hey*," I shout after them, feeling a bit out of breath and a bit manic.

They stop and wait for me to catch up, looking a bit bewildered.

"Are you okay?" Peter asks. "I'm just going into the river."

"Well, don't. I need to talk to you." I'm going about this all wrong, but I don't want him to step into those waters. It makes my skin crawl. Peter looks from me to Connie, somewhat confused, waiting for me to proceed but I can't think of the right words to say.

"Okay," he says with an edge of caution. "Why don't you stay here with Connie? I won't be long."

"No. What I'm saying is *don't* go into the water. Why do you have to do it?"

Peter looks taken aback. I've never asked him before. I have always preferred to avoid the topic because the feeling creeps me out.

"It's nothing bad," he says in a simple tone.

"No, you have to tell me more than that, brother. Because it feels wrong to me."

"What do you mean?" he asks, his expression becoming unreadable.

"I can feel it too. When you are in there, all of those souls being carried down the river... it makes my blood run cold." I wrap my arms around myself, dropping my voice to a whisper. "Why do you like it? Where are they going?"

"It's cleansing. I don't know where they are going." Peter's strong eye contact and tilted head show concern when he rounds on me slightly. "What do you mean you can feel it?"

I shake my head, rubbing my eyes. "It's kind of like an echo. What you feel when you're in there, I can feel it ripple against my skin." I look down. "It happens all of the time, Peter. Whenever you use your powers, or even when you feel an emotion strong enough, I can feel it. It's been that way since you healed yourself."

"You have to be joking." Peter's words sound hollow. "Tell me you are joking, Anna." Sounding angrier now, grabbing both of my arms, he states, "This whole time, you've kept this a secret from me?"

I stare up into his hard face, his anger catching me a little surprised. "Don't you lecture me about keeping secrets. You keep secrets from all of us. I thought I was protecting you. I am telling you now, you need to start taking some responsibility for yourself. You have to remember that you affect *all of us* around you."

"Not this crap again. Just say what you want to say to me."

I glance at Connie. I don't want to hurt her. "You have to stop," I say through gritted teeth. "You have to think about what you're doing."

"That is *all* I ever do," Peter shouts at me. "My whole fucking existence is nothing but measured steps."

I laugh, a humorless laugh. "Now you are the one who is joking. All you do is act. If it feels good, if it feels right for you, that is what you do. I can feel it, Peter."

"Are you kidding me? That is what you think of me?"

I regret what I've said in an instant as his voice becomes a deadly whisper. "Everything I do every day is to keep me from what I really am. You don't think I feel it in there." He slams his hand into his chest. "I will fight with everything I have to not become what he said I would be."

I shake my head, trying to say the words only he can hear. "You have to think of Connie."

Lightning quick, his hand becomes a vice on my jaw, his eyes hard as stone—a way my brother has never looked at me before—his face inches from mine as he growls, "Don't do that. I would never, *ever* do anything to hurt her."

I try to pull away from him, something in his expression changing.

"Where is this coming from? Did Sorcha put you up to this?"

He finally lets me go, leaving just a slight ache from where his grip was too tight. He shakes his head at me, taking my silence as my admission that, yes, Sorcha has something to do with this.

And that's when he turns his back and walks away from me.

Chapter Six

Connie

Peter and Anna not talking is weird.

Both are too stubborn to apologize to each other.

Peter is upset that Anna has kept what she's been feeling a secret for so long, but really, I know most of his hurt comes from Anna thinking so ill of him. Anna hasn't been as forthcoming with me. Not that I have much chance to speak to her at the moment, but it doesn't take much stretch of the imagination when the soft bruising of a handprint appears on her lower jaw to understand why she is still mad. Peter cannot bring himself to look at her, he is so ashamed. Another reason he is keeping his distance.

I feel so warm I don't want to wake, but I begin to peel open my eyes. The weather has taken on a chilly edge these last few days, so I know before my eyes are open that Peter is still in bed. He's lying on his side, watching me, brown eyes wide so I check my face for drool.

"How long have you been awake?"

"Not sure." Peter shrugs, moving to pull me closer. "A few hours."

"Ugh." I push my hand onto his warm chest. "You've just been watching me. That's really creepy."

Gemini

He laughs, tracing the edges of my face. "I do it all the time. You are so beautiful."

I feel the heat rise in my face, smothering my cheeks in red I am sure.

"Plus, you were snoring."

"Shut up. I don't snore."

"You do. It's not loud. More like this little growl."

I use my free hand to cover my face. "That is mortifying."

"It's adorable." He smiles.

I stretch, hearing some of my bones crack.

Peter's expression turns serious. "Connie, have I ever hurt you?" His voice laced with this much uncertainty is so rare for him.

"No. Never. Why would you ask that?" I return without hesitation, taking in the furrow of his brow.

"What I do... it doesn't hurt you?"

"You mean the electricity?" I place my hand on his face. "No, of course not. It feels good, Peter. It makes *me* feel good. I thought you knew that."

Peter closes his eyes in relief, taking my hand and bringing my wrist to his lips. "I did. I do. It's just this whole fight with Anna, it's really messing with my head." He keeps his eyes closed. "I *never* want to hurt you."

My chest constricts. It's been a long time since I've seen him look so vulnerable. He needs this fight with Anna to be over. I draw him close, wrapping my arms and legs around his body, holding him as close as I can. His strong arms wrap around me, holding me so close they threaten to choke me.

"Sadhu is back," he says into my hair after a while, pulling back. "I will go up to the roof to see him. Will you come with me?"

"Peter." I hold his face in my hands. "You go," I encourage and feel his hands tighten on me. It concerns me enough to ask, "What's going on with you? What are you scared of?"

"Everything," he says with a chuckle, closing his eyes tight. "You're right." He opens his eyes to look at me, saying his words more to himself. "I can go on my own. You get breakfast, and I will be with you soon. I won't be long."

When he moves, he takes all the warmth from the bed with him.

I take my time getting dressed before heading downstairs.

Lorna and Anna are sitting at their favorite low table in the corner of the balcony. It's been a few days since I've eaten breakfast with them.

The last week or two, it's been difficult to find a moment away from Peter. After our conversation, Lorna went to the pharmacy for a pregnancy test. I managed to sneak into the bathroom with her one afternoon to do it without Peter or Anna noticing. *Negative.* Both Lorna and I had let out a collective sigh of relief. It would've been a complication none of us needed, especially now, what with Peter and Anna falling out.

Nervous, I go and sit in front of them. "Is it okay if I join you?"

"Of course, Con." Lorna's smile is warm.

I chance a glance at Anna, who gives me a hint of a smile. It's pretty embarrassing to learn she can feel what Peter has been doing. Since finding out, he has shown more restraint where he can, trying to meditate more. I know he's glad sadhu is back. While I appreciate Anna's concern, the truth is, I don't want him to stop.

I run my finger along the edge of my jaw. "That is looking a lot better," I say to her. The bruise all but gone now.

She nods. "I see he's managed to release you from his presence for a second."

"He's suffering, Anna. Can't this fight be over?"

Anna sinks her head into her hands. "Believe me, Connie, I want it to be. It feels unnatural not to be talking to him." She looks at Lorna, who rubs her back. "I think I just need a bit more time."

I give her a nod. *Progress, I guess.*

I tuck into my omelet and coffee when Vik brings them over.

Not much later, I feel Peter slip his hands onto my shoulders from behind me, his thumbs rubbing in anxious circles.

Gemini

"Hi," he says, and I know he's talking to Anna as she glances up at him. "Anna. Your face, I'm really sorry about that."

I see Lorna's dark eyes flick up to him and then to me. I guess we both thought Anna would give in first.

"Thank you," she says, her tone stiff.

"Can we just move past this?" I hear the crack in his voice as he pleads with her.

"I'm not ready, Peter," Anna says, getting up and brushing past him.

"She'll come round," Lorna soothes, her face soft, almost in the way of an apology herself.

Peter takes a few paces and sits on the cushion next to Lorna. "I hate her being mad at me."

"You scared her." She eases the words out.

"I didn't mean to."

Lorna gives him a half smile, which must aim as reassurance. I think we all know Peter would never hurt Anna on purpose.

"I'm going to head over to the temple," he says to me. "Will you come?"

I nod as he turns to Lorna, a silent invite on his lips.

"I'd better stay here with Anna," Lorna decides.

This last week while they've not been talking, Peter and I have retreated to the sanctuary of the temple. Peter is sitting cross-legged at the back of the room, playing cards with Mahi. It's good to see him looking a little more relaxed. I make my way over to the small kitchen area to get some water. Closing the refrigerator door, Sorcha's standing there watching me.

"Hi, Connie," she says.

"Hi. I haven't seen you here in a while."

"Mmm... I have been doing a little traveling." She smooths back her hair, looking a bit uncomfortable. "I wanted to apologize to you."

That takes me by surprise. "For what?"

"For not being nicer to you." She gives a little laugh. "Truth is, I guess I am a little jealous."

I can't believe the words coming out of her mouth. "You? Are jealous? Of me? Why?" I sound like an idiot with all the dumb questions.

Sorcha shifts about, ill at ease. "Connie, don't make me say it."

Him, obviously. I don't make her say it. Perhaps if I patch things up with Sorcha, it will move things along with Peter and Anna.

"Sorcha, I am sorry too. I haven't been the friendliest either."

Sorcha gives a huge sigh of relief, taking an easy step backward. "Thank you. I'm so glad I got a moment to talk to you." She laughs. "He is very protective of you."

This makes me chuckle. *Who would have thought it?*

She gives me a brilliant smile, one that touches her eyes. "Can we start over? Try and be friends?"

"Sure," I say, deliberate but tentative. "I would like that." I don't know why I don't trust her. Everyone else seems to like her—except Peter—but it's hard to tell how Peter feels about her for real because I'm kind of too scared to ask.

As if reading my mind, Peter puts his arm around my stomach, pulling me against his chest.

"What are you talking about?" The question comes out hard, so I know it is meant for Sorcha.

She rolls her silver eyes at him. "Has it ever occurred to you that it doesn't concern you, baby god?" With a flick of her hair, she dramatically spins and exits the room.

Peter stares after her. "What did she want?" he says much nicer to me, turning me to face him.

"Erm, to be friends, I think." I pull him close. "Maybe we've been a little hard on her."

Peter raises his eyebrows.

"Maybe we should *try*, you know?"

Gemini

But Sorcha's presence back in the coven has set him on edge. Their constant glares at each other start to grate on my nerves.

I need to get out of here.

"I'm going to go back to the hostel," I say, standing.

Peter eyes me with surprise. "Okay," he agrees, a strange glint in his eyes, standing to join me.

"You can stay." I put my hand on his chest. Perhaps I need a bit of breathing room from him too, to speak to Lorna. My head is always in the clouds with him around. Peter's proximity rarely leaves me with a coherent thought in my head. And Sorcha being back sinks my thoughts into the mist even further. My ability to think straight around both of them is absolute zero.

Instead, he takes my hand, and we walk back to the hostel.

We don't talk the whole way back. With every step I take, I feel more and more of a weird charge between us. Peter's constant gaze on me is almost oppressive.

As soon as we are back in the privacy of our room, his arms are around me, turning me, his kisses coming hard and fast. Lifting me clear off the floor, he wraps me around him. I can't catch my breath. The only slight reprieve is when he drops me to the bed. The reprieve is an unwelcome one. *Who needs to breathe when it's possible to feel this good?* After yanking his T-shirt up over his head, he is on me again. His kisses are hot on my neck, and I can already feel the crackling of electricity, clouding every last one of my thoughts.

"Peter." I gasp.

"Connie," he whispers, his kisses now traveling down my chest.

Who cares about my thoughts? He feels too good.

"Connie," he continues. "I have this thought." He pulls my shirt over my head. My brain is in such a fog that I don't register what he is saying. "Of you." He kisses me. "Me." His kisses are at my neck again. "And Sorcha." His lips find mine, his hands running up my back drawing me in closer. I will give him anything he wants, but...

Sorcha?

My hand comes down heavy on his shoulder, and with all the force I can muster, I shove him off me. "What?" I demand, pulling myself together.

Peter leans back on his heels, his face the picture of innocence. "You don't want to?"

I pull my shirt back on and climb off the bed. "I don't want to what? Share you with Sorcha? No, I don't want that."

I don't know what I'm doing. Frantic, I look around for something to throw at him.

"Connie," he soothes, reaching out for my hand.

I whisk it out of his reach. "Is that what you want, Peter? You want her?"

"No, I want you." He runs his hands through his hair. "It was just a thought." He shrugs.

A thought? Like ordering pizza.

No big deal.

Has he lost his damn mind?

I look around again. There has to be something to throw at him.

My search for something to beat him with is stopped by a soft knock at the door. My stomach drops when Peter moves to open it, inching around me like I am a wild animal who might attack. I pray it isn't who I think it will be.

Sorcha.

I narrow my eyes at him. "Did you plan this?" I ask as Sorcha glides into the room, her eyes only on him.

He shakes his head, a slow and calculated movement directed at me. "Of course not." Then he turns to Sorcha, his voice smooth and serious. "Connie stays," he says with no room for argument.

I see Sorcha nod in agreement.

But my hand is already on the door handle.

Chapter Seven

Anna

Connie is not making any sense. From her place on Lorna's bed, all of her words are garbled.

Lorna looks up at me in panic.

I clamp my hand hard on Connie's shoulder, crouching to look her in the eyes. "Connie, breathe. Tell us what happened."

Connie lets out a long ragged breath. "Peter. He is with Sorcha."

Lorna's eyes flash at me.

I will kill him. I am going to murder my idiot brother.

I fly out of our room and bash my palm onto Peter's bedroom door, hammering it with all of my force. It's not needed because he answers straight away, standing there shirtless, Sorcha hovering behind him.

"What the hell are you doing?" I scream, making even him flinch.

"Nothing," he says, holding his hands up.

"Really? Because Connie is distraught."

Peter pushes past me, out of his room and into mine, coming to a stop in the doorway as Lorna stands over Connie, protecting her.

"Connie, please... come talk to me."

She shakes her head in response.

"Are you sleeping with her?" Lorna asks, nodding in Sorcha's direction, whose hip is balanced on the doorframe.

I move to stand between Peter and Connie.

"What? No. When would I have been able to do that?" Peter laughs, looking at us like we've all lost our minds before settling his eyes on Sorcha, whose eyebrows are raised. He shakes his head, ruffling his hair, trying to organize his thoughts. "Sorcha." He lets out a noise of utter frustration. "No, I am not sleeping with her. I don't know what I want. I don't know if I want to screw her or kill her."

Lorna makes a noise of disgust.

Sorcha gives a humorless laugh. "The feeling is mutual, baby god."

"*Get. Out!*" Connie screams at him. "If that is what you want, then *get out*."

"Connie. No, that is *not* what I want. I want you." His voice sounds too smooth as he approaches her. "I love you. I want you." This time, she lets him take her hands. "Why can't I have both, Connie? I want you there with me. I always want you with me. Trust me, it will be so amazing. We can make *you* feel so good. I only want it with you there."

I feel the disgust rise in my throat as I realize what has happened. Connie's face starts to soften, and I'm aghast she might even consider this. There is no way I am letting her give in to him. He cannot go through life getting *everything* he desires.

I close the distance. Two paces are all it takes to plant my palms onto his chest and shove him back into the wall. Peter's face is awash with absolute shock. So often, I feel his emotions. I only hope he can feel my fury.

"You are disgusting," I spit at him.

It's enough to make him snap out of it and look from me back to Connie's tear-stained face.

"Shit," he says, raking his hand down his face and heaving himself from his place on the wall to turn to Connie, who has taken a step away from him again. "Connie, I am so sorry. I am the biggest idiot. I'm so sorry. I would never have gone through with it." He looks back at Sorcha. "Can you just go already?"

"You want to screw her, Peter. You j-just said it in front of e-everyone." Connie's voice shakes.

"I know. It's my fault. It was a really, *really* stupid thing to say. I wish I could take it back." All of the arrogance I'd just witnessed starts to melt away. "I don't want to *be* with her. I wanted *us* to be with her. I will never, *ever* ask you something so stupid again."

Out of the corner of my eye, I can see Sorcha's eyes bulging. "Peter, what are you doing?"

"Don't you think you've done enough?" I spit at her.

This all comes down to Sorcha—why I am mad at him, why Connie is mad at him. *I am so stupid. Of course, this is all about Peter. It's always about Peter.*

"I am sorry, Peter," Sorcha says, shaking her head at him, sounding anything but. "I cannot hold my tongue anymore. Can't you see what you're doing to this poor girl? What with your incessant need to use what you have? You are wearing her out. Is that what you want, to kill her?"

"Connie, that's not true." He turns on Sorcha. "What are you trying to do to me? Why would you say that?"

As much as I hate Sorcha right now, what she says makes sense. Connie's continuing weight loss is a prime example. I'm sure Peter can tell from my expression that I'm uncertain if she is lying.

"Because it's the truth." Sorcha cocks her head at him. "It's really not fair to play with your pets like this. Besides, what can you offer her other than an addiction that will burn through her body eventually? Doesn't she deserve a human life, one where she can have a family?"

The moment the words leave her mouth, I know she's got the right hook into Peter. I can see the retreat in his face as Sorcha laughs, humorless and calculating.

"You really didn't know? I am sorry to be the one to tell you,

Peter, but you cannot father children. It is part of the cosmic joke that makes us what we are."

Peter takes a step away from Connie. "I didn't know, Connie."

Connie blinks, glancing between him and Sorcha.

"Why don't you tell her what you *do* know?" A sly smile passes across Sorcha's lips.

Peter's eyes flash back to Sorcha. "No."

"What?" Connie stares at Peter, and his eyes land on mine in sheer panic.

"Connie, you seem sweet. You deserve to know." She smiles.

As if Sorcha cares at all about Connie.

"Stop," Peter whispers, but it is too late.

"If you won't tell her, then I will." She directs her body toward Connie. "The only reason you are doing any of this, entertaining a life with him at all, is because he wants you to." Sorcha rounds on her. "You are so far under his influence that even he doesn't know whether your love is real or not."

Connie recoils away from Peter and into Lorna. "She's lying, right, Peter?"

Peter implores Sorcha. "Why are you doing this to me?"

Except Sorcha has also found the right hook to put Connie on.

"Tell me it isn't true, Peter." She forces him to look at her. "Tell me you're not using your influence on me."

Peter's face is in his hands again. "*Using* is a strong word. I can't control it." He scrambles for his words. "I am not *using* my influence on you, Connie. I never use those powers. Not on the people I l-love." His voice cracks. "I would never *knowingly* use it on you. I love you. It's because I want you so bad that I don't know for certain. I don't know if you feel the same way. Trust me when I tell you I hope it's not true."

Connie sinks to the bed and drops her head into her hands. "You *hope* it's not true? Jesus, Peter. You think I might not be able to control what I'm doing, how I'm feeling, and your reaction is to continue sleeping with me? Feeding on me, even. Make it so that, what? I am addicted to you?"

"Connie, don't do that."

I can almost feel his hurt at the accusation.

"Don't make it sound like that. How I feel about you... it's real. I love you."

"No, Peter. You don't do that to someone you love." Connie is on her feet, backing away from us all. She looks at me for the first time, the same accusation in her stare. "Did you know about this, Anna?"

"It's complicated. She's making it sound way worse than it really is, Connie."

"Oh my God," Connie whispers, clutching her chest.

Peter takes a tentative step toward her, his hands raised, complete devastation in his countenance. "Connie, Arjun said there was a spell, something to make you immune. If we could just go to the coven—"

"Arjun?" Connie's voice is shrill. "You've known this since Arjun? And you didn't say anything?" She doubles over. "I think I am going to be sick."

Peter moves to support her, but she throws her hands up and pushes him away.

"Don't you dare touch me. You don't get to do that anymore."

Lorna moves to her friend's side, supporting her as the tears come again.

"Connie." Peter's voice sounds desperate. "It's not like that. I have *never* forced you to do anything."

But I can see it, and my heart is breaking too.

He's already lost her.

Connie straightens herself up to look him in the eye. "But you *want* me, and so I have no choice but to want you back." Connie shakes her head. "I'm going to get my stuff."

"Connie, please don't g-go." His voice breaks.

"What are you doing, Peter?" She fights against her tears. "Are you going to force me to stay?"

I clutch my chest as I watch him shake his head, then lift his face to the ceiling so he doesn't have to witness her leave. As soon as she's gone, he sinks to the bed, and I'm across the room and in his arms. He's holding me so close it feels like my bones could break. My soul—his soul. I feel my own tears falling down my face. There are no words for how he feels because I feel it all too. So broken, I don't know how we will ever be whole again.

For the first time in over a year, storm clouds roll in, and lightning forks and hits the waters of the Ganges. I can't remember at what point Sorcha slipped out of the room, but I'm glad she's gone. I might have killed her myself, given half a chance.

I hold Peter at arm's length, both of our faces puffy. "You can't let her go."

"I did this," he says, his eyes distant.

"Peter," I say, shaking him. "We can't let her leave like this. It's a mistake. We have to fix it."

"Anna." He takes hold of my elbows. "I did this. I am bad for her. Didn't you hear? Even if I get her to the coven somehow, and they do the spell, and by some miracle she forgives me, you heard the rest. I am killing her, robbing her of a chance for a family."

I stand. "You're not going to fight for her?"

"I've already lost, Anna."

Screw that.

I'm out the door and back in his room in a flash where Lorna is helping Connie pack in silence.

Connie takes some money from under the mattress.

She is really doing this.

"Can we just take a minute?" I ask.

Connie looks up at me, exhausted. "I can't even look at him, Anna."

"I know..." I cross the room to implore her. "I know my brother can make you madder than you have ever been with anyone in your life. But, please believe me, he is not controlling you. *I* would be able to feel it."

"So there is no truth to any of it?" Connie raises an eyebrow.

"I know you love him." I feel the tears prick my eyes watching her.

Connie fights back her own. "Except I don't know if it's real." She pushes them down. "I can't stay, Anna. I love him and I love you, but how can I ever trust myself with him?"

"The coven, Connie. They can help." I'm begging her now, pleading for her to stay.

"I don't want it." Connie shakes her head again, fighting a fresh wave of tears. "I don't want that spell. It may not be real, but I don't want to forget all the things he's made me feel. I don't want that to happen to me."

I can't believe this is happening.

I watch Connie hug Lorna goodbye before she turns and pulls me into a hug. "Look after him, okay? It's *you* he needs."

And Connie is gone.

I have to make him follow her, bring her back.

But when I finally go back to my room, Peter is also gone.

I race up to the roof just in time to see him below.

He's wading into the river, right up to his shoulders.

I should have felt it before.

I watch him as his head goes under.

Chapter Eight

Peter

The downpour masks my drenching from the river as I drip back to my room.

I'm hollow, with no emotion to make the world react around me. Just hollow.

I'm a terrible person.

As I shuffle down the corridor, I hear Lorna and Anna talking in their room, although I can't tell what they're saying. I don't make it back to my room before Anna's door opens and her voice is at my back.

"Peter, are you okay?"

"No, Anna," I say without turning around to face her. "I'm pretty far from okay."

I retreat into my room and fall back onto my bed.

Connie is gone.

For real.

My hands rake through my hair while I try to organize my thoughts. Thoughts I have long tried to bury.

Connie.

The influence.

How much was she really under?
She could leave me.
She could walk away.
The influence is such a murky thing.
How many of my ideas has she gone along with because I wanted her to?
She was able to walk away.
Which had to count for something.
So, what do I influence? Her heart? Her emotions? Nothing at all?
I should have made that spell my priority at the coven. My fear that I control too much, too scared to remove it in case the worst-case scenario is true, held me back.
Maybe Connie never felt anything at all.
Maybe she was never mine.
The soft knock at my door brings me back.
I am so not in the mood for this.
I move to open the door. "You need professional help, Sorcha," I tell her, stepping back to let her in. *I don't know why I'm even bothering to talk to her.* At least it's a distraction, I guess.

Her eyes follow as I go and sit back down, caution filling her look, her every muscle tight with it. "Peter. I know you don't believe me, but my intention is not to hurt you or her. Not really."

A hollow laugh escapes me. I'm lost for words. Sorcha knew exactly what she was doing.

She leans against the window ledge to study me. "Trust me... I did her a kindness. And you need to learn to be more careful with your pets."

I take a deep breath. *Find your center,* I tell myself. "Do you have a death wish or something? What are you here for?"

Her stare turns hard, with her eyes now flinty. "You need to realize what you are. I'm doing you a favor. Listen to me... I have been around a lot longer than you, and over time, you will have a great many followers. Some will be your favorites, and yes, some you may even fall in love with, and it will break your heart every time they die.

Every. Single. Time." She moves closer to me, kneeling at my feet. "Peter, I was not lying. I know you care about her, but her body is not built to last. Whatever it was that you were doing, it was killing her."

I stare into her silver eyes, trying to find the lie there, and ask again, "What are you doing here, Sorcha?"

"What *were* you doing to her, out of interest?" She gives me a wry smile, avoiding my question.

She is seriously starting to aggravate me.

"Why? Do you want it?" I ask without thinking.

Her eyes gleam as she moves to stand. I watch her, and I know she wants to say yes, but she doesn't know what she is agreeing to.

Sorcha bites her lip. "It's you I want. You do know that, right?"

My heart hammers. I loathe myself, but I don't move, just freeze, as she eases a knee on either side of me, straddling my lap. I hate my body for reacting, for noticing how good her body feels. She's more substantial than Connie. At the same time, I hate that it's not Connie.

I swallow hard.

Just tell her to go.

"Your thing is plants, right? Show me." I stare up at her, indecision vibrating through me. She is magnificent. Finally, she rolls her silver eyes. "Yes, Peter, I want it," she purrs.

I sit up so quickly it catches her off guard as I grab onto her wrist. Then, I send a surge of electricity down her arm, only a little bit more than I needed to, but enough to hurt her a touch.

"Shit!" She clasps onto her arm, moving off me in a heartbeat to stare at the place where my golden electricity crackled moments before. She laughs, sounding more nervous than she wants to. "Baby god, you have been holding out on us. What was that?"

"What did it feel like?" I mock her, glad of a little payback.

She glances at the storm outside the window, shaking her head a little, eyeing me with more caution now. "But how? How do you control it?"

"Sorcha," I say, stalking over to her and taking her face in my palm, letting the static crackle there. "I control *everything*." Although

Gemini

I'm enjoying how Sorcha is trembling a bit—that what I can do is so much more than her, that it makes her fear me enough she can't help but show it—it's a lie. In this moment, I am *not* in control. "Do you still want it?" I ask.

She nods, her silver eyes penetrating me as I bring her lips to mine.

The steady rhythm of rain outside greets me when I wake. I am thankful Sorcha has already left.

I lie back in bed—Connie's and my bed—observing a few pieces of furniture I broke throwing Sorcha against. Doing all the things that have plagued my thoughts for weeks.

I officially hate myself.

The last thing I want to do is go down to breakfast. I don't want to see Anna. I also don't want to go to the coven. No doubt Sorcha has run back there to tell them all I've been hiding. It seems she has come into my life to tell the world all my secrets.

I rub my eyes. *What a mess.*

Not wanting to face anything, I decide to go back to sleep.

When I wake later, it's already dark, and the rain has subsided. It takes me a minute to realize a knock at my door is what has woken me.

I go and open it, not bothering to say hello as I retreat back under the covers.

"Jesus, Peter. You could have put some clothes on. I could've been anyone."

"Who else would it be?" I roll away from her on the bed.

"What if it was Lorna?"

"She would've gotten over it."

I feel Anna's weight on the bed next to me. "So, this is what you are going to do? You're going to sulk?"

I pull the sheet over my head. "You know what happened, right?"

"Peter." Anna sighs. "I know your heart is broken."

I peep my head back out from under the covers to look at her. Her face is full of empathy even though I have done nothing to deserve anything but animosity right now.

"I am officially a piece of shit."

Anna laughs. "Maybe you could stop making horrible decisions?"

I put my hand over my face. "The coven, Anna. What am I going to do?"

"There is this little thing called honesty, Peter. Maybe you could try it?" Anna shrugs. "Kali is reasonable. She probably already suspects there are things you're not saying. Between our mother and Arjun, she'll be understanding that we don't trust easy."

I nod. That makes sense. "Have you heard from Connie?" I ask, the lump forming in my throat.

Anna nods, averting her eyes. "She texted Lorna from the train. She's okay."

I nod, not knowing what else to say.

Connie is gone.

Anna runs her fingers through my hair. "Will you be okay?"

I let out a shaky breath. "I'm not sure. Will you stay with me?"

My sister shakes her head. "I told Lor I was just coming to check on you. I'm going to get back to her."

I give her a small smile, propping myself up on my elbow. "Are you and Lorna?" I ask, wiggling my eyebrows at her but not finishing the sentence.

"No." She pushes my shoulder. "Is that the only thing your brain thinks of?"

I catch her hand, laughing. "No? Then why are you blushing?"

"Because you are being ridiculous."

I shrug my shoulders. "I would be happy for you. One of us should be happy."

"Good night, Peter," she says as she leaves. "And take a shower. You stink."

It's more than I deserve. I decide to bask in the small victory of

Gemini

Anna talking to me again and take a shower. Anna is right. I should go to the coven tomorrow and tell them everything.

When I get out, Sorcha is already in my room, perched on the end of the bed, looking at her fingernails. I grimace at the sight of her.

"What are you doing here, Sorcha?"

Sorcha shrugs her shoulders. "I thought this had to be a nightly thing, or you, I don't know, you go *pop*."

I laugh, shaking my head as I dry myself. "I don't want to see you every night. I don't think even I can handle that level of self-loathing."

"Fine by me." She jumps up, clapping her hands together. "But I am here now. So..." Her eyes travel down my body.

Just send her away, Peter.

"So I think you should go."

"Okay." Sorcha nods, moving toward the door. "So, just to be clear. What you peddled to your girlfriend, that this was something you *had* to do to keep all that power inside of you in check, that was all bullshit?"

"Wait." I turn to her. "It wasn't bullshit. I do need to do it... to use it, to keep it balanced. What I mean Sorcha is... I can't do this with *you*. You will *never* be her. Do you understand?"

"Sure," she says. "I understand. But, I am here now," she repeats, letting the offer hang in the air.

"So come here."

Chapter Nine

Connie

The rain has followed me home.
Home.
It feels strange being back in Wixford. It's all familiar, yet it seems so far away.

As I walk up to my front door, a few short days after walking away from Peter, I'd hoped it would bring me more of a sense of relief, but right now, I still feel hollow. And incredibly tired.

I hadn't mentioned to Lorna in my texts how horrible my journey to the airport had been. My body went into some kind of shock or withdrawal. I was vomiting, had cold sweats, and had nightmares of drowning. I look worse now than I did before. No more glow, just sick and hollow, the whole journey consumed by one thought…

Peter knew.

He knew the whole time and didn't say a word.

I press the doorbell, and even that simple action seems like an effort. I called my mum from the airport in Mumbai to tell her I was coming home but can't remember the conversation. When my phone ran out of battery, I made my own way back from Heathrow, letting my tired legs carry me. It's been over a year since I've seen her.

My mum flings open the door.

Strange, all of my homesickness hits me at once. Dropping my backpack, I close the gap and am in her arms. Crying. Not for Peter, but because I have missed Mum so much. She is crying too, so much so her knees buckle, and we are basically a big sobbing heap on the floor.

I stay in my room for three days.

Three whole days of nothing but sleep, drinking cold tea Mum has left on my bedside table, and eating the three meals a day she brings up to me. I haven't seen my dad.

On the fourth day, I finally get out of bed and take a shower. A long, hot shower. I can't remember when I last had a shower so warm. Our showers in Varanasi had been lukewarm and not more than a trickle. I enjoy scrubbing my skin. It feels so good. I am quite embarrassed by the color I turn the water, but seeing the filth and grime wash away down the drain makes me feel better and more like myself again.

In the bathroom mirror, my skin still looks a bit sallow, but it's getting better. I run my hand over my belly. Not quite so flat after three days of being fed and zero movement. I smile at its softness.

I make my way downstairs to see my mum in the kitchen making breakfast, her face full of worry. The smell of the fry-up she is making makes my mouth water.

"You're out of bed. I thought you were when I heard the shower. Are you hungry?"

"Starving." I move to sit at the breakfast bar as she switches on the kettle, casting a nervous glance my way.

"Connie, I can't tell you how happy I am you're home. But... what happened? Where are the others?"

"They're still in India, Mum." I rest my hand on my chest. "Peter and I broke up."

She hands me my cup of tea. "Mmm... I see. What happened?"

"I really don't want to talk about it right now." What do I even say to her? That he cheated? I suppose it would be the easiest thing for her to understand.

"I'm just surprised you came back on your own. Why didn't Lorna come back with you?"

I suppose I hadn't thought about it. I'd been stuck to Peter like glue for so long that when I found out the truth, I needed to put some physical distance between us. I blink at my mum. Thinking about it now, the need for space kept pushing me farther away until I arrived back home. It never occurred to me to ask Lorna to come with me.

"They all have a life out there, Mum. I couldn't ask Lorna to follow me back."

My mum eyes me as she hands me breakfast. "So, what? They have no intentions of coming back?"

I shrug my shoulders, desperate to eat.

"I know Lorna's parents and I got the odd phone call, but Sally and James are beside themselves with worry."

"I thought Anna kept in touch?" I say, then bite into my piece of toast.

"Not for a long time." Her eyes turn watery. "You said you were only going for a year, to travel. But I hardly ever heard from you, and when I did, you were always distant. I've been so worried about you, Connie. We've all been."

My heart sinks. I never thought about those we left behind. "I'm sorry, Mum." I rest my hand on hers. "There was never any need to worry. I'm fine. And they are too. I'll speak to Lorna and Anna about getting in touch more."

She nods, giving me a shaky smile. I can sense all the relief radiating from her as she glances down at her cup of tea. "Constance Prinze, you are a bag of bones. I need to fatten you up a bit." She laughs.

I nod my head in agreement. "Yes, please."

She looks happy to see me demolishing my plate of food.

"Where's Dad?" I ask, looking around for a sign of him. "Is he working away?"

My mum is instantly uncomfortable. "Oh, well. Actually, Connie, your father... he moved out. A few months ago."

I almost drop my fork. "What? You and Dad aren't together anymore?"

"We'd been fighting a lot, and we both came to a decision it was best to move on with our lives separately. To be honest, I am happier. So is he."

"Is this because I wasn't here?" I ask, the panic rising in my throat. "Because I didn't come back?"

"Lord no, Connie." She moves to put her arms around me. "Things haven't been right between us for a long time. I suppose all the empty space just made us realize what had been missing for a long time."

"Wow" is all I can say.

"I am sorry, though." She fixes me with a warm look.

"Why?" I give her an extra squeeze. "Mum, I just want you to be happy, for you to do what's right for you."

She plants a kiss on my head. "Thanks, love. I am. I really am. I even got myself a little job." A proud smile transforms her face and lights her eyes.

"That's great, Mum. And, you know now that I'm back, I can do the same and help out here."

She rubs my hand. "We'll see."

Normal life is weird.

When Mum heads off to work, I sit on our comfy sofa and stare at the television screen, flicking through the channels. I can't remember the last time I watched television. Even on the plane back, I was too sick to watch anything.

I feel thankful when the doorbell rings.

"You're back." Blue eyes are the only thing I have a chance to register, with no chance to say anything in return before Jamie's arms are around me, squeezing the breath out of me. "I heard you were back, but I didn't really believe it." He holds me at arm's length to look at me. There's no trace of malice or worry in his eyes. Nothing but pure happiness to see me before he's pulling me back into his arms.

I hold him close, enjoying all his warmth. "It's really good to see you, Jamie." I feel wetness on my face, but they're not my tears. I pull back to look at him, and yes, he is crying while still looking happy. "You're crying?"

"I am so happy to see you, Con." He laughs, wiping the errant tears away. "What happened? Where are the others? Are the twins at their aunt's? She's been a mess."

"Erm..." My heart hammers. I don't know why I thought no one would miss us, that when I came back, I would become invisible like I wanted and wouldn't have to answer any questions. "Why don't you come in? It's a very long story. The extremely short version is that the others are still there. I came back on my own."

Jamie's eyes go wide as he joins me on the sofa, waiting for me to go on.

Best to say it quickly, like ripping off a Band-Aid. "Peter and I broke up. Well, I broke up with him, I guess."

Jamie's mouth drops. "Are you ready to talk about it?"

I look up at him, appreciating his choice of words. I think I am. Maybe getting it out will help me compartmentalize. My brain has been a jumble, too sick and tired to sort out how it all went so terribly wrong.

I rub my forehead. *Where to begin?* "It turns out you were right, Jay. About a lot of things."

"Okay," he says slowly, giving me a small smile. "You might have to be more specific."

So I tell him. Beginning with the whole situation involving Sorcha, as it's the easiest place to start.

Jamie, who hasn't said a word through my story, sits there intently. He takes a minute to digest, his eyes on mine, when his lips begin to stretch into a smile and then, of all things, into a laugh.

"Man." He laughs some more. "Talk about all-time backfires."

I give him a bit of a push. "Laughing? You are laughing at my pain?" But I find I'm giggling along with him too. "You know, he had the nerve when he asked to just shrug his shoulders and be like..." I put on my best Peter impression, "... 'What! You don't want to?'"

We laugh some more.

"Wow. I can't believe he thought he could pull that one off. Still, I am sorry, Con. I thought he was a lot of things, but I didn't think he was a cheater."

"Well, I suppose he didn't, technically," I admit, already feeling better for talking about it. "I left, and Anna was furious. Peter followed me straight out and was all apologies, said he took it all back."

Jamie raises his eyebrows in disbelief.

"This was after he told me how great it would be, that he only wanted to do it if I was there. He said those words to me in front of everyone, including his sister, and then I think his exact words were 'I don't know whether to kill her or screw her.'"

Jamie roars with laughter, clutching his chest. "I'm starting to like this Peter."

"Jamie." I slap his arm again. "What is this? Some sort of bro code?"

"Not at all." He wipes the tears away from his eyes. "He didn't cheat on you, Con. You do know that, right? He didn't actually sleep with her."

"He wanted to."

Jamie tries to pull his expression into a serious one. "No." He chooses his next words with care. "He wanted a threesome with you, Con." He starts chuckling again. "He may be a god or whatever, but he is a nineteen-year-old guy. Hot goddess, beautiful girlfriend. He has the arrogance to ask. Connie, maybe it would have been great."

I slap him again.

"Okay, you weren't up for it. So, he said sorry. Doesn't sound like he would have done anything about it."

I stare hard at my friend as he pulls himself together to stop laughing.

"Please tell me you didn't leave the country over that?"

I rake my hands through my hair. Typical, Jamie is able to make it all sound so reasonable. Maybe I wouldn't have reacted quite as badly if Sorcha hadn't shown up at the exact moment he made the proposition.

"Yes, I was mad about that. But it was just the start, so not the only reason I left."

Jamie waits for me to go on.

"There was a big fight, and then Sorcha told me the whole time Peter and I have been together, I've been under his influence, that I only feel the way I do because that's what he wants."

Jamie's eyes widen. "He confirmed this?"

I close my eyes, trying to remember his exact words. *He had looked so devastated.* "He just said it was complicated, that he never used it, but because it's the way he feels, he doesn't know for certain."

"So he hasn't been Jedi mind tricking you this whole time?"

"I don't know, *can't* know, for sure. He says he hasn't. But how do I trust that? Even he doesn't know himself."

"It's obvious, right?" Jamie holds up his palms. "He could have brainwashed his way into a threesome if he was."

Jamie's lips twitch, and I could strangle him. "Can you just stop saying *threesome*?"

"Sure. But, Con, think about it. You said no. You left him, left the country. Does that sound like someone being controlled?"

"When you say it like that, no. The fact is, he thinks he has that control over me, but he never talked to me about it."

Jamie thinks about it for a second before taking my hand. "Con, I don't even like Peter. I think he is an arrogant dick. But, you're him, you fall in love with this beautiful girl and you can't believe your luck that she likes you back. For a few months, everything is great, and you even convince her to do some pretty stupid stuff, which is incredible because you are such a weirdo, and then, your dead dad shows up and drops some huge bombshell on you. Not only do you have to deal with all of that mess, but now you have the paranoia that your beautiful girl might not actually, truly be *your girl*. I know that feeling, Connie, because when he showed up, and I knew I couldn't compete, I wanted to hang onto you. I mean, it's messed up, but I get it."

I breathe out, taking in everything Jamie has said, feeling a whole lot lighter. "You're right. You are so right. I didn't give him any chance to explain. I just left. It was chaos, and Sorcha kept dropping bombshell after bombshell."

"There's more?" he asks.

I nod.

"Like what?"

"Like..." I push my mind back to that afternoon, "... Peter can't have kids. We would never have been able to have a family."

"Yikes."

"Yeah, Peter looked so upset. I genuinely think he didn't know. Or that what he was doing was hurting me." I look to Jamie again, whose visage is a mixture of confused and horrified, and gulp. "That just my being with him, physically, was wearing me out. He was killing me."

"Really? What did he say?"

I shake my head. "That it wasn't true. Except I could see Anna wasn't convinced, and I knew there had to be some truth to it. I'd been losing all this weight, and my period stopped. At one point, Lorna and I thought I was pregnant. Of course, I wasn't. I hadn't told him, though. He was always so worried about all of us, and he wanted us close all of the time. Thinking about it now, it was claustrophobic. So I didn't say anything to him." *I feel horrible.* "Jay, have I made a horrible mistake?"

"No," he soothes. "Not if it's true he was killing you, whether on purpose or not. I can't believe this all came out in one fight."

"I know." I rub my forehead. "You know, looking back at it now, everything was a big mess. The whole week before had been awful. Peter and Anna weren't even talking to each other when all of this happened."

"Are you being serious? How is that even possible for those two?"

I breathe out. "Erm... they'd had this huge fight the week before, where she ended up with a big bruise on her face from him grabbing her so hard." I grab my own jaw to demonstrate.

Jamie's eyes bug out once more. "Peter put his hands on Anna, his twin?"

"He was so mad at her. She was accusing him of hurting me, and he was convinced Sorcha had put her up to it."

Jamie leans back, letting out a long breath, bringing his hands to the back of his head. "Sheesh, Con, that all sounds so dramatic."

"It really was." I breathe out too.

"I told you trouble would follow him everywhere."

"You were right." I laugh.

"You know you have all been totally played, right?"

"Right. Wait, what?"

Jamie holds his hand up like it should be obvious. "Sorcha. She's been moving you all about like chess pieces. Saying the right things at the right time to make sure you all turn on each other. Driving in a wedge and moving you all away from him."

I sink my head into my hands, annoyed with myself for letting it happen. "Argh. Where were you in Varanasi?" I say into my palms.

"It's the beauty of perspective. I hate to be the one to tell you this, Connie. While he may not have been sleeping with her before, he definitely is now."

"Jamie, don't say that to me."

"Look, she set all of those wheels in motion. Planted all of those seeds of doubt. She has made her move, trust me. And Peter is stupid enough to fall for it."

I lean my head back onto the soft sofa and stare at the ceiling. "Yeah, that sounds like him," I say, causing fresh laughter from Jamie. I laugh too. "He is like two people. His god side, that makes him say and do all of these stupid things, and then..." I look at my friend but can't laugh anymore, "... there is his other side. Peter, the man, who is really sweet, gentle, and loving." The tears sting my eyes. "And he is so lost his vulnerability could make me shake. Some nights, he would hold onto me so hard." The tears fall freely now. "He could make me feel like the only person in the world who mattered. That's the Peter I love, Jamie."

I let myself crumble into his arms and cry for everything I've lost.

"It's okay, Con. It will be okay. I'm here. You know I am here for you."

After a moment, I pull back and dry my eyes on my sleeves. "Thanks, Jay." I give him a wry smile. "After, right?"

Jamie lets out a harsh laugh and turns away from me. "Please, don't say that."

"Why? You were right?"

"Connie, I don't want to think about the things I said to you then. I was being a dick. I won't lie..." he takes a deep breath, "... it's been hard without you here."

I take his hands, wanting to return the same kindness he's shown me. "Do you want to talk about it?"

"I have." He smiles, but it doesn't quite reach his cheeks. "A lot. I put myself into therapy. There was a lot of shit to unpack."

"Why?"

Now it's Jamie's turn for his tears to prick and I watch him holding them down. "Brady died, Connie. And you were all just... gone. For a long time, I felt lost too."

I don't say anything else, simply pull him back into my arms.

While I put it off for another two days, I know it's something I have to do.

I haven't spoken to Lorna since I texted her that I was home safe a week ago. A whole week of no contact. I feel butterflies stir in my stomach as I send Lorna a text asking if she's free to Face-Time. I don't know what the butterflies are about. *Do I actually think he'll jump on the call? More than likely, he never wants to see me again.*

Almost immediately, Lorna texts me back to give her five minutes to go downstairs, where the Wi-Fi is better.

Why am I so nervous to talk to her?

Her call buzzes through and I answer, seeing Lorna's smiling face. She's in her favorite place on the balcony. I have never appreciated my friend's beautiful face more. *I miss her.*

"Connie! So good to see you. You look great. How is it being back?"

"Thanks. Honestly, it is so good to hear your voice. Sorry I have left it so long. I just needed some time to adjust. Being back is weird. You don't know how much of a bubble you live in over there."

Lorna pulls her brows together. "What do you mean?"

"I don't know..." I try to find the words. "It's like I'd forgotten life was carrying on here without us."

Lorna laughs. "Yeah, that is a weird thought. I guess I never think about it. So, what have you been up to?"

"I saw Jamie."

Lorna's eyebrows shoot up. "Oh yeah? How is he?"

"He's doing really good. He's been great, actually. It's nice to feel normal."

"That's great, Connie. I am really happy for you." Her words and expression are soft.

I might as well get this question over with. "How is he?"

Lorna lets out a long breath. "Erm..." She shifts her phone camera from her face to pan the scene off the balcony. "It's raining here, if that answers your question. Rains quite often these days." She turns the camera back to her face so she can see me. "He's sad. He misses you."

"And Anna, how is she?" I say against the pain.

I miss him so much too.

"She's okay. She cried for like a whole day when you left."

"Really?"

"Yeah, but..." Lorna shrugs, "... you know, sometimes you can never really tell what is him and what is her." Something about the way Lorna says it, with such nonchalance, as if this is an everyday thing to say, makes me realize how deep in we all were.

Actually, they still are—a life of witches, magic, covens, and twin souls.

"Lorna..." I start. I don't really know why I am doing this to myself. "Is he, you know?"

Lorna pinches her forehead.

I know she doesn't want to answer, which should be answer enough.

"Yes, he is."

Wow, that hurts more than I thought it would.

Tears spring into my eyes, and I fight to keep them down.

Damn Jamie, he knew it.

"Listen, Connie," Lorna continues. "It's not like he's with her now. We all hate her. I don't know the full story. If she's at the temple when we're there, he won't even look at her. Anna and I never talk to her. Do you really want to know?"

I nod, not daring to speak, but I feel like I need to hear this.

"She just turns up at the hostel. Sometimes we can hear them shouting at each other. It's awkward, but obviously, we know what's going on between them."

I move my hand to wipe away the stupid tears that are full-on betraying me right now.

Lorna stares out at the rain, her expression serious. "Connie, the truth is... he's a big mess. We have had so much rain and two storms. There was talk of a typhoon, which thankfully came to nothing with the help of the coven. They know all about him now, what with the uncontrollable weather and such, and they've been really good about it. He kind of threw himself at their mercy."

I make a sound somewhere between a hiccup and chuckle. "Sounds nuts."

She smiles. "Yep. Pretty wild here right now."

"Sorry to leave you all in it."

"You don't need to say sorry. I understand. And please don't worry about him. We'll take care of Peter."

"I take it he and Anna are talking again?"

"Oh yes. That was all over the second you left."

"Well, that's something."

"Connie." Lorna gives me a look. "You're not having second thoughts, are you?"

"Are you kidding? Of course I am. With the benefit of perspective, it's easy to see I might have overreacted."

Lorna gives me a sympathetic look. "Don't do that to yourself. I can say this to you now, but in all honesty, I think he's been a mess for a while. You couldn't go on being the glue holding him together. Just try to get on with your life."

Easier said than done.

I say goodbye to my friend, making her promise to call me again soon.

But she doesn't.

It takes a few weeks to pin her down again.

When I finally get to speak to her, she is baffled that it hasn't been only a few days since we last spoke. I try to ask more questions about her and stop myself from asking about him, but she only tells me that it's stopped raining.

I hold tight to the somewhat pathetic notion that the love I feel for him means he still loves *me* first.

Chapter Ten

Peter

Lying back in my bed, I close my eyes and try to picture the perfect emerald green of Connie's eyes. Try to remember the softness of her skin.

I wish I'd taken more time to memorize every curve of her body. I feel like I am already starting to forget.

I try again—starting at the top, her shiny hair and how it felt in my hands, tracing the lines of her heart-shaped face—then do it over and over again.

Because it hurts.

And that's what I want.

To hurt over and over again.

A faint knock sounds at my door. I glance out of the window where it looks light outside, but I have no idea what time it is. I grab a pair of shorts from the floor and go to open the door. It's Anna, who I can barely look at lately. I can't take the constant sympathetic look she wears. In a way, I wish she was madder at me. Which is funny because I've always hated anyone being mad at me. Now, I want to wallow in it.

"It's almost midday," she says. "Maybe you should come down and get something to eat."

I look out of the window again. At the boats sitting peacefully on the river. Sorcha was here last night. I'm tired, and a little bit sick with myself. The energy I use on her should be enough to kill a person, but she never mentions anything. Last night was different. I pushed too hard, and it hurt her. I didn't even say sorry. She was in pain, and I told her to leave. It was the closest thing to upset I've seen Sorcha get.

Anna's eyes are on me.

How long have I been standing here?

"What were you saying?" I ask.

"Some food? Come on."

A shower would be good, but I can't find the energy. It hasn't rained in a while—a week, two weeks? I try to pull it together in my brain. *How long has it been since Connie left?* It all feels foggy. After all of my sadness induced storms, the coven found a spell to force me into a deep sleep, although they said it didn't keep me under for long enough. But it had worked—it stopped the downpour and now I feel not much of anything. Except longing, to see her again, to be near her again.

This morning feels a bit different. However, a bit clearer.

A little at a time, the first wheels in my brain start to move. There is something that needs to be done. I take my seat in front of Anna, who pours me some chai, then pushes a plate of fruit toward me.

"Thanks," I tell her. "I think I am going to head over to the coven today." I take a sip, shaking my head. "I feel like I haven't been there in a while."

Lorna's eyes flash up at me.

Anna looks like she doesn't know whether to be excited or worried. "Really? You're leaving the hostel?" Anna asks.

"Uh-huh," I confirm, noticing how good the chai and the fruit taste. Fresh. It feels like I've been eating ash for weeks. "I haven't done that in a while, have I?"

"You've been pretty out of it since the spell," Lorna says, looking relieved. "Kali said it must be kind of like a hangover. You've sort of been here, but not."

"Like a zombie," Anna whispers, she can be so dramatic.

"A zombie? Really?" I laugh. "Have I eaten anyone's brains yet?" Anna and Lorna exchange wide-eyed glances, so I lean in closer to them. "Please tell me I haven't eaten a brain."

"No. Of course not." Anna giggles. "It's just... Peter, you are laughing."

I frown at her. "It's really been *that* bad?"

Anna lets out a sigh of relief that I seem to be back on the planet. "Honestly, I don't know what was worse, all the rain and your sadness, or having you existing like a robot, walking around not really being anything."

"I think the robot was slightly better." Lorna looks to Anna.

"Mmm..." She nods in agreement. "You are definitely right. The robot was better, much easier to handle."

"And certainly less wet."

They both look back at me.

What are they, a double act now?

"I wonder what snapped you out of it?" Lorna ponders, going back to her breakfast.

I feel a slight pang of guilt as my mind flashes back to Sorcha. The surge had been enough to char her skin, leaving a huge black handprint seared into her back. The thought is enough to put me off my breakfast.

Best not to say anything about that.

I shrug. "No idea. I'm still a little foggy," I say, getting to my feet. "I should get going. Sounds like Kali really came through for me. I want to say thanks. See you there?"

"Sure," Anna and Lorna say together, both looking pleased to have me back.

I am not entirely sure why, though.

Why are they so ready to forgive me for what I did, for what I'm still doing?

The temple is just as bad when I arrive not long later. Everyone looks so happy to see me, or maybe I never noticed this is how they've always looked at me, like something to be revered and respected, something good.

I spot Kali toward the front of the room, collecting flowers in baskets.

She smiles when she sees me approaching. I notice the gray hairs falling loose from her headdress. If she is Arjun's mother, I wonder how old she truly is.

"Peter, so nice to see you looking more yourself."

"Thanks," I tell her, putting my hands in my pockets. "And thank you for what you did. I don't know what I would've done if you hadn't been able to come through for me."

"That is what we are here for." Kali's expression is one full of the warmth of a mother. She then returns to her task with her flowers and baskets. "Of course, the aftereffects wouldn't have been quite so bad if you'd just slept it off and not fought against it so hard."

I don't even remember them doing the spell. I only remember feeling bad—awful—burdened with a mixture of sadness, guilt, and a self-loathing I could not contain.

"Sorry," I say, feeling a bit pathetic.

Kali waves her hand. "All is well now."

"Kali, I came here to ask—"

She cuts me off, shoving a few of the baskets in my hands. "Can you help me? I need to move all of these out into the ceremony room."

"Sure thing," I say, collecting all the baskets I can carry, and Kali picks up what she can too. "What's with all of the flowers?" I ask, now distracted from the task that brought me here.

The coven is a hive of activity today. Everyone is busy. I scan the hall for Mahi, but I can't find her. I haven't spoken to her in ages.

Gemini

I follow Kali out of the hall and along a narrow corridor I've never been down before.

"Tonight, the moon will be full, and a very special ceremony will take place." She stops and pivots toward me, an almost devilish smile passing her lips. "You can stay and watch if you wish. I don't imagine you've seen anything like it before."

"What is it?" I ask as we step into a small ornate room.

The walls shimmer almost gold, and at the front of the room is a stone altar. I'm not sure I like the sight of it.

Kali does not answer my question. Instead, she sets her baskets down and pours some of the flowers into a large copper basin. "Peter, can you help me pour these flowers into the basins?" She motions with a nod of her head to several other vessels dotted around the room. "I will get the water."

"What is this for?" I ask as I drop my baskets and follow Kali's lead, tipping the flowers into the bowls.

She joins me at my basin and tips a large urn of water in. "These flowers, which we've grown and blessed, are soothing for the spirit," she tells me as she enjoys the sight of the flowers swirling in the water.

"Kali, what is going to happen here?"

"Our service to the people." Kali grins as she continues with her task, motioning for me to do the same. "Every once in a while, we open our home to those in need. Tonight, we welcome families into this hall who require our assistance. They will have traveled far. These beasts always dwell in the most rural reaches of our country, and we will exorcise their loved ones."

I accidentally drop the whole basket of flowers into the basin I'm filling. "You are performing an exorcism here?"

"Three," Kali clarifies.

"What are you exorcising?" My heart is in my throat.

"Why, demons, of course."

"Demons are real?" I can't believe my ears, but I don't know why I am surprised.

Kali laughs at my gobsmacked reaction. "Yes, my child, they surely are. They are as real as you and me."

"What are they?"

"They are twisted souls." Kali looks a little sad. "Usually torn apart in horrible deaths. Unable to find their way to the river. Instead, they roam the Indian countryside searching for a way out of this plane and to share their suffering."

The river. My brain swims. There is so much I want to ask, but I can't find the right words.

I stand here dumbfounded.

Like an idiot.

Kali completes her task and turns back to me. "Would you like to see?"

How can I possibly say no?

Kali has a lot of preparations to make, including readying herself, but I can't stop following her around and asking her a million questions, which she answers with extreme patience. I discover that, while the whole coven is helping to prepare, only the five most senior witches, including Kali, will be there for the ceremony. If I join them, I am under strict instructions not to say or do anything. I am invited as an observer only. She also warns me against trying to interact with the demon once it is out. I have no idea why she thinks I would do this, but I readily agree.

"Kali…" I begin asking yet another question. "How exactly does an exorcism work?"

Kali chuckles from behind the screen, where she is changing. I've followed her into her personal quarters, but she doesn't seem to mind. "You will see, have patience. We will use our collective power and our strong connection to the universe to drive the demon out. Much groundwork has been laid. There will be singing, and we will call upon Vishnu."

Hearing the name makes me stop. It's a name I've heard a lot in the city. "Vishnu? You are going to call another god here? Is that a good idea with me there?"

Kali laughs again, and it's deep and hearty. "Peter, Vishnu has long since left this plane. Once, he was perhaps the most powerful god to ever be created in this world, and his ideas and beliefs are strong in this part of the world, which helps in freeing the demon. You have to understand... the old gods were so powerful their ideals still hold fast to this very day. Their effects felt for thousands of years."

I think about this for a second, feeling that dark pit in my stomach —*influence*. When I don't say anything, Kali continues, reading my expression.

"You are very young, Peter. It is not something for you to worry about. But, a small word of warning, when someone believes in you, that effect can last for lifetimes." Kali walks out from behind the screen, looking regal and serious. "What you mean to them, it can be handed down for generations. As you age, it will be natural for you to begin to amass followers. By age, I mean beyond your human lifespan. Choose your circle wisely, and what you choose to teach them."

My insides feel like ice. "Arjun said it was possible to stop the influence, to give a person immunity in a way."

Kali smiles again sympathetically. "Peter, please do not worry yourself. It will take many years for you to build the strength to have that kind of pull. And even when you do, you should understand something..." she clasps my face in her hands, "... those people will *want* to follow you. You cannot ever take away someone's free will."

"It isn't r-real, though, is it, Kali?" I can hear the crack in my voice.

Kali's expression is motherly as her thumb strokes my cheek. "My dear, young, innocent boy, you are about to witness an exorcism performed by a coven of witches in a city where the river flows to the underworld itself. Who are we to say what is real for others and what is not?"

Despite myself, I give a small laugh. "But, Arjun's spell?"

"Yes, there is a spell. It's the reason witches are protected from your charms, but the spell is performed on us when we are small children, when we are untouched. Peter, I know this has to do with your pretty friend who left, but I would not worry. You are so young, you are incomplete. The chances you have done this are incredibly small."

"But I can use it, Kali. I made my aunt talk, I stopped my uncle kicking me out, I stopped all the rumors when everyone was talking about us, and I'm pretty sure I clouded Connie's judgment on a few occasions without meaning to."

"Peter..." Kali is laughing again, "... influencing a few individual, temporary actions and inspiring lifelong devotion are two quite different things." She turns serious for a moment. "I hate to say it, as it is a cruel thing to say, but things are harder for you because you are incomplete. When you are whole, you will be able to control all of this."

I rub my eyes. "That in no way makes me feel any better."

Kali laughs, helping me up from my place on the floor. "Only eighty-something years to go and Anna lives as long and as full of a life as possible. It sounds like a long time now, but believe me, child, when you are facing lifetimes in this world, it is not."

I blow out hard and follow Kali to a table where she adorns her neck with chains of beads. I think some of them are made of bones. "I don't want to live forever."

Kali jostles my arms as if trying to cheer me up. "Peter, you will be as eternal as the sun in the sky. But, trust me, nothing truly lasts forever."

"Kali," I begin again. Why she hasn't banished me from her presence, I don't know. Maybe she also has pity for me. "If the old gods were so all-powerful, what happened to them?"

"Ah..." She raises her finger in the air, making me jump a little. "I was wondering when you were going to ask this question." The first glimmer of excitement passes her face as if this is the first question I've asked worth asking. "It is an interesting question and one we do not know the answer to. It has been over two thousand years since gods walked this Earth, so there is no one around today who could tell you. However, amongst my kin, there are two main schools of thought. The first being that, as the world changed and man became more civilized, the gods were less necessary. The tribes became less willing to sacrifice their people, and thus their power depleted. And after a while, they withered and turned to dust."

"And the second?" I prompt when Kali pauses.

She sparkles under the dim light as she takes a seat on a low bench.

"The second is a far more interesting one. Many believe the knowledge obtained by the first ancient witches of this world was taught to them by beings who put humankind here. It was they who taught us about the infinite and gave us the knowledge of how to tap into those ancient sources and call forth that power, binding it into human form. They were the first 'gods' who walked this Earth. These beings saw the terrible destruction the gods were bringing to this world, so it was them who removed the deities from this world."

I sink to the bench next to her, unable not to let my lips curl into a smile. "Really? Aliens?"

She laughs, jostling me again. "Why not? Why not believe in the fantastic if you have the chance? You will find these references across all the ancient cultures spanning the entire globe." She nudges me off the seat as I laugh.

"So when are they coming to "beam me up"?" I chuckle.

Kali rolls her eyes. "Please. You are not so big or terrible." She begins to usher me out of the room. "Now, please, enough of your questions. I have to prepare."

I relent, although I still have so much to ask. My brain swirls with all this new information. *Aliens?* It sounds too much. For the first time, I'm feeling a little bit hopeful that Kali is right, that I had no influence at all in how Connie feels about me. *Felt about me,* I check myself. I should feel happy this is true. Connie can move on with her life. The spell would be the only way to know for sure, but that's out of the question now.

I head back into the main room. Anna and Lorna are here now, lazing around, giggling, and smoking something. I don't even know what. I swear Lorna is a bad influence on Anna, but in a way, it makes me like Lorna more.

The hall is quieter now. I begin to cross it to go and get some air when I feel someone's small frame hit me from behind. *Mahi.* She is abuzz with what will happen tonight, although she cannot attend. She chatters away about how she's missed me and catches me up on how her studies are coming along. The girl is lovely. But I sense something in the way she looks at me, like I'm someone to be looked up to, and I become more uneasy that I am deceiving her. I want to shake her and tell her she shouldn't want to have anything to do with me, that she is far too good to care about me.

But I don't.

I can't bear to tell her I'm not who she thinks I am.

All too soon, Kali appears at the entrance of the narrow passageway. With a simple motion, she beckons me to follow. The anticipation of what I am about to see ripples through me.

An exorcism.

A demon.

As I join Kali, she doesn't say a word, silently leading me along the long, narrow passageway. This time pushing on a door I hadn't seen before and leading me down an even narrower dark path, so dark I can barely see where I'm treading until we come to a low sliding door. When we reach it, every hair on my body stands on end.

What's behind this door does *not* feel good.

Kali pauses a moment, then turns to me and presses her finger to her lips before she puts both hands on the door and slides it across. I'm not prepared for the sounds the room contains. Rasping and unnatural cries echo around the walls as I follow Kali, staying close and feeling way out of my depth.

The room is pitch-black except for the candles at the end of the hall. We seem to be in some sort of vestibule with small areas sectioned off by latticed partitions. I feel the wary eyes of the people on me. *I do not belong here.*

Kali stops to say a few words of comfort to those who approach her, speaking in Hindi and Bengali and offering them her hands as they weep. I feel like I'm intruding because what they are here for is private and painful.

As we near the last partition, a movement from the dark floor catches my eye. A young girl is lying with her cheek against the floor, but her legs are raised in an unnaturally high crouched position as she glides against the floor in front of me. I realize the foreign creaking sound is coming from somewhere deep inside her. I freeze, horrified, only moving when Kali returns to push me forward into the main chamber.

Once inside, the door to the vestibule is closed, and I breathe a sigh of relief to be away from the noise. I push my shaking hands through my hair.

Why did I ever agree to this?

The rest of the senior members are already here. Kali ushers me to the back of the room and shows me where to plant my feet. In the faint flickers of the candlelight, she must be able to see that I'm looking a little green.

She places a soothing hand on my shoulder. "Breathe. Steady yourself, boy. And remember, do not speak. Do not interact with the demon."

I nod and wipe the sweat from my forehead. She must be madder than I gave her credit for. I'm barely standing, let alone have any desire to interact with whatever those things are.

Kali indicates for the ceremony to start. The first is the girl I'd seen in the vestibule. She is carried in, her body contorted as she's brought to the alter. I might actually be sick. Except, when the coven starts, it is impossible to look away. I can feel the power radiate from them, the power in their words as their hands move against the girl's thrashing body, their song getting louder and louder, faster and faster until Kali pushes her palm onto the girl's raised chest, sending her flat into the alter, where the girl's body goes limp. As Kali lifts her hand away, with it comes a blackness I've never seen before, like a shining dark light rising into the air.

It looks familiar somehow. I cannot take my eyes off it, and there's a strange burn in my veins. I am looking at a twisted soul. A voice in the back of my mind tells me normal souls shine white. Something I should've pieced together long ago falls into place in my brain. What I took from Arjun, what I almost took from Lorna and Anna. It was their souls.

When the ceremony is over—the demon banished, cast toward the river—my head spins, and I am sick all over the ceremony floor.

Due to my all-too-human stomach, I'm not permitted to attend the remaining rituals.

I don't make it back to the hostel.

Instead, I curl up in a ball on some of the cushions in the main hall and fall into a deep, dreamless sleep.

When I wake up the next morning, it takes me a moment to realize where I am. The hall is deserted, so it must be early. I sit up, weariness clinging to me as I rub the sleep out of my eyes. After a few moments, the sound of movement behind me causes me to turn to Kali who's walking over with a small cup.

"How are you feeling now?" she asks, the warmth in her words betrayed by the slightest of chuckles.

"Better," I reply. "Why on earth did you think I would want to see that?" I ask, feeling grateful she is handing me what looks like green tea.

"In truth, I'm glad it was too rich for your blood." She laughs. "It was maybe a test of sorts. The sight of a soul, even a twisted one, it could have gone one of two ways."

I take a sip of tea, letting it warm me. "You thought I might want it," I say as more of a statement than a question.

With just the slightest of nods, Kali says, "It makes me glad you didn't. As far as I know, from stories passed down through the generations, the first soul to join with a new god was their twin. These two souls should be as one. It is their soul that fully binds you to this plane. But the gods of old were bloodthirsty beasts, raised by their tribes to be worshipped and consumed by the need for more power. As I said before, through human sacrifice, the souls brought the gods more and more power. Unspeakable power. So much so that some of them were not bound to their human forms any longer. They had the power to change what they were, including the very fabric of their beings."

I sink my head into my hands. "Kali, I don't think my brain can hold onto what you're telling me. It's too much."

"I know," she sympathizes. "I am sorry, my child. I'm sorry to tell you this, but you need to understand it so you do not become it."

I nod, feeling the lump rise in my throat. "Are you telling me my father's soul, it's... inside of me?"

"Like so many things, it is not that simple. It is their energy. Most souls will find their way to the great rivers of this world, where they will journey on, but the ones you take will become your power. It offers a certain... balance, if you will."

I rub my temples. "So, what you're telling me is that human sacrifice is off the table?" I glance at her. "Is this a warning?"

Kali lets out a deep belly laugh, jostling me once more and forcing me to laugh despite myself. A hundreds-of-years-old witch grandmother and her god-grandson laughing about human sacrifice. It is so ridiculous tears are rolling down my face. I think, for the most part, they're out of laughter and maybe ten percent at how wretched I truly am. Human bloody sacrifice, harvesting souls.

"Yes." She wags her finger at me as if I am a naughty schoolboy. "No human sacrifice. Otherwise, us witches will get involved. Consider yourself warned." She laughs.

I wipe the last of my tears away, then look down at my hands. *I don't want them to be bloody. I already carry so much guilt.* "Kali..." I begin in a small voice. It's a question I should have asked long ago.

"My mother, what she did... Anna told me when she knew it was me, she bound my powers, buried them deep. Could that be done again?"

Kali's warm expression leaves her face. "Why would you ask this?"

Despite myself, I feel the hot tears prick my eyes. "Because I don't want this. I thought I did for a while. I thought I could have it all. But I'm so sick of it raining every time I want to cry. I am so sick of feeling what I have inside pushing against my skin. I don't want any of it. I want it to stop."

Kali's expression is unreadable.

"Can you help?"

Kali looks away from me, deep in thought, pushing her hand to her headdress. "Peter, when your mother did that spell, you were a baby, your abilities a bud of a single flower. What you are now... it would take the collective power of the entire coven to hold you down."

I move on my knees in front of her. *There is hope.*

"It would be a dangerous task for all of my people. You fought so hard against the sleeping spell, and that wasn't an inch of the magic needed for this one. You cannot ask this lightly. Plus, once it is done, it cannot easily be undone. There would be many things to consider."

"Such as?" I press.

"Such as, when one of the coven dies, the spell would be weakened. You would need to return for new bindings."

I nod. I could do that.

"You must also consider your sister. I do not know what would happen to her or you if you are bound when she passes." Kali takes my face in her hands once more, her expression stern. "You need to understand what you ask of us. It is not a light decision, so take some time. I must also consult with the seniors and decide what is the best course of action. Consider one thing, Peter. It may bind your powers, but it will not change what you are."

For once, I am glad to be out of the temple. I hurry through the dusty streets and make my way back to the hostel. It's still early so there isn't much movement. I head straight to the roof for some room to try and clear my head. Gazing out at the waters of the Ganges—with so many souls—the cleansing, calming feeling it once brought now feels polluted.

Light steps sound on the ladder, and I turn my head to see Lorna making her way over to me.

"Hi. I thought I saw you." She perches next to me at the edge, letting her legs hang over. "How you doing?"

"Yeah, I'm good," I lie.

"Okay," she says slowly, nudging her shoulder into mine. "Once more, with feeling."

I nod, cracking a half smile. "Okay, not too good."

Her head bobs up and down while she stares at her feet.

I haven't spoken to Lorna much on her own about everything that happened. For some reason, I feel the tears rise again. "You know, Lorna, everything that happened with Connie, it really wasn't like that. You know I never forced her—"

"I know, Peter," she says gently.

I nod again. That counts for something. "I should've been more honest with her. I was just so scared of losing her, and I never expected it to come out like that. I don't blame her for leaving."

Lorna looks hard at me for a few moments. "And you?"

"Me?" I rub my face. "I am a mess."

"No kidding." Lorna laughs. "This whole thing with Sorcha?"

"Ugh, Sorcha." I lean back so I'm observing the sky. "An even bigger mess. I think I've upset her." I lower my gaze at Lorna, admitting, "I'm not very nice to her, Lor. I don't like who I am when I'm around her."

Lorna shuffles back from the edge to lie next to me on her side, her eyes wide but with no hint of judgment. "Why do you think she keeps coming back to you?"

I let out a shaky laugh and return my focus to the sky again. "I have no idea. We don't talk much, only when I tell her to leave. But

I..." I pause. "I did something pretty bad. I don't think she'll be coming back."

"Peter, did you ever think what you are doing with her isn't good for you in here?" She reaches out and places her hand on my heart.

With this simple action, and her straightforward words, I can't look her in the eye. Instead, I squeeze mine shut, feeling the tears escape them as I nod my head. I need to pull this emotion down before we have a full-blown rainstorm on our hands.

"So, it's been a day or two since you've seen her. What are you going to do?" she asks.

To be honest, I haven't thought about it. I turn back to Lorna as she moves her hand away. "I don't know. Meditate, I guess. It can help."

"Will it be enough?"

I shrug. "It will have to be."

Lorna slips her hand into mine. "I could help."

I don't move my hand from hers but immediately look back at the sky. "No. I can't ask that of you. You heard what Sorcha said before. It was killing Connie. She wasn't lying. I don't want to hurt you too."

"I want to help. Besides, it doesn't actually hurt, does it?"

"No," I say, heaving my legs up and turning my body toward her so I'm lying on my side on the flat roof too. "It feels good. Or so I'm told."

Lorna props herself up, slight concern in her eyes. "It's not sexual, is it?" she whispers.

Her serious expression is so uncharacteristic it makes me belt out a boisterous laugh, natural and real. "No. It doesn't have to be. It's just more fun that way."

Lorna gives my shoulder a small shove away, laughing too.

My face falls a little. "It will still feel like me, though. This isn't real lightning... it's me. The same way Sorcha's illusions are her."

Lorna nods in understanding.

I appreciate what she is doing for me.

It won't be much, I tell myself. *Just enough to take the edge off.* A temporary arrangement until I find a more permanent solution.

I roll onto my back, bringing the crook of my arm over my face. Anna would be so pissed off if she knew what I was about to do. Being as gentle as I can, I squeeze Lorna's hand.

Lorna's breath leaves her body in a whoosh.

I stop myself as soon as I can.

As she sits up, I keep my arm firmly clamped over my face.

Shit!

But then I hear laughing. I move my arm in time to see her lying back down next to me, her face light and relaxed, and obviously not mad.

"I will tell you one thing, Peter." She giggles, bringing her knees up to her chest. "Your shit is way better than Sorcha's."

Which makes me laugh again too—a normal-person laugh.

I don't know why, but after the last few strange days, being with Lorna is the most relaxed I've felt in a while. Maybe it's because she is so much like Connie.

I smile at her from our place on the hard concrete of the roof together. "So, you and my sister?"

"What about us?"

"I don't know. You two seem close, I guess."

She gives me a look of mock surprise. "Peter Burke, are you actually noticing what other people are doing for once?"

"It's kind of obvious, even for me," I tease her.

She gets serious. "We've shared a room for almost two years. Of course, we're close. And I adore her. You know, there is just so much going on."

I frown at her. "What is going on?"

Lorna moves her arm, raising her eyebrows as if it should be obvious.

"Me?" I clarify. "I'm miserable. That's what's going on?" I shake my head at her.

She gives me a light push again. "You take up a lot of headspace, my friend."

Chapter Eleven

Anna

Closing my eyes, I take a deep breath and try to empty my mind.

"Connect with what is in front of you. Feel it. Let it become part of you," Kali's guiding words come in my ear.

I open my eyes and focus on the small leaf in front of me. As I hover my hand a sliver above it and let it rise from the table, the leaf quivers and does as I command.

Lorna lets out a small shriek of excitement from her place at the table opposite me, which breaks my concentration and allows the leaf to drift back down to the table.

Kali laughs, giving her the slightest look of reproach before moving away from us. "You did it, Anna," she says with glee.

My smile must reach from ear to ear. After a good few days of practice, I've finally done it. I see Peter walk into the hall and shoot my hand up into the air to excitedly wave him over. "Peter, come and watch this," I tell him.

He gives Lorna a quizzical look before sitting cross-legged, like the two of us, on the cushion next to her.

I do the same again, hovering my hand right above the leaf, connecting, and allowing it to rise higher and higher into the air.

Peter and Lorna watch intently, not saying a word.

"Well?" I say, letting the leaf fall back to the table.

"You're practicing magic?" Peter asks with something of a blank expression on his face.

I roll my eyes at him. "Levitating a tiny leaf is hardly practicing. But, you know, I was interested. Kali said that nearly all magic is learned, so she showed me a few things. She said that organic matter like plants and stuff should come easier to me because they're your primary, and she was right."

"My what now?"

"Your primary. You know, your gift that came first. She also said most gods only have their primary gift for many lifetimes before any other abilities start showing. How come you have so many?" I ask, and Lorna looks at him too, also interested in finding out the answer. I can see the cogs turning in his head, trying to figure out if he should tell me off.

"Because most things are organic. It's all connected," he says quickly. "Anna, I think—"

Lorna cuts him off, asking, "What about water? That's organic, and you can make it rain. Can you do anything else? Could you make a whirlpool in the sea?"

He shakes his head. "No. I don't know, but—"

"Or..." I start, a thought popping into my head, "... maybe you could make like a giant floating bubble of water?"

He cocks his eyebrow. "Seriously?"

"Like a massive raindrop." I smile. He's getting peeved with us, but it's fun.

"Look, I am not connected to water, okay?"

"Why?" we both ask in unison.

He looks toward the ceiling as if calling on a shred of patience to deal with us. "I don't know. I learned how to use the lightning after being struck. That idiot Jamie was right... it's like muscle memory.

The second time I was hit, I knew what to do with it more. After a while, I knew how to create it." He looks from me to Lorna, hoping we are satisfied with his answer. "Now, maybe if I drown at some point, I will know how to do the same with water."

We take a while to ponder that thought.

"But, Anna, you should be careful, okay?"

"It's just a leaf, Peter," Lorna points out.

He dips his head, trying to be reasonable. "I know, but one thing leads to another. Magic is serious and dangerous."

I raise my eyebrow at him. "Really? Didn't I see you wrapping pea shoots around Mahi's arm like mehndi yesterday?"

The corners of his mouth pull up a bit. "That's different. She thought it was cute."

Lorna and I give a collective eye roll. "Yes, we all think you are very cute, Peter."

"Look, I'm not saying stop." He softens. "I am just asking you to be careful. I don't want to see you get hurt."

I give him a small smile. It's levitating a leaf, nothing more, and therefore, a promise easy to make. I tip my head toward him in assent.

In the next instant, he changes. His back stretches out and he flexes his neck in discomfort, which can only mean one thing...

... Sorcha is here.

Sure enough, a moment later, she walks into the room.

Lorna's eyes turn to Peter, who is decidedly staring at the table. I cannot stand the sight of her. Although I haven't seen her at the temple for a while, I know she slithers into my brother's bed night after night.

Lorna and I exchange wide-eyed glances when Sorcha makes her way over. She's not talked to us once since the day Connie left, and now looks nervous before she comes to a stop at our table. Lorna stares on in disbelief at me. This is a car crash waiting to happen.

"Hi, Peter," she almost whispers.

He doesn't look up but continues to stare at the table. It's not unusual for him to pretend like she doesn't exist while she's here but it is unusual for her to speak to him in front of everyone.

"I'm sorry I have been gone for a while. I know what kind of position that put you in. I just needed to take a little time after last—"

She doesn't get a chance to finish. Peter is on his feet, grabbing her arm and moving her a few paces away in a heartbeat. Not that it matters. We can still hear everything.

"I do not want to talk about this here," he mutters, his eyes cold on her.

Sorcha nods, glancing from him to us while easing her arm from his grasp. "I know. I'm sorry. But I didn't want to come back if..." She looks away, fiddling with the edge of her kaftan and making me wonder if she is scared of him. "I was going to come by later, but I didn't want to if, well, you know."

Peter seems to know, and he looks back at us. I don't think either of us has taken a breath. Watching this is better than a soap opera. All eyes on are on him, waiting for what he will say.

Eventually, he breathes out and shoves his hands through his hair. "I'm sorry about what happened."

Sorcha shifts her weight, looking a little surprised.

"You can come by later if you want to."

"Okay," Sorcha chirps, her easy smile back on her lips. "Well, I guess I'll see you later."

Without another glance at us, she is out of the room, and Peter comes back to his place next to Lorna. None of us say anything. Lorna and I look at each other, then back to Peter, who is studying the table.

I can't take the suspense anymore.

"So, what did you do?" I ask with a hint of a smile in my voice.

"Anna, please," Peter balks. "I really do not want to talk about this with you."

"She said she's been gone for a while. But I know you've been using your powers. I can feel it. So, how have you?"

Then I see it. He makes the tiniest of glances toward Lorna, who is also decidedly looking at the table now too. *I can't believe it.* Rage floods my body as I round on them.

"Are you *serious*? You two?" I shout. In my anger I stand too fast, my knee catching the low table and flipping it.

Both Peter and Lorna jump back to avoid being hit. Before I can really gear up to scream at him, Peter has closed the distance between us and is clamping his hand over my mouth. I battle against his hand, calling him every name I can think of.

"No, no, no, no, no," he says, looking into my eyes. "It is so not what you think. Stop screaming."

Everyone in the room is now gawking at us. From behind him, I see Lorna, who is bent over laughing. It's obvious he can hear her too because his panic-stricken face has changed to one of humor, and his body starts to jostle against me with his own fits of giggles. The onlookers begin to move away and leave me standing here with Peter and Lorna laughing at me.

"Thank you for that," Peter says after a bit, wiping his tears away when it is clear I'm no longer shouting. "And thank you for your incredibly low opinion of me."

"And me," Lorna says without any malice. "Him, I can understand, but surely you know I would never."

"Hey." Peter gives her a gentle shove away from him, before turning back to me. "Lorna has just been helping kind of take the edge off while Sorcha hasn't been here. Believe me, she is definitely *not* sleeping with me."

I let my stance soften. "Why didn't you say anything, then? More secrets?"

"Because you would have wanted to help." Peter clasps my arms in his loose hands. "And I don't know how your body would react to it. Look, Sorcha is back now. Lorna was doing me a favor. No harm done."

I look from my best friend back to my brother. "So if you don't need to be sleeping with Sorcha, remind me again why you are?"

"Ah!" He raises his arms in the air in frustration, walking away from me. "Because I am a masochist."

And then he is also out of the temple.

I stare after him, blinking a few times slowly, disbelief firmly written on my face.

"Don't be too hard on him." Coming to stand in front of me, Lorna takes my hands. "You know better than anyone that he hates being alone."

I let out a low breath. "He has me."

"And you have me."

"He has you too, Lor."

"Not in the same way," she says quickly. Too quickly. By the time my eyes find hers, she is looking away, the color flooding her face. "I don't know why I said that."

Now it's my turn to stare at the floor. "Do I, Lor? Have you?"

"I don't know. You're my best friend, Anna."

I glance up and she smiles, her attention somewhere in the distance.

"Yes. You do have me, in that way."

My heart does a little summersault as I bring myself to make eye contact with her. I try to form the right words to say back to her.

"Stop," she says, taking a slight step back. "Let's just leave that there for a minute. Don't say anything, Anna. Just take a minute for you to feel how *you* feel about that. Like I said, you are one of my best friends and nothing will change that, okay? I won't allow it. So, take a minute." Lorna gives me a large warm smile, as if she can be anything else, and she too walks out of the temple.

So, I do. I take a minute and try to let the notion sink in.

Lorna is mine. Really. Just mine.

I kneel down and start to clean up the debris from the table, and realize I'm unable to keep the smile from my face.

Lorna is mine.

We've been through so much together that I never want to not have her by my side.

Without a word, I leave the temple and float back to the hostel.
Lorna is mine.

The more I think about it, the happier it makes me feel. All the confusion I felt when I was with Brady, I never feel around Lorna.

I make my way upstairs and let my feet take me to the person I want so desperately to talk to about this.

I only hope he is alone.

With a light tap, my knuckles strike his door.

Please be alone.

He looks a bit annoyed to see me. "If you're here to give me a lecture, I would rather not."

I drift in past him, going over to the window and turning to face him as he closes the door behind me. "So, Lorna said a thing to me."

All traces of exasperation are gone from his face and he looks bemused by my expression. "Yeah?"

I nod, my heart racing. "She said... she's mine."

Peter laughs, taking a seat on his bed. "Wow. She actually had the balls to tell you."

I move to sit next to him. "You knew? And you didn't say anything?"

"For once, this was a secret that wasn't mine to tell." He smiles, taking my hand. "So, why are you sitting here telling me this rather than being in there with an amazing girl who's just told you she likes you?"

My eyes widen. "Because it's a lot. You know, I need to think about this. Our whole friendship. She means so much to me. I need time. She said she would give me some time."

Peter takes my face in both of his hands. His eyes look bottomless and weary.

"You think too much. Why wouldn't it be anything other than wonderful? I know I'm not the poster child for well-thought-out decisions, but from the outside, you and Lorna are perfect for each other."

I pull him in close. "Thank you, Peter. Since when do you have such words of wisdom?"

Gemini

He laughs—it sounds a little off—then pulls me in tighter. "I don't want you to forget to live your life. You need to stop putting it on hold for me."

I hold him for what seems like an age.

I peel myself away from my brother and return to my room, but Lorna isn't here or on the balcony of the hostel, so I make my way up to the roof, where she sits with her cigarette, watching the sunset. I take my place next to her, taking the cigarette out of her hand when she offers it to me.

"You don't need to give me time," I say. Her round eyes turn to me, and I smile down at my hands. "I'm yours too."

"Yeah?" she asks.

Such a simple word, but I can hear her happiness in it.

"Yeah," I confirm with a nod, raising my eyes to meet her smile before we both look back at the sunset, falling into silence. Not an uncomfortable silence but one filled with anticipation. "Just..." I start after a while, "... baby steps, okay? Lor, you mean so much to me. We can't mess this up."

"I totally agree." Lorna bobs her head, taking the cigarette from me again. "I know exactly how you feel."

We take a moment's silence once more.

"What, shit scared?" I ask after a while.

Lorna descends into laughter. "Yes, exactly that," she says, peeking over at me as I laugh with her.

We've said it.

It's out in the open now.

We both know it.

What we have will never be the same, which is incredibly exciting and scary at the same time.

Heavy steps sound on the ladder and Peter joins us.

"You missed the sunset," Lorna tells him as he takes a seat on the other side of her.

He shrugs. "I think I prefer this part more, the way the light looks now. How the Earth's atmosphere catches the sun's final rays of the day."

"Mm-hmm. Pretty," Lorna agrees as Peter sets his head onto her shoulder and they watch the dying light.

I take a moment to look at them, the two people who mean the most to me in this entire world.

My family.

I rest my head on Lorna's other shoulder.

Chapter Twelve

Peter

As I stare at the ceiling, I become aware how it's tinged yellow. The beginnings of cracks are showing.

I wish there was something to do about this feeling—a feeling like I am dead inside.

Maybe the coven has one of those sacred silver knives like Arjun had. Maybe, if I ask them nicely, they would do us all a favor and kill me.

I'm too selfish to die.

My gaze shifts over to Sorcha. She's not looking at me, expecting me to tell her to leave at any moment, I assume. When I roll onto my side to face her, she eyes me with suspicion. In all honesty, she's the most incredible-looking person I have ever seen. Her dark skin is flawless, and with her full lips and silver eyes, this woman looks like a goddess, and I have no idea what she sees in me.

"Tell me something real, Sorcha. Something about you."

The look on her face—genuine surprise that I've asked her a question about herself—would be comical if it didn't make me feel awful.

"What do you want to know?" She still sounds unsure.

"Anything," I say, closing my eyes, not knowing if I genuinely want to go here.

"Okay," she says after a while, propping herself up on her elbow. "My name isn't really Sorcha."

"What?" I ask, intrigued. That her name is not her own is not what I was expecting, although I am not sure exactly what I was expecting. "What's your real name?"

She shakes her head. "It doesn't matter. It's not who I am anymore. Trust me, after a while, you will need to change yours too. I promise you, give it time, and you won't go by Peter anymore."

"So where did Sorcha come from?"

"Erm..." Sorcha smiles, the fondness at the memory shining through. "It's Irish. There is a coven there. Well, there used to be a coven there, and they were really good to me when I was young. They took me in. The high priestess took one look and immediately named me Sorcha. It means brightness." She twiddles with the ends of her white hair. "Anyway, it kind of stuck. I've been Sorcha since."

I pry the hair from her fingers, rubbing it between my own. "Your hair is incredible," I say in quiet awe.

She pushes her fingers through my own much darker hair. "It is a sign of what we are. Marked by the universe." She looks down again, her expression darkening. "Unnatural beings."

I take a moment to consider her words. I've never thought of Sorcha as anything other than vicious. Certainly never sad or capable of any real human emotion. "What you said before, how I can't father children, does that mean you also cannot have children?"

"Yes," she confirms, rolling onto her back with a sigh. "It means I am the same. For everything I am, and all that I can do, including the gift of unending life, I cannot create it. I am cursed to spend my life alone. A cosmic joke. All in the name of balance."

"A cosmic joke," I whisper back.

That is what we both are.

Relics who do not belong here.

She turns her silver eyes on me once more, with softness and vulnerability. "That is why fate has brought us together, Peter."

Oh no.

I close my eyes, wishing more than anything that she is not saying these words.

"We are the only two gods on this Earth. We were made for one another."

I sit up, turning away from her and dragging my hands down my face. "Sorcha..." I start.

But she is moving to her knees, grasping my face and forcing me to look at her. "Why are you fighting me, Peter? I know you can feel it too." I give in and look into her eyes. "I have spent so many years alone. You do not have to share the same fate."

Her lips find mine, coaxing me to her. Yet it feels wrong. It always has, despite the gravity between us. Perhaps a primal, ancient need to move toward the one thing that is the same as me.

But my heart.

My broken heart.

I ease her away from me. "Sorcha, I can't." I stare into her eyes, perhaps seeing for the first time how unfair I have been to her. She's been believing I would eventually come around. "This is over... you and me. I can't do this," I say with as much kindness as I can.

We stay this way for a minute, staring at each other.

"You just need more time," she says after a while.

"Christ, Sorcha," I almost yell while getting out of bed, needing to put some distance between us and pulling on the nearest available clothes. "Can you hear yourself? Just because we're two of a kind does not mean we are made for each other."

Sorcha's eyes turn hard. "So, what? Are you really so pathetic you're just going to pine for her for all of eternity?"

I rake my hands through my hair. "I would rather spend all of eternity pining after her than spend another second of it with you. What was I thinking? I must have lost my damn mind."

"You are not one of them, Peter." Sorcha points her finger at me before imploring, "Why can't you just accept it, revel in what you are? I know you want to."

"Revel in it?" My hands cover my eyes as if rubbing them will help me comprehend what she is saying. "How can I possibly do that? I have no peace from it. Not a moment, and I'm told the only peace I can look forward to is when my sister... the person who means more to me than anything else in this world... is dead. So don't stand here and tell me to revel in it!"

"You know nothing of this world, baby god. What true cruelty is. I never knew my brother. He was taken from me. You don't understand all you have," Sorcha yells. "You know nothing, *nothing*. You *will* lose your mind. When they die... and they all die... you *will* be alone." Sorcha turns to implore me once more, pushing hard on my shoulders. "We are not meant to be alone. We were made to be loved, worshipped, and feared. But everything you will ever have from them is temporary. Peter, you and I—"

"Get. Out," I scream. "There is *no* me and you. I am not the same as you. I don't want you, Sorcha. *Get. Out.*"

"You need me!" She spits the words in my face. "We both know you are in control of nothing. All of that power will spill out of you without me."

I snap, and in an instant, my hand is around her throat, squeezing hard enough to make her shut the hell up. I pull her face close to mine as she grapples at my fingers, trying to tear them away. "I will say this one... more... time," I whisper through gritted teeth. "You are *nothing* to me. You were an itch I needed to scratch. Nothing more."

In one swift move, I throw her out of my grasp, and she lands on the floor with a heavy thump. I turn away from her to look out the window, marking the graying of the skies.

Sorcha's breath comes hard behind me.

I do not want to hear anything else she has to say. "Before you state whatever you are thinking, Sorcha, *don't*." I take a deep breath. "Just go."

I feel rather than watch her leave.

Sorcha is gone.

Is this who I am now? Someone who throws women to the floor. I should be elated that she is gone—*for good*—but instead, I'm furious. Furious at her for thinking she has some sort of claim on me, furious at Connie for giving me up so easily, and above all, furious at myself for letting *any* of it happen.

In a heartbeat, I want to destroy everything.

But more than anything, I want to destroy myself.

Leaving my room, I make my way up the stairs to the roof, where I can scream without attracting too much attention. It is already raining when I get there, the black storm clouds rolling over the river.

I am so sick of my agony being a gaping hole for everybody to see. If I suffer, everyone else also has to. Even my own goddamn pain cannot be mine alone.

For a moment, I stand there taking in the rain, listening to the storm roll in, the low earthy grumble of thunder getting closer. I close my eyes, raising my arms to the sky. I long to feel something different, something physical, instead of sheer worthlessness and self-loathing.

I know one lightning strike won't hurt.

But two? *Let two come.*

One hits my neck, the other the top of my back. The force is enough to send me to my knees, but not enough to hurt, not really.

Three.

Three hurts.

More.

Is agony.

More, I think. *Don't stop, Peter.*

I try to hold my concentration and keep from passing out as I call the strikes down again and again. Hitting me in my neck, my back, my chest, my face while I keep myself teetering on the blackened edge of consciousness.

I don't notice when I can't hold myself up anymore or that it's my own screams I hear over the deafening cracking sound of the lightning hitting my body. I can smell it, my skin burning. The purple forks travel down my arms in front of my eyes, turning black and starting to char.

The pain is good, I tell myself. *The pain is real. Now all you need to do is die, Peter.*

But I hear something else.

A new sound.

Someone calling my name.

I open my eyes to see Anna and Lorna on the roof, running toward me.

The lightning stops as I hold up my weak arm. "Stop!" Even my voice seems to buzz under all of the electricity I am carrying. "Don't touch me," I manage to get out, my arm flopping back to the ground.

"Peter, what have you done?" Anna cries and I wonder who is screaming.

It's me.

The sound is coming from me.

Goddamn! I think I'm burning from the inside.

Darkness takes me.

I don't know how long I was out for, but I am on my feet, moving and walking. Two sets of arms are around me, helping me forward. I'm covered with blankets, so I can't see where I am going. I don't know who is moving me.

A glance down at my hands reveals charcoal-like skin as electricity ripples and rushes across my body.

I fall down in agony, darkness taking me again.

On my feet again. Barely. I feel so heavy like I could burst. I look down at my feet, and the ground looks like I'm passing the entrance to the coven. I take two steps and collapse to the ground for good this time.

Sweet relief inside the darkness.

Gemini

When I wake, the pain is gone. I'm on a thin mat in a small windowless room I have never seen before.

I rub my eyes. My body aches, but I can sense there is someone else in the room. "My head h-hurts." My voice cracks when I speak.

"Mmm..." Kali's soothing tone washes over me. "So I would expect from someone who swallowed a few billion volts." Her words are gentle, but her face is harsh, the ragged noise of her breaths sounding more bull like than priestess. "I hope you know the trouble you've caused. You've been lighting up this room like a firework and have scared every single person here. It's taken much to ground what you consumed, and there is still some left, but the fact that you are awake now is a good sign. Your sister will be pleased to see you, but I would advise you not to touch her, or anyone else, for the moment."

"Sorry," I say in a small voice. It seems I apologize a lot to Kali, who places a cup of water next to me. I readily take it up as my throat is parched. "How long was I out?"

"Three days," she replies, drawing symbols in the dust around me rather than looking at me.

"What are you doing?" I ask, regretting my decision to attempt sitting up. The black charring is gone now, but faint purple bruising remains everywhere.

"I am protecting this coven."

"From what?"

"From you." Her stern eyes find mine. "We have decided to reject your request to be bound. It is too dangerous."

My eyes widen. "Kali, but what I did... surely it shows how much I need it."

"It is because of what you did that your request has been denied. I cannot risk the safety of this coven, and I don't believe you will accept the binding."

"I will, I promise." I rise to beg her. "I was just angry."

"And what will happen when you become angry while bound? Will you take a knife to your own skin? Will your sister forever be dressing your wounds? Or will it be worse? Will it be someone else's? The binding does not change *what* you are, Peter."

I blink at her, lost for words. "I'm sorry," I say again quietly, my eyes wet. "Arjun, before, he almost killed me with what he called a sacred knife."

Kali's expression remains unreadable.

"Do you..." I start, then stop. "If you cannot bind me, if it really is too dangerous, is there a way you can kill me? One where it won't hurt Anna."

Kali kneels by my side as I blink back tears, determined not to cause another storm.

"I don't want to hurt anyone else," I whisper.

Kali's eyes return to the gentle gaze they usually hold. "My child, the only person you are hurting is yourself."

"What can I do?" I ask. "How do I live with it?"

"By becoming a student." Kali touches my cheek, not minding the faint remnant of electricity that crackles down her arm. "You have an entire coven at your disposal. I know you enjoy entertaining the youngsters here, but now it is time for you to start truly learning and understanding the magic that is woven into you. Show me you can learn, and then we will talk again about binding." Her eyes become hard. "You need to stop putting so much stock in what my son told you. You are not so easy to kill, as you now well know, and the sacred blades were not made for killing gods."

I want to ask more, but Kali motions for me to rest and leaves me to my thoughts. Not long after, Anna comes in, wringing her hands while coming to sit next to me. I shuffle to the edge of the mat to maintain my distance.

"Best not to come too close," I say to the ceiling. "Kali tells me I'm still radioactive."

"I can't believe how quickly you've healed. You looked like you had been on a barbecue."

"Mmm..." I snort, looking into her concerned face. "A few billion volts floating around your body will do that to a person."

"Not many people would walk away with their lives. It was scary to see that happen to you, Peter."

"You shouldn't be scared," I say, turning back to the ceiling. "I'm three attempts down and still here."

"Attempts?" Anna asks.

"Mm-hmm." I shrug. "My own father stabbed me, a fatal car crash was not fatal enough, and apparently, a few billion volts isn't enough to finish me off either."

"Attempts, Peter?" she says a little louder, and I catch my mistake from *how* she is saying it. "These are 'attempts'?" She staggers to her feet and looms over me.

I shuffle myself a little bit away from her, holding my hands up. "Well, not the being stabbed so much," I say in a weak attempt at calming her.

Anna stomps her foot, sending a puff of dust into the air. "I cannot believe you."

I wince at being shouted at.

"Attempts, Peter? Frigging *attempts*! How could you do that to me? You selfish piece of shit." In the heat of her anger, Anna reaches out, placing both hands on my bare chest to push me.

The second her hands connect, the blue crackles of electricity transfer from me to cover her skin, causing her to step back a few paces. The static makes her hair stand on end.

"Whoa. What was that?" she exclaims.

I'm on my feet, now trying to dodge her as she lunges to grab me again. "Stop it. I haven't had a chance to get a handle on it yet. It's dangerous, Anna. Can you just stop?" I plead while we continue to dance around.

"Why?" Anna laughs. "You share it with everyone else."

"Can you just stop for a second and I will explain?"

Anna stops circling me like a vulture and stands with her hands on her hips, waiting for me to go on.

"First of all, this is real. Natural electricity, from nature, is way stronger than what I can create myself. Now, I can control it, but I've only just woken up. I took on a lot, and there isn't much left, but if I transferred it all at once, it would still be enough to kill you."

Anna considers me for a few moments. "It didn't feel bad. It felt strong, powerful." The corners of her mouth upturning. "Is this what you make them feel like?"

I roll my eyes at her, then dip my head and sit back down as Anna starts to chuckle.

"Well, now at least I know what everyone sees in you."

"Oh, thanks." I roll my eyes again before giving her a dry laugh. "You mean you thought women like me for my winning personality?"

She snorts again, coming to sit by my side but keeping her distance. "Attempts, Peter? Please talk to me."

I feel her dark brown eyes on me and know there will be nothing but empathy in them now, so I can't look at her. "It was a poor choice of words. I've never set out to do it. I didn't ask for our father or for the crash. Just, in those moments, I hoped it would happen. I hoped I would close my eyes and slip away. But it doesn't stick. My eyes open again, and every time they do, my life is more shit than it was before. The lightning..." I continue in a shameful murmur, "... I suppose was the first 'attempt.'"

"*Wow*," she mouths, turning her face to the ceiling before whispering, "You are such an asshole."

"What?" I laugh. "I'm suicidal, and you are calling me an asshole?"

"You are such an asshole." Anna chortles, flashing her brilliant grin at me. "I love you more than anything, and you want to leave me? What happened to not being able to live without one another?"

"Sorry." The word is barely audible as I bring myself to face her, my inescapable mirror.

"You die, I die, remember?" she whispers back, and I nod. "You need to live. Do it for me. I want to live and be happy, and I want you to do the same. You can start by forgiving yourself for everything you think you have or haven't done."

I look down at her hand, desperate to take it and to feel the comfort she brings.

"No more self-destruct, Peter."

I nod, my eyes feeling hot again.

Anna continues, her voice sounding cautious. "Maybe it's time we listen to what everyone has been saying to us. Something we have always joked about ourselves."

"What do you mean?" I meet her eyes again.

"That we are a whole. I am the head, and you are the heart. But all this time, *you* have carried the burden, Peter. Why don't you try to let me carry it with you?" Anna shifts her hand toward mine. "I trust you, brother." She shakes her head as if coming to her senses. "I can't believe I didn't see it before." Her fingertips are so close. "This is meant for me."

I don't move. I hold my breath, trying to pull myself together so the shock doesn't stop her heart. Anna eases her hand into mine.

The electricity rises in my blood at once, but I am prepared for her touch so I'm able to control it, careful not to share too much as our fingers thread together. Anna's eyes drop to our hands to watch the charge pass from my skin to hers. After a minute, I stop. Her face is not giving anything away.

"How do you feel?" I ask.

Anna doesn't respond straight away, releasing my hand and looking at hers like she should see something there. As I'm about to tell her all she will do is ground the charge, I see a small blueish wave of electric current pass over her palm.

Anna looks from her hand back to me. "Cool," she says with a smile.

Chapter Thirteen

Anna

Peter and I giggle, holding our forearms out from the elbow, so close they are almost touching. Peter smiles down at me, once again sending a wave of golden yellow fizzing across his palm and down his arm before it dissipates. I concentrate hard on my hand. With some effort, I follow suit, and a small wave of faint blue passes over my hand and down to my elbow. I laugh again, kicking my legs out with glee from my place on the floor with my back against the cold wall next to my brother.

"This is so awesome," I tell him with a giggle. "Do it again."

Without any sign of effort, Peter lets the golden wave rush over his skin again, and I look back down at my own, pushing it out, the blue light fizzing even fainter this time.

"I wonder why mine is gold and yours is blue," he muses, eyeing my arm. "I've never seen that happen before."

I shrug. "Who knows? Yet another thing to add to the list. It's starting to fade, though." Already, the buzzing in my veins is starting to die down. "It's still grounding through me. It's just that I can use it too." I look up at my brother, trying to read his expression. "I think it means I can do both."

Gemini

Peter regards his own arm. "You can do both," he repeats in quiet awe. "How is that possible?"

I give him a small smile, nudging my shoulder to his. "Perhaps being your human half means more than we originally thought." His expression is unreadable, so I push on. "Peter, this is good news. This means you don't need Sorcha anymore or even to ask Lorna. Any power you can't contain, just give it all to me, Peter. It is meant for me."

"How can you possibly know that?" He sounds so uncertain, but I've never been more sure of anything in my life. "How do you know it won't hurt you like it did with Connie?"

"Call it twin's intuition." I look him square in the eye, trying to reassure him. "Peter, this feels right."

Peter closes his eyes, banging his head against the wall. "Anna, that's what they all say." He adds, "It's part and parcel of the horror of what I am. It makes you think I'm good, but in reality, I am poison."

I get to my knees, taking his face in my hands. "This is you and me. This is totally different from them. I am different. You listen to me now for a change." I take his hands, holding them as hard as I can, and his eyes don't leave mine. "This is not about what *you* are anymore. It's about what *we* are. Okay?" I see the water rise in his eyes as he nods his head in agreement. "You are not alone."

He simply nods again, unable to find the words. My own tears prick my eyes as I pull him in close to me. He wraps his arms around my body, holding me as close as he can, and I do the same. I want to crush him—I need him so close.

I don't know when Peter first decided to put the distance between us. After the crash was when I felt it most, but in truth, it started before that.

Arjun. All roads lead back to him.

The moment Arjun told Peter he needed to kill me, the distance started to grow between us. I do know deep down inside that Peter feels the inevitability of Arjun's plans for him around his neck like a noose he cannot break free from. And all of this comes down to one inescapable fact, one core belief of Peter's that our father was able to shatter—Peter is good.

After a while, he breaks away from me with a sigh. "So, what now then, boss?"

I give him a shove. "We talk to Kali," I say, not actually knowing what we should do with this new information. "She'll be able to tell us more. And we will take it real slow, you know, with me. The coven should monitor us for now, make sure what you transfer doesn't hurt me, and also help me to channel it, right? We'll learn these things together, okay?"

He nods, letting out a low breath. "Sure. That sounds like a solid plan. But not today. I'm still pretty tired. I think you took the last of it, so I'm going to sleep some more. Why don't you come back tomorrow, and we will talk to Kali together then?"

"Are you sure?" I eye him with some skepticism. "You've been in this room for three days. Why don't we take a walk? It would be good for you to be outside, see the sky. If you come back to the hostel, you will have a room with a window."

"I don't want to," he says, his tone hushed. "I just want to rest, maybe take a shower."

I still don't know what happened with Sorcha, or if she has gone for good. All we know is whatever was said or done between the two of them was enough for Peter to hit self-destruct. I should have seen it coming—he'd been heading that way for a while. I'm about to argue with him about staying here, insist the first step on his road to recovery is to take care of himself, but I don't have a chance as Lorna comes into the room.

"Hi," she says, trying to keep her voice cheerful. "You've been quite a while, so I just wanted to check that everything is okay. It's so good to see you awake, Peter, and only a little purple."

"Thanks." Peter smiles warmly at her. "I think I'm pretty much back to normal now."

"That's good to hear." She smiles.

"Lor, watch this," I say, turning to her. Focusing on my hand with great effort, I force the last bit of electricity from my fingertips. It's not enough for a wave, more of a crackle, but it's enough to make Lorna's eyes widen.

"How are you doing that?" she asks me, her excitement evident.

Before I have a chance to explain, Peter clears his throat, indicating he wants us to leave. So we tell him goodbye and head out of the coven.

I try to catch her up with my new theory about how we have been going about this all wrong. That the power is not Peter's burden alone, and we have been on two separate paths when we should be thinking of them as one. I barely even notice we've made it back to the hostel as Lorna flops down onto her bed.

"I mean, he is just so scared of what it means, in that one day I'm destined to become part of him, that he hasn't even considered the possibilities of what I can do apart from him." I pace our room as my thoughts now flow freely out of my mouth. "Do you know what I mean? Can you imagine?" I look to Lorna for confirmation and she's smiling. "Maybe I can have the best of both worlds? You know, access all of this insane power he has, but also just be able to live a regular human life."

"That would sure be something, kind of like a real-life superhero."

I stop my pacing and look down at her. "You're making fun of me."

"Not at all." She laughs and stands. "You are right. We should have thought of it before." Lorna takes both of my hands. The look she's giving me feels like a caress across my skin. "Just go slow, okay? What you are saying makes sense to me, but I don't want you to get hurt."

I stop myself from rolling my eyes. "You're starting to sound like Peter."

She tightens her grip on my hands, pulling me a fraction closer. "That's because you mean the world to him. You mean the world to both of us."

Her words make the color rise in my cheeks. I try to tell her thanks, but when my eyes meet hers, I am lost for words. I see only her deep brown eyes. It seems Lorna has lost the ability to speak too as the air thickens between us.

I have always been one to think, even overthink, but standing here, looking at Lorna, I have never been surer about what I want. I let go of her hands, closing the distance between us and placing my hands on either side of her face, and bringing her lips to mine.

Lorna's hesitation is momentary before she kisses me back, her arms wrapping around me to deepen our kiss, and that's when the butterflies explode in my stomach. She feels good, right, like home. Kissing Lorna is the most natural thing in the world.

I feel like I could kiss her forever.

When I pull back, although I miss her, I can delight in the look on her face.

Every single thing we'd been scared about now seems to have melted away.

"Wow," she says through a shaky breath, her eyes sparkling as she tucks a strand of hair behind my ear. "That was even more amazing than I imagined it would be. I can't believe you are mine, Anna."

At her admission, I let out a giggle. "Yes," I say, beaming while holding her close. "I am yours, all of me, in every way."

I kiss her again.

The next day, I wake in nervous excitement, the anticipation of talking Kali through my new theory about Peter's excess powers zinging through me. I can barely keep my thoughts straight. I've never felt anything but ordinary next to my brother. Not that I ever

Gemini

wanted his abilities—I've never been envious of him. We are both so different, and I have always accepted how things were.

Part of me is cautious about what Kali will think. The high priestess has been so patient with how increasingly volatile Peter is, but I'm not sure how she will feel about another unknown variable.

"I've been thinking," Lorna begins as we are getting ready. "I'm going to hang back today, just chill here, maybe go to the market for some things."

"What? Why?" I pop my head out of our bathroom, where I'm brushing my teeth.

Lorna continues to tidy some of her clothes. "Just while you have this conversation with Kali." Lorna turns her eyes on me, and they're filled with nothing but compassion. "Peter needs you right now, Anna. He's not in good shape. Go, be with your brother. I will be here, and you can tell me all about it when you get back."

I give her a long look before nodding in agreement. She makes total sense. It's a weird thing. Lorna seems to somehow understand him better than I can sometimes. There are moments when my logic is a little too much at the front of my mind, and I don't give enough thought to the emotion. Peter has always been our protector, and seeing him so fragile is difficult. I don't know what else to do but to try and fix it.

When I arrive at the coven, I linger in the doorway, scanning the main hall for him, but I can't see him anywhere. I spot Mahi in a far corner and make my way over to her.

"Hi, Mahi," I greet.

She offers me a wide toothy grin in return.

"Have you seen Peter this morning?"

She shakes her head. "I haven't seen him at all. He's still in his room. My mother took some breakfast to him earlier."

I stick out my bottom lip. I wish he would get out of these four walls.

"There he is."

My gaze follows Mahi's pointing finger across the room to one of the corridors that leads into the underground rooms.

In the light of the main hall, I can see all but the faintest traces of bruising have healed now. All in what, four days? Peter's skin had been charred beyond recognition when Lorna and I carried him here, or rather, dragged him here. Great black scars covered his face. It was horrific. One hundred times worse than the singed smell when he was hit first, the overpowering stench of burning flesh even worse than the ghats. Peter's knees buckled every few paces, immobilized, and he screamed when we were first moving him, falling clean off the ladder from the roof and landing in a heap. He must have taken over a hundred hits.

Now, just a few faint forks of purple remain across his cheek.

He scans the room, finding me before sauntering over, his expression serious.

"Hey, kid," he greets Mahi with a ruffling of her hair.

She giggles as she pushes his hand away, but there is a definite wariness to her expression I've never seen before.

Kali told me Peter's screams echoed through the entire coven when they first moved him to the room in the basement. The amount of electricity in his body kept discharging out all over the room, and Kali became worried it would start a fire. Together, Kali and the senior witches worked together, using their magic and trees from their small fruit garden to allow it to ground. She also shared that Peter turned their bark to ash in seconds. After that, it was up to the seniors to siphon it off as safely as they could.

I don't think Peter even remembers.

I look around. There is a slight change in the witches, a wariness in their eyes in their stolen glances. A danger they never saw in him before. I try to push the words our father had spoken to us out of my mind about how Peter is a ticking time bomb for everyone around him. I shake that thought away. It's different now. I feel certain my theory is right, and the balance he needs is all to do with me. I can bring it to him in life, not just in my death.

"Are you ready for this?" he asks solemnly.

"Yes, I think so." I nod.

We walk side by side toward Kali, who sits in her seat at the front of the room. I work to keep my nerves under control, and Peter's face remains serious. I know he isn't convinced this is a good idea as he wants to protect me above all else.

Kali lifts her eyes to us in our place before her. I don't know where to start. It seems like the eyes of the whole coven are on us.

"Kali," I begin. "We would like to talk to you. Maybe, more like get your advice on something."

Kali raises her eyebrows, her eyes flicking to Peter and then back to me. "Of course. Please tell me what is on your mind, Anna."

I am about to go on, but my brother's voice rings out beside me. "Can we do this alone, Kali? The three of us."

Kali's eyes narrow and her expression becomes stern when she turns to him. "My child, this coven is a collective. There is nothing you can say that is not permitted for everyone's ears."

I see him rolling his eyes from my peripheral. *I wish he wouldn't do that.* He is on thin ice as it is.

So I take a seat on the step in front of Kali and try to calm the swirling atmosphere with a clear but tranquil voice. "Something happened yesterday, Kali, when I was with Peter. I touched him, and some of the electricity passed on to me." I glance at him, but he's not looking at me, instead watching Kali for her reaction. "Only, it didn't ground straight away. I could use it." I move my eyes back to Kali's masked expression. "I'm starting to think the excess power Peter has is meant for me."

Kali remains silent but presses her fingers to her lips.

"It would make sense, right? If technically we are part of a whole, then the power, which can be such a burden, well... what if I'm supposed to share it with him?"

Kali regards me for several moments before looking back at Peter. "Do you share your sister's beliefs?"

Peter takes a long time to answer. "It's true. I saw her use it, but she didn't just use it. It was changed and became her own."

"How so?" Kali cocks her head at him.

Peter shrugs. "It burns a different color."

Kali's eyes flick back to mine. "How interesting. Anna, you have to understand there is no precedent for this in all of our history. You are the first and last of your kind."

I take a shaky breath. Being the first and last of something is a lot of pressure. "So, what do you think? Can you help? Can you help us make it work?"

Kali is about to rise when Peter moves forward, taking two slow steps so he is standing above her. In a way, it feels like he is somehow making himself taller by towering above her. "Before you say anything else, Kali, I want to make one thing crystal clear." His voice slow and serious as he warns, "If any harm comes to my sister because of this, if any advice you give leads her to injury, then I will tear this coven down. I don't care if I go down with it. Do you understand me?"

I cannot believe what he is saying. He is in no position to be threatening Kali. I try to gather my thoughts to tell him to stop being so ridiculous and apologize, but Kali speaks first. "Yes. I understand that, Peter," she says smoothly.

I look around and note that everyone in the coven has stopped. All their eyes are on him. I've never seen anyone address Kali this way—no one has ever stood over her. I reach out and gently place my hand into his, urging him back. Kali's eyes don't leave him as he takes his place by my side.

"So, what first?" I ask, desperate for some of the tension to dissipate.

"Let us see the two of you in action." Kali motions.

I instinctively look to Peter, who is far from convinced.

"Everything you took from the sky is now grounded, yes?" she asks and he nods. "The excess, what form does it take?"

Peter shrugs again, thinking, taking his time to answer. It's a bit irritating that he has never thought about it before, as it all comes so natural to him. "The form I choose. I guess electricity is easier, especially when it comes to transferring it to somebody else. If I'm transferring to ground, I suppose it doesn't take a form, but rather it's my energy that makes things grow." He mulls things over again and his eyes take on a new depth. "It's hard to put into words."

"And you always need contact?"

Peter glances back at me before answering. "Mostly."

I give him a hard look—he needs to be honest.

After a minute, he rolls his eyes. "Fine. I don't need contact, not anymore. It's more that I *like* the contact." He moves his head to the side, a sure sign he is weighing up his words. "I guess it feels better to do it that way. In certain situations, it feels more... intimate." He looks back to Kali, who now seems a little concerned. Peter clears his throat, perhaps only now realizing he is thinking out loud, the slightest hint of red coloring his cheeks. "Plus, it's easier to control the transfer with contact to steady the flow," he says toward his feet.

Kali's expression is thoughtful. "Could you transfer the energy to Anna without it becoming electricity? The way you do with the earth."

"I don't know," Peter replies, considering.

"Come." Kali ushers us from our place on the steps, and we move to sit on a couple of cushions facing each other on the floor. A few of the senior witches gather close, watching on in silence. "Why don't the two of you link hands?"

We do as she asks. I almost expect there to be an instant connection, but there isn't, only the warmth of his hands in mine.

Kali turns to Peter, giving him a tender look. "Peter, I know you do not find this comfortable, to be pushed, but it seems you must be a teacher as well as a student."

He keeps his eyes on her, waiting for her to continue.

"This excess energy, as you call it... what you cannot contain, can you feel it now?"

Peter nods.

"What does it feel like?"

Peter closes his eyes, taking a deep breath. "It feels like pressure under my skin, like water in a dam, ready to burst."

"That is good, Peter," Kali soothes. "That is a strong image. Hold onto it. Imagine the dam. It is strong, with high walls. It is not about to burst, though." Kali kneels beside us, placing a hand over each of our joined ones. "This dam has a small overflow floodgate to cope with its reservoir. Picture it, Peter, in your mind, a small gate where a stream will flow. You can open that gate now."

I feel Peter's fingers flex in mine. "I don't know if I can."

"It is small, Peter, but it is strong. It will help when it floods."

Peter's fingers clamp down harder and I try not to wince, but when he breathes out, I feel it. Warmth. I close my eyes as the heat radiates in my hands and starts to rise. This feels like a wave too, washing up my arms and hitting my chest before rolling down my belly and into my legs. I grasp onto his hands to stop myself from falling back. I can't see it, but it almost feels golden, confusing my senses. Not intoxicating but definitely powerful.

I can't say how long it lasts. Maybe time stands still. For the first time in our whole lives, we are connected in the way we were born to be—as one.

I feel so warm it takes me a moment to realize Peter has released my hands.

"How do you feel?" Kali asks him.

"Better," he replies with a weak grin.

"And you?" Kali asks me.

"Strong," I say, surprised by the conviction in my own voice.

Kali chuckles, getting up from her spot to pace. "How very peculiar." She taps Peter on the shoulder. "This is the way. You keep your transfer pure, and it should not harm her. However, I would suggest you continue to do the transaction here in view of the coven so we can monitor it for the time being. Just to be sure." Kali turns back to me with a grin. "It looks like you were right, my child. This power *is* yours too. He is its conduit."

I let out a low breath. "You could see it?" *I wonder if it was golden.*

But Kali shakes her head, still smiling. "There was nothing to see, but I could feel it." She glances around at the other witches, who are observing. "We could all feel it. It is quite a thing."

The witches all dip their heads in agreement.

Kali faces Peter, placing her hand on his arm, the anticipation clear on her face. "Are you ready for your second lesson today? Let us teach your sister how to use the power she is holding?"

"Erm, sure." He gives me an uncertain look. "I don't know how to do that, though."

Kali raises her eyebrow toward me. "Maybe it's time you learned a little of yourself, Peter. Not just that which comes naturally." One of the witches hands Kali a small pot of dirt, which she places between us. "What is in this pot?"

Peter reaches out to put his hands around the pot before looking back at her. "They are pansy seeds."

"Mmm..." She nods. "And how do you know that?"

Peter looks back at them and then at me and shrugs. "I don't know. I just *know*."

Kali is thoughtful for a moment. "And you *know* how to force them along their journey? Bring them into bloom before our eyes." Peter gives a small nod, and she continues to push. "So, why don't you tell your sister how to do it?" He opens his mouth to protest, but Kali raises her hand to stop him. "I do not want to hear... 'I don't know how.' Try. Explain."

Peter takes a moment to observe the pot, moving up onto his knees. Closing his eyes again, I imagine he is attempting to gather the right words together. After a minute, he guides my hands so my thumbs dig into the small pot. Taking his own hands away, he looks me in the eyes with a tentative smile. "Right. Feel that soil, Anna. It is part of you now. You have to connect to it."

I keep my eyes on his and let my thumbs slowly rotate the cool earth.

"Find the seeds in there, all of them. Breathe. All of that energy, draw it up high. Imagine it in your shoulders." With his words, I can feel it reacting, although I'm not sure if it's his command or mine. "Now. When you breathe out, it is going to wash out down your arms and past your fingers into the earth."

I breathe out. With a shudder, I feel it happen. The power moves out of me and into the pot. Three pansies sprout into life, revealing their purple petals. I can't fight my smile at the sight of them. Neither can Peter.

"Shit," he exclaims. "I can't believe that actually worked."

"Beats levitating leaves." Kali smiles at me, once again taking a seat next to us. "This challenges everything we previously believed. We knew the human twin soul binds the god soul to this plane. We would never have guessed you truly come as two halves. Every aspect of yourselves, every personality trait, is all drawn in balance." Kali shakes her head the slightest touch, pointing to me, to label me. "Reason." Then to Peter. "Intuition." Before back to me. "Mortal." To Peter. "Immortal." Resting her fingers on my arm, she says, "Life." Settling her eyes back on Peter, she murmurs, "Death."

Perhaps Kali is thinking out loud, but it's the wrong thing to say. Peter is on his feet in a flash. "Death? Really? I am not death. In fact, I saved Anna and Connie." He jabs his finger into his chest. "I am life, Kali. I am the one to give life. It is my power. *Mine.*"

His little outburst leaves Kali and me quite speechless. Frustrated by the silence he is met with, Peter throws his arms up in the air and stalks off, I am guessing back to his room in the basement.

What on earth was that all about?

I get up to follow, but Kali's gentle grip on my arm stops me. "Leave him, child. That is enough practice for today. Why don't you come back tomorrow? And bring your friend. He will be glad to see her."

I nod and give her a warm smile. "Thank you so much, Kali, for everything today." Then I add quietly, "And for everything you are doing for him. He may not seem grateful, but I know he is."

Kali smiles, but something makes her avert her gaze. "I am glad that you came to me. I hope you always will."

It feels strange leaving him here again. It goes against everything I know about him. Not only does he want to be alone, but he is retreating to a windowless room by his own choice. I don't even know if he's been outside yet.

I'll deal with him tomorrow.

For now, I want to get back to Lorna.

She's in our room, reading, when I reach the hostel.

"You've been gone a while. How did it go?" she asks when I burst in.

I'm so excited to tell her about everything that I squeeze onto the bed next to her and gush with all that has happened. How Kali agrees with my theory, that she thinks Peter and I are split down the middle, and I can use his power in a safe way. I almost can't contain my excitement when telling her about how I used it to grow the flowers. *Me. I did that.*

"It felt so natural, Lor. Like I was made for this."

"Wow." Lorna smiles, propping herself up on her elbow. "This is so incredible. Kind of the answer to all of Peter's problems. You were under his nose the whole time."

"I'm not sure how he's taking it, to be honest."

"What do you mean?"

Her earnest expression is so piercing that I am hit with the reality of how close we are. "I'm not sure. Maybe he's a little envious that I can be both?" I look down at my fingers weaving with Lorna's, hyper-aware of her body next to mine. "He'll be okay. He will come around. Once he has all this mess with Connie and Sorcha out of his system, he'll get better." I peer up at her face and smile. "Our connection is so strong, Lorna. I felt it today, like being whole in a way where you didn't realize you were incomplete before. I can fix this. I can fix him."

Lorna's eyes sparkle as she looks at me, more like into me. "You are amazing, Anna," she says, tracing her finger down my face. "I love you."

Chapter Fourteen

Connie

For what feels like the hundredth time today, I rub my cloth over the dark wood counter, appreciating the way it shines. The coffee shop's aroma is comforting and familiar, like a blanket wrapped around me. I'd been so happy when Mike gave me the job in the coffee shop, as it allows me to feel closer to Brady again, and that brings me a great deal of peace. Bringing back only happy memories of many afternoons spent at the shop. Working here is a tribute to Brady, a small gesture I'm able to make. It feels both good and painful at the same time. Strangely, I feel like I haven't been able to access my grief for him for a long time.

With the benefit of distance, I am starting to think Peter's influence works differently from how even he suspects. Affecting everybody close to him, not just me. His desire to protect us meant our own grief was kept at bay, allowing us to only feel the fringes of it while Peter absorbed its full force. It would explain Lorna's seeming inability to keep track of time, and why Anna never thinks to contact their aunt. Peter doesn't think these things are important, so when in his bubble, everyone forgets about them too. I realize none of it is intentional. He doesn't know, and even if he did, it can't be helped. How does one just stop feeling? Even him.

I was hoping the now seemingly slow passage of time would help heal the feeling of missing Peter, but in a way, I feel it more every day I don't hear from any of them. Their lives are carrying on without me, and even though I'm the one who left, I can't fight the hunch that, somehow, I am the person left behind.

My phone buzzes in my back pocket. Luckily, Mike is relaxed about me using my phone as long as it's not busy. Of course, it's only Jamie who texts me these days, but when I pull it out, I see Lorna's name flash up on the screen for the first time in weeks.

Lorna: *Hi, Con. How's things back in the UK? Are you free to catch up? I really need your advice about something.*

I stare at the screen, my heart in my throat. On the one hand, I am so happy to hear from her, but on the other hand, I can't help being a little annoyed how, after weeks of radio silence, she is acting like no time has passed. I wonder what she could possibly need my advice about. I try to avoid the sinking feeling in my stomach that it is something to do with Peter and Sorcha. I quickly type out a response.

Me: *I can, but I don't finish work until five. So it will be late if that is okay with you? About eleven your time.*

Lorna: *Speak to you then. Xxx*

A part of me wishes I'd just asked Mike for a break and called her straight away. I'm intrigued, but also, in a pathetic kind of way, I want to make her wait for me.

I glance toward the door as Jamie comes in with Lauren, a friend of his from school. They look deep in conversation as she bats her eyelashes up at him. She motions to a nearby table, and he makes his way over to the counter.

"Hi." I smile at him. "How come you're with Lauren?"

"Oh, I just met her outside. She's back from uni for the weekend. I haven't seen her in ages."

"Right. I forgot she moved away. What is she studying again?"

Jamie shrugs his shoulders. "I forget." He rubs his forehead. "She just told me as well."

I laugh. "Well, I think you'll be forgiven. It's obvious she likes you."

Jamie's eyebrows shoot up in surprise. "You think?" he asks, looking back to where she's sitting and messing with her phone.

"Definitely." I smile as he turns back to me. "I saw the way she was looking at you."

Jamie gives a small nod, seeming pleased with himself, then stops to study my face. "What's up with you? You look all flushed."

"Oh, I heard from Lorna just now." I wave my hand, hoping at nonchalance.

"And?"

"And nothing. She asked if I was free to talk, and I told her I would call her later. No biggie."

Even talking about it makes my heart race, and Jamie is clearly not convinced. "Connie—"

"Actually, what are you doing later? Maybe we could go out for dinner? Have a few drinks at The Fish? My treat."

I'm not sure why I've asked him out, but I don't want to have to think about speaking to Lorna or speculate on what she wants to talk to me about anymore.

Jamie wears a mixture of expressions. I'm not sure whether it's shock or confusion, but eventually, he stammers out, "S-sure. That sounds really nice."

"Amazing." I force myself to beam at him. "I doubt I'll speak to Lorna much more than half an hour, so why don't you pick me up at half six? And let me take your order. You don't want to keep Lauren waiting."

Jamie is all flustered but manages to get his order out, which I busy myself making while cringing inside. No doubt he thinks I've asked him out on a date in response to seeing Lauren giving him puppy dog eyes. The last thing I want to do is lead Jamie on when he's been so good to me since I got back. He's nothing more than a good friend, though. He lets me cry when I need to, but more than anything, he has been cheerful and worked extra hard to help take my mind off the car crash of my last moments with Peter. He's also pretty much the one person in my life I call a friend right now.

While walking home after my shift is finished, I text Lorna with shaking hands to let her know I'll call her in five minutes. I don't know why I feel so sick at the thought of speaking to her.

Why am I so nervous?

Neither Peter nor Anna have made any attempts to contact me, so I doubt they'll be there. I feel ridiculous when I press her name, my hand trembling while I FaceTime her from the privacy of my room.

"Hey, Connie. So good to see you. I know it's been a while. How is everything with you?"

Lorna, also appearing nervous, only deepens my feeling of dread.

"I'm good. I started working at the coffee shop, which is really nice." I steady my hand on the desk in front of me.

"Really? That's cool. Yep, that's cool." She nods before slipping into an uncomfortable silence.

The suspense might kill me. "So, what's new over there, Lor? You look all edgy."

Lorna gives a nervous laugh. "Yeah, quite a bit actually. Erm... I think I might have done something a bit stupid."

This takes me by surprise. "You?" I let the hint of a smile cross my lips. "What have you done?" She is a pretty levelheaded person most days.

Gemini

Lorna runs a hand through her hair. "So, before I tell you, you should probably know that Anna and I are together now."

That is certainly not what I was expecting, and it shocks all the nervousness right out of me. "What? As in... together, together?"

"Yep." She smiles. "Together, together for a few weeks now. We've been taking things slow, super slow. Like snail's pace."

I look hard at my friend, waiting for her to go on, but she doesn't. "So, what? You think that it was a mistake?"

"Oh, no, no." She shakes her head. "Anna is great. We agreed slow was the best way because we don't want to ruin our friendship. But, I said something." Lorna lets out a deep breath, closing her eyes. "I told her I love her, Connie. That is not taking it slow. I totally broke the taking-it-slow rule. She was on this roll talking, being amazing and, well, it just came out."

"Oh, Lor." I let out a long breath, smiling at my friend, feeling like it's been no time at all. "You love her? I didn't even know."

"I know. It's been such a long time coming on, so gradual. But, yes, I think I really do love her." Her cheeks turn rosy.

"I am so happy for you." I beam. "Does Peter know?" I have to ask.

"Actually, it was Peter who gave me the courage to go for it," Lorna says, her apprehension melting away too. "But I shouldn't have said it. It's too soon."

"Lor." I cock my head at her. "Who doesn't want to hear that? What did she say?"

"Nothing. I freaked out and told her not to say it back, that I just got caught up in the moment. She was being all noble. We kind of laughed it off, but I can't stop thinking about it."

"Are things awkward since? Where is she now?"

"No, they aren't awkward, but we haven't talked about it since. You know, there is a lot going on to distract her, and whenever I am left to my own devices, I can't help but overplay it in my head."

"Why are you being left to your own devices? Where are they?"

Lorna looks a bit awkward again. "Oh. She is at the coven with

Peter. I've been giving them some breathing room. He's been staying there lately." Lorna looks down.

My heart is in my throat again. "With Sorcha?" I ask, trying to keep my voice even.

"Oh God, no," Lorna says with relief. "That is over, thankfully. But, well, I guess there has been a new development. Erm... so we kind of discovered that Anna can use Peter's powers."

"What?"

"Yeah." Lorna smiles again. "She's pretty impressive. Kali has been teaching Peter how to pass it over to Anna without hurting her, and he and Kali have been teaching Anna how to use it. It's all been a pretty steep learning curve. She's getting stronger, but I think it frustrates her when he doesn't have to think about it. About as much as it frustrates him having to explain it." Lorna laughs. "They are literally two halves, split." She makes a motion with her hands as if breaking a cookie. "Right down the middle. I find it best to stay out of the way sometimes."

I give a small shake, wrapping my head around it. Anna with powers and Sorcha out of the picture. The second part makes me happier than it should.

"So, why is Peter staying there?"

Lorna glances away. Maybe I should stop asking questions, but it seems so out of character to keep himself away from his sister.

"Connie," she hedges, still looking out into the night. "I'm not sure he would want me to tell you."

My pulse quickens again. "Why?"

Lorna gives a big sigh. "Can we just talk about something else? What's going on with you and Jay? Are you two together now?"

"No, we're still just friends. Jamie has been great, though. A real friend to me." For some reason, her evasiveness has my back straight. "I don't hear from any of you. Just because I left doesn't mean I stopped caring. I love you all." Annoying tears prick my eyes.

Lorna rubs her eyes. "Connie," she teases out my name. "I don't know why he's staying there and neither does Anna, but it's probably for the best. It seems to be where he needs to be right now, where there are more eyes to keep an eye on him."

"Lorna, what do you mean?"

Lorna's expression is defeated, and from that simple look, I can tell she's sad. "Are you sure you want to know? You're a million miles away. There is nothing you can do. You are home. You have a job, Jamie."

"Lorna." I'm verging on panic now. "I will obsess over this unless you tell me. I still care about him. I want to know."

Lorna squeezes her eyes shut. "We didn't know at the time what he'd tried to do when we found him. But, Peter hurt himself, really bad. He's fine now, Connie. Within a few days, he was up and walking around." Lorna shakes her head. "And, of course, he just got up and carried on like nothing happened. His scars healed so quickly."

"You mean he..." I whisper into my hand. I don't remember putting my hand to my mouth. The tears that were already there are now spill freely down my face.

Lorna nods.

"But, Anna," I manage to say.

"I know." Lorna holds up a hand. "It's not good. He does seem a little better. He's quiet, as usual." Lorna shakes her head again. "But, I don't know. We are lucky we discovered Anna can tap into it... the power. She can take some from him. Con, I think he would go nuclear without it."

"This is all my fault." I shake.

"No." Lorna shakes her head. "No, Connie. That is *so* not true. This goes so much deeper than you. There is so much I don't know. He doesn't talk to me about it all that much. Even with Anna, it's only bits and pieces. He's been primed his whole life to keep everything in. You know he's complicated. It has been hard, but he's been working with Kali a lot lately, which is the best thing for him. I think the coven and Anna are helping set him on the right path now. It will get better. Please don't blame yourself. That's why I didn't want to tell you."

"No, it's better that I know." I dry my eyes. "Believe me, it's better than not knowing."

Lorna fixes me with a sympathetic gaze, but then her eye is caught as she waves to someone who must have come up the stairs. "I'm just speaking to Connie," she says.

My heart is hammering, although I know it won't be him. Sure enough, Anna's heavily tanned face enters the screen.

"Hi, Connie." She beams, and my breath is pretty much taken away by the sight of her.

Her skin is so tanned now, her shoulder-length hair even lighter, and her dark eyes sparkle. She looks so incredibly like him that it makes my heart ache.

"How are you? It feels like forever."

"You're telling me." I smile at her. "I miss you all."

"Aw... we miss you too. We all do," she says.

We make small talk, and I make her promise to call her aunt. She finds it vaguely amusing that her aunt cares, but she promises me anyway. I wonder if she's not inherited some of Peter's personality after all.

After a while, they click off the call once they assure me it won't be so long next time. Something tells me that won't be the case, though. I stare at my phone, feeling empty.

I miss them.

I miss *him*.

A gentle knock on my bedroom door makes me jump a mile, and Jamie pops his head around the door.

"I was calling for ages. Didn't you hear me?"

"Sorry. I was lost in thought."

"Are you okay?" he asks and takes a seat next to me. "How was the call with Lorna?"

"I'll tell you over dinner," I say, in no hurry to retell the call. I look down, realizing I'm still in my apron and work shirt. I can get away with my black jeans.

Going to my wardrobe, I start rooting around for something to wear, settling on a Breton top. I throw my apron over the back of my chair as I turn back to Jamie, desperate for a change of pace.

"So, you and Lauren? Are you thinking of asking her out while she is back?"

Except, Jamie isn't answering. He's staring at me and going ever redder in the face.

It's then that it dawns on me what I'm doing as my fingers undo the last of my shirt buttons. "Whoops." I chuckle, turning my back to him, my turn to go red now. "Old habits."

"I don't mind." He laughs.

"Can you maybe turn around?" I peek back over my shoulder to ensure he is doing as asked and whip my shirt off before pulling the clean top over my head. "All done."

Jamie does a good job of avoiding the subject of my call with Lorna until we're sitting in the restaurant with a drink.

He takes a long sip of his beer before saying, "Okay. Take a sip of your wine and then talk."

I'd thought about this on the way over and decided to only share the good news part of the call. So, that's what I do. I tell him all about Lorna and Anna being together now.

Jamie almost chokes on his beer. "So, Lorna likes girls now?"

I shrug. "I'm not sure she ever entirely liked boys. She was never interested in anyone around her, not that there's much choice." I give him a wry smile, which he returns.

"Still, for you to have no idea. You've known her forever."

I shrug it off, determined to keep our conversation light and to keep the knowledge that Peter tried to take his own life out of my head. "You know those two. They could make anyone fall in love with them."

It's the wrong thing to say as Jamie looks at me hard. "And what of Peter? Where is he in all of this?"

"He approves, I'm told," I say, focusing on keeping my hand steady while I take another sip of wine. "Lorna says Anna and Peter have found a way to share his power, and Anna is learning how to use it, so that's also good news."

Jamie shakes his head and stares down at the menu. "Your friend's lives are weird."

I take another sip of wine. *Ain't that the truth?* It kind of hurts how, without the presence of Brady, Jamie doesn't consider them his friends too. Maybe as much as the fact they're barely my friends anymore. With Peter all but moving into the coven, Anna will never leave him, and Lorna will not leave Anna. I doubt they will ever come back to Wixford.

"Let's talk about something else," I tell Jamie before sinking what's left in my glass.

Two courses and a bottle of wine later, and I'm thoroughly merry.

As Jamie walks me home, we move to one of his favorite subjects —Brady. Which is one of mine too. Talking about Brady with Jamie is never sad. He only talks about the good stuff.

Jamie is practically crying with laughter as we stroll along discussing the funny things Brady used to do when we were kids. "Do you remember the time when he went down that big hill on Lorna's micro scooter?"

I laugh, nodding and stumbling. I remember it well. Brady's family had taken us all on holiday with them.

"He flew right down that hill," he continues.

"I've never seen anything move that fast. He might as well have been flying." I cry with laughter while holding onto Jamie.

"It was like a rocket." Jamie can hardly speak. "And then he couldn't make the corner and went straight into the bush."

I double over, fighting to breathe. "Lorna was so mad he broke her scooter."

"You were crying." Jamie wags his finger at me.

"I was concerned." I bat it away. "Did you see what he looked like when he came out of that bush? He looked like the scarecrow from *The Wizard of Oz*."

With that, we're both clutching our stomachs, laughing so hard we might as well be rolling around on the floor.

Jamie dries his eyes as we arrive at my house. "He never cried, even though it must have hurt like hell. He just laughed it off," he says and turns to me.

"That was Brady." I smile.

Jamie makes a small noise of agreement. He doesn't move, and neither do I. We stare at each other for a moment as our smiles fade. His head makes the smallest of inclinations toward me.

"Jaaay," I draw out his name, putting my hand on his chest. "It's not fair on you. I'm not over him. Honestly, it's going to take a while."

"I know," he says, putting his hand over mine. "I take full responsibility for my feelings getting hurt."

I sway on the spot, looking into his pale blue eyes. "I can't lose you."

"You won't," he whispers.

He moves so slow as he lowers his lips to mine, his palms moving to hold my face. It's a gentle kiss full of warmth and nostalgia, and exactly what I need right now.

I bite my lip as I back away toward my house. "Good night, Jamie."

"Good night, Connie," he says, looking every bit like the cat who got the cream.

I greet my mum, who is still up watching television with her own glass of wine. She looks pleased I'm home and doesn't grill me too much for information. I heave myself up the stairs, noticing how drunk I am now that I'm inside.

I throw myself onto my bed and, against all my better judgment, take my phone out. Before I have a chance to think about what I'm doing, I hit *his* number. For a few seconds, butterflies explode at the thought of talking to him.

I should have expected the out-of-service tone I get instead.

Annoyed more at myself than anything else, I let my phone fall out of my hand and drop to the floor.

My eyes begin to slip closed.

Then I hear it buzz against the wooden floor.

I lean down, hoping that somehow, it's him. But it's Jamie.

Jamie: *I had fun tonight. We should do it again sometime. X.*
Me: *Anytime xxx.*

The screen looks a little blurry as I type my reply.

Chapter Fifteen

Peter

"Are you kidding me, Peter?"

I'm not even awake yet, and all I can hear are the visceral sounds of my sister shouting at me. I turn my back on her from my place on the small mat on the floor, pulling my blanket over my head.

"Leave me alone," I mutter.

I'm not sure what time it is. It's hard to tell in my windowless room, but it feels like it should be morning. I rarely know what time of day it is these days.

Anna closes the distance and whips the blanket off me as if some form of punishment. "You seriously moved everything out of the hostel without telling me? I thought we were past this?"

"Past what?" I bite as I turn back to see her towering above me. "It's just a room, and I don't want to go back there. I've been staying here anyway. What's the difference? I paid for your room for the month."

"You could have told me. I had to see Vik checking new people into your room. You're really staying here? In the basement?"

"Maybe if I'm a good boy, they'll give me a room with a view." I smirk at her.

Anna rolls her eyes but softens. The worry is back on her face now that she's less mad. "Do you think they are still worried?"

I shrug. "I don't care."

"Then why stay here?"

"I told you. I *do not* want to go back to that room, Anna," I shout at her.

"Okay, fine," she mumbles, coming to sit next to me. "No need to be such an asshole." Her tone is haughty.

"You were shouting at me while I slept. You, sister, are the asshole." The corners of my mouth are twitching, trying not to laugh. Anna's are too.

"You snuck into the hostel to check out without me noticing."

"Are we really going to play *who is the bigger asshole*?" I grin.

"There really is no competition. You would win that game every time." She pushes me without any real effort behind it.

I give a large sigh, my expression softening. *If only I could get past this.* "I miss her, Anna."

"I know." She strokes my hair with tenderness. "You need to give it time."

"I have nothing but time."

"But I don't," she laments. "You said it yourself. I need to live my life. I want to live it, with Lorna, with you. I need my brother."

I take her hand in mine and kiss the back of it. "You have me, always."

"Promise?"

"I promise," I say, gazing into her dark eyes, so like my own, which are so hopeful it hurts.

I usher Anna out of the room while I go to take a shower.

She's right, and I hate it when she is right.

Time to start moving on.

The water washes over me, and I tell myself it is healing. All the scars are gone from my body, leaving no sign of what I did. Vanished. It's as if they were never there.

I swallow the hollowness that threatens to consume me by pretending it doesn't exist.

It's time to stop being selfish and think of Anna, to let Anna live her years as happy as they can possibly be. Years where I am not what she has to worry about all the time.

This is who I will be from now on. Not the awful god creature, but just the brother Anna needs me to be.

Now if I can just hold onto that thought.

I am Anna's brother. I am Anna's brother. Nothing more.

When I enter the main hall, Anna and Lorna are standing at the front, chatting with Kali. I make my way over, placing my arm around Anna's shoulder.

"Forget practice for this morning," I say. "Let's go get some breakfast."

"But, the transfer?" she asks, uncertain.

"It can wait."

She eyes me with suspicion.

"I'm fine, Anna. More balanced than I've been in a long time, thanks to you. Let's go and enjoy a nice morning together. A few hours won't hurt."

Anna looks to Lorna like I've sprouted a new head. Even Kali's expression is somewhat stern.

I guess none of them quite trust me right now. Something else I will have to work on. *You are Anna's brother*, I think to myself, giving them the most genuine smile I can muster.

We find a small restaurant off the dusty, busy road where we sit at a table outside. The light of the morning sun feels accusing. I pretend I don't notice Anna and Lorna's glances as I read the menu. I keep forgetting to be normal. I have to try harder.

I order an omelet, Anna some fruit, and Lorna just a coffee.

"We already ate at the hostel," Lorna explains.

I give her a nod, and they both watch me, waiting.

"Can you both not look at me like that? I really am okay. Can we try to be normal?"

"Sure," Anna says, popping her elbows up onto the table. "So, talk. Why don't you want to go back to your own room in the hostel?"

I run my hands through my hair. *I suppose I walked into this.* "Because that was mine and Connie's bed, then mine and Sorcha's, and now they are both gone. I need a fresh start. Like you said. You are both right. I need to face up to everything at some point."

"Makes sense to me." Lorna gives me a small smile.

"Can we not talk about me?" I ask as my breakfast arrives. "How are things with you two?"

"Peter," Anna proceeds with caution. "You need to talk. Keeping everything in is what gets you in trouble."

I hold up my hand to stop her. "I know. I promise. You make all of the decisions from now on," I say between chews before giving a shrug. "Actually, it feels quite liberating. What with the transfers, and you using my powers, it's getting better. I promise."

"Fine. I am in charge, then." Anna relaxes a bit.

"Good. You are the brains, after all. I don't know why you all listened to me for so long anyway. You're way more sensible. You all need to stop trusting me so much," I add quickly, and Anna rolls her eyes, but I go on before she can interrupt. "Come on, then. Your turn." I look between the two of them. "What's going on with you two?"

They smile at each other, Lorna taking her hand as Anna says, "Not much to tell. We are taking it slow, but, yes, we are together now."

I can almost feel it coming out of Anna, her happiness. And it's all I want for her.

"That's amazing. I am so happy for you both." I fix Lorna with a mock-serious expression and tease her. "I hope you know what you're getting yourself into. I hear the family is psychotic."

"Pah!" Lorna laughs with a flick of a hand. "Who needs normal?"

We share some small talk for a while.

Gemini

I can do this.

Over the next couple of days of transfers, the coven finds no outward signs that I am causing my sister harm nor any indication the power is wearing Anna out. The long-term effects remains to be seen.

The days become a routine of transfer, practice, and then lessons with Kali. Lessons about the universe I'm so connected to. The cosmic. Kali says it's not just about nature anymore. I am part of something much bigger. That while I am bound in human form, what I really am, my soul, is part of the energy that has been around since before the birth of the universe itself. An ancient source of creation, something that is part of everything. This is where the gods are brought from, across spacetime. Our lessons make my head hurt. It's difficult to fathom what she is saying, and in truth, it doesn't bring me any comfort. Rather than making me understand more, the information makes me feel even more alone.

I keep smiling for Anna, though. We do the transfer and we practice. I take it slow, show her how to grow the pansy seeds. I can feel her becoming more familiar with their biological signature, becoming more aware of it myself the longer I have to learn it through Anna. I add more seeds to her pot, instructing her to find them all while directing the energy rather than firing it all at once and hoping for the best. When we are practicing like this, sometimes I get glimmers, faint vibrations, and can almost smell the sweetness of her soul while she channels the powers. It makes me feel sick and hungry at the same time but I don't mention anything.

Just swallow it, Peter.

When not with Anna or Kali, I retreat to my room in the basement. I assure Kali the transfers are good, that between them and the lessons, I'm tired. I don't know or care if she believes me.

At night, I think of Connie while trying not to dwell too much on her body, or having her, how thin she was in the end, or how what I was doing was killing her.

Don't think those thoughts.

Remember her eyes, those emerald eyes, and how they sparkled. How they sparkled for me. So green. Mine. For a while. I allow myself to feel that agony.

When longing to be extra masochistic, I think about Sorcha. How sad she was. How I couldn't stand the sight of her, my mirror, another wretched creature. Beautiful. Toxic. Caught in a loop of wanting her and wanting to kill her.

Every day that passes, I can stand myself less and less. When Connie left, I think I stopped being human.

"Kali," I ask when we are alone one evening. "Why is it that human souls give me, or rather, would give me, more power?"

Kali studies me for a moment. "What is a soul but pure energy? Everything has a cycle, even souls. When you absorb them, rather than making their way back to the source to be recycled, they become owned by you. Forever. You break the great cycle."

I rub some of the leftover seeds Anna had been practicing with between my fingers, cracking them into life and sending spirals of pansy leaves down my arm. "Why?"

"Balance. There has to be balance in all things, Peter."

"Balance sucks," I say absentmindedly, watching the delicate leaves grow over my knuckles.

Kali chuckles. "It may seem that way to you. I am afraid you were born out of your time." She pats my arm, cleaning up some of the soil. "I am sure you would have been quite magnificent if you had been born a millennia ago."

"So much for small victories." I grin. Lying back on a cushion, a thought occurs to me. "I haven't told Anna," I begin, making Kali eye me curiously. "That it was his soul I took, not just his life."

Kali lowers herself beside me.

"There is something I should tell you about the day I killed him, Kali." I don't look at her, focusing on the ceiling instead. "He stabbed me with that sacred blade, and I was dying. I didn't have anything left to give, so I used Anna to heal myself. I didn't realize it at the time, but it was part of her soul." I look back to Kali. "It's why she can do all of this now, right? She's more connected to me because of what I took from her."

"Ah..." Kali dips her head, now understanding an element of Anna's mysterious abilities.

"He was right, wasn't he? She will never be able to live apart from me. That bit wasn't a lie. I will have to stay close her whole life."

Kali looks sympathetic. "I believe that to be so. But why would she want it any other way?"

"It's fine now, but what about when she is thirty, with her own family? Or fifty, watching her kids grow up. Or seventy? What will I even look like then? Will I look old like she will?"

"It depends on many things, Peter. I only have one other to compare it to."

"Sorcha." I nod. She has probably been around since long before Kali was born. "How old is she?"

"Let us just say she has outlived her human years."

I wonder how many lives have been sacrificed to her. How many was too many before it was no longer what she wanted? How she could walk away from it?

"What are you thinking?" Kali asks as I let the leaves that have been wrapping around my arm wither and die.

"I just thought... the knife Arjun used on me. You said before that they were not made for killing gods, but I almost died. Is that because I am incomplete? Or am I just weak?"

Kali lets out a snort despite herself. "Peter, that knife would never have killed you."

My mouth flops open then closed like a goldfish.

Kali stares at her hands for a while, weighing up her words. "Peter. I have never known a creature like you. You are more like a half god. Sorcha was always raised to be what she is, but..." She pauses, deciding on what to say. It is not like Kali to waver. "That blade was not made to kill you. It was made for *your* sacrifices. For blood to be spilled by your hands."

I rake my hands through my hair. *Just fantastic. More good news. Not.*

"Peter, I know you've chosen a different path than what your father wanted. Just as Sorcha came to that same path, she did not want innocent blood on her hands either. She suffers for what was done in her name." Kali places her hands in mine, her touch too kind for me to bear. "I am sorry. Sorry for what my son did, sorry for your suffering. But I am not sorry to have you here with us."

"I hate it, Kali. I hate what I am," I admit it to her in a near-whisper.

"Peter." Kali moves my face so I look into her familiar dark eyes. "You choose your fate. You are not what he said you are."

I put my hands over hers, holding them to me. *I need to make her understand.* "I can see it in all of your eyes, Kali. I can see the fear there. You need to bind me." Protest blazes in her eyes as she opens her mouth to speak, and I cut her off. "At least tell me you will think about it? It's the only way I can give my sister a normal life. If you know only one thing about me, know that I love my sister."

Kali nods. "I will think about it. But you should talk to her as this also affects her now. She is getting better with her skills. You said yourself that she helps with the balance."

"Doesn't she deserve a life where she doesn't have to? Don't I deserve that? If I get to choose my fate, then this is the one I want. I choose a life without my abilities. They are a curse."

With reluctance, Kali agrees to consider it but will only do so with Anna's input on the matter. She wants me to really think it through, be sure my sadness is not a motivation for the decision. I don't tell her that being bound again was the whole reason we began our search for the coven in the first place. That, over a year ago, it was my every intention to live without my powers and return to Wixford. Anna could live a normal life with Brady, and I could live a normal life with Connie. Somewhere along the line, I'd come to enjoy it, the growing power at my fingertips. Teetering on the edge of control. I foolishly thought Connie would always be there to cling to. I realize if I am truly my mother's son, if Anna and I are opposites in every way, then she is sanity and I am madness. I need to swallow all that pride and accept the binding for all of our sakes.

The next day, Anna comes alone to the temple, so after the transfer, I sneak out and make my way back to the hostel. I already know where I will find her, enjoying the warmest part of the day from the privacy of the roof. She looks up, taking her headphones off her head as she sees me approaching.

"Hey. What are you doing here?" she asks, full of Lorna warmth.

"I snuck out." I plonk myself down next to her. "It's like being back at school. Lessons and learning. It can all get so boring."

She chuckles. "Anna's loving it."

"That figures." I shrug. "Why do you stay away?"

Lorna leans her shoulder into mine. "Maybe I'm more like you than Anna would like to admit."

I really cackle at that. "Heaven forbid."

Lorna looks pensive. "It seems like what you both need right now... to have that proximity. I don't want to get in the way."

"You could never be in the way, Lorna," I say, holding her gaze.

She squirms, but I don't care. I never want her to feel that way. I love Lorna in a way I've never been able to love anyone else. She is one hundred percent my friend, and she doesn't want anything from me.

"You can do me a favor, though."

She eyes me suspiciously while waiting for me to go on.

"I need to see her."

Lorna looks far from convinced. "I really don't think that is a good idea, for either of you. What happened to a fresh start?"

"I know. I mean it, but everything between us ended so horribly. I've never stopped loving her. I just had to put those feelings away. This is part of moving forward. I would like to know she is okay and to apologize. Really apologize."

"She's okay. I spoke to her recently."

I look down at Lorna's earnest face, her wide, honest eyes. Maybe I should listen to her, but I feel guilty that months have passed without speaking to Connie, the thought of doing so too painful. *Maybe it's better this way. Maybe she prefers it like this.* I close my eyes, longing to see those green eyes again. I hate that I'm starting to forget. That every time I picture them, the shade will be off until they look nothing like Connie's eyes at all.

"Please, Lor. Maybe you could call her first and ask if she wants to speak to me? If she says no, then I won't ask you again, but if you think there is a chance she wants to talk, then... *please.*"

I can see the defeat in Lorna's eyes. When Lorna spoke with her, she must have asked about me, the way I can never bear to ask about her.

"Fine," she agrees. "I'll call her first. I don't want to catch her off guard."

My heart is in my throat as I follow Lorna downstairs to grab her phone and then head to the balcony. It must be late morning in Wixford. I sit opposite Lorna while she holds her phone in front of her face before giving me a final glance to ensure I want to do this.

I nod, letting my knees bounce. I am nervous. I *never* feel nervous.

What if she is still unbelievably mad? What if she asks about Sorcha?

Maybe she already knows, so she'll tell Lorna flat out she never wants to see me again.

The phone rings once. Twice. Three times.

She won't answer.

Lorna looks up at me, opening her mouth to speak.

"Hi, Lor."

I hear Connie's voice chime as Lorna returns her attention to her phone to greet her friend. The familiar sound of Connie's voice ripples against my skin. *I miss her so much.* More than I allow myself to feel. In this moment, I wish I had made her stay. Reached out and used every terrible part of me to force her to stay, and become the very thing she accused me of that day.

"I didn't think I would hear from you so soon. Is everything okay?"

"Sure." Lorna smiles, looking over at me. "But I do have something to ask you."

"Really?" Connie asks, and my heart hammers in my chest. "Oh, hold that thought. I have someone who wants to say hi."

Confusion crosses Lorna's face for a split second.

"Hiya, Lorna. It's nice to see you after so long."

My stomach turns to ice.

Lorna glances in my direction again. "Jamie, hi. Wow, it's been too long."

"I know. Almost two years. You look great, by the way."

"Thanks, Jamie." Lorna smiles back, the nerves obvious on her face as her eyes dart my way yet again.

"Is Anna there with you?" Connie asks.

I give my head a vehement shake at Lorna, making a cutting motion across my neck. There is no way I am sharing this moment with him. Which, in a certain sick irony, serves me right.

"Erm... no. It was just Vik bringing me a coffee."

"That's a shame," Jamie says, but I am already getting to my feet.

"So what was your question?" Connie asks.

With only a slight pang of guilt, I shake my head at Lorna and start to move away from the table, leaving her to make up whatever bullshit story she needs to. At least this answers my question about whether she's been able to move on.

Maybe she does ask about me.

Maybe she does still care.

But she has moved on, as she should.

Like *I* should.

This is a good thing, I try to tell myself.

It can't be more than two minutes later when Lorna joins me on the roof. "It probably doesn't mean what you think," she offers. "When I asked what they were doing, she said watching a film."

"It's about eleven there, Lor. Why would he be there so early watching a film unless he stayed over?" I'm getting worked up, I can't help myself.

"Peter, the last time I spoke to her, she said they were just friends."

"Were they in her room?"

"Peter—"

"Were they?" I demand a little louder than necessary as the wind rolls in from the river, indicating my mood.

Lorna closes the distance between us, taking my hands as the wind whips her hair into a frenzy. "Peter, stop," she urges, looking around without any alarm. "Get this under control. You need to stop. You need to let her go."

I take a deep breath. Find my center.

Lorna closes the gap, bringing me into a hug. And that works too. I hold her close to me, forcing her onto her tip toes to wrap her arms around my neck while the winds begin to die down around us.

"I am so screwed," I whisper into her ear.

Lorna gives a small chuckle, putting me back at arm's length. "I feel for you. It's tough when the whole world witnesses your emotions. You can't fall apart like the rest of us."

I give a shaky laugh. "It's a curse."

Lorna nods. "So it would seem."

I tell Lorna I should get back to the coven before I am missed. I need to be on my best behavior, and impromptu storms of any kind are no way of proving to Kali I am in control enough to be bound. Thinking back to life with our mother, when I'd been bound before, my emotions were tied with the binding. When she died, Anna had screamed and cried and beat me as I dragged her away from the room, but I hadn't cried. Gradually, as the binding came loose, the horror of everything came back to me. It took me a long time to even register that anything had happened to us. When you live a certain way for so long, it's just normal. All my life, I never was allowed to feel much of anything. I thought I'd been happy, but it wasn't until Connie that I knew what true happiness felt like.

If the restrictions of the coven's binding are anything like my mother's, then my emotions will disappear with my power. *I can't wait to be rid of them.*

I find Anna near the front with some senior witches, trying to help a poor bitter gourd seed into life, her palms pushing deep into the soil. I smirk. She hasn't noticed me getting closer. I place the tip of my finger into the soil and, within seconds, a fully grown gourd is in her hands.

"You're moving on from pansies?" I ask, unable to keep the smile out of my voice.

"And where have you been?" she snaps at me.

Out of nowhere, Kali is at my side, shaking her head. Showing off. I shouldn't be doing that right now. On instinct, I ease my hand back into the soil, soaking up the rich nutrients of the bitter gourd. It's not as easy, but a few moments later, the bitter gourd is back to its seed state.

"Sorry," I tell Anna. "There, you can try again."

Anna stares at her pot.

Kali's eyes are on the tiny seed, and the senior witches are staring at me.

I laugh. "I've never shown you that before, have I?"

"Explain," Kali demands.

"I can't." I hold my hands up, but Kali puts her hands on her hips, and I peer around at all of their serious faces.

They didn't look this mad when I told them I could control the weather. Even Anna looks a bit confused about why they all think it's such a big deal.

"I can give it, and I can take it away. It's the same cycle, just backward," I say, trying to find the best way to explain.

Kali's eyes shift to the seniors, who whisper something to each other. The feeling makes me uneasy, so I look at Anna, who gives an almost invisible shrug.

"What's wrong?" she asks, looking up at Kali.

Kali softens a fraction at her. "Nothing. It was just unexpected." She looks back at me. "You are full of surprises, Peter."

I can't help thinking that's not a good thing. *It's never a good thing.*

She motions for Anna and me to join her, and I fall into step with her. "Kali, did I do something wrong? With the seed?"

Kali glances from me to Anna, who is listening intently.

For the first time, I notice Kali looks weary, bearing a few lines in her forehead I don't recall seeing there before.

"I'm not sure. Us witches pride ourselves on our connection to nature and the universe. We can bend a lot of rules, but there are universal truths which cannot be bent. The great cycle of this world, Peter, it only moves in one direction. Forward and not backward."

I can't help but laugh. "It was a seed. All I did was put it back."

Kali's eyes turn dark, hard as they fixate on me. "You didn't even flinch."

I feel my blood run cold. "What does it mean? That I can do that?"

"I do not know," she says as she turns away from us.

Anna's expression furrows and my heart sinks. Yet another reason for Kali to turn down the binding. We never should have come here. Ignorance was better than this.

"Is that something I will be able to learn?" Anna asks, now sitting at Kali's feet and not understanding why what I did was so bad. *It was only a seed.*

"My child, that is something you should not learn."

"Why?"

"Because it is against the natural order," I answer, reading Kali's mind. "That is what you were going to say, right?"

Kali dips her head. "It is a skill not easily accessed and one associated with dark magic."

"I am an abomination," I mutter and sink to the steps.

Anna gives my arm a gentle rub. "You didn't know," she soothes.

"You continue to surprise," Kali seems a little more collected now. "We are no experts in the ways of the gods, Peter. I cannot pretend I am. But your gifts, they are more vast than we could have ever expected for one who..." She trails off and looks at me, her expression a mixture of sadness and trepidation.

"For someone with only one sacrifice under his belt," I confirm.

Kali closes her eyes for a few seconds before turning to Anna. "We should continue your training with great caution. The level of power you have access to, we may have underestimated your natural abilities, Anna. We should take nothing off the table going forward."

Alarmed, Anna looks from me and back to Kali.

Being told I'm a terrible thing is nothing new to me, but it is a new sensation for my sister.

"What do you mean?" she queries.

"We know little about the nature of your brother, Anna, but even less of yours. Our purest understanding of a god is to imagine them as a star. After all, our sun was the first god mankind ever worshipped. The bigger the star, the stronger the gravity, the greater their effect on their surroundings. If he is the sun, then you are his solar system, a planet in your own right, with your own gravity."

"I-I don't understand."

For a change, my sister is receiving one of Kali's unfathomable teachings. After experiencing many of them already, I'm catching her drift. The one thing I have zero control over. My most hated and ingrained ability.

"You, like your brother, have an impact on everything in your path."

Anna's eyes turn to me, struggling to keep up.

"The influence, Anna," I tell her in as gentle a voice as I can.

Chapter Sixteen

Anna

When I laugh, it doesn't feel connected to me. An echo of an echo.

I don't remember standing up or looking down at Kali and my brother, who are both eyeing me cautiously and with sympathy. My stomach turns, a bit of retribution on Peter's part for all the sympathetic looks I've given him over the last month. Not that he would mean it that way.

"Th-that can't be true," I stammer, then laugh again. "That is preposterous. I have no influence. I have never been able to sway a decision or an outcome."

Kali tries to soothe my rising panic. "It would probably look different on you, Anna, like charisma or a natural leader. Someone who is easy to fall in love with."

"What?" I whisper and see Peter close his eyes at her words. I know enough about him and his worst fears for him to know what my mind will jump to. "Are you saying Lorna and Brady, they fell in love with me because Peter is my brother?"

"Of course that's *not* what I am saying." Kali rises to her feet while mine carry me backward. "Your power is your own, Anna, separate from Peter. You will attract others wherever you go." Her warm eyes crinkle, and I know she means it as a compliment.

"But this is just a theory, right?" I can hear the panic in my voice as I look between the two of them.

"Yes, it is only a theory. Theory is all we have when it comes to you." Kali tries to reach out to me. "Anna, this isn't a bad thing. My intention was not to upset you."

The heat is rising in my cheeks as I try to hold in my tears. "No, it's fine. I just need to take a moment."

I feel out of my body as I walk away.

But I am just ordinary.

Kali must have started to follow me because I hear Peter tell her to let me go.

It's just a theory. This is not true. I am human. There is nothing extraordinary about me, except for being the twin of a god.

I have always been happy in his shadow. He's always wanted me close, even when we were kids standing on the highest branches of the trees hanging low enough to get over the glistening lake. He always wanted me to watch as he spun and dived into the waters. He wanted me to clap, to laugh, to be impressed. Always. I was always telling him not to climb too high. Not to get hurt. I never knew he was invulnerable. In the back of my mind always worried. *What if something happened to him? What would I do?*

I close my eyes. I was the shadow. *I feel more like the moon than a solar system.*

My feet lead me, and after a while, I figure out I'm moving in the direction of the hostel. It is true, I have been having fun lately while learning how to use his power. A funny side effect of being his twin but nothing more. Feeling relief, if anything, that Kali thinks we are split down the middle, perfectly balanced. It's a good thing, in my mind. It meant I could fix him, bring my brother back, and force him to live.

Peter's influence has never brought him anything but heartache and constant worry that those around him are only there because it is what he wants. I can't not think of Lorna, about the night she told me she loved me—it was the first day Peter fully transferred his power to me. Could the transfers have made the influence stronger? Urged her to say it because the power clung to me and made her *think* she loves me.

"You're back early," Lorna exclaims, jumping up from the bed. "What's wrong?"

I should have gone to the roof to clear my head, to try and shake the thoughts out, so I wouldn't have to do it in front of her.

"Oh, there was a bit of drama at the coven today."

"More drama?" She rolls her eyes, moving to take my hands.

I find I can't take them, and she notices the brush off.

"What's happened? Is Peter okay?"

I nod, trying to make myself busy with the throw on my bed. "Typical Peter stuff. I just need a break. Actually, Lor, I have a really big headache. I think I need a quiet, dark room for a bit. Is that okay?"

"Whatever you need." Her words are clipped as she motions toward the door. "I was just heading out for dinner. Are you sure you don't want anything?"

I wave her off, trying to ignore the concerned look on her face, and curl up into a ball in my bed. I'm grateful I fall asleep quickly.

At some point in the night, I wake to find Lorna asleep in the bed opposite me.

From then on, my night becomes a restless one.

When I wake in the morning, Lorna is sitting by my side, stroking my hair away from my face. For a moment, it makes me forget.

"Hey," she coos. "You've been tossing and turning."

Her hands feel soft and warm, gently soothing me. "Bzzz," I whisper.

"What?" She giggles.

"Busy thoughts." I smile up at her. It's impossible not to smile at her as I gaze into her dark, round eyes. I know I love her too, which brings with it the return of the sinking feeling in my stomach. "I think I need to go back, check in with Peter."

I hate how I'm lying to her.

"I take it he told you?" Her face drops a little.

"Told me what?"

Her brow furrows. "About Connie, how he came here to talk to her."

I sit up to look at her. "He did what?"

"I thought that must've been what you were talking about yesterday. He didn't end up speaking to her. Jamie was there, so naturally, Peter assumes they are together now."

My eyebrows shoot up. "Are they?"

Lorna shrugs.

I get ready in a rush, eager to avoid any further questions from Lorna.

It's early, the city is still waking up. Almost no one is awake at the coven. I deftly make my way down to the small basement room where Peter is still staying. I hate it, but I'm glad to be away from others this morning. I find him asleep—something about this room seems to force him to sleep.

He looks so peaceful stretched out on one side, nothing more than a thin blanket over him despite the cool room. I lie down next to him, tentative as I trace his features with the barest tips of my fingers, so like my own, apart from being a little broader with a few freckles on his nose I don't have.

"I've been told it's creepy to watch people when they sleep," he says quietly, reaching out and wrapping his arms around my waist.

I bury my head against his chest, his warmth enveloping me. For our first seventeen years, we'd slept like this, lived like this, right next to each other. "I miss you," I whisper.

He pushes me back to hold me at arm's length, searching my face. "What do you mean?"

"I miss having you so close to me. I'm not saying I want to go back. I don't think what our mother did to you was right, but it was simpler, wasn't it, when it was just the two of us?"

"Anna—" Peter begins, but I cut him off, moving to be able to see into his eyes.

"How do you live with it, Peter? The not knowing? Not knowing if what people feel for you is just a lie. How were you with Connie for so long with it hanging over you?"

Peter takes a sharp breath in, his eyes turning hard, the way they once did when I accused him of hurting her. "You bury it." His voice sounds like ice.

It takes me by surprise. Of course, I don't know what I was expecting. "You bury it?"

Peter grabs onto my hand, holding tight to it, and looks me square in the eyes. "Anna, you push that bile down so far you can't taste it anymore. You bury it deep. There is nothing you can do, so the fact that you love *them* has to be enough."

"Is that really what it's like for you?" I whisper.

"There is nothing pure about what I am, Anna. I would never wish this on you."

"It might not be that way though, right? Even if what we are is what attracts people to us, they might still really love us for... you know... *us.*" Peter looks at me hard, like I'm being foolish. "Why are you so ready to believe the worst about yourself, Peter?"

"Because I can feel it," he says, moving my hand to cover his heart, where I can feel it beating against my palm. "Deep down inside, I can feel the darkness. It is there, waiting, ready to swallow me whole. I am dark and you are light, remember?"

"It's not that simple. We are still people, but there are always shades of gray."

He closes his eyes again. "It's different. It calls me."

Gemini

"But you fight it."

"Yes. I fight it." His expression becomes distant. "But I am so tired, Anna."

He pulls me close to him again.

"What can I do to help?" I say into his chest.

"You are already doing so much for me," he murmurs.

I get the feeling there is something else he wants to say, but he doesn't. He only holds me. My restless night and Peter's body heat make me drowsy. I wish he knew what he means to me, how much I need him. Peter's breathing becomes deep, and it doesn't take long for me to fall back under too into a peaceful sleep.

Someone is clearing their throat and wake to the noise. My face is still pushed against his chest, his arm and leg over me, his head resting on top of mine, like a personal heater wrapped around me.

"Are you two getting up at some point today?" It's Kali's voice.

I struggle against Peter's vice-like grip to look up at her. "Sorry, Kali. I didn't sleep well last night," I tell her.

Peter starts to come around, rubbing his eyes.

"I understand." She smiles. "But it is almost two in the afternoon. And Peter... you did promise you would help to replenish the garden."

"Sure. I am awake." He releases me and rolls onto his back.

I sit up, trying to flatten the bird's nest on the side of my head from where my face has been sweating against his chest.

Kali gives a small nod and leaves the room.

"Do you want to help? With the garden?" he asks while rubbing his eyes.

"I would love to," I tell him, glad of the distraction.

Peter seems to notice my still pensive expression.

"You'll need this," he says, then grabs onto my arm, taking me by surprise. The rush of power rolls into me like a wave. A moment later, he is on his feet, laughing and leaving me wondering what happened. "Anna, you should see your face."

I get up and playfully slap him as he pulls his T-shirt on. "You can't just spring that on me. We're meant to do that in full view of the coven."

Peter rolls his eyes and shrugs.

"I swear sometimes you like pissing them off."

"Nope!" He taunts me. "Sometimes I like pissing *you* off. Isn't that what brothers are for?"

I slap his arm again as we make our way into the main hall. Despite the slight change of tone toward him in the coven, Peter has made himself quite at home here. And even though Kali has given him a task, he is obviously procrastinating—talking to Mahi, getting himself chai, and taking his sweet time getting around to it.

Kali glances at him every now and then.

For someone on his best behavior, he knows how to test his limits. Even though he says I am in charge of our decisions, I know he doesn't like being told what to do. I watch him lean against the kitchen counter, eating pistachios and laughing with Mahi, and feel a pang of worry knowing he will never willingly follow anyone's orders. Not if he doesn't really want to. Peter will always rule Peter.

"Peter, the garden?" I remind him after he helps himself to his second cup of chai. I'm also conscious of how the power he transfers to me fades over time.

He doesn't say anything. Only rolls his eyes and takes my hand to lead me toward a far corridor, which eventually leads down to an outside area I've never seen before. A small stone space with a long, trickling, manmade waterfall follows a narrow footpath along the side of the hill, opening up to a large grove full of cheerfully flowing flower beds and vegetable patches. Aside from the large banyan trees flanking on either side of the grove, the garden is conspicuous in its absence of fruit trees.

The witches had sacrificed them, enabling Peter to burn through them so he could ground safely.

Apparently, it was now time to repay the favor and replenish their stores.

"So, what are you growing for them?" I ask as Peter takes up a wooden box of seeds, swirling them around in his hands.

"*We* are going to grow mango, apple, lychee, orange, and papaya."

"That's a lot of trees."

Peter nods with a small smile. "It is a lot of trees."

"Are you going to be able to manage all of that? There was a time when you couldn't have."

Peter shrugs, selecting a seed. "Maybe. It feels like a long time ago. When our mother died, her spell died with her, but I guess I'd been bound for so long it took time to unravel. Kali said my ability to still use some of my powers while being bound could mean a few things. Including that the spell was unstable, which is possible given our mother was completely unstable."

"Or?" I push.

"Or," he says slowly. "How did Kali put it? 'Your gifts were too great to be fully contained.'" He shakes his head. "They trickled out despite the binding. Either way, it's been a long time since I felt any aftereffects of using them. Except, of course, when I…" He doesn't need to finish.

"What does Kali think?" I ask, not wanting him to dwell on those thoughts. Then I pick up a seed, trying to figure out which is which.

"A combination of both." He sees my bemused expression, and I guess he's trying to figure out why I look so confused. "Are you attached to it? Now that you are starting to learn all of this, would you give it up?"

I think over my answer. "I would say attached is a strong word. I'm only starting to come to grips with it." I move over and sit by a patch of dirt that was once home for a tree. "I can't say it hasn't been fun. It's a pretty amazing feeling, but I do understand that what I'm doing doesn't come with all of the baggage."

Peter snorts and sits next to me, placing the seed he is holding into the ground. "What a perfectly reasonable answer."

"What seed is that?" I ask, peering into its new home.

Peter looks at me in genuine surprise. "It's lychee. Can't you tell? You don't even need to know the signature. The seeds all look different, no magic needed." I shake my head, and he looks a bit baffled by my ignorance. "Anyway..." he turns back to his task, "... I can understand why they want them. They can be tricky things to grow. I'm sure witch trees always bear fruit. They must have ways of doing that, but I imagine they were annoyed to lose them. Lychee trees can take years to grow and produce fruit. It must've taken many years to nurture them. The coven are children of nature, so it would have hurt them to see it all burn. What?" he asks again at my bemused expression. "I thought you wanted to help?"

"I do." I laugh. "But how do you know this? Have you ever eaten a lychee? We never had them at home."

"I'm not sure, to be honest," he says, looking back at the seed. "When I hold the seeds, I always know what the process should look like. It doesn't matter if I've seen them before. If I have the seed, I just know."

I smile. "This really is your thing, isn't it? I haven't seen you do it much while you've been here, but you were always happiest in the garden."

He sinks his hands into the soil, giving a fraction of a smile. "There is something beautiful about it. Watching something living come alive because of you, to witness a journey that should take weeks or months, or even years, take only minutes. To really give." His smile falters. "Anyway, I'll take care of this one since you don't know what you're aiming for."

I don't have time to feel annoyed or wonder if that was an insult because watching the seed transform from tiny sprouting leaves to a fully realized tree with clusters of plump red lychees is magic on a scale I've never seen before. Something totally beautiful. Like a miracle. I have never seen him grow a whole tree before. I look back at him, and even he can't keep the smile off his lips as the tree grows. It makes me think of being kids, when our mother wasn't looking, and he'd say, *"Watch me, watch me, Anna,"* then tap the edges of wildflowers, sending them into life. He'd always been so beautiful. All of the destruction came so much later—he was so different after she died.

"Let's try them," Peter says, grabbing two lychees and handing me one.

They taste amazing.

It turns out Peter is right. Knowing what you are aiming for is crucial in forcing the trees into life. A big part is trying to visualize in my mind what I want the tree to look like. Having never seen a lychee tree before, I can only imagine Peter's. For now, it's too hard, and I only manage a small seedling before Peter has to finish the job. He reassures me the lychees are harder and I should try an apple instead. It's his fault. He should have started easier, but he wanted to try the lychee to see how they taste.

An apple tree is still as hard in my mind, even though I know what to picture. I've certainly seen enough apple trees in my time. It takes a lot of concentration, even with Peter coaxing me through it.

Like blood from a stone.

I'm sure my face is turning pink. I finally stand back to look at my small, fruitless apple tree. He's making a valiant attempt at holding his laughter at me in.

"You did like ninety-nine percent of it," he says, rubbing my weary shoulders. "Here..." He rests his fingers against some low branches, and small, blush apples appear on its branches.

Gasps from behind us alert us to a few of the coven who've come outside to witness what we're doing.

"It's cute," he tells me with a grin.

"You can do the next one," I tell him, feeling a bit worn out and more nervous now that we have a small audience.

Peter obliges, taking up a mango seed—one I *do* recognize—and producing a fully formed mango tree in about five minutes.

A mini cluster of applause erupts from the observing witches, and Peter folds his body forward in a small bow, much to their delight.

"Your turn." He holds out a mango seed to me.

"I don't think I can," I tell him. "I don't think I have anything left."

"Just try," he whispers.

I appreciate his belief in me, but I can feel it almost as soon as I put my hands into the earth—I don't have enough to grow a full tree, let alone produce fruit. Perhaps sensing I'm done, he puts his warm hand on my shoulder as his forefinger connects with the skin on my neck. Even the small connection is enough to feel the warm ocean of his golden power wash through me, tingling down my neck. He's giving me more, replenishing me, so I have enough to finish what I've started. Only this feels different. I can tell Peter is thinking about what I need to do too. Like wordless instructions. With the resurgence of energy, he also enlightens me, so I know what to do. The growing crowd of the coven gives me a little cheer as I finish. I graciously accept with a little courtesy.

I wonder if it feels this way for him, too, when we transfer. Like we are one. He's never mentioned it. Maybe it makes him sad. Kali says he is the conduit, but the larger part of me suspects he does not feel it at all, which makes me a little sad.

However, right now, I am definitely done.

I feel like I could drop on the spot.

I tell Peter to carry on, though. It's good to see the coven's building concerns fade away watching him do something so good. It emits beauty, not destruction. Abundant and pure. He takes small flourished bows and hands them the fruit to try. Smiles again.

Peter is so wrong, he has so much good in him. He may not take orders well, but making the coven happy is beneficial for him. It makes me realize exactly what I need to do. Lorna should be here with us, seeing this. Hiding part of myself from her is the wrong thing to do.

I am going to tell her everything.

"You feeling okay?" he asks as we walk back into the main hall.

"Actually, I feel great." I smile. "How did you know how to do that? When you touched me?"

Peter shrugs. "I figured you needed more."

A thought occurs to me. "So, what does that mean for you? You'd given me all of your excess this morning. Where did more come from?"

"Well, that was this morning. Time passes, and it starts to build up again."

"That quickly?"

"It's constant, Anna." He cocks his eyebrow at me, taking in my concerned expression. "Look, I just grew a boatload of trees. I am fine."

Except something about him seems a little off.

"Are you sure? Because that was amazing, Peter. You were amazing. I think you are well and truly in their good books."

"You think?" he asks, raking his hand through his hair.

"Talk to me. What's going on with you?"

"You know what I think? It has taken more out of me than I thought. I'm going to go and lie down. Maybe bring Lorna back tomorrow? I would like to see her."

I bring him into a hug before watching him disappear down to his room.

My all-around good feeling starts to dissipate as I get closer to the hostel and remember what kind of mood I was in this morning when I left Lorna. I feel guilty for having left on that note. Lorna has done nothing wrong, and neither have I, but I can't help what I am. Here's hoping Lorna sees it that way.

I'm glad she is in our room when I arrive. It's already dark outside since I've been gone for the whole day and she is immediately on her feet.

"Where have you been? I've been worried sick. I was going to come to the temple, but I was almost scared about what I would find."

"I'm sorry. We need to talk." I motion to her bed as I take a seat on mine.

"Oh, sweet baby Jesus," she whispers, looking at the ceiling and holding her breath.

And I tell her.

She listens while I explain the coven's reaction to Peter's growing list of unexpected powers and Kali's concerns for what that might mean for me. What I fear it means for Lorna and me. Her expression gives nothing away.

"You are saying you're worried you made me like you? The same way Peter thinks he did with Connie."

"Not quite the same way. Kali's analogy is that it's like gravity, more of a way of pulling people to you."

"Hmm..." Lorna says. The cogs of her brain are whirring. None of her thoughts does she chose to share with me.

"Lor, please talk to me."

"Do you care?" she asks suddenly, her dark eyes passionate.

"What do you mean? Of course I care."

"Do you not want to be with me anymore?"

I'm so confused by her question for a second, as it seems out of place. "Of course I want to be with you, Lor." I kneel at her feet, taking her hands. "What I don't want is for you to feel trapped. I thought you might not want to be with me."

"I don't care." She smiles, the relief washing over her face. "Gravity or no gravity. My feelings for you are real, Anna. More real than I have ever had for anyone."

This is all the reassurance I need. I lift myself up to kiss her, all the earlier worries gone, my fears allayed. Lorna knows and doesn't care, and that's enough for me.

It is such a huge weight off my shoulders.

Still reeling and buzzing from earlier, Lorna and I stay up late chatting, kissing, holding each other. I can't contain my excitement while recounting today's events of growing trees. She's sorry to have missed it. I promise myself I will never keep anything from her again.

We both sit bolt-upright when there is a small knock at the door in the early hours. I warily rise while Lorna moves into a crouch position, ready to jump on whoever it is. Although, I am sure if they were here to attack us, they wouldn't have knocked.

"Peter," I exclaim, taking a big step back to let him in as he sheepishly moves into the room, casting apologetic glances at Lorna while I throw myself back into my bed.

"Can I stay with you tonight?" he asks.

"Sure." I nod.

Relief washes over his face as he flicks off his shoes and climbs onto my bed behind me. At first, he doesn't say anything, only wraps his arm around my waist. He feels tense. I look up to see Lorna's large eyes on me.

"*Should I go?*" she mouths.

I widen my eyes because, in truth, I have no idea.

"You know I would follow you anywhere, Anna," he says out of nowhere, his voice as tense as his body feels. "We could leave India. Go somewhere where no one knows any of us, and you could have a normal life with Lorna. I will come. I will follow you there."

"Where is this coming from?" I wiggle around and cup his cheek.

His eyes are wide, looking right through me. "All of this has to stop. I want it to stop being about me. I want *you* to be happy. I want *you* to have a life. I want to watch *you* grow old, get married, and have a fa... family." Against his will, his voice trembles. "And I will love all of your children so much, Anna. Even though it will be so unbelievably hard, because it's everything I want, and I will envy everything you have. But I will be so, so happy to just be there with you. That's all I want anymore."

I am trying to push him up, to make him look at me because he is scaring me, but Peter pushes his face into the mattress so I can't see him, only hear that he is sobbing. Huge, uncontrollable sobs, the likes of which I've never seen from him before. So painful, their agony rips into my own chest. I can't help but notice Lorna because we're both doing the same thing—looking out the window, watching the huge storm cloud roll in across the river.

Lorna starts to get up. "I should go for a minute."

"No," Peter says between gasps. "Please. Please, don't leave because of me. I don't want to be alone."

I smooth his hair back. "What is all of this?" I ask. "Talk to us, Peter. You have t... to talk t... to us." I hear the tremble in my own voice and don't know what to do. I don't know how to take his pain away.

Peter's hand clamps down hard against my waist. "I hate what I am, Anna. I wish I were human." I can feel him holding back his need to cry again. "I need it to end."

He loses his battle, his sobs coming hard again while his body shakes against mine. I don't know what else to do except hold him tight and let my own tears fall as I rock him in my arms. If I could take it all off him, I would. He has carried this for so long. It's not fair. So I simply hold him as there is little else I can do.

Our mother always took just enough to make him useful to us. Peter did everything. He's the one who kept us alive. He grew all our food, cooked, and cleaned for us as best he could. She rambled about the stars while he cleaned her burns. She always told him off if he pushed too far. It wasn't natural. He was special, but there was an order, a cycle, something he had to maintain. That he had to promise her to be good. Maybe even she didn't notice in the end—I didn't until afterward—that he kept our house warm and our summers long. Peter didn't always run so hot, but multiple years of generating heat, so his family didn't freeze is the only scar of the binding. He always protected us. And I have no way of returning the favor.

His crying doesn't slow. It keeps coming in long deep sobs.

Gemini

Lorna moves around the bed, sliding down the wall around the other side of him to hold onto him as hard as she can too.

We let him cry, listening to the storm outside that only dies down when he eventually falls asleep in our arms.

Some peace comes to him again while the quiet rain against our window doesn't let up.

We try not to move, and I think Lorna falls asleep before I even close my eyes.

Chapter Seventeen

Peter

Anna and Lorna are wrapped around me when I wake up fully clothed and sweating. Anna's head is buried against my chest, Lorna's arm around my waist, all of us squeezed onto my sister's single bed. The sun is shining in through the window with no hint of the rainstorm in sight. With any luck, the coven passed it off as a genuine rainstorm and nothing to do with me.

As gently as possible, I begin prizing myself out of their grip, easing Lorna's arm from my waist. Almost immediately, Lorna lets out a large breath, pushing against me and almost sending Anna off the edge. Forcing herself up from her small space, Lorna moves off the end of the bed.

"Jesus, Peter, it's like sleeping in an oven," she says, grabbing herself a bottle of water and trying to flatten her knotted silky hair.

Anna stirs in my arms, looking up at me with a sleepy smile. "Good morning," she tells me before her expression turns serious.

I imagine she's remembered last night.

I feel a lot better for having slept next to her, but I know I have some explaining to do.

"I guess we need to talk," I concede, still holding her close.

"What happened? I thought we had such a nice day together yesterday. What you did made the coven so happy. I don't understand." She clings onto my T-shirt as if I will slip away from her if she doesn't.

"They were. Kali even thanked me for what I did, even though I was the one who burned all their trees in the first place. You were right, it seemed like they were coming back around. But..." I pause, trying to take a breath, "... I realized after you were gone it's all just bullshit. I liked spending the day with you, Anna. Of course I did. In a way, I wanted to keep pushing for you to do it, but you seemed so tired. After a while, it was frustrating. Seeing them clapping... it was all so frustrating."

"But you made everyone so happy, Peter. It was beautiful."

I swallow hard, forcing myself to look at my sister. I wish I could believe her. "It's the tip of an iceberg, Anna."

Her eyes search mine.

"It's not enough anymore. I have to do what they want in the way they want it. I can't be like you. I can't push my limits, not with that. Anna, after you were done, I could've put my hand on the earth and raised it all in seconds. *Seconds*. It is that easy for me. But I knew I shouldn't. It would freak them all out, so I showed restraint. Did it nice and slow, in a way that wouldn't scare everyone."

"But you didn't scare anyone."

"The point is that I can, and part of me wants to do it. Anna, I am one mistake away from them all turning on me."

"Peter..." she starts, the familiar soft look back in her eyes. *Pity*.

Lorna, who has been observing from the side, gets up. "I think I might go down for breakfast," she says.

"Lorna, stay," I tell her, moving from my place and making Anna sit up. "You are part of this family now. You should hear all of this."

Anna sits next to her, and I face them both, trying to keep my thoughts organized so I can say everything I want to while they exchange glances of trepidation.

"What if we left? Moved on from Varanasi. Not back to Wixford but find somewhere new to make our home."

"Peter, the coven has been nothing but helpful. I think we still need them, for my training and especially while you're still coming to terms with everything. You were able to show restraint yesterday. I understand how frustrating that feels, but you were able to do it. I'm not saying we can't leave, but we need to know how to manage before we're on our own."

By manage, she means manage *me*.

This is my chance.

"What if we didn't need to? To manage." I regard them carefully. "I'm the problem here. I've asked them to bind me again as our mother did. But properly this time. I will have no magic, no powers, none of it."

Anna and Lorna exchange glances.

"Once the binding is done, we could go. I would have to come back every now and then to ensure the spell holds. But then we could be done with this. We could live in peace, be normal." I half laugh. "You two could have a regular life together, and I can at least pass as human and not worry about causing a storm every time I'm upset."

They don't say anything for several minutes.

"Are you sure you want this?" Lorna asks after a while, and I nod.

"You've been through a horrible time recently. Maybe you should wait until you are out the other side." Lorna looks hard at me. "You will still be you, Peter. No spell can change that. You will still think the same things, feel the same way."

I nod again. "I know. I know my head is not right, and I promise I'll work on it, but I really need to be away from magic." I sink my head into my hands. "Lor, I am so tired of it. Tired of feeling it pushing against my skin."

There is another moment's silence before Anna speaks, "What aren't you telling us?"

I look up at her, taking another breath.

All cards on the table.

"There are risks." I pause when her mouth draws into a thin line. "Plus, it would also mean, well... if I have no power, then you would have no power."

"And the risks?" she presses.

"Obviously, like Lorna said, I would be powerless, but it doesn't change what I am, so I would still be immortal, which poses its own challenges. I would go with you wherever you want, but I wouldn't be able to stay in one place forever. People would notice my lack of aging, so we would need to move. That means you would be uprooting your life every once in a while. You'd still be making sacrifices for me, for both of your lives. I know it's a lot to ask, but I figure we could have five good years and then see—"

"Peter, can you get to the point?" Anna says firmly.

"Kali doesn't know what will happen when you die. Whether your soul will still bind to mine, or if the binding will stop it, or something worse."

Anna considers me for a while. "What else?" she asks. "Why is Kali so hesitant?"

"Kali is so hesitant because she doesn't think I will accept it. She said it needs a lot of energy behind the spell, from the whole coven, and if I fight it, then it could be dangerous for them."

"Why would you fight it if it's what you want?"

I shrug. "Instinct. Self-preservation? I don't know. But she's made it clear she won't even consider it without your say-so."

"Really?" Anna asks, her eyes going wide. "Why?"

"Because you are the brains, dummy."

Anna stares at me. I wait, holding my breath, and eventually, Lorna turns to watch her too. We both know she is not used to being the decision-maker.

"Where would we even go?" she asks after a while.

I let the hint of a smile tug at my cheeks. *It isn't a no.* "Where do you want to go?"

Anna shrugs, so we both turn to Lorna for her input.

"Me?" Lorna puts her hand on her chest under the weight of the decision being left up to her. "Don't ask me." She laughs, shaking her head.

"Why not?" I push. "Connie said the both of you always used to play that far-away game. Where did you want to go? Just somewhere that is not a city, preferably. It would be nice to be somewhere without so many people."

Lorna's face cracks into a smile. "How far are we talking?"

"Wherever your heart desires." I laugh. "Within reason, of course. Our money from the house will run out at some point. You may even have to get jobs."

"We? Why can't *you* get a job?" Lorna laughs.

"Let's just take a minute," Anna says, bringing us back down. "Peter, are you sure? Is this really what you want? This decision... it won't affect me. I don't care about the powers. This decision is yours."

"It is what we came for," I say, feeling lighter when it looks like Anna will say yes. "It's what I want."

Anna gives a gentle nod. "Then tell Kali I said yes. I just want you to be okay, Peter."

I'm on my feet in an instant, throwing my arms around her and Lorna, sending them shrieking backward.

I don't want to lose any time.

Now, all I need to do is convince Kali.

Kali is in her usual spot on her stone chair at the front of the temple, reading while others busy themselves around the main room. No one pays me much attention as I make my way up the few earth steps and sit at her feet.

She lowers her book to look at me, waiting for me to talk.

"Kali?"

"Yes, Peter."

My heart hammers in my chest with anticipation. "Anna said yes.

She said she agrees to the binding." I stare up at her, hoping, praying, for her to say yes.

To give me relief.

Comfort.

Support.

Her eyes stay on mine.

My influence is useless on her, but I still think the words over and over again. *Please say yes. Please say yes.*

After a moment, she heaves a big sigh. "I have been giving this a lot of thought. I cannot lie, Peter. I do believe it is your humanity which rules you that you love, and you have much capacity for it. But, I can no longer deny what is right in front of me. Your power frightens many members of this coven. We've known Sorcha for a great many years. For a long time, she was our only knowledge of a god in this modern age. Her skills are impressive, but you..." she shakes her head, "... I do not know how your father did it. But what he created in you is the most powerful creature to walk the face of this Earth in a millennia." Kali's eyes gloss over. "I believe you have so much potential for good, but there are some here who believe containing you is the best course of action."

I take her hand with reverence, the relief washing through me. "You have to, Kali. It is the best thing to do."

"The binding, it is a powerful spell, Peter," she reminds me. "I do not want blood on my hands, and the seniors want reassurances should the spell fail. If you do not accept the bindings, then we will have to destroy you. The fallout from the spell failing will be too great otherwise. It could kill every witch here."

Every hair my body stands on end at the threat.

Swallow it, Peter.

I can't speak the words so I simply nod.

Taking in her words, the world grows quiet around us. "Is there anything you can do to break the bond between Anna and me, so she can live if I die?"

Kali shakes her head, furrowing her brow. "I do not think so."

"Can you try?" I plead. "Please don't let that happen."

"I can try. But, Peter... you already have part of her soul. It would mean splitting it. That is extremely dark magic, something I am not permitted to practice."

My throat becomes thick. "Anna doesn't deserve to die, Kali."

"I will look into it. But I can't promise anything." Kali's eyes are soft on me. "Neither of you deserves to die, child. There is something I can do, although it won't be pleasant. To ensure you accept the binding, I could weaken you. It will not be nice for you. It will feel like your human form is dying. Day by day, weakening your body more and more. Your powers will still be there, and you will still need to transfer, but you should be too weak to fight the binding. Once bound, I will let the poison heal out of your system."

I look into Kali's eyes, trying to find any hint this is some sort of trap. *Why would she want that?*

"Do it," I tell her.

Once agreed, she informs me she'll need two days to prepare the poison and then another week for her and the seniors to prepare the spell while I become weakened enough. It seems like a long wait. However, in seven days, I will be bound and, after a brief recovery, we can leave India. Make a new start somewhere else.

Before I leave, I ask her for one final favor, one spell I would like to know. Just in case I should ever have the opportunity to use it.

Anna is not at all thrilled when I get back to the hotel and tell her the plan—well, most of the plan. I don't tell her Kali is searching for a way to sever our bond should the spell fail and the coven needs to kill me. I try not to think about how this means splitting Anna's soul. Whatever I already have, I cannot give back.

Don't think about that. The spell will work, and I will be bound. No need to frighten her.

She kicks off about the use of poison to weaken me enough to accept the spell, asking me a million questions about which poison and what exactly it will do. Of course, I hadn't thought to ask those questions, only wanting the result. *An end.*

Gemini

I stay with Anna and Lorna again.

For two nights, I sleep side by side with my sister once more. I stay with them at the hostel, steering clear of the temple until the poison is ready. This will be something new and unknown. I've never been unwell before, not really. Never had the flu or any kind of illness. I can't help worrying about what it will be like. The pain from all the lightning was repressed somewhere deep inside of me, so I don't remember how much it hurt. Besides, nature is something my body is made for, compatible—the poison will not be. Kali has made it with the intention to wound.

Anna wanted to come with me, but I told her no. I don't want her to see this. Whatever it is going to be, it will be ugly.

As I make my way through the markets, I almost miss a small figure tucked between stalls, hiding behind a rack of bright paisley material, motioning to me, a large hood up over their head.

I make my way over and tug back their hood.

"Mahi." I smile. I've never seen her outside of the coven.

"I have been waiting for you." She glances around, nervous. "Please, I wanted to warn you."

"Mahi, what's wrong?" I ask, placing my hand on her shoulder to calm her fidgeting.

"I do not want you to get hurt." She looks up at me with honest eyes. "Please, Peter. I overheard them talking. I know what you are doing."

"Mahi." I sigh, pulling her into a hug. "It's for the best."

"No!" She pushes me to arm's length. "What I heard some of them saying. They don't want the spell to work. They think it would be better to use the opportunity when you are weak to kill you. Kali says it is not the way and that Anna is innocent, and to spill her blood would be a crime, but they're saying it would be for the greater good. There is no way to sever her from you."

I regard her. "Do you think they would defy Kali?"

Mahi looks around again. She is taking a great risk in telling me all of this. "No. I don't think they would."

"Mahi." I lower myself to look into her frantic eyes. "It's okay. Kali will not let Anna get hurt. The spell will work. We will both be okay."

Mahi's eyes look pleading. "Kali hasn't told you the truth about everything. I heard her as well. I didn't mean to pry, but they've talked about you a lot recently."

"What hasn't she told me?"

"Sorcha. She is not an ancient god, Peter. I heard one of the others arguing with Kali about why she sent her away."

"Kali sent Sorcha away?"

Mahi nods. "She said something happened between you. She also said Sorcha was an experiment of Arjun's from before... in a different coven. He oversaw the ceremony, but her parents died because of it." My stomach sinks as Mahi's eyes become watery, her bottom lip trembling. "He was your father, wasn't he? Kali said he raised her, forced sacrifices on her, but he abandoned Sorcha when she was young because she wasn't strong enough. She's probably only around one hundred years old. Sorcha is why Arjun was cast out of the coven. They are saying he succeeded with you where he failed with her. He found your mother, fathered you himself. He was a bad man."

I push my hands through my hair, steadying my breath. Typical, terrible timing. *It doesn't matter*, I tell myself. *Why does any of this matter?* I take Mahi's arms. "Thank you. I appreciate the risk you took in telling me this, but listen to me, Mahi. Your seniors, they are right. I am nothing good." Her eyes swim as I go on. "What they are doing for me, it is the right thing. But these next few days, you should stay away from me, okay?"

Tearful, Mahi nods, and I continue on the path to the temple.

Sorcha, another creation of my father's. Something from a hundred years before me, someone he raised to be a god. I wonder how many sacrifices he made for her, trying to turn her into a terrible creature. Except, she was a disappointment, not terrible enough for him, so he created another—he created me. *Maybe this is the claim she sought* on me, to know why he wanted me so badly when he had discarded her.

I am the terrible creature she could never be.

Part of me wants to run back to Anna, to go back on everything I've said. It's an old instinct, to run. The three of us should go now and never look back on this terrible place.

But it feels too late.

The wheels are in motion.

Against that instinct, my feet carry me forward into the temple. Eyes follow me to the front of the hall, where I meet Kali as she rises out of the chair, a small reassuring smile on her lips.

A senior witch hands her a small vial.

"What is it?" I ask, motioning toward the black liquid swirling inside.

"Hemlock root, amongst other things." Kali looks at the glistening concoction.

My stomach does a little somersault. I know what hemlock is.

"Peter, this is the first of five doses. You will need a dose every day to keep up the progression. You may stay with your sister, if you wish, but you will need to come back every day. On the fifth day, we will gather to perform the binding ritual. I take it you know the side effects of hemlock?" she asks as she hands me the vial.

I nod. She does not need to explain.

"You may feel disorientated and confused after a few days. That will be normal."

I dip my head again.

"Are you sure this is what you want?" she asks one final time.

I don't answer.

I swallow the contents of the vial.

Chapter Eighteen

Anna

It has been the longest four days of my life.

With every day that ticks by, I become more sure that this plan is flawed and a bad one.

Peter's grip on reality is totally gone.

He drifts in and out of this world.

As the days pass, I begin to feel a hysteria of my own. A growing feeling that something awful is about to happen. I so desperately want to tell him this is all a big mistake, that the binding tomorrow is *not* a good idea. But it's what he wants. This final piece of suffering before he has some peace, and I'm terrified if I put doubts into his mind, it will be my fault if the binding goes wrong.

For the most part, he has retreated to the waters of the Ganges. It seems to be the only thing that can soothe him from whatever nightmare he is trapped in. His powers are still as strong, and the transfers have been made when he has been able to do them. Sometimes multiple times a day to ease some of his torture.

I wonder if the madness has infected me.

Kali assures me this is not the case and that his suffering is temporary.

Peter has not stayed at the coven, but Lorna and I have had to escort him there and back every day to make sure he does not get lost.

He is a walking corpse, having ingested enough hemlock to kill someone three times over. Peter stopped being able to eat after two days, although that hasn't stopped the vomiting. Kali has given us solutions to help him drink and keep his body hydrated. His skin is on fire, his heart races as wild and furious as he looks, and his eyes dart around the room in an attempt to comprehend where he is. Nighttime brings seizures, where Lorna and I have had to restrain him with our hands and bedsheets as he lashes against us while trying to talk him out of the nightmares that are blurred into his reality. There is lots of talk of death, blood, souls, and Peter not being a god but the devil.

It is a horror unlike any I have ever experienced.

When he is asleep, I cry over how I should never have allowed this. Lorna tries to comfort me, and sometimes she cries too.

I desperately want to tell him to stop.

But we are so close.

I have this feeling.

This sinking feeling tomorrow, something awful will happen.

Lorna and I have been sleeping in her bed, letting Peter take mine as sleeping next to him would be near on impossible with his constant shaking.

He's been napping for a while, thankfully, so we've taken the opportunity to get some rest too. Lorna is wrapped around me.

As my eyes start to blink open, I see Peter staring at the ceiling, beads of sweat rolling off his face.

Lorna must have noticed me wake because she moves her head to whisper in my ear, "Can you hear what he is saying?"

Peering closer, I see his lips moving, repeating the same thing. "*I have come to lead you to the other shore, into eternal darkness, into fire and ice.*" He whispers the words over and over again, staring into nothingness.

"What is that?" I ask her. We've been keeping the curtains closed for him, trying to keep the heat out. I should've predicted Varanasi would heat up with his physical changes.

She shrugs. "I'm not sure. Dante? Maybe?"

I ease out of her arms to sit next to him, caressing his face. He doesn't seem to see me. Another side effect of the poison is enormous winding black vines have etched themselves onto his skin, covering his arms and neck. With his pupils in a state of constant dilation, he looks terrifying. I can almost smell his skin rotting under the effects of the hemlock. He's been coughing up bits of blood and muscle, the hemlock wasting his insides faster than he can regenerate them.

He catches my arm, bringing me close to him. "Am I in hell?" he whispers.

"No, Peter," I soothe, forcing myself close to him. "You are here with me, and with Lorna. We are both here with you."

My words seem to calm him. He closes his eyes before looking toward the window, the small shaft of light there. "I think I will die," his words gargle in his throat.

"No," I say. "You can't die, remember? It feels that way now, but you'll be okay."

Peter turns back to me, a maniacal grin on his face now. "No, I really am going to die. They're going to kill me."

"No. They are going to bind you. Once it's done, you will feel better. It's almost over. Just hang in there, okay?"

Peter starts to laugh. It's an unsettling creaking laugh, displaying blood between his teeth. I try not to look away.

"It's all a trick, dummy. They won't do it. They will kill me instead. Mahi told me before. She tried to warn me, but I didn't listen." He takes my hand. "They'll probably kill you too. Do you think you will go to heaven, and I'll go to hell?"

It is just delirium, I tell myself, but when I look at Lorna, she is worried as well.

I try to grasp his face, to look into his eyes in an attempt to understand, but his eyes can't focus. His skin is so hot it is almost unbearable to touch. "Peter," I say and slap his face as his head lolls about, trying not to let my own hysteria allow me to hit him too hard. "Peter, this is serious. Is that true? Did you see Mahi?"

Peter's brow furrows, trying to comprehend my words. "Mahi. I saw Mahi. She was waiting for me." He nods. "But I am death. Pale, so pale. It needs to be done, Anna." His head bobs again. "Before it's too late, before I destroy it all. I am death." He closes his eyes, shuddering before curling into a ball and turning away from me with a quiet, "It hurts."

I shift my gaze to Lorna, who motions toward the door. I follow her out into the corridor, where we talk in hushed tones.

"What are you thinking?" she asks.

"I'm not sure." I run my clammy hands through my hair, and they get caught in its ends. "I'm wondering if we're not feeling a little paranoid ourselves. He's said a lot wilder things over the last couple of days."

Lorna nods. "You're right. But..." she hesitates to finish. "This has a hint of reality to it, doesn't it?"

"Why would he go through with it if he thought they would kill him, kill me?"

Lorna looks at the floor. "Anna, Peter was suicidal. We can't really account for what kind of harm he would put himself in, or you. He did it before."

I feel sick. I rub my eyes until I am seeing stars, trying to think. "This is all my fault."

I wanted things to be easier for him so badly that I didn't think it through.

"No." She grabs my arms hard, shaking me a little.

Her palms feel sweaty. The heat of being in this room must be making us delirious also.

"This is so not your fault. It is chaos. We need our own plan, Anna. If this goes wrong, what are *we* going to do?"

"Okay." I nod, frantic, and grasp onto Lorna's face, needing to anchor myself. "That is good thinking. We need a plan. I need to be there for the spell. Tomorrow, he will need the final dose of hemlock right before the binding spell. I will stay, and if it starts to go south, I will get us both out."

Lorna takes her hands in mine. "Okay. How, though? How will you be able to take on the whole coven?"

"I don't need to. Just enough to get us out." I look around. It's not enough. *If things start to go wrong, they won't just let me walk him out.* "The powers, the transfer... I'll take more. He's all over the place. He won't notice if he gives me more. We'll do it the old-fashioned way. It's more powerful."

"Anna, I don't know..."

I can feel my bones begin to shake at the thought of what we're beginning to account for—an attack from the coven, our friends. "Let's just be prepared for the worst and hope I don't have to use it."

"Will you be able to channel it? The way he can?"

"Let's hope we don't have to test that theory."

"I don't like it." Lorna's eyes are wide with fear, her entire body trembling.

"What else do you think we can do?"

Lorna has nothing to suggest.

Peter's body is weak from the poison. I don't know if weak is the right word. He's confused, in agony, and I honestly don't know if the binding will work. His confusion is causing distrust.

"Lorna, I need you to stay here tomorrow."

"No." She shakes, holding me close to her. "I am not letting you walk in there alone."

"I need you here. If it goes wrong, I'll need to focus on getting Peter and me out. We'll meet you back here. I *will* come back for you. Be ready to leave."

Lorna's eyes fill with tears as she grasps onto me. "I'm so scared."

I pull her into a tight hug, the walls seeming so close.

Everything is closing in on us.

It will be over soon.

"Me too. It's almost over. We all just need to hold on a little longer. We'll be okay. We've been here before, with my father. My brother and I, we'll be okay again."

Lorna nods. "If you take too long, though, I am coming for you."

She looks so scared, but I know she is telling the truth. She is fiercely loyal.

"I love you," I confess, the words out of my mouth before I have a chance to think about them. It seems like terrible timing, but Lorna's face stretches into a huge smile, so beautiful and so pure in our darkest moment. I'm glad to have said it.

"I love you too," she says, fresh tears springing from her eyes before she leans in to kiss me. Really kiss me, like our lives depend on it.

We creep back into the room, where Peter is still curled up in a ball. I move over to him, rolling him back to look at me. He tries to look around, bewildered, unable to focus on my face. "Peter, listen to me. It's time to transfer, okay? Do you hear me?" I slip my hand into his. "Only this time, you need to use your electricity, Peter. Not too much, just enough to make me strong, okay?"

Peter's teeth chatter, and he rakes his hand down his face, wiping away the sweat. "No. No, I don't think that's what I'm supposed to do." He squeezes his eyes shut. "It will hurt you."

"It's okay," I soothe, while Lorna stands on her bed watching, ready to do I don't know what. "Don't you remember? This is part of the plan. You need to make me strong, Peter."

He looks like a wild thing, his pupils widening and contracting as he attempts to focus on me. He doesn't say anything else, but the surge of electricity passes into me. Rolling back, the wave of energy this time feels totally different more like a drug that makes my head spin, crackling under my fingertips. We take the same approach as the hemlock, doing multiple transfers to build up the energy. My body hums. After the third transfer, it is too much for my body to handle, and I heave, becoming violently sick. My vomit tastes burned on the way out.

"Anna, you need to stop now." Lorna holds my hair and rubs my back. "Kali will see what you're planning a mile off if you walk in there like this."

"We'll do one more in the morning. Just to be safe."

Lorna does not look convinced but doesn't say anything, she simply leads me back to bed.

I don't think any of us sleep much.

Peter and I toss and turn, shivering through the night before our bodies give in and we fall into slumber.

An uneasy slumber in anticipation of what tomorrow brings.

Lorna is wrapped around me, the sun shining through the crack in the curtain when I wake.

Peter is not in his bed.

The panic rising in a second, I scramble out of bed, jolting Lorna awake.

"Oh my God. Where is he?" For some reason, I push the bed covers back like he is somehow hiding under them.

"Relax," Lorna says, pulling on her leggings. "He's probably in the river. Let's go and look."

I take a shaky breath as we make our way up to the roof. He's not here, but sure enough, as Lorna predicted, we spot him way out in the river, floating around on his back. Whenever he gets dragged out by the current, he gets back to his feet and walks back a little before resuming his floating position. The buzzing in my veins is making it hard to concentrate on anything else.

Lorna gives me a sideward glance. "You look a little wired."

"I feel it." I smile at her.

She turns to face me full-on, taking both of my hands and trying to look reassuring, although I can feel her shake. "Go and get him. The sooner this is over, the better."

I nod, fighting down the urge to be sick again.

"Maybe you don't need another transfer," she suggests.

I agree with her. Whether it's the electricity or nerves, I barely know where to put myself.

"I love you," she tells me again.

I tell her the same, then walk her back to our room, giving her a final kiss before making my way to the riverbank.

In just a few hours, this will all be over.

It feels like I've forgotten how to walk. I don't think I have ever felt so nervous.

Still, I smile a little as I approach the Ganges' edge, the sun bouncing off its calm waters. It looks magical and peaceful. Peter appears serene in his little place floating on the surface. I can barely see the black vines that creep up his neck from here.

I steel myself.

This has to work.

I call out to him, motioning it is time.

He looks a little better today, perhaps even lucid enough to comprehend this is almost over. Peter gives me a broad smile as he gets to his feet, waving at me.

His wave slows.

His eyes narrow as if not trusting what he is seeing.

The world seems too quiet for a moment, right before Peter's booming voice carries across the water. A resounding "No!" accompanies his outstretched hands toward me.

I don't have a chance to look around, I only feel it, the sharp pain entering my back. A vice-like grip holds my shoulder, keeping me standing as a hot voice whispers into my ear, "Stupid boy. He should know by now he is powerless in those waters."

Hot tears leave my eyes, almost as hot as the knife in my back. A small voice tells me that the fact this doesn't hurt worse is not a good sign. I watch Peter fight against the current, trying to make it to me, but it's taking too long. Throwing out his hands, he tries desperately to bring the lightning against the nullifying effects of the waters.

Sorcha calls out to him, over my shoulder, "I curse you, Peter. Curse you to this half-life. You will know no peace."

I've never been stabbed before, but something about the feeling of this knife as she pulls the blade from my spine feels wrong.

Sorcha moves her hand to the wound, the heat gathering there, creating a tugging feeling somewhere deep down inside of me that I can't place. My hand clutches to my chest the instant I realize what she is trying to take from me, from him.

My tears taste a mixture of salty and burned.

There will be no spell.

That is over now.

With what force I have left, I turn to face her, my one foot barely able to keep me upright. I dig my fingers into Sorcha's face as hard as I can, hating her with everything I am. I let it go—all of that hate, every ounce of power I have absorbed from my brother. The force of it leaves me in screams. I hold on for as long as I can, wanting to hurt her for every last terrible second.

Until, finally, the force sends her hurtling away from me.

And me backward from her.

There's a slight shooting pain as I move backward. My legs are like jelly.

I register Peter moving past me. Free of the waters, he is only a series of blinding lights as he rounds on Sorcha, whose screams seem far away.

I'm not in control of my lower half. My feet move of their own accord, and I stumble over the edge, plunging into the cold waters of the Ganges.

"Peter." I can't shout, it's only a whisper. I struggle to keep my head up while tears come freely. I'm slipping away, the current taking me farther from the shore. I gulp for air at the surface. I can feel them now. The souls. The feeling somewhere deep inside of me starting to pull again.

I am *going to die.*

"Peter!" I gasp.

This time, he is at my side, yanking me back to the water's surface. Dragging me back toward the bank. The tug inside of me gets stronger. There isn't enough time. I gaze up into his face and wish he didn't look like this. I wish the black vines weren't covering his skin. This is not my beautiful, sad, show-off brother.

"Please," I splutter. "Don't let it end like this. Don't let it be her who does this to us."

Peter's tears fall onto my face, his pupils still contracting wildly. "It's okay. I will get you back to the shore. I can heal you just... *hang on*."

I dig my nails as hard as I can into his arms. I need to make him understand. "It's too late. That knife... if you pull me out now, it will go to her." I shout but it's more like a whisper, "Peter, if you don't do something, my soul will travel down the river." I wish I was stronger, and my face crumples as I plead with him, "Don't let it go down the river with the rest of them. I don't want to go that way."

"Anna." He is still trying to haul me out. "No. This isn't supposed to happen."

"Stop. Peter, stop," I say as loud as I can muster. "Please." I force him to look at me with his wide, scared eyes. "I want it to be you. I am so sorry. I am so sorry for everything, Peter. So sorry it has to be you."

For the first time, his grim acceptance comes on a sob that leaves his chest as he nods his head. A wave of relief and fear wash over me. I wish I could tell him all the ways I love him. I wish we had more time. I hope he feels me with him always. I hope being whole brings him some kind of peace.

"I am sorry you didn't get to live," he says. "That I couldn't save you."

I bring my hand up to stop his chin from shaking. Until now, I hadn't noticed the sky turning black above us. As black as the poison vines.

"I love you," I whisper.

His strong, hot palm on my chest pushes me under the water.

Chapter Nineteen

Peter

My feet seem to know where they are going whereas my brain does not.
Is this real?
Am I real?
Did I kill Sorcha?
Did I kill Anna?
I stumble forward.

The sensation hits me in waves. The slight taste of fresh berries against the choking taste of hemlock. Anna's soul fighting against the delirium and the poison Kali has been feeding me.

It stretches, wrapping itself around me. Binding. A different type of binding. I am not being held down, rather things are slipping into place.

It's confusing.

The feeling of goodness—the energy of Anna's soul finally at peace with my own—battles against the poison still coursing through me.

In the end, I am the one to force Anna's last breath. To keep her soul from traveling down the river when she died.

I had to make it my sacrifice.

She was my sacrifice.

I hold my hands on my knees, shaking my head as my vision blurs and shakes. *Her soul is now mine.* She was dying already—there was no way to save her. I did what she asked me to do.

But I failed her, and now, I am whole. Or I will be whole once I burn through the poison.

I lift the dead weight of my feet forward and stumble down the narrow pathway crossing the invisible barrier of the coven.

Why did I come here?

I trudge onward, everyone turning to look at me. I realize I'm drenched, wearing no shoes, only my T-shirt and trousers clinging to my skin.

Was it raining outside?

I look down at my hands. The black vines of the poison still cover me, but they shudder, trying to retain their hold. Or my eyes could be playing tricks on me.

I wish my head would stop spinning.

I want to vomit.

The blackness of the poison and the light of Anna's soul war inside me. I feel like I'm being pulled apart. I sway on the spot just over the threshold of the coven's main hall. But it is all inside. The world remains in its place. No shuddering roots, no claps of thunder rolling in the distance.

It's different.

I can feel it.

Waiting for me.

Whispering.

I shake my head. I can't think. Yet I can feel it all, waiting. I only need to ask.

New sensations. New things start to coil. Burning and thrashing, they push and pull through my body. Like I am being ripped apart. I'm going to collapse. My body shakes, the force trying to send me to my knees. Gravity—she always called it gravity. I'm going to collapse underneath it.

It is overwhelming.

The light rolls through my body once more, fighting back the poison. It's edging forward, starting to win. I notice the sounds I am making with the sheer effort of remaining on my feet.

"Peter?" Kali's voice sounds cautious.

I focus on her and take deliberate steps forward.

"Where is she?" My words come out slurred like I haven't spoken in a long time.

"Who?"

"Sorcha," I say.

I don't know why I am asking.

Did I kill her already? I want to rip her apart.

A flicker of confusion crosses Kali's face. "Sorcha is not here. You are befuddled, Peter. It is almost time."

She moves to collect the last vial of hemlock as I glance around.

They are all still. Too still. They must know something is wrong.

Why are they pretending?

If they aren't with Sorcha, then they can't know for sure what has happened. They don't know Anna is dead.

For some reason, I laugh—a strange, strained sound. I move close to Kali, the coven closing in around me. Then I start to feel it, their magic rippling around the room. Warding spells, protection. They must think there is still a chance I can be bound while the poison is in my system.

I spot Kali's fingers twirling underneath her robe. Whatever she is doing ripples against my skin.

"That isn't going to work," I tell her.

Stopping to focus on her, my vision blurs once again. Goose bumps charge over my skin. Maybe the fact Anna and I have lived side by side for so long has slowed the process, or maybe this is just the way it works.

My sister is dead.

I killed her.

I may not have started it, but I finished it.

She is dead, and I feel free, connected to everything. Every single thing in this room. All that power. All of them. It makes my mouth water.

Kali clasps onto her vial of hemlock. "Peter. You are so close to achieving what you want."

The poison recedes again when I look into Kali's eyes, so like my father's.

I take my time to speak slowly so as not to slur my words, "Kali. My sister is dead."

The collective coven gasp. Even if they were not part of it, they know exactly what it means. All except Kali try to flee, heading to any exit. The roots that lie in the walls and floors are all too easy to control. I bring them all down, blocking them all in with me. My eyes are fixed on Kali.

I drown out the cries of the witches who've been caught by the falling rubble. My focus on Kali, my body still wages the battle against the poison slowly being fought off. I am sick of the poison clouding and confusing my mind. It will be clearer when the poison is gone.

Kali's eyes never leave me.

I lick my lips. I know one thing that will help me fight it off. They are all trapped in here with me, and I don't know why I wanted this. I need to think clearly.

It should be Kali, a voice tells me.

The rest are okay. I can feel them all. All but one.

That's when I hear the cry. It isn't just a cry but a name. I am pulled back to myself, wrenching my eyes away from Kali. Turning around to the back of the room, where some of the witches have gathered.

No.

No, no, no.

I am at her side in a heartbeat.

Mahi's mother clutches her lifeless body buried under the rocks.

"Shit." Hot tears rise in my eyes as I kneel on the ground beside her. "I didn't mean..." I put my hands on Mahi's young face. The girl was thirteen.

Her mother slaps me away, telling me not to touch her in Hindi.

I sink my head into my hands beside her.

"Peter," Kali says. "We are not with Sorcha. We did not do this to you."

But I hear the tremble in her voice, and I know she is scared.

"Let us help you. Mahi was an accident."

I look at my young friend's lifeless body.

Everyone I love dies.

I kill them.

I am death.

I slowly rise to face her again, the hardness gone. It is all just so inevitable.

"Kali. We both know I am beyond help. You tried. But you were right, I am death." My voice doesn't sound like my own.

My hand clamps onto Kali's neck and the coven braces. I can feel them all, all their power. I feel their magic tear at my skin. Kali's hands wrestle with mine as I walk her to the front of the room.

"Peter," she whispers, choking into my grasp. "You choose your fate. You do not have to become this." But I can feel her, what she is. Her years are closer to three hundred. Anna only lived to see nineteen. It's not fair.

"You don't understand," I tell her. "It is already what I am."

It's almost too easy to snap her neck. Her lifeless body drops to the floor at my feet. The coven falls into silence. Their leader is gone. Three hundred years on the planet, and in the end, her death was so easy.

Now that she is dead, she looks even more like my father.

I crouch down at her side, looking into those cold, dead eyes. My heart hammers as I reach down, tentative, and place my hand on her broken neck to take what I want. The brilliant white glow starts to form between my fingers, then begins to wind up my arms.

Kali's power, her life, her soul. *All mine.* The faint taste of pomegranate and dirt. Her power, overwhelming. I drop to my knees beside her, breathing it in. My chest heaving. When I look at my hands, the writhing poison vines disappear from my skin.

I am free.

The new soul rushes through my body, making it hard to stay steady on my feet.

I stagger into a turn at the top of the dirt steps to look out at the terrified coven.

They are all too shocked to move.

A real, live, human sacrifice, right in front of their eyes in their very coven.

Their high priestess.

Better than any drug, it feels too good. I laugh. The power of Kali's soul is so great, contorting my body as it contains it. I wobble on the stone steps, trying to make my way back down toward the rest of them. I only wanted Kali to stop the poison, to heal.

Everything is blurry. I cannot see them, only sense them. They are all so scared. I realize I don't want to let them all go.

I'm so hungry.

I shouldn't laugh.

I am going to kill them all.

I stop laughing and the silence echoes everywhere. I try to focus on their faces, but the rushing makes it hard. They're scared, yes, but they aren't giving up without a fight. It only lasts a second, a fraction of a second, before they descend on me.

Trying everything to take me down.

In every possible way.

With magic or with weapons, the remaining witches swoop on me.

It's a blur.

A blur of blood and dirt.

Their bones break with ease. What I don't do with my hands, the tearing roots of the trees from the hillside take care of. I barely need to talk to them. It's more like they are an extended part of me—my weapons.

Their spells are not doing much except slicing my human skin. I know the knife in my hand is from someone stabbing me, not a sacred blade, but a kitchen knife I've seen them chopping food with.

I don't know how long it takes—not long.

It's not long until there is no one left, only the sound of my hard breaths. I move quick on purpose. I don't want any to escape. I don't have much time before the souls are on their way to the river. Outstretching my palms, I call them all to me. The lives I have claimed. The pure white of their souls rising and hitting me the way the lightning once had.

All eighteen souls.

All claimed except Mahi. She can go on.

My body shudders, the feeling almost too much. So different from my father's. He was evil. The goodness of the coven. They were all good. *The good ones must taste better.* I almost can't stand up, clutching onto the stone steps.

I am drunk on souls.

I can't get a handle on it.

Despite the poison being gone, my vision is still blurry. I still cannot see the sights around me.

All I know is that Anna is dead.

Anna is dead.

Anna is dead.

I sink my head into my hands, trying to steady myself on my knees.

Anna is dead, Peter.

She is gone, and I am whole.

I am whole, but I still feel so fucking lost. My chest heaves, and I start to sob again, resting my back into Kali's body to do so. There it is. I am whole with no way to die, burdened with all this power.

Right now, my only gift is death.

It is the only thing I have to give.

The sound of tumbling rocks has me on my feet.

I strain to see to see a small figure in the corner. When I was busy butchering the coven, vines and roots that found their way in must have disrupted the exits I'd blocked, and she found a way in.

I can see her shake as she moves into the room. The hems of her cream-colored linen trousers are tinged with crimson as she takes in the sight around her.

"Peter, what did you do?" she whispers, her eyes wide in horror as she looks up at me on my place on the steps.

I take a shaky step toward her. "Anna is dead, Lorna."

The noise that comes from her isn't words. It's a sound from deep within where she clutches her chest. "No." She cries, getting closer. "The coven, what happened to them?" She has stopped walking toward me, looking at them all, all I have done, and she is scared.

Scared of me.

I feel my chin shake, all of me shake, and I close the distance between us, grateful she doesn't move away. "I had to make someone pay. She is gone."

I crumble into Lorna's arms, forcing us to the ground, and weep into her lap. She clutches her arms around me, crying too, for what we have lost, for what is around us. I feel like I'm seeing it for the first time, all the blood. There is so much blood.

I don't know how long we stay like this, but eventually, Lorna's tears turn to panic. "Peter, what are we going to do? How are we..." She can't bring herself to say the words as I release her to look at her tear-stained face. "There are so many bodies here. Where is Anna's?"

"She is by the river," I tell her, the memory of placing her there only just coming back to me.

"Peter, there is so much blood. How are we ever..."

I look into her round brown eyes, swallowing hard. It's hard even for me to see so much death in the room, considering I am the one who caused it all, but to see Lorna look at me with honest eyes and ask me how *we* are going to get away with it is heartbreaking. The tears rise in her eyes again. I take hold of her face, accidentally smearing the blood on my hands all over her.

"Don't worry, Lor. I have it all under control." Lorna's panicked eyes meet mine, but I can hear the panic in my own voice. I nod my head, an idea forming. "I can feel it all now. It will be okay," I tell her, moving her back a little to press my palm into the blood-soaked earth, using something I have never felt before. *I am so much more now.*

I look back at Lorna, whose eyes widen once more as I say, "I am going to burn it all down."

The flames lick around my hands without burning my skin, the growing deadly fire traveling and dancing along the pools of blood. I watch Lorna stare at the dancing orange and yellow blaze for a moment, see the huge golden orbs reflected back in the blacks of her eyes.

Chapter Twenty

Connie

I'm not quite sure why I feel so nervous.

I hold my shiny new guitar in my hands, trying to think of what to sing later. For the last two weeks, I've sung a short spot on Thursday nights. They've gone down reasonably well. There's been a nice little turnout of people who have seemed to enjoy the songs. Always upbeat.

Of course, Jamie and my mum are my biggest fans. They even sit together now. My mum likes him, and he is so good with her, just the right level of cheeky. I've never sung that Cat Power song again, not since the night over two years ago when I serenaded Peter in the coffee shop.

I reach out and touch my phone, thinking of my friends so many miles away from me. It's been a while since I heard from Lorna. I woke up the other night thinking about her and sent her a text to check in, but so far, nothing. That's not unusual, though. I wonder if there will come a day when she stops replying altogether. When I'll no longer call her my friend. I never imagined this would happen to us. It's a strange feeling to mourn a friendship. Even more so when she is out living her life with Anna and Peter. I'm beginning to feel bitter that they got to keep her.

There's a knock at the front door, and I bound to my feet to get it. I'm glad Jamie is here to take my mind off her. The grief I felt over Peter was so great when I first left that it took me a while to recognize I was grieving for Lorna as well.

"Hi," he greets me, planting a kiss on my lips. Handing me a bunch of daffodils, he moves into the hallway.

"Oh, you're cute." I smile, taking them off him and walking into the kitchen to put them in water.

"So, how are you feeling about the big performance this week?"

"Actually, I feel really nervy. I can't decide what to sing. What do you think I should do?" I ask, wrapping my arms around his waist, leaning him slightly into the refrigerator door.

"You're taking requests now?"

"My brain is on holiday today." I smile.

"Hmm…" he says with a mock-serious expression, pushing the hair off my face. "That implies you had one to begin with."

I give him a gentle shove, but he pulls me close, kissing me again. After taking a seat on the sofa, I do demand he give me at least one song to sing, but every suggestion he offers is an obvious joke. He is starting to get on my nerves a little.

"Jay. What song do you want me to sing? I'll even dedicate it to you."

I poke him playfully with my foot, which he catches.

"Lord, Connie. Do not do that. I would die of embarrassment."

I raise my eyebrows. "Isn't it romantic?"

"Hmm… I'm not a very romantic person."

"You have your moments." I smirk at him. He massages the foot he is holding, which he pretends not to notice when I snatch it away.

Jamie has been the most patient person in the world. Kissing him seems to be fine in a way, sweet, quick kisses that feel good. Normal. They taste like Jamie. Anything more and my mind races and floods

Gemini

with Peter. Even from halfway across the world, the memories of him are overwhelming. It is beyond frustrating.

"Is your mum coming?" he asks, letting me tuck my feet back under me.

I look at the clock on the wall. "Yeah, she's a little late actually. She should be home soon."

Right on cue, she bursts through the door looking flustered. Dropping her bag onto the floor, she leaves the door wide open behind her.

"Mum." I scramble to my feet. "What's wrong?"

"I've just seen Lorna's mum."

My heart sinks, and Jamie is on his feet as my mother sweeps into the living room, grabbing the television remote.

"Have you seen the news?" She's clicking through the channels, trying to find what she is looking for.

As she does, Jamie's fingers push through mine. I can feel the color drain from my face, along with Jamie's eyes on me, not on the scene on the television in front of us. I quietly lower myself onto the coffee table so I don't fall over or pass out.

Destruction.

Everywhere.

Varanasi is under water.

I can't hear what the newscaster is saying, only the dull thump of my own heartbeat. My free hand clutches my chest as if my heart will burst out otherwise. It all looks familiar. I'm pretty sure Vik's hostel is gone. The banks of the Ganges have burst in a huge flood. The residents have been forced to flee, their homes destroyed.

My mother takes a seat beside me, wrapping her arms around my shoulders. "Lorna's parents can't get hold of her. When did you last hear from her?"

"A week or two ago." I breathe heavily and look at my phone, my hands shaking. A little over a week ago, she called me. I can't remember what we spoke about. It was a short call. I hit her name, putting the phone to my ear.

Please pick up.

It goes straight to voicemail.

"Voicemail." I look up at my mum.

"Can you try Anna and Peter? I am sorry to ask, love, but they might respond to you."

I nod, finding Anna's name first, but both their numbers have the same out-of-service message. "I'm s-sorry." I hear my voice shake. "No answer. It sounds like they aren't switched on."

I feel numb, a sinking feeling in my stomach. I dreamed of Lorna a few nights ago, but I can't remember it.

Please don't let them be dead. What was my dream?

I remember waking up and feeling like I should text her. I wanted to know if she was okay. She was so scared in my dream.

But it was just a dream.

"Are there any fatalities?" Jamie asks.

"Not according to the news," my mum says, turning to me again. "If you hear from her, please let her parents know straight away, Connie."

I nod as my mother leaves. Jamie looks at me like I might snap, "Don't, Con. Don't do what you are doing."

"What?"

"Jumping to the worst possible conclusion."

I rub my eyes, trying to listen to him.

He lowers his tone. "The one good thing you know is that Peter would not let them get hurt. They are okay, Connie."

I look back at the destruction on the screen. Checking that my mum is out of earshot, I ask, "Look at that, Jay. What if it *is* him?"

Jamie looks at me like I've lost my mind. "That is a flood, Connie. A force of nature, not the wind or a bit of rain. Trust me, they are all fine. They'll have left the city, and Lorna will find a way to get in touch when she can. Your mum said there haven't been any fatalities."

I nod. He's right. There is nothing left to do but wait for Lorna to get in touch. She'll have to get in touch. They must be with the thousands evacuating."

I try to calm myself. "Yes, you're right. They're just getting out. Lorna will know we're all worried. She will get in touch." I meet his eyes. "But, Jay, I dreamed about Lorna only two nights ago, and she was scared. She was looking right at me."

"Connie, it was just a dream," he says, rubbing my shoulders. "It looks scary. There's nothing we can do from here, though. So let's just sit tight."

"Okay." I nod.

I'm being ridiculous, having been around magic for far too long. My dreams don't mean anything. I dream about Peter all of the time.

"Let's get back to deciding what I should sing tonight."

"You're still going to play?"

I shrug. "Why not?"

Jamie doesn't look convinced but doesn't argue.

It's a quiet journey to the coffee shop, and my mother is also wracked with worry. She's known Lorna since she was little. The news about the three of them missing has spread fast, even for this village's standards. The mood in the coffee shop is somber. It's quiet, full of whispers. No one can quite meet my eye.

In the end, I play one song. The only one I can think of.

I can't keep the big bulbous tears from rolling down my face.

Please don't let them be dead. Please don't let him be dead.

I know in my heart I wish I'd never left. I felt mad and claustrophobic, but I should never have left.

Even if it wasn't real, it was better than this, and now, I have lost him. I've lost all of them.

As I finish my song, Jamie meets me, putting his arm around my waist and leading me outside while I weep. I bury my head into his chest as we walk. He smells nice, like fresh laundry.

He is all I have left.

My only friend.

My one source of comfort, of warmth.

"What are you doing to yourself, Con? Why did you sing that?" I look up at him through my teary lashes, and he almost rolls his eyes at me as he gives me a squeeze. "You are so oblivious. He wasn't the only person to ever notice you. I know that's the song you sang when he was here."

The color floods my face. "Jay. I'm sorry."

"Don't be sorry. I understand how you must be feeling, but try not to worry. They will be fine. Trust me."

"Will you stay with me tonight? I don't want to be alone right now." The color pools in his cheeks and mine follows suit as I avert my eyes to his chest. "You don't have to. Sorry, that was a stupid thing to ask."

"No, of course I'll stay. It's just..." he shifts about uncomfortably, "... what will your mum say?"

I scoff, waving him off. "Please, she loves you." I can't meet his eyes, instead playing with one of the buttons on his shirt. "But, you know, it will just be to stay. No funny business."

He holds his hands up in indignation that I would even suggest the notion of any funny business crossed his mind.

Funny business or not, I realize this is a bad idea when Jamie lies next to me in bed, his arm wrapped around me. Despite Peter being considerably taller than Jamie, my single bed never seemed to be a problem. Peter felt like water around me. This does not feel the same.

I can't sleep, and I can tell he is not asleep either. It feels strange to have him here, awkward, and I feel guilty I'm comparing everything about him to Peter.

Which is so unfair of me. I can't go through life comparing everything to Peter.

I close my eyes and take a deep breath. I know Jamie would like more, and in a way, I do too. My stupid brain gets in the way, telling me, of course, Jamie can't compare. *He's only human, after all.* What a ridiculous thought. *Only human.* It's like I have set the bar at god now, and no mere mortals shall share my bed. Stupid brain.

Gemini

Jamie is probably thinking the same thing.

If Peter were here, there would be no hesitation. I would know exactly what he wanted. I would know what to do. He would be everywhere, filling my vision, his hands on my body. It would all be so free and natural. It always came so easy to him.

I rake my hand over my face.

Stop thinking these thoughts, Connie.

It's the worst possible time to think about him. How different it is to lie next to Jamie in my fluffy pajamas, how he asked my mum if it was okay for him to stay, too shy to make a move.

Don't think about Peter, how he always radiated heat, him climbing in through the window, drawing constellations on my naked back, telling me he was addicted to me.

I let out a deep breath and wiggle around so I'm facing Jamie. I can just about make out his blue eyes in the dim light, and they're full of concern. Taking his hands off me, he gives me some space. He is so good. Too good for me, actually.

"Are you okay?" he whispers into the night.

I remember Peter telling me once how he wanted his name to be the only one I whispered into the night.

"No," I admit. "I am so not okay."

Before he can say anything else that is good and comforting and the right thing to say, I bring my lips to his. He kisses me back, slow and cautious, but at this point, I need to do something to hit reset. I can't spend my life only thinking of Peter. There has to be something else, someone else.

Jamie follows where I lead, only resisting at first, as I pull his T-shirt over his head. His conscience raises a red flag perhaps, but it only lasts for a moment.

When I wake, I pop my eyes open in time to see him getting dressed. *Is he sneaking out?* He must think last night was a huge mistake.

Well done, Connie, another friendship completely ruined.

He turns to look at me but catches me squeezing my eyes shut. "I know you're awake." He laughs.

I open one eye, covering my face in embarrassment. I'm sure I have the worst bedhead. "Are you leaving?"

"Total honesty? I was hoping to make the romantic gesture of bringing you tea in bed. Is that lame?"

"No. I love it." I smile, one hundred percent glad he is not running away.

"Okay, well... I'll be back."

He trudges off downstairs, and I jump out of bed to pull some leggings and a T-shirt on, then try to sort out whatever is going on with my hair before switching some music on. When he comes back up with two mugs of tea, I jump back onto my bed.

Jamie's friendly exterior changes to something more serious as he hands me my mug. "Do we need to talk about last night?" he asks, looking at his feet.

I start to feel nervous again. "What about last night? Didn't you have fun?" I try to say it lightly—it doesn't sound good on me.

Jamie's expression is unreadable. "Connie, I know you must be feeling vulnerable right now." He shakes his head, smoothing out his dark hair. "And I know I took responsibility for my feelings getting hurt, but last night..." he looks around, uncomfortable, "... that meant something to me. I realize I'm in deeper than I thought, and I don't want to get my heart broken. So, I guess I just want to say, if you want to draw a line under what happened last night, then that is okay with me. I'm more than happy to be your friend who comforted you, Connie. I am okay with that. People you care about are in danger. I get it. But I can't keep doing this. Because what we did, I can't keep doing that and have it not mean anything to me."

"I understand." I nod, wrapping my hands around my drink, appreciating its warmth. "Is that what you want? To draw a line under it."

Jamie laughs. "Connie, you have no idea how much I wanted last night to happen. For way longer than I'd like to admit. But I don't want to be 'after,' that's bullshit. I want to be who you choose, not what you are left with."

I chance a brief grin at him. "When did you get so good with words?"

Jamie shrugs. "I've always been good with words. You've just never noticed before."

He takes a long sip of tea and I realize I haven't answered him.

"It meant something to me too, Jamie."

He beams.

"But..." I add, drawing the word out, "... you are right. My head is all over the place. I am so worried about them, *all of them*. Not just him. I need to know they're okay. When we have news, and I can put my mind at rest, then we can figure this out." I motion between the two of us.

His gaze shifts to the floor as he chews his lip, and a twinge of guilt squeezes my heart because it is not what he wants to hear, but it's the best I can do for now.

"And, I promise in the meantime, I will keep my hands to myself." I attempt to lift his spirits with light humor.

"Ah..." He smiles, coming to sit next to me. "I already regret saying that."

I chuckle, nudging my shoulder into his. "Probably the right call, though."

He gazes down into my eyes—a longing look—and I can tell he doesn't want to stick to what he has said.

Against both of our better judgments, I close the gap and kiss him.

Days pass, and there is still no word. I call and text Lorna around the clock, and do the same with Peter and Anna. I even try Lorna's email and her social media. It has been months since she's been active on any of them.

She used to love that stuff.

I feel like I am losing my mind with worry. I flip between wanting to cry great salty tears until I have nothing left to give because I am so certain something horrible has befallen them, to raging with so much fury they are fine as Jamie says, only they can't be bothered to text me to let me know they made it out of Varanasi.

I'm also aware of the growing impression that my body is making promises to Jamie my heart can't keep. I miss Peter more, not less. I hate myself. I try to convince myself that if I knew they were all okay, then I would feel better.

Please don't be dead.

Please don't be dead.

The mantra runs through my head over and over.

I think it on repeat.

Until I start to think if Peter is dead, at least I could move on. Maybe. I cast the thought out of my head. It's the waiting that is killing me. *Why hasn't Lorna gotten in touch? Peter doesn't owe me anything. But Lorna, what would stop her from letting us know she is okay?*

My plans have become pretty drastic. *I need to go back.*

The only problem is I don't have enough money for the flight, and I need about a week to organize a visa. Providing I'm not banned from overstaying my last one. It's a risk, but I have to try.

My request to borrow money from my mum has not gone down well, and Jamie's visit comes at the wrong time.

She almost throws the door off its hinges when she answers it. "Can you please talk some sense into her?"

"Mum, please! I haven't even had the chance to talk to him about it." I storm after her, but she is already upstairs and away from me as Jamie catches my arm, twirling me toward him.

"Talk to me about what?" Jamie questions.

"I'm going back to India," I say as firmly as I can, looking over his shoulder, so I don't have to look at the rising anger in his eyes.

"You're what now?"

"I have to find them, Jay. I am losing my mind."

"Connie, you are not going back to India." He stares at me like I've sprouted a second head. "The city is still flooded. It will be like looking for a needle in a haystack. What if they're on their way home as we speak?"

"I spoke to Lorna's mum. She spoke to the embassy today, and none of their passports have been picked up at the airport." I hold onto him, trying to implore him. "I can't do nothing. And I can't shake the feeling something bad has happened to them." I can tell he wants to be angry, but as the days have passed, even he has started to worry. Lorna's parents are a wreck, and James and Sally are too. "Come with me?"

Jamie's eyes widen. "You want me to come with you to look for your ex-boyfriend?"

"I want you to come with me to look for our friends."

Jamie considers me for a second, softened by the fact I've asked, I'm sure. "I don't think so. If, by some miracle, we find them, I am the last person he will want to see. And we'd tell him, what? That we traveled thousands of miles to find him and say we're together now."

I flap my arms, exasperated. "That wouldn't be our opening line. Besides, he doesn't hate you. You were the one who didn't like him." When Jamie still doesn't look convinced, I narrow my eyes at him and ask, "Jamie, are you scared of him?"

"Con." He chortles. "I watched that dude get hit by lightning and walk away. I helped him dispose of his own dad's body at a pig farm. Yeah, he's a bit scary. I don't want some kind of showdown with him."

I suppose he has a point.

I ease a laugh, softening to lean against him. He does such a good job of bringing me back to Earth. To make everything seem a little less crazy. I don't think I ever realized how dramatic Peter is, or rather, was.

Kerry Williams

"I have to go," I insist. "I would prefer it if you came. For me, it would be less scary with you there. You help keep me grounded."

But my mind is made up.

I am going back with or without Jamie.

I won't rest until I find them.

Eventually Jamie nods his head.

Chapter Twenty-One

Connie

My mum remains adamant I should *not* go back and refuses to lend me the money. However, Jamie, being the star he is, gives in and agrees to not only come with me but to pay for our flights. I imagine his mother agreed to give him at least some of the money. She would do anything for him. After Jamie calls me to give me the news, the idea I am really going back to India starts to sink in. It's a restless night. I have a whole day to kill before Jamie can come over and we book the flight.

I wander around my house, not knowing what to do with myself. I know it's a long shot. Varanasi is still deep underwater, with no one able to get in. I suppose we'll need to get as close as possible and find where the people who've been displaced have moved to.

I pour over my guidebook, thinking about the route we took. The trains will be a no-go. I search for nearby towns and cities that might be good starting points.

Why hasn't Lorna called? Please don't let them be dead.

At long last, my concentration is broken by a knock at the door. I glance at the clock. Maybe it's a parcel for Mum, or Jamie finished work early to come over and get things in motion. I feel like we're wasting valuable time.

Pulling the door open, I freeze.

"I thought you should know Lorna is okay. She is back, at her parents' house. I just thought you would want to know."

I struggle to process what I'm seeing.

He's here, standing back a little ways off my porch.

He looks good, usual Peter, dressed in jeans and a long-sleeved T-shirt. Somehow, he looks taller. Golden skin and paler hair with those big, bottomless brown eyes.

My hand moves to my chest, but my feet are frozen. I don't know what to say or do. "You? You just got back?" I don't know whether to laugh or cry.

All that worry.

He is here.

"This morning." Peter nods. "I went to see my aunt. Took a shower and got changed. It's been a long trip back." He grimaces.

It's only now I'm noticing something different about him. He's cautious, keeping his distance, standing back from the door, and his eyes look distant, cold even. He won't make eye contact with me.

"Erm... sorry to just drop in, but my aunt said you'd been round, that you have been worried."

"We've all been so worried." My voice comes out in gasps.

Peter seems to swallow hard, then he takes a step backward.

"What happened?"

Peter holds my gaze for a split second before turning away. "This is a bad idea." He puts his hands into his jeans pockets. "I'm sorry, Connie. Look, Lorna is okay. But I should go."

"Peter," I shout, moving out in front of him. "No, you don't get to do that. You don't get to show up here and then just walk away."

"Connie..." he starts, really looking at me for the first time.

But now that I'm moving, I am mad. All my emotions and frustration bubble up to the surface as I scream, "I was terrified. I was so scared. I saw on the news what happened. And what? You couldn't have called? Or texted? Not even Lorna? What happened?" I advance on him.

Peter seems keen to keep his distance, still backing up, but now he is backing into my house.

"We came back with nothing. No phones, nothing. Lorna is exhausted. I can't explain right now." No more Peter vulnerability. Now he's just guarded.

"Why not?" I demand, furious. Furious I've never gotten the real truth from him. "Why not, Peter? Why is everything a big secret?"

He holds his hands up. "Connie—"

"Tell me. What did you do?" My rage bubbles over the surface, and I push him as hard as I can, then do it again.

"Connie, stop," he says, his voice gentle, though his cold eyes betray him.

But I push him yet again, the tears starting to spill. "What happened? What did you do?"

I keep pushing him until his feet have taken him into the kitchen.

"Stop. Do not push me." The coolness of his eyes enters his voice.

I'm too mad at him, and in seconds, my whole world is crashing down again. "Or what?" I push him again. "No more secrets, no more lies, Peter."

When I push him again, he catches my wrists. "Connie, do not push me." His voice sounds like ice as his stare bores into me.

"Why?" I spit, looking up into his cold eyes. "What are you going to do?"

He grits his teeth, tightening his grip on my wrists. "Why? Because I am a whole fucking god. Because if you push me, I will tear the moon out of the sky and burn this village down. Because Anna is dead, Connie." He mellows for the first time, loosening his grip, throwing my hands away from him. "Anna is dead. And I..." He lets me go and moves to the counter, putting his head into his hands. "I killed them all."

I stand there and look at him, hunched over. "Who?"

"The coven. I killed the coven."

"You killed them, Peter? Why? Did they hurt Anna? Did they kill her?" I move to place my hand on his shoulder, which he dodges.

"Don't," he seethes. "Don't fucking touch me."

"What is wrong with you?"

"I can smell him on you, Connie," he says through gritted teeth, shaking his head. "You are so very predictable."

I've never seen him so cold and it sends a shiver down my spine.

"Excuse me. How dare you?" I swivel away from him, starting to walk toward the hallway.

"That's right, Connie. Walk away. You're good at that." He follows me.

I spin on my heels. "How you dare you say *that* to me? I wasn't even on the flight home and you were screwing *her*, weren't you?"

"My heart was *broken*," he shouts.

"So was mine," I scream at him, a literal scream. "Get. Out. Get out of my house, Peter." I fling the door open, my chest heaving.

Peter holds my glare. "Gladly," he spits before stalking out.

I slam the door as hard as I can behind him before banging my back against it, letting my legs give way and sink to the floor. I don't cry. I scream. As loud as my lungs will allow.

When I am done screaming, I get back to my feet, throwing the door open and moving as fast as they will take me away from my house. It's a long walk. I half run, half jog, out of breath, having to stop every now and then. I should've taken my bike but, in a way, I need the pain of my muscles burning, anything to distract me from what's just happened.

At last, I round on Lorna's house, almost unable to breathe.

"Connie," Lorna's mother greets me. "You've heard? I was just about to call you. I'm afraid Lorna has gone to bed. She's been through a terrible ordeal."

"I need to see her, Sita." I pant.

She looks at me sympathetically, then lets me up.

I'm in such a rush to see her that I don't bother knocking on her bedroom door. As I throw the door open, I see Lorna isn't sleeping.

Gemini

She's sitting at her window smoking. She jumps at the sound of me opening the door and throws away her cigarette in a panic. The second she recognizes it's me, she closes the gap in two steps, throwing herself into my arms.

"I am so happy to see you," she cries into my hair, holding me as tight as she can.

Lorna isn't vibrant and healthy-looking like Peter. She's thin with huge bags under her eyes, with her hair all bedraggled.

She releases me, holding me at arm's length, to get a good look at me. "Damn, you look good. I look like shit." Lorna laughs, taking another cigarette from the packet with a shaky hand. "Did my mum call you?" She pulls out a bottle of what looks like tequila from a plastic bag and takes a large swig.

"Where did you get that from?" I motion to the bottle. Now that I'm catching my breath, Lorna's nervous energy is perhaps even more overwhelming than Peter's coldness.

"We stole it." Lorna laughs. "Going through customs. I don't think I've been sober since we got on the plane."

I nod, going to sit beside her. She seems manic. "I saw Peter. He told me you were here."

"Wow." Lorna takes another swig. "He didn't waste any time."

She hands me the bottle.

Why not?

I take it from her and tip it up for a long swig, then confess, "We had a big fight."

Lorna snorts. "Figures."

After another swig of tequila, I hand the bottle back to her. "Lor, what happened? We saw the flood on the news. Peter said Anna died... that he killed the coven."

Lorna takes a long drag on her cigarette, a manic laugh playing on her lips. "Killed the coven?" She shakes her head. "Connie, it was a blood bath. There were... parts..." She shakes the memory out of her head.

"Why did he do it?"

"Why?" She laughs, and it's a little unhinged. "Erm... I don't know. Because his sister just died, because he was furious, because he was whole for the first time, because he wanted to, because he enjoyed it, because he was half driven mad by poison. I don't know, take your pick."

"Poison?"

Lorna rolls her eyes at me. "Please don't make me relive it, Connie. It's been a week from actual hell." She rocks forward. "Like true, seven circles, deepest hell, haven't slept, death and bullshit, hell. A hell Peter created, yes, but one he also pulled me out of. Pulled us both out of." Her brown eyes look into mine, the desperation running deep in them. "I know you want to know, but I can't." She laughs a little. "I don't even want to know what he said to you. I only know I can't go through it all right now. It's just *too much*, Connie."

I put my hand over hers. "It's okay, Lor. Don't worry. You're home now."

She gives me a weak smile, then drinks more tequila. "I just need to have a hot shower and about a week of sleep, maybe some Xanax or something." Her laugh is hollow.

I smile. "I am so glad you're here."

Her eyes glass over. "I'm so glad you came." She puts her other hand over mine. "Peter..." she pauses, "... I know he probably said something incredibly shit to you, but he's just lost her, Con. I'm not making excuses, he also just killed a *lot* of people." She laughs. "It is insanity." Her eyes go wide. "There were so many bodies, Connie. After a while, he started to come back to himself, and he seems like himself again now. But, wow." She rubs her forehead. "What he can do now, that shit is biblical." She laughs again, shaking her head. "Sorry. I am so, so tired. I just need to sleep, okay? But, you know, if you do see him again, he just lost her, so, you know." She nods at me. "You know?"

I nod, not knowing who is more confusing to talk to at this point.

After I leave Lorna to get some sleep, the guilt starts to creep in. Seeing him so suddenly was the emotional equivalent of jumping in the deep end and not knowing how to swim. All my unresolved feelings came straight back to the surface. In the process of being mad at him, I lost sight of the fact that Anna has died.

I clutch my chest again.

Anna's dead.

His world has fallen apart.

How can he cope without her?

Anna was his life.

I realize my feet have not taken me home as my hand rests on the gate of Sally and James' house. I'm not sure if he'll even want to see me because he probably hates me right now.

I knock on the door anyway.

Sally opens, her face is all red and puffy. "Connie." She smiles through her sadness. "Please come in."

As she moves the door back for me to enter, Peter comes to stand behind his aunt. A protective arm goes across her shoulder, but his eyes are hard on me.

She grasps his hand, giving it a gentle shake and looking up at him warmly. "I'll give you two some space." With that, she retreats to the living room.

Peter crosses his arms in front of his chest, waiting for me to speak.

I don't think I've ever seen him mad at me and certainly never cold toward me. All of the fragility there ever was about him seems to be gone. "How is she?" I motion toward the living room. Now that I'm here, I don't know what to say.

"Not so good," he says, looking in the direction she left.

"What did you tell her? About how Anna died?"

Peter glares at me. "I told her she drowned in the floods."

"That's not what happened, though, right?" I all but whisper.

He doesn't say anything for a while, just stares. Then he motions his head for me to follow him into the kitchen, where he moves away from me and sits up on the counter.

"No, she didn't drown in the floods. The flood came after." His voice sounds flat as he stares at the floor.

"Peter, I didn't come for another fight. I came to say I'm sorry. I can't even imagine how you are feeling. You came to tell me your sister died, and I ended up screaming at you. I'm sorry about that too. I guess there were a lot of things left unsaid between us. Again, I am sorry, so sorry, about Anna."

Peter looks at me almost in surprise but doesn't say anything.

Which is bad because it means now I have to fill the silence. "About Jamie—"

"Stop." He holds up his hand. "You really do not have to explain yourself to me. I was out of line. It was just a bit of a shock."

I give him a small smile. "That it was. You were the last person I was expecting to see today." I lean back against the table, trying to relax. "You know, I was coming to find you."

The corners of his lips twitch. "You were what?"

I cross my arms, letting out a large breath. "I was going to get on a flight and go find you all."

"How were you planning on doing that?" His smile widens again, some of the ice starting to thaw.

"I might not have had the finer details of my plan laid out, but I would've done it somehow. I can be very resourceful." I nod, letting my lips stretch into a grin also.

He lowers himself down onto his bare feet, slow, almost slithering. "That, I have no doubt about. You were coming to India to rescue *me*?"

"To rescue all of you," I clarify, and he steps closer. "You seem so different." I grip the edges of the table to keep myself in place. "What you must be feeling, and no rain, no storms?"

He is within reaching distance now, and he towers above me.

"I am different. Those storms, they rage inside me now. And I feel different like I'm connected to everything." His dark eyes dance over my face. "I can feel your heart beating." The corner of his mouth pulls up a little. "Very fast."

He takes his final step toward me, only inches away now. He is so perfect it's painful. His lips, so inviting. I can feel his heat from where I stand. I can't believe I'd almost forgotten how it feels to be around him. Overwhelming. Consuming. I grip the table harder.

My heart is beating so fast that all I can do is look at him—so different and yet exactly the same. My phone buzzes in my back pocket, and I pull it out to see Jamie is calling. I click it off to ignore and look back to Peter, who has given me a little breathing room.

"Look," I tell him, pulling myself together. "Today has been a lot to take in. But you should know, Jamie and me..." I murmur the words, "... I am with him now, Peter. I'd like us to be friends, though, if we can. If you would like that?"

Peter seems to consider this for a while. I wish he didn't look so good. "Mmm... you really think that could work? You and me, *just* friends?"

"Why not?" I tilt my head at him. My phone buzzes again, and I automatically click it off. "Maybe that's what you need right now? A friend."

"Okay." He gives a slow nod. "Let's be friends." He moves a little closer, seeming puzzled by the notion. "You really want that, to be my friend? Even with what I did, to the coven, to people you knew."

It sounds insane, but I don't know what to say. I think back to Lorna, who is currently a wreck, and flap my arms at my sides. "What do you want me to say, Peter? That you're a psycho and I don't want to see you again?"

"That would be the sane response." He half laughs.

"Do you want to be friends or not?" I put my hands on my hips, starting to become a bit peeved.

"Fine." He holds his hands up in defeat. "Yes. I want to be your friend. I would *love* to be your friend."

He looks like he is making fun of me, but I feel a little better knowing we are no longer screaming at each other.

After a few minutes, I start the long walk home, feeling something close to whiplash. The last few hours have been a lot to take in.

I text Jamie, letting him know I'm on my way home and he should meet me at mine. He is already there when I arrive, hovering at the front door like my mother.

"Where have you been? Your mum called me to say Lorna is home with Peter."

I nod. "Yes, I saw them." I go into the living room to sit down, suddenly exhausted.

"And Anna isn't with them, is it true? Is Anna... did she die?"

All I can do is nod again.

"Holy shit. What happened?"

"Erm... she died in the flood." I look down at my hands.

Jamie stares at me for a second. "So Peter didn't cause the flood?"

"You were right," I hear myself say. I have no idea why I'm lying or why it comes quite this easy. "But to tell you the truth, they were both super out of it. Peter was distant and Lorna was a little manic. I think they'll both need time to adjust."

We all will. As much as I have missed them, I suppose it'll take some figuring out how they fit into my life now. Peter in particular.

Jamie takes his time studying me before he asks, "Connie, what does this mean for us?"

"What do you mean?"

"Now that he is back? Will you want to get back together with him?"

"No." I take his hands. "I told him you and I are together now. He knows. No showdown needed. But, his sister has died, and I'd like to be his friend if I can. He could really use one right now."

Chapter Twenty-Two

Peter

Sleeping in my old bed is weird.
    Or it would be if I could sleep.
    Instead, I lie here listening to my aunt crying through the adjoining wall.

The sound is like nails on a chalkboard. I hate to do it, but I cannot stand it any longer. I slip out of bed and move into her room slowly, so I don't frighten her. I put my hands out a little as if approaching a skittish animal, and her crying eases at the sight of me coming nearer.

As light as a feather, I place my hand on her forehead. "Shh," I tell her, and her eyelids flutter while I watch as she falls into a peaceful sleep.

I look up to see James' wide eyes watching me in the dark. I reposition and trace my fingers down his temple, allowing sleep to come to him as well.

If only I could do the same for myself.

No such luck.

All roads in my mind lead back to Connie. I can't stay in this village for long. I just need some time to plan what to do next. And how to get there. So, for the time being, I'll enjoy Connie's company, make the most of being around her, and try not to wallow too much in the feeling that, once again, I will be losing her.

The morning is a gray and drizzly thing. I have nowhere to go, but I can't stay in this house. Outside, it's not a pelting, cleansing rain. Instead, everything is just wet.

I pound on Lorna's front door and after a couple of minutes, her mother answers.

"Peter, hi."

"Hello, Mrs. Jain. Is she in?" I give her the most charming smile I can manage.

"Still asleep."

"Can I go up?" I ask, then think, *Just let me go up.*

"Sure." She smiles, opening the door for me. "Straight up the stairs. It's the second door on the right."

"Thanks."

I bound up the stairs and enter, not bothering to knock. As suspected, Lorna is not asleep but lying in her bed smoking, staring out the window.

"Sheesh. This weather is shit. I thought it was supposed to be spring." I throw my wet jacket onto her floor, kicking my shoes off, and land heavily on the bed next to her.

"Welcome to the real world." She doesn't look surprised to see me, only a little annoyed I'm now taking up her bed space.

"Right. I have to make it happen these days. Should I make it sunny?"

"Don't bother," she tells me. "This weather better suits *my* mood for a change."

We stay here for a moment, not saying a word, Lorna inhaling and exhaling the only sound.

Finally, I blow out a large breath. "Normal life is shit," I say to the ceiling.

"I'll say." She laughs. "It feels so weird being here. I thought it would be better, and I didn't know where else to go. Sorry I made you come back."

"It's okay. Better that your parents know you are alive."

She nods before turning to me and saying, "I feel like I don't know how to be here anymore, Peter."

"It will get easier. I felt the same when we first came here after my mother died. Every day, you get a little more used to it. And if you don't, then you can leave and start again somewhere new. Be a new version of yourself." I turn toward her too. "Shall we find every drug we can and take them all, and then we can forget all the bullshit we've been through?"

Lorna laughs. "I don't know about that, but there is some tequila left around here somewhere."

I get off her bed and root around for the bottle. There isn't much left, so I drain it, then ask, "So, what are you doing?"

"Erm... I'm just lying here. I'm shattered, Peter."

"Come on. You should get out of the house."

"And do what?"

"I don't know, assimilate?"

Lorna laughs again, propping herself up. "We could go and get coffee?"

I drop my hands to my sides. "That's the best you've got?"

"Fine. You choose." She huffs, dropping herself back into bed.

"I'm sorry," I tell her, grabbing her hand and half pulling her off her bed. "Coffee it is. Get up."

She reluctantly indulges me, although she makes sure she takes her time getting ready to show me she's not pleased about being forced to leave the house. By the time we're out of the house, Lorna is looking a little more like herself and not like the wild thing she'd become to survive with me the last week.

The rain stops as we walk to the high street. Lorna gives me a knowing look as we stroll.

"What?" I laugh. "It wasn't even the good sort of rain."

She shakes her head but doesn't look too bothered.

I look at the ground for what I am about to say next. "Lorna, I want to say thank you. For sticking by me. For pulling me back from a cliff edge."

Lorna snorts. "You mean that wasn't you going completely off the deep end? You destroyed a city."

I nod, grimacing. "I know. But it could have been a lot worse if it weren't for you. So, thank you. And I am sorry, for all you saw, for everything I put you through. You lost her too," I add in a quiet tone.

Lorna sniffs, the humor in her face gone. "In a sick kind of way, I was glad of the distraction. Seeing you like that made me forget my own pain. It still doesn't feel real, you know?"

I nod. Except it's not true. For me, it feels all too real. I'm glad to get Lorna out of her bedroom with nothing but her own thoughts. As we approach the coffee shop, she gives the closest thing to a genuine smile she can while we enter.

"Connie!" Lorna rushes to hug her over the counter, which is a confusing sight.

Connie looks equally confused at the sight of Lorna and me together.

"I totally forgot you work here now."

Connie smiles at the both of us, her initial confusion now masked. "Do you want your usual, Lor?"

"Yes, please." Lorna rubs her hands together in delight. "I can't believe it's been two years since I had one."

Her green eyes turn onto me as she queries, "What would you like?"

I'm almost annoyed with myself for forgetting how they sparkle. There was a time when it only happened for me. I would like nothing more than to taste her again, but she is not on the menu.

I sink my elbows onto the counter, sliding closer to her, pretending to read the menu. "What's good here?"

Connie raises her eyebrows a fraction before leaning closer, her hands gripping the edge of the counter. "Do you want to try the sugar-laden monstrosity?"

"I'm not sure?" I tilt my head, my lips pulling upward. "Do you think I can handle it?"

Lorna rolls her eyes beside me. "I'm going to find a table. Have fun, you two."

Lorna moves away and Connie pulls back, a bit more caution in her eyes. "You really want one?"

"Why not? Two sugar-laden monstrosities, please."

When she looks at me for a second, I notice. "I like your fringe," I tell her.

"Oh." She nervously dusts her hair with her fingers. "Really? I'm not so sure about it. You know, I thought I should just give it a try. My hair is so boring. Although, I'm not so sure. Might grow it out."

Connie looks good. Different from what she usually wears, her all-black uniform and tight-fitting shirt draw my attention.

"You look good," I tell her, unable to keep my eyes off her.

The pink rises in her cheeks a little.

"Peter, don't do that."

"What?" I smile, moving back a little. "I thought we were friends now? I can't give you a compliment? You look good. I like your hair." I shrug. "Friendly stuff, no?"

She considers me for a second, then starts busying herself. "We're friends. So thank you for the compliment." She blushes again as her green eyes flash at me. "You look good too. Your hair's so much lighter."

"Mmm..." is all I say, looking at my reflection in the mirror behind her.

In the days after I'd absorbed the souls of the coven, Lorna noticed the change. The only outward sign of what I'd done was my hair turning a shade or two lighter. It reminds me of Sorcha's pure white hair and makes me wonder how much sacrifice she had to endure.

The bell of the coffee shop door dings.

I don't bother to look at first because I can't drag my eyes away from her. I only check to see who it is because of the look of panic that crosses her face. He's not looking at her, but he is looking at me.

I straighten up. "Hi, Jamie," I say with the most genuine smile I can muster.

His eyes flick between the two of us. "Hi."

He holds out his hand for me to shake. I don't hesitate to take it, the most fleeting of desires to crush it passing through my mind.

"Good to have you back."

I know his words are a big lie. He hates the sight of me.

"I'm really sorry for your loss."

"Thanks."

"Erm... Peter. I can just bring your coffees over," Connie says.

"I don't mind waiting," I tell her.

Jamie's attention turns from me to Connie. "Hi." He gives her a big smile, leaning over the counter to give her a quick kiss.

He's lucky I'm in control of everything now. I owe him a few thousand volts. "Are you almost on break?"

"Yep. Just making these." Connie is making a mess of everything, spilling milk all over the place. "Can you just take a seat, Jay? Please."

With a warning look at me, he moves over to the table where Lorna is sitting.

Connie, who is mopping up milk, leans over the counter, speaking in a hushed voice, "Peter, please don't do this. Don't make my life difficult."

I lean in closer, whispering back, "Me? I didn't do anything."

"You don't have to. You just have to stand there."

I half laugh. "I can't stand here?"

"No." Her lips twitch. "You can't stand there. Listen, I can't put up with any territorial bullshit again from either of you."

I give her my best mock-hurt look. "I'm not territorial."

"Like you didn't parade me in front of him?" she whispers.

"Connie," I whisper back. "I would parade you everywhere."

Connie giggles, but it's cut short when glancing across the room. I follow it to see Jamie staring daggers at me. She goes back to making my drinks and tries her best not to look in my direction again. He shouldn't push his luck—it would be all too easy to smite him.

The daggers he is throwing me can only mean he doesn't know I am guilty of mass murder. I look back to Connie. Here she is, keeping my secrets. *Again.*

When I make my way over to Lorna, Jamie immediately gets up and leaves. He and Connie disappear, and Lorna shakes her head at me, pulling her drink closer.

"You really can't help yourself, can you?"

"What?" I ask, feigning total innocence but I can't keep the stupid grin off my face.

"She is happy."

"Then he has nothing to worry about."

"Peter..." her expression turns serious, "... you aren't planning on staying here, are you?"

I look down at the monstrous drink in front of me. I haven't discussed my plans with her yet, mainly because they don't exist. "No," I admit.

"Then try not to be a total catastrophe while you're here, or anywhere else for that matter."

"Thanks, mate," I tell her with a fake smile.

She gives me one back. "That's what I am here for. To pull you back from that cliff edge, remember?"

"Mmm..." is all I have to say. Taking my first long sip of the drink, Lorna is already halfway through hers. "Oh wow. That's disgusting." I push it away from me.

"All the more for me." Lorna pulls it toward her with glee.

I think about Lorna's words. The last thing I want to do is mess up the life Connie has built for herself. Seeing her again, I know how much I still love her. Probably always will love her. Except we can never go back there. I want to be selfish, enjoy being with her for a while, even if it can't be in the way I want. Simply to be around her, to see her smile, it will have to be enough. I leave her alone for the rest of the time Lorna and I are in the coffee shop.

Lorna gives her a wave goodbye as we leave, and I do the same.

She moves out from behind the counter, asking, "You're leaving?"

I see the flicker of disappointment cross her face.

"Yeah, I'm really busy, you see," I joke.

She puts her hands on her hips. "Doing what?"

"It's a secret." I put my finger against my lips.

She rolls her eyes. "Goodbye, Peter."

"Goodbye, Connie." I smile.

It's a little after midnight.

I lie in bed, staring at the ceiling and wishing I could sleep.

I get up and pull my clothes on and go outside. Lorna will kill me if I go and annoy her again, so I go to the only other place I know.

From down in her garden, I look up at the darkened room. My heart hammers as I focus in on her. There is only one heartbeat in the room. Thankfully, *he* is not here. I've never had much to feel nostalgic about, but it feels like only yesterday I was doing this. Standing in her garden, throwing acorns at her window.

Eventually, a nightlight comes on and she opens the window to see me smiling up at her.

"Want to come for a walk?"

"What happened to not making my life difficult?" she whispers.

"I'm not, I promise. I know he isn't here. Come on, Connie."

She chews her lip. "Fine. Give me a minute."

It doesn't take long before she's out in the garden, her big coat wrapped around her, looking only a tad irritated.

"What?" she demands.

"Humor me." I smile. "Please. Do you want me to beg?"

"No, Peter. I don't want you to do anything."

I know she is trying to sound annoyed, but she's also attempting not to smile.

It feels so strange not touching her.

We walk side by side out of her garden into the night, like we've done so many times before. For once, it seems she doesn't have much to say.

"Feeling nostalgic?" I ask after a while, and she gives me a sideward glance.

"I guess I am." I hold up my hands. "Just as friends, let's go and sit under the stars the way we used to, when everything was so much simpler."

"Okay," she agrees.

We make our way to our little spot although it looks different now.

The wheat is much higher.

We walk out a little way, and I wilt a patch big enough for us to lie down with enough distance so we're not touching. I simply hold my heat around her, keeping her warm as we peer up.

"You're losing your touch." She smiles. "Not a star in the sky."

I glance at her.

Drink in every inch of her.

I wish I could make her happy, really happy. "Look again," I say.

Her reaction is priceless. She clasps her hands to her cheeks, laughing. Every cloud has vanished to reveal the night, our night. She shakes her head, her eyes sparkling at me. "Show-off."

I laugh.

"Always."

The ache in my heart will always make me think of my sister. But the ache is welcome. I could survive for eons and it would feel the same. I always hoped when our souls *were* one, it would feel like she was always with me, but it doesn't.

"So," she says after a few moments of silence. "You're in control of everything now?"

"Mmm... you mean all of my powers don't just spill out anymore?

Then, yes, I am in control of everything I had before and even more."

"That means the flood..." she suggests.

"Yes," I confirm, watching closely for her reaction. For when she realizes what I am, that she should want nothing to do with me. "I meant to do that. I caused that flood on purpose. In my grief and sadness, I wanted to destroy everything."

We stare at each other for a while. I wish I knew what she was thinking, or at least why she isn't running. She rotates a little on her side so she is no longer looking at the stars but right at me.

"What does it feel like?" she asks.

"What, to kill everyone?" I frown.

"No, why would I ask that, you psycho?" She laughs. "What does it feel like to be so connected with everything?"

"Oh." I chuckle, rolling my body so that it inches closer to hers. The action isn't lost on her as I feel her heart pick up its pace, forcing mine to do the same. "It's weird. Before, it was always like I could do things without trying, without really knowing. But now, it's almost as if things can talk back. Like, everything."

"What do you mean?"

"So," I point back out into the sky, a shudder of excitement going through me, flexing my reach. "See that bright dot? That is Venus. I can feel the spin of its axis. I can feel the worms move underneath us. I can feel the rain thirty miles away, the high tide of the sea in Wales where we swam."

She doesn't look scared, more enraptured.

"If you asked me to, I could pull that sea straight to us."

"How?"

"Kali explained it like gravity. Kind of like the sun. I have an orbit that affects everything around me. I just didn't realize quite how far it reached until, you know, Anna died." I stare back out into the stars.

"How far does it reach?" Connie asks.

"I don't want to say."

"Why not?"

"You'll think it's weird."

Connie giggles. "You are weird. Tell me. How far? Venus? You could knock Venus out of balance? Tell me." She laughs again. "Why are you embarrassed?"

"I'm not embarrassed." Yet I falter and have to cover my face with my palms to say it out loud. "Neptune, okay."

Connie starts cracking up.

"If I try hard enough, I can reach as far as Neptune. Stop laughing at me."

Her laughter is contagious, though, because it is ridiculous.

"That is wild, Peter," she cries. "You could take out our entire solar system."

I'm cracking up now too. "I don't know about that. I can just…" I search for the right word, "… interact with it."

Our laughter dies down, and Connie seems more content now, peering out at the stars in comfortable silence.

I swallow hard. "Connie, I do have a bit of an agenda being here."

She narrows her eyes at me, waiting for me to go on.

"I have the spell. The one which can take my influence off you."

She takes a sharp intake of breath. "I know you are with Jamie now, and if you've moved on and you don't feel anything for me, then that is great. The spell is not needed. But if you…" I can barely say it. "If you do still love me, then I can make it stop."

Connie's expression is unreadable for a second, her breathing hard. She moves so quickly I don't even have a chance to sit up. Before I know it, she is on her feet and stepping over me.

"Fuck you, Peter."

She marches off into the night, leaving me little time to wonder what I did wrong.

I am on my feet, chasing after her. "What? Connie, stop." I try to grab onto her, but she shrugs me off. "Please, Connie. I just don't want you to have to live with me in your head. I'm trying to help."

Connie swings around on her heel. "I was doing fine before you showed back up. I *was* moving on, and now you are here, and I am right back to square one. I don't want your stupid spell."

She is right in my face, only now she has run out of steam. She's so close and breathless, I close my hands into fists to stop myself from reaching out to her. Her green eyes are locked onto mine.

"Connie," I whisper. All I need to do is close the gap. *Just kiss her,* my brain tells me. But I can't move.

Connie closes her eyes. "Go home, Peter," she orders, turning away.

So I walk back to my aunt's house, which is so very far from home.

The next morning, I am in a monstrous bad mood. I don't even say hello to Lorna's mum when she lets me in. Instead, I stomp past her and up the stairs. Lorna is sitting in front of her mirror, putting makeup on.

"You again?" she greets me, her expression deadpan.

I flap my arms to my side. "Good morning to you too."

"It's like two in the afternoon."

"Whatever. I didn't sleep well."

Lorna eyes me suspiciously. "Really? Because I've had Connie on the phone."

"Argh." I shake my hands through my hair, lying back on her bed. "I was trying to be helpful. Why doesn't she want the spell?"

Lorna plonks herself beside me. "You are both as bad as each other. She thinks you just want to make yourself feel better so you can forget about her."

My eyes bulge. "Are you serious?" I move my hands over my face. This means she does still have feelings for me. I want to be happy but can't find it in myself. "She is better off with Jamie, though, as much as I can't stand him. He can at least, you know, give her kids, grow old with her. He's not a monster."

"You are not a monster."

I stare at her, incredulous.

"Okay, you sort of are. But isn't it Connie's choice?"

"But that's just it. It's not, is it? I'm still in love with her, so we'll never know if I am the reason she loves me back unless she lets me do the spell."

"Can't you just take her word for it?"

I look down at my friend. "Does that sound like me?"

She gives a small shrug of agreement.

"Besides, she'd be giving up too much for me to live with being able to take that away from her without knowing."

"You're making my head hurt." She mock slaps her head.

"Urgh." I rub my face. "What am I doing here, Lorna? I should go before I do any real damage. I have no idea where to go, though."

Lorna stares at the ceiling. "Okay. Just stay a little longer. I don't think my parents will forgive me if I disappear again so soon."

I remove my fingers from my face. "What do you mean?"

"I'm obviously coming with you."

"You are?"

"I can't stay here. Not now, not after everything we've been through. Plus, I know you're trying to be all noble by saying you'll leave to make everyone's life here easier, but I think we both know you can't be left on your own," she adds with a poke to my ribs.

I chuckle. "You sure? Like you said, I'm pretty much a catastrophe wherever I go. Things will get easier here if you stay. You will learn to fit back in."

"Peter, I am with you." Her eyes become watery. "I don't think I could ever leave you. I thought it would be painful... you look so much like her. But, honestly, being around you, it makes me feel like she is still with me. That part of her, however small, I can't give it up. I can't give up on you."

I swallow hard. "I think that is pretty much the biggest compliment you could ever give me."

Slowly, Lorna wraps her arms around my waist and I follow suit, holding her close as she buries her face against my chest.

Chapter Twenty-Three

Connie

It feels like history repeating itself.

It's been a week, and I'm getting the distinct feeling of being left behind all over again. Every time I call Lorna's house, she is not in. I haven't seen Peter again since our night under the stars. I try to tell myself it has only been a week and they need time to readjust, but it still stings. I don't want to moan to Jamie about feeling left out, and I get the impression he is glad about it anyway. Maybe 'glad' is too strong a word, but he is a little too diplomatic in pretending not to notice me glaring at my phone screen.

I decide to call Sally's house. Peter's not in.

So I call Lorna's house. She isn't in either.

But Lorna's mum does let me know she has a new phone and gives me the number, which I call. It rings for ages, but as I'm about to hang up, she finally answers.

"Hello?"

"Hi. What's happened to you? I've not heard from you." I don't particularly like how I sound so possessive of my friend. Maybe I'm jealous since I can only assume she is with Peter.

Gemini

"Connie?"

"Yes, Connie. Obviously. Where are you?"

"We're at the tree." *She sounds funny.*

"Brady's tree?"

"Yep. Why don't you come down?"

I hang up, already on my way. Even cycling, it feels like it takes too long to get there. It isn't particularly hot, but I am sweating by the time I arrive. Not my most attractive look. I throw my bike to the ground and walk the rest of the way to the field, trying to compose myself. From the top of the field, I spot Lorna under the tree. It looks like she is dancing around. Yes, she is definitely dancing. As I get closer, I hear music playing from her phone, something I don't recognize.

When she sees me, she runs over and throws her arms around me. "Connie."

I sway under her weight and notice that she seems unsteady on her feet.

"You found us."

"Us?" I look around her. "Is Peter here?"

She rolls her eyes dramatically, pointing upward.

I look up to see Peter high in the tree. He's standing on a high branch, and there's no way he could have climbed up there . When he notices me, he begins his descent. As he walks—or should I say stagger—down to greet me, new branches form under his feet, creating steps. Yet, he misses the last step, falling face-first into the ground.

Lorna doubles over in laughter while Peter chuckles with his face still planted in the ground.

"Lightweight," she tells him.

As he gets to his feet, there's a huge scrape mark down his face. He gives her a gentle shove, sending her stumbling a few paces.

"Are you two drunk?"

"No," Peter says while Lorna nods her head sloppily. He looks at her, slinging his arm over her shoulder. She staggers under his weight as he admits, "Yes... I am drunk." He grins at me, the cuts on his face healing in front of my eyes.

Lorna pushes him off her and comes over to me, taking me by the arms. "Are you okay?"

I don't really know what to say. "Lor, I was worried about you. I still am. I feel like I'm losing you."

She looks back to Peter, who waves her away. "You go." He turns back to the tree. "I'm fine."

Lorna puts her arm around me, and we go back through the field. "Let's get coffee," she suggests.

The walk does an excellent job of sobering her up. I cycle slowly beside her after convincing her she is in no state to ride my bike. For a while, she sings at the top of her lungs, then chats about her family driving her crazy. By the time we reach the coffee shop, she seems a lot more with it, if not now a little sleepy.

She takes a sip of her black coffee. "Wow. That's strong."

"Talk to me, Lor. What's going on?"

She shrugs, not looking at me. "What do you mean?"

God, she even sounds like him.

"You and Peter? Why the distance?"

"Connie, it's only been a week." She fidgets with the handle of her mug. "He doesn't have anyone else."

"So, what? You two have just been getting smashed? Drinking your feelings? You do realize you are totally enabling him?"

I can almost see the steam leave Lorna's ears, the heat building in her eyes as she lets loose on me. "Let me ask you something, Connie. Why won't you just let him do the spell?" I stutter on my answer, unable to get anything out, so she continues, "Because *you* left. *You* wanted out and *you* got it. But let me tell *you* something right here and now..." she stabs her finger onto the table multiple times to make her point, "... I was the one there picking up the pieces. I am *still* picking up the pieces. So, while you were here, building yourself a life, I..." Tears rise in her eyes, and she blinks them away. "He is my life now. I am sorry, but he is all I have too."

"Lor, you have me." I reach across to take her hand, and she squeezes it hard.

"It feels like hell being here." She cries fat tears that roll down her cheeks. "I don't know why, but it all feels far away. Like I don't fit. I feel so lost without her. And I can't let him go because, if I do, then it will feel like none of it was real. Just a distant dream. One I don't want to let go of."

I wrap my arms around her, starting to catch her meaning. "You're both leaving again?"

"Not now." She pulls back to look at me while swiping at the tears then she takes a sip of coffee. "He said he'll wait. You know... my family are so happy to have me back. I don't want to upset them again so soon." She takes another big sip of coffee. "I am sorry, Connie, that I've been avoiding you."

I'm relieved I am not going crazy. "I knew it." I smile. "I'm not just obsessing."

"Oh, you definitely are obsessing." She laughs. "You know, you are both so alike. There must be something in my blood that makes me a glutton for punishment."

"What does that mean?"

"I've been avoiding you because of Peter. He's trying to stay away from you. But obsessive is his middle name too, Connie. You are both here, in the same tiny village, avoiding each other, obsessing about each other, and I am caught in the middle."

"I am not avoiding him." I try to defend myself.

"You told him to fuck off." She laughs.

"Actually, I said fuck you," I correct, smiling.

"Either way. Don't worry, it will only be a matter of time before he gives in and knocks on your door again. You know what he's like." The color rises in my face, and Lorna's eyes turn serious. "Why don't you want the spell? If you don't want to be with him, what have you got to lose?"

"I don't know," I admit. "It's complicated. I suppose there's a part of me that doesn't want to let him go. I wish you weren't leaving. Both of you. I feel like I just got you back. I know there will be an adjustment period—" Lorna's puzzled look stops me, and I ask, "What?"

"Why? Con, you are actually moving on. The sooner we go, the better for you. Having Peter here will only complicate things for you."

"I want him in my life, Lor. He doesn't need to feel like he needs to stay away."

Lorna looks at me hard for a while, opening her mouth before thinking better of whatever she was about to say, and takes another sip of her coffee.

"What?" I push.

"*Connie...*" She draws out my name, looking at the ceiling. "Are you sure about that? I know part of the reason you left was because he gave you no breathing room. You were suffocating, I could see it. I get it. He is intense. Being his friend is intense, let alone his lover. Are you sure you want to invite that back into your life? He doesn't see clearly when it comes to you. What I am trying to say is, he will always lean on you. If you let him."

My breath catches in my throat, a dull ache forming in my chest. While Lorna is right in a sense, all I did was miss him when he was gone.

Lorna looks at me sympathetically before draining the last of her coffee. "Just think carefully about what you really want, Connie. I get the feeling that if you let him back in, there will be no turning back."

I don't press her on quite what she means by that. Peter is different now. Whole. More in control.

While probably a bad idea, it doesn't stop me from calling Peter after Lorna leaves the coffee shop. The spring sky starts to turn dark as I lean against my bike, chewing my lip as the phone rings.

"Hello?"

"Hi, Sally, it's Connie. Is he in?" I ask, not holding much hope. Let's face it, he's probably still up a tree somewhere.

"Sure, honey. Just give me a second."

My heart starts to hammer, so I take a deep centering breath.

I am playing with fire here.

"Hello?" He sounds confused.

"Hi. It's Connie."

"Yeah, I know."

"Right..." I pause. "You do realize we're not doing so great at this being friends thing."

"Mmm... I have noticed."

"How about we give it another try? I'm walking in your direction."

I text my mum that I'm with Lorna and arrive at his house twenty minutes later. He opens the door only in his tracksuit bottoms and I roll my eyes.

Definitely playing with fire, Connie.

At this point, I am making my own life more complicated.

"Can you put some clothes on?"

"Why does it bother you?" he asks but pulls on his hoodie while chuckling. "I just got out of the shower. I thought I best sober up when you called."

"And? Are you?" I ask as I follow him into his kitchen.

He motions with his head. "Sorta." He hops up onto the kitchen counter. "How was Lorna? Did she tell you off?"

My eyes go wide at him. "Yes. Did you tell her to?"

Peter laughs, popping a grape into his mouth. "No. But she's always telling me off, so I figured it was your turn."

"Well, consider me put in my place."

He eyes me up and down. "What did she tell you off about?"

"Erm... for being jealous," I admit, tucking my hair behind my ear. His eyebrows raise in surprise as he eats another grape. "That you've stolen my best friend."

"Oh, right." He throws his next grape at me, but I dodge it. "And not jealous that your best friend is spending time with your ex-boyfriend?"

"Don't flatter yourself." I throw his grape back at him, which he catches and eats.

He chews his thumb for a moment, watching me and for no reason, I feel the color rise in my cheeks.

He hops down from his perch. "I am not good at this, Connie. Being your friend. I don't know if I can."

"Peter..." I groan and edge a little closer to him. "You haven't even tried. Can't you just give it a while?" I look at the floor. "Lorna mentioned you were leaving." I can't keep the hurt out of my voice.

"Not yet." He closes some of the distance between us making him reachable. "We have no plan and no passports. We aren't leaving tomorrow. I am not stealing her," he says gently.

All the coldness I've seen in him is gone, leaving soft, big brown eyes. I shift closer to him. "I don't want *you* to go either. I just got you back in my life."

I can feel the words falling out of my mouth without even meaning them to while inviting him straight back in as Lorna had explicitly warned me not to.

Peter closes his eyes, grimacing. "What are you doing to me?" he asks before he locks his eyes on mine, and all the air leaves the room. He takes a few steps forward, backing me into the corner of the counter, lowering his head so his eyes draw level with my own. "Do you want to know how it feels to be around you again? To have you this close?" His eyes sparkle, rich with desire.

I try to talk, but my mouth is dry, and nothing but a mumble emerges from my throat.

"It feels like being alive again," he whispers, the hunger in his eyes consuming my body before settling on my lips.

His voice is too inviting. It's like velvet I want to wrap myself in and feel the comfort envelop me.

"Do you have any idea of all the things I want to do to you?"

I shake my head infinitesimally, and my breath catches in my throat. The thrill of his words vibrates through me as I grip the hard surface of the counter, turning my knuckles white so I don't dig my nails into him. My skin could be on fire from his radiant heat alone.

Peter moves his right arm across me, blocking my escape and leaving me nowhere to look but into his eyes. His head tilts, inching closer until I can feel his hot breath on my neck. Then his nose ghosts along my jaw, sending a shiver jolting down my spine. "Even the scent of him on you, do you know what that does to me, Connie?"

My body trembles as he brings his face to mine, and I could fall forever into his eyes. I don't know what I will do if he doesn't touch me soon.

His pupils bloom in front of me. "Do you want me to show you? Do you want me to show you right now all of the ways that you are still mine?" His eyes are desperate, so all-consuming, I might pass out.

I still can't answer him.

"Say yes," he whispers, his chest rising against mine. "Don't you miss it? Feeling my skin on yours? Do you miss saying my name? I know I miss it. I miss it so fucking much. Just say yes, Connie."

God, I am so stupid.

I've forgotten how overwhelming Peter is and how much my body craves his. I've lit a match for the purpose of watching the world burn. I close my eyes because there is nothing else to do, our chests rising and falling in time with each other. My lips part to meet his, but he still hasn't touched me, and I think it might kill me.

I can't breathe or think.

I am drowning in him once again.

He makes a hissing noise and, in a flash, he has thought better of it and retreated to the other side of the kitchen. My knees are physically shaking as he pushes his hands through his hair, not daring to look at me, his gaze fixated on the window.

I have no idea where to put myself.

What to think.

My throat is still so damn dry.

"*Connie...*" He draws my name out like he is tasting it. "I'll stick around for as long as Lorna needs, and I promise I won't avoid you if that's what you want. But without that spell, you will get no peace with me here." I can see the pain in his eyes as he turns back toward me. "I can see it written all over you. It is so hard not to have you when I know I could." He rubs his eyes. "If we try to be friends, it's only a matter of time before things blow up between us. So let's just keep it civil and..." he shakes his head, hardly believing his own words, "... keep it public."

I nod and leave, feeling horrible.

As I float home on a river of rejection and guilt, I promise myself he's right, and it is hurting us both to pretend we can be friends. My tears betray that what he's said is for the best.

"Hey. Did you forget I was coming?" Jamie greets me when I get home. "Did you know your mum has gone out on a date?"

"Really?" Although it comes out all wrong, I laugh and hope the air from the ride home has cleared up any evidence I've been crying. "No. I did not know that."

"She was adorable. Like so nervous." He chuckles as I follow him into the kitchen, where it looks like he is cooking dinner.

"What is all of this?" I ask.

"Your mum said you were out with Lorna. I know we made plans, but you know... I know you've been worried about her. I figured you would be hungry when you got home."

My eyes prick with tears, and I close the distance and kiss him, wrapping my arms tightly around him. He returns my kisses. With a little titter as I pull away, he says, "It's only bolognese, Connie. If I'd known this would be your reaction, I would cook for you more often." He moves back to stirring sauce on the stove.

"You've never even entertained the idea that you are too good for me, have you?"

Jamie raises his eyebrows. "What happened?"

"Nothing," I say, wrapping my arms around myself. "Just seeing Lorna. I guess she's doing a lot for Peter at the moment, and that's why she's been absent. It's intense, what is going on with them. And with Anna's passing, they seem to think the answer is at the bottom of

Gemini

a bottle." All lies fall out of my mouth, which shocks me at how easily they escape. I pour myself a big glass of wine, seeming to also find the need to jump on the alcohol train. My opinion of myself couldn't be lower right now.

"Will you stay tonight, Jamie?"

Chapter Twenty-Four

Connie

When Jamie leaves for work the next day, I spend about half an hour in the shower. Just my face under the spray, thinking of nothing but the water on my skin. I have the day off today—a whole day to spend by myself with nothing but my thoughts. I am considering calling Mike to see if I can pick up a shift, but then decide I would rather mope.

Lorna is right.

Peter is right.

He needs to leave.

We *can't* be friends.

I wear a simple black dress and look at myself in the mirror. My dark hair, past my shoulders, now frames my face, which seems utterly sullen today. I smooth my hands along my fuller curves and belly, which is a little softer. I can't concentrate on anything. Even after playing my guitar, I realize I am not playing anymore, just grazing my fingers over the scar on my collarbone.

After a while, I decide to treat myself to a day of doing nothing.

A knock on my front door breaks me out of my reverie. I wonder if Lorna has decided to follow through on her promise to come and see me.

When I open the door, Peter is standing there with his hands against the porch posts, and a giant fake grin is plastered on his face.

I put my hand on my hip. "What are you doing?"

"An apology?" he says through the grin. "Can I come in?"

I open the door for him to enter, and he gives me a wide berth and looks somewhat embarrassed.

"Not so public in here, Peter."

"I know." He drags his feet as he walks into the kitchen, maintaining a safe space between us. "I was way out of line yesterday. I should not have said those things to you. I was drunk, and I am sorry."

I cross my arms, and he leans his elbows on the breakfast bar. "Go on," I tell him.

"Connie, I shouldn't have cornered you like that. It was unfair." He clears his throat, and I shift about, feeling uncomfortable as we both remember what he said.

I nod.

"Connie, I do want to be your friend." He looks at his hands, and seeing him look embarrassed is too much. He is painfully beautiful.

"It's obvious I won't be able to stay away from you. But I won't lie, I don't quite know how to do this."

I let a deep breath out. "I forget how exhausting you are."

He chances a half smile. "This time, it's me who needs to practice being around you. I'm sorry if I've caused you any trouble with Jamie."

"Don't," I say. "I don't want to talk about Jamie with you."

"Okay." He holds his hands up. "Shall I go? Are you annoyed?"

"No, you can stay." I breathe out heavily and move to put the kettle on. "Do you want tea?"

"Sure," he says, looking relieved. "Where is your mum?"

"Oh, she got herself a job. Erm... actually, her and my dad split up." He raises his eyebrows as I move around him. "Yeah, it happened when I was away."

"Shit. Are you okay?"

"Yeah." I give a little wave. "They were barely married anyway. It's been a long time coming, I guess."

He looks down at his hands. "I take it Jamie doesn't know. About the time you've spent with me?"

I look at him out of the corner of my eye. "No. Nor about what you did in India. So, do me a favor and don't mention it to him."

He nods again. "Sure." His eyes stay on me as I pass him his tea. "Con..." he gets up slowly, "... the spell—"

I slam my palm on the counter. "Peter, I *don't* want the spell."

He shrugs, moving a little closer. "It would just make things so much easier. Look at what happened last night. The spell would make it much easier for us to really be friends."

"I said *no*."

"I don't understand. I'm telling you I want to be your friend. I will even stay if it makes you happy. This is a good thing. I want no power over you, Connie. You can move on, really move on. What happened last night was inexcusable. I wouldn't have let it get that far."

I slam my palm down again, furious now. "I don't want to stop loving you, Peter. I want you just as much as you want me."

Peter stops talking.

He opens his mouth to say something but decides against it.

As he looks from me down to his hands, I close my eyes.

Damn! I wish I could take those words back.

I need to put some distance between us again, but as I turn to move away from him, he is also trying to move away, and I collide straight into his chest.

I don't move. Standing here breathing him in, he smells so good. His hands linger on my hips while he decides whether to push me away or not. This is the first time his hands have been on me since he's been back. He draws in a solid intake of breath, waiting for me to move away.

Ever so slowly he moves a hand up my back. I don't breathe. My heart is beating so fast, and I know he can feel it. His hand finds its way into my hair, his fingers entwining with the strands, pulling it back and forcing me to look at him. His dark eyes dance over my face, his breaths heavy, before his eyes settle on my lips. I might die if he doesn't kiss me, so I don't give him a chance to move. My own hands move quickly up to his neck, bringing him to me.

It takes him no time at all to respond by crushing his lips to mine.

The world disappears.

Peter's hands on my hips again, lifting me to wrap my legs around him, placing me on the kitchen counter. His fingers dig into my legs as he pushes my dress up. I am all sensation as one of his thumbs drags down the soft skin of my inner thigh, his other hand on my throat. We are all heat and hands and messy in our desire for each other. I wrap myself tightly around him, feeling him, feeling what I am doing to him, lifting his T-shirt over his head.

His hands are on my hips again, and his lips on my throat.

There is no stopping.

No going back.

I only want him.

My legs are like jelly, and my hands shake as I collect the shards of the teacup from the floor. I hadn't even heard the cup smash, too wrapped up in him to notice we knocked it off the counter.

Peter is kneeling at my side, mopping up the spilled tea, but his eyes are intently on me. "Are you okay?"

"Erm..." I don't know how I feel. My body tingles, but my brain is an absolute mess. I throw the broken cup into the bin and turn to look at Peter. "I'm not sure."

His large eyes are full of vulnerability once again. I guess he's waiting for me to tell him to leave, but instead, I hand him his T-shirt.

"Con," he says wearily, pulling his top on. "I'm sorry. I shouldn't have kissed you."

"I think I kissed you, actually."

"I should have stopped. This is on me."

"Peter, it was a bit more than a kiss. It's on me as well."

I run a shaky hand across my face, noticing that not only is his T-shirt inside out but also backward. I laugh. A big, bad god in my kitchen with his T-shirt on backward, looking totally adorable and waiting for me to blow my top.

I ping his label, smiling. "You look ridiculous," I tell him.

He looks down, chuckles, then he rectifies his mistake. "Do you want to pretend that didn't happen?"

"Peter." I sink my head into my hands on the counter. "Ouch!" Glancing down, my foot is starting to ooze red. I must have missed a bit of teacup.

"Let me get that." Peter motions, kneeling and lifting my foot to remove the shard. He carefully runs his finger down the cut, a slight golden glow emitting from his fingertip. "There, good as new." He smiles up at me, his hand sliding up from my foot and wrapping around my ankle. His smile fades as he bites his lip, tugging me toward him.

Sighing, I think, *I am in so much trouble.*

"Peter. You need to go."

Once he's left, I frantically clean the kitchen until all traces of my bloody foot are gone, taking extra care with the spot where I'd had sex with Peter. The same place where, only the night before, Jamie had cooked me dinner.

Afterward, I get back in the shower.

I feel sick with myself. After everything, I am doing the one thing I didn't want to do—hurt Jamie. I need to tell him. But, of course, a part of me thinks we could pretend it didn't happen. Maybe Jamie doesn't have to know.

That is a horrible idea. You cannot treat someone you care about like that.

I pull out my phone, then chicken out, instead texting Jamie that I don't feel well and he shouldn't come around tonight.

Gemini

Jamie: *I hope it wasn't the bolognese!*

His reply makes my heart hurt.

Faking a bad stomach is also a good reason for staying in my room and avoiding my mum.

We're going to pretend it didn't happen, Connie. Go back to the public places plan. Avoid being alone with him. Avoid thinking about him and how good he feels. Avoid how it feels to wrap myself around him, for him to give himself totally to me. Avoid the feeling of him coming undone and how he bit down on my shoulder. On my kitchen counter. Definitely don't think about that.

I squeeze my eyes shut, but even my dreams betray me—they are filled with Peter.

When I wake up for a second, I'm disappointed he isn't here. Something seems off, so I check my clock—it's a little after midnight. Phew. At least I'm not dreaming anymore. Then I hear the tiny *click* on the glass.

I jump out of bed, opening my window wide to stare down at Peter standing there, his hands in his pockets.

"Want to come for a walk?"

"Not really," I reply with a hint of a smile.

Totally back to square one.

He moves back a few paces. "Shouldn't we, I don't know, talk about it? You seemed freaked out earlier. Are you rethinking the friends bit?"

"Are you?" I whisper back.

"Can't you come down?"

I shake my head and motion for him to come up, then stand back from the window. But he doesn't come up. I peek my head back out to see him still on the ground, walking in a little circle. I swear he is talking to himself.

"Are you coming up or not?"

He looks up, hesitating for a second before moving to the trellis.

A few moments later, he's in my room, standing over me but not too close. He looks around at the familiar room, his gaze lingering on my bed before settling his eyes on me. "This probably isn't a good idea."

"I feel awful," I whisper.

He nods, moving to sit in my computer chair. "I'm sorry. Look, whatever you want to do, I'll go along with it. Jamie doesn't have to know. We can be friends. I promise it won't happen again. Or, if you want me to go, then I can go."

I stay rooted on the spot. "Why are you being so nice?"

He puts his hands in his pockets. "Because I love you," he says toward the floor.

I take a deep breath. "And I love you," I whisper, watching him rise to stand in front of me.

"Tell me what you want, Connie. You just have to tell me, and you can have it."

"You," I say simply. "I want you."

He runs his thumb along my jaw. "I miss you so much," he murmurs before his lips find mine.

I clutch onto his arms, holding him flush to my chest. I want him so much it hurts. Squeezing my eyes, tears escape their corners because I know I shouldn't be doing this. Not like this. But he feels so good. He is mine, and I don't know how to say no. I can't let him go. I just need to learn to live with the fire, with his impossible heat, because I need him.

I need him as much as he needs me.

When I wake, the bright spring morning is shining in through my window. Although it feels like the height of summer with Peter's possessive arm wrapped across my chest. *This is where I'm supposed to be.* I wiggle around so I'm facing him and can't fight my smile. It feels like no time has passed as it's the most normal thing for him to be here.

"It's just too easy, isn't it?" he says without opening his eyes.

"Mmm..." is all I respond with, but I hold him closer while placing kisses along his collarbone.

"I thought you would be kicking me out," he states with some surprise, opening his eyes to look at me for the first time this morning.

"Not yet." I giggle. "Peter, when I said I wanted you, I didn't mean for the night. I meant I want you back."

He props himself up on his elbow, looking elated but a bit confused. "Really? I'm so sorry about what happened with Sorcha and everything. I screwed up so bad. But you want me back? Really?"

I shake my head a little. "I should never have left. Sorcha got into my head."

Peter dips his head and kisses my neck, starting at my ear and trailing down, sending goose bumps everywhere. "Never again. I should've talked to you."

"Peter?" I start, a thought occurring to me—a painful one. "Lorna told me about what you did."

"Hmm... you will have to be more specific." His lips are on my earlobe again.

I push him back to look at me so I won't get distracted. "That you tried to, um... take your own life. Do you still feel that way?" I whisper.

He smooths the hair from my face, looking a little sad. "You know about that?"

I nod.

"Do you think I am pathetic?"

I shake my head, waiting for him to continue.

"No. I don't feel that way anymore. It's complicated. I still feel like the same messed-up kid who lived outside, has no idea what he is doing, and is scared of being alone." He looks down. "But, at the same time, when Anna died, a lot of things shifted into place. So much *balance*. She wanted to live while I wanted to die. A cruel joke, right? How, when she died, I stopped feeling that way."

I take his face to force him to look at me, my heart aching for him. "Peter, I am so sorry."

"There is something wrong with me, Connie. There is a part of me, a small part, that is glad she died and took those feelings with her. I miss her so much, but I also never want to feel those things again. How we were split, I didn't realize all of the madness I felt was just the absence of her. How do I reconcile that?"

"No one can understand all you have lost. I don't judge you for your feelings. I know you loved her more than anything."

I pull him closer, and he shifts his weight on top of me, pushing my hair back as I wrap my leg around him.

"Peter, you're with me, right? You are not going to leave me?"

He frowns, looking like he is going to say something else, but I'm distracted by my mother calling my name up the stairs, followed by the sound of her footsteps ascending.

"Connie, I am leaving for work now. Just wanted to check that you—"

I cut her off, calling out, "Mum, I'm fine. You don't need—"

But it's too late.

My bedroom door swings open, leaving us no more time than for Peter to jump to his feet so my mother doesn't catch him actually between my legs. Rather, he's standing in the middle of my room with half a duvet wrapped around his waist, me clutching the other half to me.

"P-Peter?" she stammers.

I don't think she has seen him once since he and Lorna arrived back.

She plants her hands on her hips, and her face goes beet red.

I brace myself, but instead, Peter holds up a hand to her.

"Shh, Mrs. Prinze." He smiles his most charming smile. "It's okay. There is no reason to get mad. Don't you remember? You saw me come in this morning? You opened the door. I came to check how Connie was. She was really ill last night, wasn't she?"

My mother looks a bit confused but nods her head.

"Luckily, she is feeling so much better. A good night's sleep works wonders, right?" He lowers his arm. "Why don't you get on your way to work now? Oh, and Mrs. Prinze, don't tell anybody I was here, okay?"

Mum shuts the door, and I stare at Peter, who is putting his boxers on, not meeting my eye.

"Did you just fully Jedi mind trick my mother?" I laugh.

"Like I said, the focus is insane, Connie." He shakes his head. "How else do you think we got on the plane?"

"You Jedi-ed your way onto the plane?"

Peter regards me. "I have no idea what you are talking about. What's a Jedi? But, yes, I mind-controlled our way onto the plane, although it was a lot sketchier than what you just saw. I think Lorna took about four Valium."

"Show me."

Peter's eyes widen as he pulls on his jeans. "Con, you are the last person I would do that to."

I pout. "Why are you putting your clothes on?"

He drops his T-shirt back onto the floor. "Erm... I just assumed that I should get going." He motions to the window.

I roll my eyes at him. "You can't climb out of the window in broad daylight. My mum is about to leave. Just walk out the front door like a human being when she's gone." I roll up onto my knees to face him. "Besides, I'm not done with you yet."

His dark eyes flash as he kneels, planting his legs to either side of me. "Is that a fact?" He grins, his fingers tracing down my back, emitting the slightest electric currents from his fingertips.

"Mmm..." I arch my back into him. "That feels good. How come you didn't do that last night? Before."

"I don't need to anymore," he says quietly as I move my hands up his chest.

"What if I wanted you to? What if I want you to do that to me?"

He makes a small noise of satisfaction, grabbing onto my hair and kissing my neck again. "It's bad for you, Connie." His breath comes hot in my ear.

I'm about to say something smart about knowing what is bad for me, but he doesn't give me the chance. He pulls my hair back, kissing me hard on the mouth. The kind of kiss that makes me forget my own name. His legs keep me pinned, leaving me nothing else to do but return the kiss, driving my nails hard down his back.

"Con, I brought you soup—"

It takes me three seconds to realize someone else is in my room. My brain barely registering, I only feel Peter turn around.

He takes one look at who it is and says, "You have got to be joking," before moving off me.

Jamie's eyes flick from me to Peter like he's not sure who to scream at first.

I catch Peter giving me a probing look, as if asking permission to Jedi Jamie too, but I shake my head a fraction. This is the worst possible outcome, but I can't do that to Jamie—

just make him forget—that would be even more horrible than what he's walked in on.

"So, I made you soup, Con." *That's what he settles on?* "Although, I am assuming now you being ill is a lie, right?"

"I should go." Peter scoops his discarded T-shirt up off the floor again.

I nod my head, my heart firmly lodged in my throat. I have no possible defense for what Jamie has just seen, but he holds out his arm to stop Peter.

"No. Why don't you stay, Peter?" Some of the old Jamie malice creeps back into his voice. "Perhaps both of you can explain what the *hell* is going on here."

Peter flaps his arms by his sides. "Come on, man, you're not blind. Do you need me to spell it out?"

I shoot Peter a warning glance that this is not the time.

"Yes, I slept with Connie. What more is there to say?" He gives him a sly smile, tracing his fingers over his lips. "Do you want me to describe how she tastes? Does she taste sweet, like honey, to you too, Jamie?"

"Peter," I admonish and reach out to slap his arm.

Jamie turns a shade of purple as he rounds on me. "Has this been going on the whole time?"

"No, Jay—"

"Since when?"

I look back at Peter, who has made the wise decision to keep quiet and follow my lead.

"Since when, Connie?"

"Yesterday," I say, my voice barely above a whisper and full of shame.

"Yesterday," he repeats. "So, when you canceled your plans with me, it was because you were making them with him?" His accusing eyes stay on me, the comprehension dawning there. "Oh, I see. That is why you canceled them." He rubs his head. "I am such an idiot. That night when you came home and asked me to stay, you hadn't been with Lorna, had you?"

"No, I had. I'd been with her, but I did see Peter too. Nothing happened that night. I promise."

"Why? Why ask me to stay? You were with him, what? Hours after I left yesterday? Seriously, that's sick, Connie." He looks at Peter. "Did you know? That she was with me yesterday morning?"

Peter's jaw clenches.

"You know what, don't answer that. You probably get off on that kind of thing."

"Jay, please. I am so sorry. I didn't want you to find out like this." My eyes well up with tears. "I'm sorry. I can't help myself with him."

Jamie turns back to me. "That is bullshit, Connie," he spits out. "You don't *want* to help yourself with him. You are just as bad as he is. All you think about is yourself."

"Hey, that is enough now."

Peter steps toward Jamie, but I push him back.

"You know what?" Jamie looks between the two of us. "You two deserve each other." He storms out of the room, slamming the door and making me jump a mile before I sink onto the bed and bury my head in my hands.

I feel nauseous.

That could not have gone any worse.

Peter sits next to me.

"*Describe how she tastes.* Really? What the hell was that about?" I turn on him.

"I know." He looks up at the ceiling. "It was a shitty thing to say. I just don't think I should have to explain myself to him."

"Well, *I* certainly should. I'm the one in the wrong here."

Peter studies me for a minute. "Do you want me to go find him? I could..." he searches for the words, "... make him think it was a dream or something."

"No. It's better that he knows." I sigh. "It's just... I wish I could have done it better. You know... spoken to him first and not put him through seeing it firsthand. Turns out you're not the only terrible thing in this room." I laugh a humorless laugh.

"You are a good person, Connie." Peter wraps his arm around me. "It's me. What does Lorna call me? A walking catastrophe. I love you, but a life with me will never be easy. I don't know if I can do that to you."

"Peter..." I look up into his eyes, pushing my hands into his hair. "I believe in the good in you."

"How can you say that?" He moves away from me, rubbing his hands over his face. "I committed mass murder, I killed my own father, my own grandmother. I literally snapped Kali's neck with my bare hands. How can you live with that, Connie? Listen, my bad decisions will follow you everywhere."

He moves to stand at the window. "When Anna died, it felt like the earth shifted. Amongst all that destruction, I realized I had decided to stop fighting it, what I am. To not hate it anymore, to accept it, to understand there is a big part of me that does enjoy it, the destruction I can cause. I'm not proud of what I did, Connie. I am not proud of killing those people or destroying that city. But do I regret it?" He looks back at me. "No, I don't think I do. I do care that my sister died, I definitely care Lorna was traumatized, I care that I did that to her, and I care about you. I swear I would burn the world down for you. But—"

I cut off his flow. "I get it now," I say, the realization dawning on me. What this is all about. "The spell. The reason why you've been pushing it. It's for you. You will never believe I love you, will you? You will never be able to let it go. Every bad thing I do, you will blame yourself."

He sits beside me again. "I am too selfish to let you go, though. I can't do it until you send me away. I will love you, always."

"Okay. I'll do it," I say, taking his hand, my stomach doing a little flip at the thought. "I will do the spell, and when it works and this control you think you have is over... when I still love you... this ends, Peter. You accept it, okay? I get to decide what's best for me. My bad decisions are to be my own."

So this is it.

Our fate is in the hands of the spell, the one I've never wanted. But the one we need to risk in order to be together. For us both to know, once and for all. It's a strange thought, knowing my feelings might not be my own, but I feel sure I do love him, really love him. Yet that small voice still sounds at the back of my mind, especially after seeing him with my mum.

What if he does the spell and I forget this feeling?

That feeling of wanting someone so much it hurts.

I must've been cleaning the same spot on the coffee shop counter for about twenty minutes because I keep zoning out.

What will happen if the spell lifts and I don't love him? Will I forget the last two years? Will I feel like I have been a prisoner?

"Hey," a familiar voice says.

I look up to see Lorna smiling at me over the counter.

"You looked a million miles away."

"Sorry. A lot on my mind. What can I get you?" Lorna looks like a different person from the one I first saw when they got back. Maybe a little slimmer, but back to her pristine exterior.

"I know," she says as she peruses the cake stand. "He sent me to check on you."

"So you know what happened?" I ask.

"Yep. I'm not here to judge." She leans her elbows onto the counter. "Besides, Peter glossed over all of the Jamie stuff. He focused more on you wanting him back and agreeing to the spell. I'm not sure if he is happy or terrified. How are you?"

"I don't know. It's been a wild twenty-four hours." I chuckle nervously.

"Welcome back to the life." She grins.

"I feel so bad. I don't know if Jamie will ever forgive me. I haven't tried to call him yet. I'm thinking he needs some time to cool down." I start busying myself, making a cinnamon latte for Lorna, her eyes following me.

"I wouldn't expect too much from him, Con."

"I know." I exhale a large breath. "I went about everything wrong. I never should have let things go so far. I was kidding myself. I used him for comfort. Our friendship was doomed the second I let that happen."

"Well, I can think of one other person who has made such a lapse in judgment." She casts me a wicked glance.

I don't say anything, only give her a bit of a glare. "So, if he's not with you, where is he?"

"Getting supplies for the spell." She takes the drink from me. "Can I have a blueberry muffin too? How do you feel about that? I know you never really wanted it."

I hand her the pastry. "No. But he will always be paranoid if I don't. I feel like I need to do this to move past what happened before. But, I don't know... I can't not be nervous. I don't feel like I am under anything, but..." I look around to check no one is in earshot, "... I saw him do it to my mum this morning, and it was *insane*. Like full Jedi."

Lorna's eyes go wide. "It's weird. I've seen him doing some crazy stuff but watching that gets me every time. My heart would stop."

"He said he got you onto the plane."

"Yep." Lorna leans in closer. "No passports, nothing."

"How?"

"When we left Varanasi, I was in full-on panic mode. Everything was left behind in the chaos. Peter had kind of calmed down by then and started to realize I wasn't okay. So he asked me what I wanted to do. At the time, I wanted to be somewhere familiar, so I said we had to get home. I was panicking that all of our money was gone, we had no phones, and we had no passports. Anyway, he just was like, 'Don't worry, I'm going to get you back.' I think he was glad for something to do. And it started from there. We would get on a bus and Peter would push me on, and when someone asked if we'd paid, he would say, 'Yes, we already paid,' or someone would ask for a ticket, and Peter would say something like, 'Oh, we don't need one,' and they'd simply accept his word. But as we got closer to the airport, I knew he was getting nervous about getting us through security and on the plane. But somehow, it all worked. It's like an illusion direct from *Star Wars*. Honest to God, "These aren't the droids you're looking for" shit. But even his nerves were shot by the time we were on the flight, and we must've drunk every miniature they had." Lorna laughs. "When we got through customs and on the other side, he literally walked into duty-free, picked up that bottle of tequila, told them he was taking it and walked out."

It takes me a minute to let it sink in. "That is nothing like before."

"No. A lot has changed." She laughs again. "I know he still doesn't like it, the influence. He only did all of that to get us home, me home rather."

I give her a hard look. "What do you think, Lor? About the spell?"

"Yikes. Don't ask me that, Con. I don't know anything about magic."

"No, but you know me better than anyone. And you seem to get him, like... really get him. So, what do you think?"

"Connie, I don't know." She takes my hand across the counter. "I didn't really know what was going on with you when you two first got together." I can see her weighing things up in her head before she smiles. "I do believe he did *not* make you love him. I think you fell for him all on your own, Constance Prinze. I saw the twinkle in your eye way back then. I think you loved that boy who was full of mystery, who played right into that imagination of yours, who always indulged you and encouraged your wild streak that never really saw the light of day before."

It's a nice thought.

I bite my lip. "Lor, will you cover for me tonight?"

She looks a little confused but agrees. I pull out my phone and text my mum that I won't be home tonight and am staying at Lorna's.

For some reason, I feel nervous. The spring evening is fresh and quiet, only turning dark as I reach his house.

When I knock on the door, Sally answers with a look of surprise.

"Is he in?" I ask, unsure why my heart is pounding.

She nods. "He's upstairs. Do you want me to call him?"

Peter probably heard my heart beating from the drive as he appears at the top of the stairs looking a bit dirty. "Are you okay?" he asks, dusting his hands. "I've been sorting Sally's garden out. I was just about to take a shower."

I nod because, like usual, my mouth is dry. "Can I come up?"

Peter glances toward Sally. She opens the door to let me in, and I follow Peter upstairs to his room. I've forgotten how small it is. Seemingly even smaller with Peter in it, dressed in all black, with dirt smudged over his face. He's glorious with his perfect tanned skin and sun-kissed golden hair, which is scruffy enough to be adorable.

I take two steps closer to him, enough to see the spattering of freckles over his nose, and gaze into his deep, big brown eyes. *You need to remember this, Connie, how perfect he is to you.*

"Are you scared?" I whisper. "For tomorrow?"

"Terrified." He smiles, cupping my face with his hand.

I lean into it, closing my eyes so I don't look at him when I say it. Trying to call upon the side of me only he knows, I take a deep breath. "Peter, if this is it, if this is our last night, then I don't want to spend it apart." I open my eyes to look into his. "I want to feel every second. I want you in every possible way." I feel myself trembling. "I don't want to forget. So make it count." I give a short nod. "I don't want my feet to touch the ground."

I wait for him to talk, to say something, but he doesn't. Ever so slowly, he lowers his mouth to mine, taking his time to savor the way I taste. He pushes me into the wall and removes my hands from the back of his neck to press them hard above my head, keeping me pinned, kissing me. It all feels like a dream.

My body shudders in anticipation at what even I know is only the beginning.

Chapter Twenty-Five

Peter

"Peter! We are so late." Connie is shaking me awake, and it takes me a minute to realize I'm outside as I see bright blue sky through the trees above me. "I can't find my shoes," she says in a panic.

"They'll be around somewhere." I get to my feet, stretching out my back and watching her. She looks pretty funny walking around the woods barefoot, frantically scouring for her shoes while only wearing her leggings and my hoodie. Her silky hair is all ruffled and filled with leaves.

"We told Lorna we'd meet her half an hour ago, and my phone just ran out of battery." She looks around. "Where even are we?"

"Not far from my old house."

She straightens as she takes me in for the first time this morning, putting her hands on her hips. "How do you do that?"

"Do what?" I make my way over to her.

"Look so good."

I laugh because she actually sounds upset.

"You look beautiful," I tell her, picking a leaf from her hair. "I

Gemini

hate to tell you this, but we need to go back to mine first. We've got to get the stuff for the spell."

Connie makes a face.

"And I will need this back." I tug on the front of the hoodie, pulling her toward me. "I don't think I'll fit into your shirt."

Connie pouts but lets me pull her into a kiss. In the end, she is so stressed about being late that we abandon the search for her shoes, and I carry her piggyback to mine and then all the way back to her house. She spends a good five minutes moaning over how she loved those boots. Not that I mind. It's a small price to pay—I've always enjoyed Connie outside.

After a while, she seems to have gotten over it and is happy to chat away in my ear, making me laugh. It feels so normal, so natural, to be with her. She starts giving me requests to test how she prefers to be carried. We try a fireman's lift, her least favorite. Carried like a princess, which I quite like. But we finally go back to piggyback as we round up on her house where Lorna is sitting on the step, waiting for us.

"I have been waiting for over an hour." Lorna stomps toward us, her eyes narrowed.

"Sorry," we say in unison.

Lorna gives Connie—still wrapped around my back—a funny look. "Where have you been? What happened to your shoes, Con?" she asks, sounding more confused than anything.

"Don't ask," Connie replies as I lower her onto the porch.

Lorna raises her eyebrow at me as I struggle to wipe the smile off my face, giving her a small shrug.

"Let's have a drink first. I am so thirsty."

"Peter." Connie shrieks after catching her reflection in the hallway in horror, turning to me as she points at her leaf-strewn head. "You carried me halfway across the village like this?"

"You were in a rush," I say, struggling not to laugh. "Besides, we only saw, like, a handful of people. I am sure they were looking at your feet and not your head."

"Ugh." She stomps her feet, struggling to remove the leaves.

Lorna helps her while also laughing.

"I'll make the drinks," I tell her.

"No, you won't," she calls after me. "I've tasted your tea, and it's rubbish."

I laugh, rolling my eyes. "Fine. You and your tea. I'll start getting things set up."

I place my backpack on the side. Starting to unpack the supplies brings me back to the task at hand. One thing has not changed about me—my weak stomach. I feel nauseous over what I'm about to do, so I try and steady myself. I could just enjoy Connie, for say, the next ten years. She would still have a chance at a normal life from then on. She'd only be thirty, still plenty of time to start a family. Ten good years together. But I am lying to myself if I think I could ever let her go, even if she wished me gone. I'd always be lurking somewhere, looking for any reason to go back to her.

It's better to do this, despite the risks.

Better to know for both of us.

"Everything okay?" she asks as she comes into the kitchen.

I'm standing with my hands braced against the counter, my head hung between my shoulder blades. I tilt my head up and attempt to give her a comforting grin, but I am afraid that it comes out more of a grimace.

"So how did you get the spell?" Lorna follows her in, leaning against a cupboard.

"Kali," I tell her as I continue to unpack.

Connie starts making tea while Lorna twirls a sprig of hawthorn between her fingers, glancing up at me.

"When did she tell you that?"

I meet Lorna's eyes only for a second. I forgot I hadn't told her and Anna.

"Before," I say, taking out the last of the hawthorn. "Before the hemlock, I asked her for it."

Connie's eyes flick between us. "What's hemlock?"

Gemini

"Nothing," I say with a tad too much haste, and Connie opens her mouth to argue, so I cut her off. "It's what I was taking before I lost my mind and killed everyone, right before Anna died."

Connie opens and closes her mouth like a goldfish, and Lorna is busy checking her fingernails. We've not gotten around to speaking about that week. It's something I don't want to think about. "Con..." I breathe out, knowing she won't let it go. "Before Anna died, the coven was working a spell to bind me again, like my mother did when I was a baby. To make the spell stick, I had to be weakened. They were doing it with poison, which I was taking willingly. Can we leave it there?"

Connie looks between the two of us again, detecting this is a subject neither Lorna nor myself want to relive. It's clear it bothers her a little that Lorna and I now have experiences connecting us. Events, no matter how traumatic that she is not part of.

"So, the binding spell?" she hedges.

"There is no chance it would work now," I clarify. "It probably never would have. I would've killed the coven no matter what." My voice comes out matter-of-fact, and only I can feel the tremors in it. I take Lorna's hawthorn from her, twirling it myself for a moment, allowing it to blossom a bit more. Despite what I said to Connie before, I would rather be creation than destruction. "Do you have bowls? We need bowls, with water in them, and probably somewhere with more space than in here."

We set up in the living room. They watch me pour water into four bowls, three of them forming a triangle with the last in the center. Shaking the hawthorn flowers into each one, I place a clear quartz crystal in the center. They remind me a little of my sister when she was with Lorna.

Connie and Lorna ask so many questions.

"It's just plain water?" Connie asks.

"Yes," I answer. "Just regular water. It's a universal constant."

"What does that mean?"

"Kind of like a natural lubricant. Needed for life, transporting in death." *I don't know how to explain it.* "Just water."

"And the crystals?" Lorna asks. "What are they?"

"Clear quartz," I reply. "Gives clarity, purifying for the soul."

Lorna nudges into Connie and teases her. "You have a dirty soul." She giggles.

"I think that's it," I tell them.

"Is that all?" Connie looks around at the bowls.

"I know the words, or chant. Usually, it would need more people, but I have more than enough magic to do it by myself." I move Connie to the center of the triangle, put a bowl into her hands, and turn her to face me.

"Lorna." I motion for her to move behind Connie and take my hands, then look back at Connie. "Kali taught me in Hindi, so you won't understand." I give her a smile. "Try not to laugh at my singing."

"I promise," she says, her face serious now. Her heart rate picks up, and mine does too. I recall the words Kali taught me, along with my grandmother's gentle face. Without realizing, a tear rolls down my cheek, and I try hard not to think about Kali or Mahi as Connie smooths the tear away.

I shake off the emotions and begin to chant—half chant, half sing—gripping onto Lorna's fingers and starting to feel the vibrations. My words lifting, a faint glow emits from the crystals as the cleansing energy rises from them, twisting beautifully into the air like radiant vines. It must be something to do with me. My magic takes on vine form, earth being the element I am most in tune with.

The vines twist their way toward Connie. In nearing her, they change form, transforming into small bobbing orbs, like dancing fairies. With a sudden *whoosh*, they speed straight into her, through her eyes, morphing from white light to a green that matches her eye color, before the light dies down and Connie stumbles back into Lorna.

Connie doubles over, rubbing at her eyes, attempting to peel them open. Lorna lets go of me and holds onto Connie, rubbing her back.

"Connie, are you okay?"

"My head." She still hasn't been able to prize open her eyes. "My eyes feel sore. Like I haven't opened them in ages."

I crouch down in front of her, steadying her shoulder. "Open your eyes, Connie. Let me see you."

She blinks her eyes open, taking a moment to focus on my face.

"How do you feel?" I ask, my heart in my throat.

She looks a bit dazed, but her lips begin to stretch into a smile. "I feel... like I still love you."

I don't waste a second. I push my lips up to hers, lifting her off the ground. Relief doesn't even come close as she laughs and returns my kiss, wrapping her legs around me.

"You really love me?"

"I really love you." She beams in a half giggle.

I kiss her again. Almost two years of guilt and paranoia melt away. *It wasn't all a lie. She really is mine, mine for good this time.*

"Erm... guys. Still here." Lorna coughs.

"Sorry," I say, dropping Connie to her feet but not wiping the smile off my face.

"It's okay." Lorna relents. "This is good, but let's take a second." She pulls Connie toward the sofa and makes her sit down. "Con, talk. Do you feel any different?"

Connie looks from Lorna to me. "Yes. I feel different."

I move and kneel next to her, waiting for her to go on.

She gazes at me. "I definitely love you, like crazy love you. I am so happy I remember everything. In a way, I think I love you more now." She traces her fingers down my face, and I can't hold back my surprise.

"What do you mean, now?" I ask. "You mean, I influenced you to love me less?"

Her face is radiant as she takes the biggest sigh of relief before answering, "It's hard to explain. It feels so weird. I guess, yes, in a way. It's like you have this way of making people forget what you don't want them to remember. Like, I didn't have any head space for anything other than you." She looks to Lorna. "We always forgot there were people at home. It's like that. Like not being able to remember what day of the week it is. I think even time passes differently around you." She laughs again.

I see Lorna blink twice, and my stomach sinks a little. "You think I have it too?" Lorna asks.

"I am almost certain of it. But it's not how you think. I'm not saying you are in love with him, Lor. You love him in a different way," Connie says, her expression light. "It's not a bad thing." She takes my hand, seeing my rising panic.

Anna was right. I infect everything.

"It's not a bad thing, Peter. I think it only works for the people you care about, and the people who care about you in return."

I glance over at Lorna, who is also looking a bit panicked. "We could do the spell again. For you, this time," I offer, but Connie pulls hard on my arm.

"Peter, I'm telling you, it's not a bad thing. You have never made me feel anything I didn't already feel." She sinks onto her knees beside me, her eyes brimming with tears. "I can tell you, now, all the things you *did* do that I couldn't see before. You saved my life, you pulled my bones back together when they were broken, and I never really said thank you. You soaked up so much of my grief so I wouldn't be in pain when I lost my friend."

She looks over to Lorna. "And I know you are doing the same for her, even though it was your sister you both lost, which must hurt you more than anything. You've been everything I ever needed, I ever wanted. Peter, for all of us, you become what we need. It wasn't control, Peter. It was comfort. You're not so terrible. I know there is this whole side of you that you don't want me to see, but believe me, I see you, all of you. Even the ugly side. And I love all of you."

I don't have any words, nothing to say that will do what she has said any justice. So I just kiss her. A simple, slow kiss.

Gemini

She takes my face in her hands. "We do this, Peter, and it's fifty-fifty, okay? Me and you. No more secrets, no more lies."

"Okay." I nod. "No more secrets." I lean my arm up onto the sofa to look at Lorna, feeling a tiny bit awkward. "So, what do you think? You want to do the spell?"

Lorna waves her hand in the air. "Nah, I would rather not risk having to make such a speech to you. I'll stick with the comfort for now."

"Okay." I let a deep breath out, giving her a half smile. I almost don't know what to do next. The relief is so intense I could practically sleep for a week.

Now what? Do I dare believe that, despite everything, despite of what I have done, I now have what I want?

I look back into Connie's glittering green eyes, the smile stretching across my face. She mirrors it while threading her fingers into mine.

Here's to happy ever after.

Chapter Twenty-Six

Connie

The clarity of real life is even more dreamlike than the gentle haze Peter's influence kept me under. What he is was always at the fringes of my mind, while never giving too much thought to the creature lying deep within. These days, it is all too easy to see it. Sometimes, when he looks at me, I see just a flash—a devilish glint in his eyes—the thrill of danger knowing he could destroy me in a heartbeat. Under the light of the moon, in the darkest part of the night, I like to imagine that beast when his fingers are wrapped around mine and hold fast to the knowledge, the certainty, that his heart is mine. I own the heart of a creature capable of such terrible things.

He has woken something in myself I'd never recognized before, a desire. To revel in it. To let go. To be consumed.

It's still hard to concentrate.

On particular on days like these, when I'm working and Lorna is busy, Peter hangs around the coffee shop, being distracting. Not like he has to do much. We've discovered the only way he likes coffee is black, which is fine, but it does make him extra chatty. So he gabs away to me about whatever is coming to his mind, sometimes slipping into his twin language where I can't quite catch all he's saying because he is talking so fast.

He's slipped into a habit of taking my cloth from me across the counter and wiping down the tables. Lucky for me, Mike is pretty chill about Peter hanging around all the time and thinks it's quite funny to say I have him wrapped around my little finger and doing half my job for me. Mike says he is fine with Peter being here as long as he doesn't scare off the customers. And yet, I've begun noticing we always seem to be busier when he is around. Eyes gravitate toward him. Not women alone—it's everyone. They all watch him.

"So, I've been thinking about your birthday," he leans over the counter and says when the queue has died down.

"My birthday was two months ago," I remind him.

"I know, and I missed it. Plus, I missed the previous two. I've never really celebrated birthdays before, so, I was thinking I should make it up to you."

"And how do you propose that?" I smile at him, dropping my elbows to the counter to slide closer.

"Paris," he whispers, leaning in. "Let me take you to Paris. Let's go, next week. You and me, a luxury king-sized bed, in a room with a view of the Eiffel tower and lots of champagne."

I giggle. "It's a nice thought, but we don't have that kind of money."

"Connie, I have money. I still have loads left from the house. I just got my passport back. You've always wanted to go."

"You should save your money. I doubt anyone will ever give you a job."

"Con." He catches my hand, bringing me in closer. "I could rob a bank tomorrow and no one would care."

"You are *not* going to rob a bank."

"No." He moves his face closer to mine. "But I could definitely 'talk' us into a five-star hotel."

"Really?"

He nods, biting on his lip. "Say yes. Let me take you to Paris."

I feel the color flood into my face as I nod. I don't make a habit of kissing him at work, but I make an exception and pull him across the counter, getting a few whoops from the patrons, sending me even redder.

Peter laughs. "Okay, I will book us flights." He holds up his new phone. "On this thing. And we will figure out the rest when we get there."

"Is that a good idea? Shouldn't we book ahead."

"That is a benefit of understanding every language on the planet," he says absentmindedly, trying to work out his phone. "You can kind of wing it wherever you go. Can I have another coffee?"

"Absolutely not." I laugh. "You cannot handle your caffeine."

The bell of the door rings, and we both glance over to see Jamie walk in with Lauren. I haven't seen Jamie since he stormed out of my house over a month ago. I texted him once to apologize but never heard anything back.

Peter puts a bit of distance between us and says, "Do you think I should go?"

I shake my head. "No, but maybe you could go and sit down," I whisper as I hand him a bottle of water. I've made the mistake of giving him too much coffee before, and I do not fancy another sleepless night of Peter jitters with him explaining to me the push and pull of Io. I glance at him and try not to be unnerved by the fact he can feel the moons volcanic explosions all the way from Jupiters orbit. He takes a seat at the front of the café, returning his attention to his phone.

Jamie motions to a table for Lauren to sit and approaches the counter, making my heart hammer. Peter glances up at me. It's a little unsettling how he will forever more know when I am nervous. Jamie doesn't look happy, but I doubt he'll cause a scene where I work. He's had almost a month to cool off.

"Hi." I try to sound normal, but it sounds forced.

Jamie motions to Lauren. "Lauren wanted to come in. I wouldn't have come in otherwise."

Gemini

"That's okay. You don't have to avoid this place. Jay, I'm so sorry. I've wanted to call so many times and say how sorry I am. You were right. I was being selfish. I should never have let things get that far between us."

"Right," he says, deadpan.

"What can I get you?" I ask, now desperate to be busy.

Jamie places his order, which I try to be quick about making, as he glances back to Peter, who is engrossed with his phone.

"So, it's all official then? You two are back together? All is forgiven?"

I nod.

Jamie looks down at the counter. "So, the killing you thing? That isn't true? It won't kill you being with him?"

I look at him softly. "No, he's not hurting me."

Jamie dips his head a fraction.

"Jamie—"

"I can't, Connie," he cuts me off, his blue eyes filled with sadness. "I can't be there for you again. There is no after this time. When he breaks your heart again, I won't be there."

I push down the rising tears.

Peter leaves it a decent amount of time before approaching me. Jamie's eyes flash in his direction sometimes, but Peter doesn't acknowledge him. His inability to use his phone seems to have attracted the attention of one of the young mothers who frequents the coffee shop. It appears she's helping with something, and his laugh echoes through the shop. He looks a little older than his nineteen years, and I can see his smiles are making her a bit giggly while irritating Jamie.

I roll my eyes and clean the coffee machine.

"How was that?" Peter asks, leaning over the machine to speak to me when Jamie and Lauren are deep in conversation.

"It wasn't great, but it wasn't awful. Thank you for not making it worse. I know how that pains you," I tease him.

He makes a mock-wounded expression over his heart, handing

me his phone to show me the screen. "I may have had some help, but flights are booked."

I stare at the screen, barely able to contain my excitement. "Two weeks from now, so you should let Mike know you need some time off." I do a little dance on the spot, and Peter beams. "I won't kiss you now, but we *are* celebrating later."

"Okay." I smile, and it literally could not be any bigger.

"I'm going to go, okay? Lorna is home, so I'll annoy her for a bit and then I'll be at yours after you finish. I'll bring champagne." He winks.

"Okay," I say again, unable to move the grin from my face. I don't think it leaves my face the rest of my shift. I smile wildly at everyone who comes in, probably looking a bit deranged, but I don't care. *I'm going to Paris.*

I am still on cloud nine when I arrive home later to find my mum cooking dinner in the kitchen.

"Bonjour," I greet her. "This smells nice."

"You're in a good mood. Are you hungry?"

"Nope," I tell her, unable to keep my feet still. "I'm too excited to eat."

She smiles in bemusement, stopping her stirring. "What's going on?"

"Peter is taking me to Paris," I squeal, jumping up and down.

My mother, however, does not look happy. "Paris? When? Since when?"

"Since this afternoon." I go to the refrigerator and grab a beer, needing to calm down a bit. "We are going in two weeks. He'll be here soon." I stop and look at her serious expression. "It's only for a week, Mum. We'll be back."

"Isn't it too soon for you two to be taking a trip together, Connie? Besides, where does Peter have the money to go to Paris?"

"I told you, he has an inheritance, from his mum."

"Shouldn't he be saving that for his future?"

Gemini

"Mum." I roll my eyes at her. "I'm really excited. Can't you be happy for me?"

She softens a little bit, then tells me, like she has done repeatedly the last two weeks, to be careful. My mother certainly wasn't thrilled when I told her Jamie and I had broken up, and even less so when, in the same conversation, I let her know I broke things off with Jamie for Peter. She's not remembered the morning she caught us, so it all came as a genuine surprise to her, and I know she is still team Jamie. I carry some guilt over how I kind of led her to believe I left India because Peter cheated on me. She's also read between the lines that I cheated on Jamie with him, so I can't say she is a massive Peter fan at the moment.

Not that Peter helps himself sometimes. He's an hour later than I thought he would be. When I open the door, he gingerly steps in, a bottle of champagne in one hand, using the other to pull me to him and lift me off the floor for a kiss.

"Where were you?" I ask between kisses, tasting the alcohol already on his lips. His feet guide me backward, toward the stairs, my toes grazing the floor.

"This was originally two bottles of champagne," he says against my lips. "It's a beautiful night. There is a full moon. Do you want to go and look?" Except his feet are already on the stairs, pushing me upward, his free hand hot and grasping under my shirt.

I give a small laugh. "You are going in the wrong direction."

"Mmm... I've changed my mind. The moon can wait. I need you," he says before lifting me off my feet.

The tips of his fingers trace patterns down my arm as I sit up to take a long sip of champagne before turning back to him. "Just think, in two short weeks, we will be in Paris."

"We should try to get a penthouse, or something with a balcony, so we can do this under the stars." He grins.

"Sounds too good to be true." I laugh. "I may have to force you into some sightseeing, though."

"I think I can live with that. If it makes you happy." He rolls onto his back to look up at me. "We could do that, you know? Float around to every place on that pinboard of yours, see everything you've ever wanted to see. I could give you all of that, for as long as you want me."

"I will always want you, Peter."

He smiles his most brilliant smile. "Then you shall always have me." He kisses the back of my hand.

But my own smile falters a little. "You won't always have me, though, will you?"

"Connie. Don't go there. We have many, so many, years together to look forward to. So let's not bring your mortality into it."

Maybe the champagne is going to my head a little. "Peter, can I ask you something? Total honesty."

"Sure."

"How did Sorcha know? About what you thought about your influence?"

"Connie." He lets out a long sigh. "You want to talk about Sorcha now?"

"Yes. I want you to be honest." I take another sip of my champagne as he sits up to face me.

"Total honesty." His brown eyes are wide, as he toys with the edge of my finger. "I told her. I told her what I was scared of. It was in the early days when she used to come over and party. I never wanted to let you go, but whenever you were distracted talking to Anna or dancing with Lorna, we would talk. At first, it was because she was the same as me. She understood. She wanted to know about me, about you. How I was feeling was starting to become complicated, and then part of me realized what she was doing. So I just put up more walls, when I should have spoken to you, told you how I was feeling. I will regret that forever."

I look into those big eyes. "You were attracted to her."

"Con..." He closes his eyes, hiding them from me. "Please, it's not the same. I love you. I always will. Sorcha was a huge mistake."

I swallow hard. "Do you think you might go back to her one day, when I am gone?"

"Of course not." Peter takes my arms, making me look at him. "I would never go back to her. Not now, not ever."

"But I will die. One day, I will be gone."

"Connie, you're twenty." He chuckles. "It won't happen tomorrow. We could be together for eighty years before that day comes."

"Yet, I will still die. This is temporary."

"It is nothing to fear. Connie, you get to go on. To see the great beyond. I envy you that." He smiles. "I can heal pretty much everything, so when that day comes, we will be together and it will be peaceful and beautiful, and natural, Connie. I can heal your body, but I cannot stop time."

"You will be alone."

"Yes, so I don't want to waste our time feeling sad about this. This is so far ahead, Con. I can give you a lifetime of your feet not touching the ground, if you'll let me."

I feel slightly bad, seeing him losing his sparkle. Despite his reassurances, he has thought about this.

I bite my lip. "I don't want to die."

"It's the natural order of things, something even I can't defy."

I drain the last of my champagne, filling up my glass, then topping up Peter's too. A slight smile on my face, my heart does a skip as my brain starts to catch up, feeling a little giddy. "Are you really saying that you, Peter, the most powerful creature on this planet, a god who could pull the planets down, there is nothing in your power, *nothing* you could do?"

Peter narrows his eyes. "It's not natural."

"Does that mean you can't do it?"

Peter turns to look at me, really look at me, the glint coming back into his eyes, the danger flashing there. "You would really want that?" A sly smirk stretches across his face. "Kali, she mentioned something before about the old gods, ancient ones who were so powerful they could transform their human forms. What if I didn't transform myself, but instead used that power to transform you?"

"You think you could do that? What would happen? Would I be a god too?"

"No." He shakes his head. "No, you would be something else. Something new. Pure creation." He bites his lip, and I can tell he's getting excited, the glimmer of a possibility growing. Moving onto his knees to look at me, he adds, "But, Connie, the kind of power needed for that, the level of sacrifices. That's a lot of firepower."

"I don't want you to have to kill anyone." I chew my lip. "Like you said, we have time, lots of time, to figure it out, for you to cheat my death for me, make it so I can live forever with you."

Peter's fingertips crackle against my skin, his pupils dilating. "You should know, it would be crossing a line if I do this, if I figure out how to make you immortal. It goes against the natural order."

I slink my arms around his neck, urging him closer. "Does that mean you won't?"

That devilish grin flashes again. "Hell no. Screw the natural order."

My heart flutters in my chest.

He is going to make me immortal.

Chapter Twenty-Seven

Peter

Connie brushes her fingers over the bridge of my nose, tracing down the edges of my face, so I don't open my eyes straight away. In the light of the morning, without so much champagne in my system, I have no idea how to pull off what Connie has asked. Even with an arsenal of sacrifices at my hands, I wouldn't quite know what I was doing. Transforming Connie into something immortal, well, there is no precedent to follow. No example in nature for me to imitate. I'm sure the old gods were already thousands of years old when they were able to transfer their human forms, with thousands of years of amassed knowledge. Thousands of years of sacrifice. Even then, it would be one thing to transform myself. I'm not human, just old, powerful energy, so much so it sparked the birth of a universe. I am bound to a human body to keep me strapped to this plane.

To transform Connie—her pure, human, fragile body—into something else, I have no clue how. Especially without bloodshed. It will take time and research, something I'm not great at.

I wish Anna were here. She was always so much better at this stuff, at learning.

I can't fight it anymore. I snake my arms around Connie, bringing her closer to me. "You know, I think this is my favorite part of you."

I can hear the smile in her voice.

"What?" I open my eyes to look at her.

"Your freckles." She moves herself over me to kiss the bridge of my nose. "They're adorable." A small satisfied noise squeaks out of her before making her way out of bed. "I have work, so you can stay here if you want. I'm going to take a shower."

"Can't we just stay in bed all day?" I pout.

"While a tempting offer, I have to go. I'm off tomorrow. We can do that then?" She smiles, giving me a quick kiss as she wraps her dressing gown around her. "Maybe you could actually be here when I get home? It would be something to see you playing house for a while." She laughs.

"I'm sure your mum would love that."

"You could try making an effort." She winks at me as she leaves the room. "But no Jedi stuff."

"I still don't know what that means," I call after her.

I lie there for a moment. Connie's mother is already out of the house. Her dislike of me radiates out of her when I am close. It pisses me off more than it should. I know a large part of it is fear that I will take her daughter somewhere far away again. A life with Jamie would have meant she stayed close, lived nearby, the way everyone around here seems to do. A life with me means, not only will I take her far from here but she won't be human anymore. Maybe there's a way of keeping her human while extending her life. The way the witches do. Although I could feel from Kali's soul that it was not a permanent fixture. The natural cycle would have claimed her at some point. As it will do with Connie.

Thoughts for a different day. There is hardly any rush. Better to think it through.

I get out of bed and make my way into the bathroom, joining Connie in the small shower cubical.

"*Peter...*" She draws my name out. "I don't want to be late."

Gemini

I grin, moving myself under the hot water. Pushing wet hair off her face, I bring it back behind to expose her neck. Then I ease Connie back against the cool tiles, making her gasp.

"Do you want me to beg?" I murmur.

"Yes, Peter," she jokes. "I want you on your knees."

I know she's only joking, but I happily comply.

Connie is having a full-on tizzy fit and is quite late when I walk her to work. Even our goodbye kiss on the edge of the main high street gets a little out of control. I'm glad that even though I have no influence over her now, it hasn't seemed to change the effect I have on her. My problem is how little I have to do when she's not around.

I pull out my phone and call Lorna. "Hey, I'm on my way over," I tell her when she picks up, as I walk into the mini market. "Do you want something to drink?"

"It's like eleven in the morning," she chides.

"Hmm... and?" I ask while perusing the wine aisle. "I think I have a taste for champagne."

"You have expensive tastes." She titters.

"Do you want anything?"

The line goes a little quiet for a while, then she says, "I could drink champagne."

"Meet you outside," I say, then plonk the bottle on the counter, giving the cashier a broad grin. "Can I have this?"

"Sure." She smiles back.

"Great," I tell her, collecting the champagne. About to make my exit, I stop and look down at the bottle. It's nothing big, just a bottle of wine. Hardly a soul, hardly killing anyone, but then I look back at the lady behind the counter, who is still smiling at me. She probably owns the place. I turn back around and place the bottle back down, shaking my head. "Silly me. I almost walked out of here without paying for this."

By the time I reach Lorna's, I'm half a bottle of champagne down. I should have bought two. Lorna is leaning against her gate post, engrossed with her phone, but gives me an eye roll when she catches sight of me.

"Are you chugging a bottle of Moët?"

"I'm classy that way." I hand her the bottle.

She glances back to her house, then motions for me to follow. Side-eyeing me, she takes a sip as we walk. "Not that this isn't fun, but I'm starting to think my liver can't take champagne before noon. Is this you now, Peter? This is your way of coping?"

I take the bottle from her hands. "I am truly my mother's son," I declare and help myself to another long swig, giving her a half smile. "At the time, I thought I would never want to touch alcohol. The stench of what she used to make..." I shudder. "I suppose it was closest to gin. Just thinking about it, I can almost smell it. But, knowing what I know now, I understand why she wanted to not feel. To forget about my father, about what I am, about what she did."

Lorna looks thoughtful. "You don't talk much about her, your mother."

"Not much to tell." I take a seat next to Lorna on the bench we sometimes use.

"I find that hard to believe. It was just the two of you and her for so long."

I shake my head. "Honestly, Lor. Looking back, it feels like a different life. Like it's an old film I saw once... grainy with the sound turned down. Just drunken mumbles, eating honey, running through the woods, sleeping outside, living in rags, and days upon days where none of us spoke."

Lorna's eyes stay fixed on me. "You should talk about these things. No matter what you are, they happened to you. Not all scars are physical."

"You sound like my therapist."

Not that we continued to see her after we turned eighteen. It's weird still thinking of us as a "we."

Gemini

"Besides, I had Anna, so I was never alone. We always had each other."

"And now?"

I shrug. "I have Connie. And you. There will always be a cliff edge I need pulling back from, Lor. I'm starting to think Connie is liable to jump off too. So, lucky you, you have two of us to manage." I laugh, but she doesn't join me.

Instead, she takes the bottle out of my hands, looking down at the ground. "I want to say thank you."

I look at her, a little confused. She's probably in for a lifetime of cleaning up Connie and my messes.

"For not leaving me, for bringing me home when I asked you to, for doing whatever it is that you are doing right now, making sure I don't feel alone. Connie is right. You're not so terrible."

I can't help but laugh. She hates this stuff as much as I do. "What happened to wanting the skip the mushy speech?"

"We were having a moment." She shoves me. "You were sharing. I was trying to say thank you. You are such an—"

Lorna doesn't finish. Her phone buzzes in her pocket, and whatever she sees there causes her to frown.

"Hi, Connie? Oh, Suzie. Sorry, I thought you were Connie for a minute. No, I haven't seen her." Her eyes turn on me, looking serious. "No need to. I am actually with Peter right now. One sec." Lorna takes the phone away from her ear and asks me, "Have you seen Connie today?"

"Yeah," I say, becoming concerned. "I walked her to work."

Lorna looks even more confused, putting the phone back to her ear. "Peter said he walked her to work." She looks back to me. "The coffee shop called Suzie at work. Connie didn't show."

The hackles rise on my neck. I close my eyes, searching for her.

"Sure, sure. Maybe call Jamie, see if he's seen her," Lorna says and hangs up.

I'm already on my feet, Lorna rising to meet me. "Peter, let's not panic. We're in Wixford, not Varanasi."

"Something's wrong, Lor. I can't feel her. I can't find her. Which means only one thing... *witches*."

"But..." The color drains from her face.

I know what she's trying to say—*I killed all the witches*. But the only thing I know can hide from me are witches.

"Lorna, you go and check out the coffee shop. Call Jamie on the way. See if he has seen her."

"Where are you going?" she asks, clutching onto me.

"There is something I need to get. I'll meet you there, okay?"

Lorna leaves, and I head back out in the direction of Brady's, far out of the village. Somewhere I didn't think I would ever go back to, but there's something I want. My pace turns into a run, and as I near, I hop around to remove my shoes and socks. This will work better if I'm connected to the earth.

I am right.

As soon as my soles hit the dirt fields, I can feel it calling to me. I cut through the fields allowing me to take a quicker route than the road I traveled last time. It's a place I've only been to with Jamie, of all people.

I near its resting place, sweat covering every inch of me, and drop to my knees to dig into the earth with my bare hands. Some sense of relief hits me when I finally feel it in my hands, the cool metal and sense of belonging. Like my connection to the earth, I am connected to it. I know every cut I make with it will mark that soul as mine.

The powers resting inside me rise and crash against my skin. Not just the earth or electricity, but also fire and ice. I push my hand into the ground, a small voice in the back of my head telling me to just start.

Burn it all. No one will stop you. Feed it, Peter. Feed what is inside of you.

I run my hand over the grass, first burning, then healing before burning again.

When everything is dead, you can grow it all back.

The slightest sound of a footstep behind me makes me jump to my feet. My sacred blade is out of my hand, thrown the direction of the intruder—stupid idea, of course.

Sorcha catches it with ease as it flies close to her face. There must be magic protecting her for me not to feel her so close.

"Didn't I kill you?" I ask, straightening up to take her in.

"Baby god, we do not kill so easily. You left your mark, though." She stretches out her neck to show me the scorch marks scarred there, then eyes me for a while. "You are all grown up now, aren't you?"

"You have about five seconds before I rip you to shreds." I glower at her.

"You probably shouldn't do that. I know where *she* is."

I don't move. Instead, I send the flames smoldering in the grass to surround her, hold Sorcha in a fiery prison.

"This is new." She muses, her stance is casual and unfazed as I stalk up to her, circling the flames.

"One of a few *new* things about me," I tell her.

"Mmm..." She purrs from inside the flames. "I am sure you would love nothing more than to show me. Test what my body could endure under all that you are. I can only imagine all the ways you could show me what you've become."

I step into the flames, once again face to face with Socha's otherworldly silver eyes. Then, not moving too fast, I reach out and take my knife back. "I am taking this," I tell her.

She doesn't put up any resistance. However, being this close, her confidence falters, and she looks away, over my shoulder, as the flames lick around me.

"I will tell you where she is. It is you they want, not her." She looks back at me, the first sign of any emotion there. "To pay for the blood you shed. They were peaceful, innocent."

"*You...*" I can barely keep the rage inside of me. Their deaths are on her too. I raise my knife to her face, dragging it down her lips, not enough for her to taste her own blood, just shudder under its cold touch. "You let me in," I tell her. Her eyes are full of defiance. "When I kill you, it will be so slow, Sorcha."

"Promises, promises," she whispers, licking her lips.

Like instinct—terrible instinct—I do the same, fighting the urge to kill her right then. Take my time. Enjoy myself.

Her silver eyes are like their own galaxy, swirling like nebulas exploding into glittery stars, the birth place of a thousand suns.

I need to get to Connie.

"Where is she?"

Chapter Twenty-Eight

Connie

For a moment, I think I must be in Brady's barn.

It feels so familiar as I blink in the world around me.

Except, it can't be.

There are no bales of hay stacked high. I'm in an empty barn, rays of sunlight filtering through the wooden slats.

How did I get here?

I try to rub my head, which feels all fuzzy, but my hands are tied around my back.

"She is waking up." A beautiful face, who looks sympathetic, appears in front of me with the most flawless skin I have ever seen. "Shh," she cautions against my struggles. "We won't hurt you. There is no need to be afraid."

Two more figures move to stand behind her—a man and a woman appear a little less friendly. The woman, with dark tattoos on her face, eyes me with suspicion. The man's brow is furrowed with deep lines.

"Where am I? What do you want with me?"

A beautiful Japanese girl touches my bare forearm, and I feel relaxed instantly. "Just a little something to ease your anxiety." She smiles. "We are not in the business of hurting innocents." Her smile falters a little. "We're not sure how much you know, about the one you were with, but it seems you know enough. We are not here to hurt you, Connie, but that thing you were with... it is very dangerous."

Of course.

"What do you want with him?" I glare.

She glances back at the two standing behind her, then turns to me. "He committed a terrible crime." She looks deep into my eyes. "An entire coven perished at his hands. It was an unprovoked attack on peaceful people. They were no danger to anyone. Do you understand what I am saying?"

I'm not sure I am. *Maybe she thinks I don't know, so I should be shocked.*

"That is not entirely true, is it. His sister had just died," I reply, unsure if I should be saying anything.

"Be that as it may," the blonde behind her speaks for the first time in a broad Irish accent. "Unprovoked or not, it was an atrocity. Every action has an equal and opposite reaction. We cannot let it stand. He must be destroyed."

"You're witches, right?" I look between them.

"Yes," the Asian witch confirms. "I am Rue. This is Roisin and Caleb. We are told you are aware you're under his control."

I look between the three of them again. They stare back as hard at me. I can't help it. They look so serious, the three of them standing there waiting for me to, what? Be scared?

A cackle bubbles inside of me and erupts.

Roisin and Caleb look between each other like I've gone mad.

"This is it? The three of *you* think you can take him on?"

"Seven," Caleb corrects me. "There are more..." he motions toward the door, "... outside. Waiting for him."

"Seven." I shake my head. "Fine! You seven think you can take him down? Seriously?"

"We are not your peaceful, defenseless Varanasi tribe whom he slaughtered. We are warriors. And *we* are ready for *him*." Roisin glowers down at me.

A thrill of fear travels down me as I look up at her. "He is the sun. Do you think that matters? It is he who will destroy you if you do not stop now."

Roisin and Caleb laugh. However, Rue moves her face a little closer, whispering, "That boy is no sun. He is a black hole. He will destroy everything in his path... not just us... if we allow him to continue." Her fingers ripple down my face. "Including you. He will consume us all. We need to stop him now before it is too late. He does *not* belong here."

She looks so young. I figure she can't be much more than eighteen. "I am not under his control," I tell her. "I love him. He is *not* what you think."

Rue cocks her head, considering my words.

"What happened in Varanasi was a one-off. It won't happen again, I promise."

"Foolish girl." Caleb laughs and glances between his coven mates. "Who does she think she is?" His eyes, like daggers, land on me. "He is *not* a man. He is a creature, and you are nothing more than his pet."

"Caleb," Rue chides, her face searching mine.

I hold her gaze and plead with her, "Let me go. Just let me go, and I will convince him it has all been a mistake. He doesn't want this. But if you keep me here, he will find me, and you will all pay."

"Girl, we want him to find you." Roisin shakes her head at my stupidity for missing that this is a trap. "We know much more about his kind than the others did. He is not so powerful yet."

Rue's eyes stay on me.

I struggle against the ropes fastening me to the chair. "Please, Rue. I am not under his control. He released me from it. The spell he used, it involved clear quartz and a flower. They were in bowls, erm... hawthorn."

Roisin and Caleb's eyes flash toward the back of Rue's head.

Despite her looking about ten years younger, she is the obvious one in charge here.

"Please," I ask again. "We just want to be left alone."

Rue regards me for a while, and for a minute, I think she will let me go, but she turns away, saying, "I am sorry, Connie. As much as I would love for that to be true, I cannot allow him to live. The risk is too great. Even if your love is enough, it too will pass. We need to strike now while we are able."

"No," I whisper.

I have no time to form arguments as the ground tremors beneath us and the barn walls shudder, but the witches don't look alarmed. There is no fear in their eyes.

Rue places her hand on Roisin's shoulder. "There he is," she says before turning to Caleb. "Watch her." She motions toward me. "Keep her out of harm's way."

Rue leaves the barn in the direction of the growing noise, the earth still shaking.

"Is Peter doing that?" I ask.

"In a sense," Caleb answers, looking down at his hands. He seems to be turning something in his fingers. "They are our wardings." He graces me with a hint of a smile. "We know his primary power is from the earth, and we can turn that against him."

This time, my fear comes for Peter.

Their lack of concern is alarming me.

"How do you know that about him?"

But they don't answer, just exchange looks.

Then the penny drops.

"Sorcha." I laugh. "You are here at Sorcha's bidding."

"We do not do Sorcha's bidding. We are here at the command of our high priestess," Roisin says as she takes a step back from the doorway.

The ground tremors, rumbling from deep within the earth, along with the sound of muffled voices outside. The daylight outside plunges into darkness, and for the first time, they exchange worried

Gemini

glances. The voices die down, the rumbling and tremors coming to a stop.

My heart hammers in my chest not knowing what to do.

They start to approach the barn doors, but a second later, they're flying open, Rue seeming to have opened them with the force of her hands. The doors go back to allow four witches I don't recognize a wide birth.

As she moves into the barn, I see Peter walking between them all. The four witches have him tied with what resembles thin golden strings.

As his eyes fall on me, his expression changes—his eyes go soft, relief washing over him knowing I am unharmed. His muscles, which had been flexing against his bonds, relax.

Rue adjusts to stand back and watch the change in his countenance. She motions to the witches holding the golden strings to the far wall, where they maintain him fast.

Peter's eyes remain on mine, only relief there that I am okay.

I swallow hard.

I want to see him fighting.

Rue slowly approaches Peter, but he doesn't see her, only me. His eyes stay on me. She lifts his T-shirt, removing the knife from his waistband.

"Tut-tut-tut." Roisin waggles it in the air. "You won't be needing this."

Peter doesn't acknowledge her, his eyes still on me. "I'm so sorry," he whispers.

My eyes spring with tears. "No," I whisper, shaking my head.

"Let her go," he says.

Rue clasps his chin, turning Peter to face her. "Soon. I promise I will not let her see. But I am not stupid. I need assurances."

He swallows. "I have surrendered. What more do you want?"

"How about some retribution?" Caleb spits, slamming a large vial of swirling black liquid onto the table next to me. "For their suffering."

299

Peter's eyes go wide at the sight of the liquid, and he reflexively pulls on the gold strings.

The witches fall in a little closer at his sudden movement.

"No." He pulls back, looking back to Rue. "I've surrendered. You said she would be safe."

Rue cocks her head, and Caleb picks up and tosses the vial to her. "It's not for her."

Peter pulls against the bindings again. They seem to shimmer and spark. "No, no, no." He tries to back into the wall, but there is nowhere else for him to go. "You don't need to do that. Don't give me that. I'm not fighting you. I said I wouldn't fight. My life for hers, that was the deal."

Rue moves closer, the vial gripped in her hand.

Peter glances back at me before looking back to her and asking again, "Please don't give me that."

Rue looks back to her cohort. "Get her out, Caleb."

Caleb moves to untie me so I don't have to witness what they are about to do. His arm wraps around me, pulling me up from the chair and moving me toward the door. I can't look away, though. They are going to kill him, and I cannot look away. I stumble backward in what feels like slow motion while Rue forces the black liquid into Peter's mouth. The sound of his cry echoes all around the barn, and the gold ties holding him in place flicker and fade, then shine bright again. The witches holding onto his bonds stagger a few paces, increasing their grip to restrain him.

Even Caleb stops.

The results are instant.

Thick, black sludgy vines wind their way through his skin. Peter's cries die down, his head hanging forward. Whatever it is it's meant to hurt, but Peter begins to cackle. An odd noise comes from his throat as he lifts his head, revealing black vines crossing his face. His stare is now fixed on Rue.

She and Roisin shift about, somewhat vexed.

"What is so funny?" Roisin seethes while Rue forces more of the liquid down.

For a few moments, Peter chokes down the liquid in pain. Some of the black liquid oozes down his chin and onto his neck. Peter shakes his head for a moment, then laughs again—if the noise can be called that—as he straightens up to look at Rue, licking his lips.

"Your soul smells of sage and thyme, witch."

The black vines winding around his neck and arms shiver, almost vibrating off his skin and taking on a life of their own before settling back into his skin.

Rue and Roisin exchange looks.

"What's happening, Rue?" Caleb calls out from beside me.

Peter is still laughing maniacally then he shakes his head. "I am going to tear you apart..." he rasps, his grin vicious, "... and *eat* your soul."

His muscles tense, and the vines of the poison shiver and rip from his skin, wrapping around the nearest witch holding his bonds. Black vines snake and wind, finding their way into the witch's skin, settling in like tattoos and spreading the madness. The witch tears at his skin, trying to be rid of them, dropping the golden string.

"No," Rue screams. "Those bonds need to hold."

"I need my knife back now." Peter laughs at Roisin. The poisonous black vines deliver the infected witch to Peter, his hands wrapping around their neck.

"Kill him now, Rue," Caleb screams.

I hear the witch's bones crunch under Peter's grasp.

Rue takes a few paces backward, throwing her arms back in what seems to be a summoning of power. The shadows stretch around her.

I'm aware enough to realize that Caleb is distracted, and his grip around me has loosened. *Obviously, this is not going how they planned this going.* They'd thought the liquid would hurt and they hadn't expected Peter to overcome it.

I need to do something.

With all the force I can muster, I throw myself backward, sending us both into the wall behind us.

Chapter Twenty-Nine

Peter

The bones in my hands crunch.

This witch was not ancient, still in their human years.

The body barely hits the ground before I'm distracted by movement at the back of the room. Even the two witches in front of me stop and turn to look at the clattering sound.

Connie.

She and the witch that was holding her are grappling on the floor.

I'd thought they'd removed her.

Her eyes meet mine as I push out the poison. Like everything else now, it's all extensions of me. It doesn't feel nice. I can taste the delirium, but I can also use it. I throw it out, catching the witches holding me down, the terrible vines wrapping around them too. The delirium overtakes them, forcing them to loosen their grip on me as they try to shake off the awful feeling.

But I don't have enough time, not to really move. I'm barely free of the golden bonds. The little witch, Rue, is drawing up the darkness, her keen eyes on mine. Desperate to move quicker than her, I wrap my hand around a vine and yank the next witch into my grasp, snapping the golden bonds along with their neck.

I'm not going to make it.

I can feel what she is doing—tearing a hole in the fabric of this world.

I am not going to die—I am facing oblivion. Cast back into the chaos from whence I came.

Roisin, who's been holding my blade, throws it, and it hits me in the chest, sending me back. I hit the barn wall with a splat, cool metal searing my insides once again.

Connie is screaming, trying to run to me.

I take one last look at her.

The witch, Caleb, is reaching out and pulling her back toward him.

Her eyes are locked on me, resisting his hold, but they start closing.

She can't watch.

I can't either so I close my eyes.

Extracting the knife from my chest brings instant relief from the burning sensation, but the next scream I hear isn't my own.

It's Caleb's.

My eyes snap open to see him backing into the wall in shock. Connie has sunk her teeth into his arm, tearing at him like a wild animal.

Rue is looking on in horror.

Everyone is watching on in horror.

Watching as Connie mauls his arm.

Except me.

Destructive and terrible. That's *my girl*.

The knife is in my hand. I slice through the last of my bonds before slamming it into the neck of the witch closest to me. The copper taste of their blood sprays across my face, and in the next instant, I bring it down into the chest of the remaining witch, his blood spilling out across my feet and onto the barn floor.

Free of the bonds, I send lightning out to push Caleb hurtling backward before turning on Roisin.

Roisin—*she is not worthy of my knife.*

So I push my fist through her chest, crushing her heart and smiling when meeting her wide, petrified eyes. I mark her face with the knife before I turn on Rue.

Rue is struggling to open the portal, but it's not working. The strength of the spells is dying with each one, but Rue is different. She's special. Old. Gifted. Her movements are cat-like as she tries to maneuver around me, darkness flickering above her.

I flip the knife in my hand. Then, giving her a small smile, I send the remaining hemlock vines across to her skin, watching them wrap around her tiny arms. Her alarm grows as she abandons the darkness in an attempt to pull them off—trying and not succeeding.

I close the gap between us in a couple of strides.

"That is a talent, Rue," I tell her. Then, taking her small neck, I lick my lips. Her eyes meet mine, and the fear there is too sweet. "I know you will taste *so* good."

I raise my knife to her neck and relish its cool blade on her skin as I watch the blood drip until I cover the wound with my hand, drawing out her delicious soul. She is old—not as old as Kali, but more gifted. She tastes like sage, ancient and powerful.

Her lifeless body drops in a heap, and only then do I look around at the other bodies. Their souls are all ripe for taking, so I open my palms, calling them to me.

They fill me up, like eating an exceptional meal. So strong and powerful. It seems the Irish witches taste like roasted barley.

I'm instantly drunk—a better drunk than I could ever obtain through alcohol.

There is only one witch left and he's quivering at Connie's feet.

Connie's back is to the wall in the far corner, her hands still tied behind her back. Her green eyes are fixated on me, and her chest is heaving. The witch's blood is all over her face and down her shirt, marking her like some sort of ritualistic ceremony.

She looks wild, not agitated, but emotionally turbulent with fury.

Gemini

Her eyes, wide and alert, are swirling, marking every step I make toward her.

The raw power of the witches course through me. Rue's power—so much more than any other witch I have ever met—is truly cosmic.

Connie doesn't say anything, keeping her eyes on mine as I draw close. I must look wild, too, covered in blood once again. My hands, my arms, my chest. My face is splattered. *This is probably the closest thing to my truest form.*

I take her face in my hand, my palm connecting with every precious cell that resides in the blood that coats her chin. I press my foot onto the neck of the witch dying at our feet, exerting slow, steady pressure as he dies then I push his soul into Connie.

That's when Connie's breath hitches in her throat.

Swallowing it down, I understand that overwhelming feeling.

As her eyes open, I see the faint tinge of black creep into the outer rings of her emerald eyes.

Marking her.

Chapter Thirty

Connie

Everything is different now.

My body shakes despite the spring evening being far from cold.

I watch Peter drag the bodies into a neat pile in the middle of the barn. He appears fine. Well, as fine as a person can look while drenched in blood. Absentmindedly, I look down at my shirt, the blood there almost indistinguishable against the black material. I close my eyes when another wave of rushing floods me. Not as strong as the one before from the force of Caleb's soul entering my body. My knees feel weak again. Yet Peter seems to be handling six strong souls just fine. I wrap my arms around myself.

Peter drags Rue's lifeless form into place, stopping to kneel next to her for a heartbeat before glancing up at me. Then Peter starts to make his way over.

Maybe he does look different. His hair is a tad lighter, his whole body seems to vibrate, and the dark parts of his eyes are so wide his whole eyes look black. He tugs at his torn T-shirt, to better show the hole where the knife had gone through it, giving me a half smile.

"I'm starting to see a pattern here." He cautiously closes the distance between us. "It's a good thing you saw this, Connie. Now you know. Now you *really* know what I am. This..." he motions to the bloody scene in the barn behind him, "... this will always call me. No matter how hard I try, it will always be there. This is who I am."

Being so close to him makes me shiver even more. It's a new kind of connection, something I don't have words to explain.

His eyes scorch into me. "I am going to burn these bodies. And then I am going to incinerate it all, the same way I did in Varanasi."

I slowly nod.

"Are you scared?" he whispers, searching my face.

I give the slightest of headshakes.

"Are you with me?" he asks.

I nod. "Always," I whisper.

"Good." The corners of his mouth turn up into a smile, his hands snaking around my back. "Then I will do it. I will find a way to make you immortal, and we will never have to be apart again."

His hand moves to my face to kiss me, not minding the blood he tastes there. I wrap my arms around him, recognizing the truth in his words.

It's him and me now.

"Stay here," he instructs, turning away from me to stalk back into the barn.

Placing his hands onto the ground underneath Rue, I gasp and take an instinctive step back at what I am seeing. Golden flames grow, curling and licking around Rue's limbs and spreading to the rest of the witches. Peter stands unharmed by the flames, watching for a moment before removing his blood-soaked shirt and throwing it into the fire.

The smell reminds me of the ghats.

After a while, Peter turns back to me, taking his place by my side as his flames begin to claim the whole barn. Peter puts his arm around me, and we watch the fire burn well into the night. Undisturbed. At peace. Just us and the fire and the stars in the sky. Strangely, it feels like a sign of things to come.

Peter stands with his arm around me, his head leaning on top of mine. The rushing sensation has leveled out, and I can focus again. His flames glow more golden than normal fire. So typically Peter—incredible beauty in his destruction.

"This is all yours," he says after a while. "Everything I have is yours. I meant what I said, Connie. I would burn this whole world for you."

I lean further into his chest, pulling him close, accepting the promise in his words. But I do not feel scared, the feeling is more about being protected and safe, belonging even.

If what Rue said is true and he is not the sun in the sky but the black hole at the center of everything, if he is destruction, then I will stand at his side and revel in his devastation.

Forever.

About the Author

Kerry Williams is an emerging UK author and writer of magical romance, Other Nature being her debut paranormal romance novel. Told from multiple points of view, it will keep you hooked with its twisty plot and boy obsessed.

Copywriter by day, she gets lost in a world of magic at night, either in her writing or in what she reads. Her creative roots cultivated by the writing of the unforgettable Anne Rice, she also adores the work of Erin Morgenstern, Holly Black and J. K. Rowling.

She is an avid cat lady, die hard tea drinker and eternal star gazer. Always known to her family as a daydreamer, her and her young daughter, Ivy, can often be found looking at the moon.

Printed in Great Britain
by Amazon